Born in 1957, Andrea Japp trained as a toxicologist and is the author of twenty novels. She is the French translator of Patricia Cornwell and has also written for television.

Lorenza Garcia translates from French and Spanish.

The Lady Agnès Mystery:

Volume 1

The Season of the Beast
The Breath of the Rose

The Lady Agnès Mystery:

Volume 1

The Season of the Beast
The Breath of the Rose

ANDREA JAPP
Translated from the French by Lorenza Garcia

Gallic Books
London

This book is published with support from the French Ministry of
Culture/Centre National du Livre and from the Institut français
(Royaume-Uni) as part of the Burgess programme
(www.frenchbooknews.com).

A Gallic Book

First published in France as *La Dame Sans Terre 1: Les Chemins de la Bête*
Copyright © Calmann-Lévy, 2006

and *La Dame Sans Terre 2: Le Souffle de la Rose* by Calmann-Lévy
Copyright © Calmann-Lévy, 2006

First published in Great Britain as *The Season of the Beast*, 2008
English translation copyright © Gallic Books, 2008

and *The Breath of the Rose*, 2009
English translation copyright © Gallic Books, 2009

This omnibus edition first published in 2015
by Gallic Books, 59 Ebury Street, London SW1W 0NZ
© Gallic Books, 2015

A CIP record for this book is available from the British Library

ISBN 978-1-910477-16-8

Typeset in Fournier MT by Gallic Books
Printed by CPI (CR0 4YY)

2 4 6 8 10 9 7 5 3 1

CONTENTS

AUTHOR'S NOTE

Words marked with an asterisk (*) are explained in the Historical References starting on page 582; those marked with a plus sign (⁺) are explained in the Glossary starting on page 593.

Part One:
The Season of the Beast

Mr Feng,
Tender and serious little soul,
Friendly wind,
This tale from far ago is for you.

Agnès de Souarcy stood before the hearth in her chamber calmly contemplating the last dying embers. During the past weeks both man and beast had been beset by a deadly cold that seemed intent on putting an end to all living things. So many had already succumbed that there was barely enough wood to make coffins, and those left alive preferred to use what little there was to warm themselves. The people shivered with cold, their insides ravaged by straw-alcohol, their hunger only briefly kept at bay with pellets of suet and sawdust or the last slices of famine bread made from straw, clay, bark or acorn flour. They crowded into the rooms they shared with the animals, lying down beside them and curling up beneath their thick, steamy breath.

Agnès had given her serfs permission to hunt on her land for seventeen days, or until the next new moon, on condition they distribute half the game they killed among the rest of the community, beginning with widows, expectant mothers, the young and the elderly. A quarter of what remained would go to her and the members of her household and the rest to the hunter and his family. Two men had already flouted Agnès de Souarcy's orders, and at her behest the bailiffs had given them a public beating in the village square. Everybody had praised the lady's leniency, but some expressed private disapproval; surely the perpetrators of such a heinous crime deserved execution or the excision of hands or noses – the customary sentences for poaching. Game was their last chance of survival.

Souarcy-en-Perche had buried a third of its peasants in a communal grave, hastily dug at a distance from the hamlet for fear that an epidemic of cholera might infect those wraiths still walking. They had been sprinkled with quicklime like animal carcasses or plague victims.

In the icy chapel next to the manor house the survivors prayed day and night for an improbable miracle, blaming their ill luck on the recent death of their master, Hugues, Seigneur de Souarcy, who had been gored by an injured stag the previous autumn, leaving Agnès widowed, and no male offspring to inherit his title and estate.

They had prayed to heaven until one evening a woman collapsed, knocking over the altar she had been clinging to, and taking with her the ornamental hanging. Dead. Finished off by hunger, fever and cold. Since that day the chapel had remained empty.

Agnès studied the cinders in the grate. The charred wood was coated in places with a silvery film. That was all, no red glow that would have enabled her to postpone any longer the ultimatum she had given herself that morning. It was the last of the wood, the last night. She sighed impatiently at the self-pity she felt. Agnès de Souarcy had turned sixteen three days before, on Christmas Day.

It was strange how afraid she had been to visit the mad old crone; so much so that she had all but slapped her lady's maid, Sybille, in an attempt to oblige the girl to go with her. The hovel that served as a lair for this evil spirit reeked of rancid mutton fat. Agnès had reeled at the stench of filth and perspiration emanating from the soothsayer's rags as she approached to snatch the basket of meagre offerings: a loaf of bread, a bottle of fresh cider, a scrap of bacon and a boiling fowl.

'What use is this to me, pretty one?' the woman had hissed.

'Why, the humblest peasant could offer me more. It's silver I want, or jewels – you must surely have some of those. Or why not that handsome fur-lined cloak of yours?' she added, reaching out to touch the long cape lined with otter skin, Agnès's protection.

The young girl had fought against her impulse to draw back, and had held the gaze of this creature they said was a formidable witch.

She had been so afraid up until the woman had reached out and touched her, scrutinised her. A look of spiteful glee had flashed across the soothsayer's face, and she had spat out her words like poison.

Hugues de Souarcy would have no posthumous heir. Nothing could save her now.

Agnès had stood motionless, incredulous. Incredulous because the terror that had gripped her those past months had suddenly faded into the distance. There was nothing more to do, nothing more to say.

And then, as the young girl pulled the fur-lined hood up over her head, preparing to leave the hovel, something curious happened.

The soothsayer's mouth froze in a grimace and she turned away, crying out:

'Leave here! Leave here at once, and take your basket with you. I want nothing of yours. Be off with you, I say!'

The evil crone's triumphant hatred had been replaced by a bizarre panic which Agnès was at a loss to understand. She had tried reasoning with her:

'I have walked a long way, witch, and …'

The woman had wailed like a fury, lifting her apron up over her bonnet to hide her eyes.

'Be off with you, you have no business here. Out of my sight! Out of my hut! And don't come back, don't ever come back, do you hear?'

If the fear consuming Agnès for many moons had not been replaced by deep despair, she would certainly have told the crone to calm down and explain herself. The extraordinary outburst would have certainly intrigued, not to say alarmed her. But as it was, she had walked away, a sudden, intense weariness weighing down her every step. She had struggled with the urge to surrender, right there in the mud soiled with pig excrement, to sleep, to die perhaps.

The icy cold, which had been pushed out towards the bare stone walls when there had been a fire in the enormous hearth, now enveloped her, claiming its revenge. She pulled her fur-lined cloak tightly round her and removed her slippers of boiled wool. Mathilde, her one-and-a-half-year-old daughter, would be wearing these in a few years' time if God saw fit to spare her life.

Agnès walked barefoot down the spiral staircase leading from the vestibule beside her bedchamber into the main hall. She crossed the black flagstones. Only the dull echo of her feet seemed real, the rest of the world had died away, leaving her with no other course of action, no other purpose than the moments that were about to follow. She smiled at the pale skin on her hands turning blue, at her heels sticking to the frost on the granite floor. Soon the biting cold would stop. Soon something else would replace this pointless waiting. Soon.

The chapel. It seemed as though a wave of ice had stopped time within those sombre walls. A frail shadow stood out against one of its wall. Sybille. She walked towards Agnès, her cheeks bloodless from the cold, from hardship and also from fear. She wore a long thin tunic that stretched over her belly, revealing the life that had grown big inside her and would soon be clamouring to see the light. She stretched out her bony hands towards the

Dame de Souarcy and her face broke into an ecstatic smile:

'Death will be sweet, Madame. We shall enter the light. My body is weighed down, so impure. It was already unclean before I soiled it even more.'

'Hush,' Agnès commanded.

She obeyed, bowing her head. She was overwhelmed by a perfect peace, like a longing. All that mattered to her now was the infinite gratitude she felt towards Agnès, her angel, with whom she was about to leave this world, this corrupted flesh, saving herself from the worst fate and saving, too, this beautiful, kind woman who had seen fit to take her in, to protect her from the evil hordes. They would die a thousand deaths and weep tears of blood when they realised their terrible mistake, but at least she would have saved Agnès's dove-like soul, at least she would be saved, she and this child she could feel moving with such force below her breast. Thanks to her, her lady would enter the infinite and eternal joy of Christ. Thanks to her, this child she did not want would never be born. It would become light before ever having to suffer the unbearable burden of the flesh.

'Come along,' Agnès continued in a whisper.

'Are you afraid, Madame?'

'Hush, Sybille.'

They approached the altar that had been hurriedly set straight. Agnès untied her cloak, which dragged behind her for a moment like a ghostly train before falling to the floor. As she walked, she unfastened the fine leather thong around her waist and stepped out of her robe. At first she felt almost numb. Then her naked skin began to prickle, burning her almost. The unrelenting cold brought tears to her eyes. She gritted her teeth, fixing her gaze on the painted wooden crucifix, no longer conscious of her thoughts, and slumped to her knees. As though in a dream, she watched the tremors shaking Sybille's deathly-pale little body. The young woman rolled herself up in a ball below the altar and began repeating the same incessant prayer: *Adoramus te, Christe. Adoramus te, Christe. Adoramus te, Christe.*[1]

Sybille's body went into a spasm. She stumbled over the words of the prayer, seemingly unable to breathe, then repeated it once more:

'*Ado ... ramus te ... Christe.*'

There was a gasp, followed by a cry and a long-drawn-out sigh, and the emaciated legs of her lady's maid went limp.

Was that death? Was it so simple?

It seemed as though an eternity had passed before Agnès felt her body fall forwards. The icy stone floor received her without mercy. The flesh on her belly protested, but she silenced it, stretching her arms out to form a cross, and waiting. There was nowhere else for her to surrender.

How long did she spend praying for Mathilde's life, how long accepting that she was sinning against her body and soul and deserved no mercy? And yet one was granted her as she gradually lost consciousness. She no longer felt the relentless cold of the stone floor biting into her. The blood no longer pulsed through the veins in her neck. She would soon be asleep, with no fear of ever waking up.

'Stand up! Stand up this instant.'

Agnès smiled at the voice whose words she did not understand. A hand roughly grasped her hair, which spread out in a silky wave across the stone floor.

'Stand up. It is a crime. You will be damned and your child will suffer for your sins.'

Agnès turned her head the other way; perhaps then the voice would stop.

A heavy layer of warmth covered her back. A rush of hot air burned her neck and two hands burrowed under her belly in order to turn her over. It was the weight of another body lying on top of hers in order to warm her.

The nursemaid, Gisèle, struggled with the young girl's rigid body. She wrapped her coat around her and tried to pull her to her feet. Agnès fought with every last fibre of her frail body against being saved. Tears of rage and exhaustion rolled down her cheeks, turning to ice on her lips.

She murmured:

'Sybille?'

'She will soon be dead. And she's better off that way. You will stand up if I have to thrash you. It is a sin, and unworthy of one of your lineage.'

'And the child?'

'Presently.'

Eleven-year-old Mathilde was circling the honey spice-cake which Mabile had just removed from the stone oven. She shifted restlessly about the room, eager for the arrival of her uncle who so captivated her. Clément, the ill-fated child Sybille had pushed from her womb before finally expiring, and who was nearly ten now, was quiet as usual, his big blue-green eyes fixed on Agnès. Gisèle had taken the newborn baby and, after cutting the umbilical cord, had wrapped him in her cloak to keep him from freezing to death. Agnès and the nursemaid had feared the child would not survive his terrible birth, but life already held him firmly in its grip. It had, however, released Gisèle the previous winter, despite the care Agnès had lavished on her and the ministrations of her half-brother Eudes de Larnay's physic, whom Agnès had implored him to send; thè practitioner's celery decoctions and leeches had not been enough to cure the old woman of the fevers of pleuro-pneumonia, and she had succumbed at dawn, her head resting in the lap of her mistress who had lain beside her to provide extra warmth.

To begin with, the passing of this formidable pillar of strength, who had protected and ordered Agnès's life for so long, grieved her to the point where she lost all desire to eat. However, her grief was soon replaced by a feeling of relief – so soon, in fact, that the young woman had a sense of shame. She was alone now and in danger, but for the first time there was nothing to link her to the past besides her daughter, who was still so young. Gisèle, the last remaining witness to that night of horror in the icy chapel long ago, had gone to her grave.

Agnès sat bolt upright at the end of the long kitchen table, trying to control the anxiety she had been feeling since she learned of Eudes's visit. Mabile, sent as a gift by her half-brother following Gisèle's death, cast occasional glances at her. She was obedient and hard-working, but the Dame de Souarcy disliked the girl, whose presence was a constant, niggling reminder of Eudes. She suspected that the gentle Clément, despite his extreme youth, shared her misgivings. Had he not said to her one day in a mischievous voice, which his serious expression belied:

'Mabile is in your room, Madame. She is tidying your things – again, taking them out and carefully examining them before replacing them. But how can she rearrange your registers if, as she claims, she cannot read?'

Agnès needed no clarification in order to grasp the child's meaning: Mabile had been sent by her former master to spy on her. Not that this came as any surprise – indeed, it explained rather better than compassion her brother's persistent generosity.

Clément's extraordinary precocity astounded Agnès. His keen intelligence, his relentless powers of observation and his remarkable ability to learn and memorise caused her on occasion to forget how young he was in years. Scarcely had Agnès finished teaching him the rudiments of the alphabet than he knew how to read and write. In contrast, her daughter Mathilde's indifference to the advantages of knowledge meant she was at pains to recite even the simplest prayer. Mathilde possessed the grace and delicacy of a butterfly and the complexities of life quickly bored her. Perhaps the explanation lay in Clément's strange birth. Mathilde was still a child, whereas it seemed to Agnès sometimes that Clément was becoming more and more like a companion upon whom she could depend. To what extent had the child understood Eudes's wicked scheming? How conscious was he of the threat hanging over the three of them? Did he know the cruel fate that awaited him if his true origin were ever brought to light? The bastard progeny of a violated servant girl, the orphan of a suicide seduced by the fables of heresy, who had escaped torture and burning at the stake thanks to Agnès's unwitting collusion. And what if someone were to suspect what the child knew he must conceal? She shuddered at the thought. How could she have been so oblivious to Sybille's asceticism that she attributed her compulsive behaviour to the pregnancy forced on her by a common brute? Had she been blind? And yet in all honesty, what would she have done had she known? Nothing, to be sure. She would certainly not have turned the poor wretched girl out. As for denouncing her – that was a vile, wicked act to which Agnès would never have stooped.

'Will my good master, the Baron de Larnay, be passing the night here, Madame? If so, I should send Adeline to prepare his quarters,' Mabile observed, lowering her gaze.

'I know not whether he intends to honour us with his presence tonight.'

'The journey is nearly seven or eight leagues.[+] He and his steed will doubtless be weary. I don't suppose they will arrive here until after none,[+] or even vespers,'[+] she lamented.

What a relief it would be if he lost his way in the forest and never came out! Agnès thought, and declared:

'Indeed, what a tiring journey, and how kind of him to undertake it in order to pay us a visit.'

Mabile gave a little nod of approval at her new mistress's observation, adding:

'How true. You have an admirable brother, Madame.'

Agnès's eyes met Clément's and the boy quickly turned away, concentrating his gaze on the glowing embers in the huge hearth.

Whole stags had been roasted there when Hugues was still of this world.

Agnès had never loved her husband while he was alive; the idea of forming an emotional bond with this man to whom she was being given in matrimony had never crossed her mind. At just thirteen, she was of age,[2] and was obliged to wed the pious, courteous gentleman. He showed her the same respect as he would if her true mother had been the Baroness de Larnay rather than her lady-in-waiting. In any event, he had been gracious enough never to remind her that she was the last illegitimate child of noble birth sired by Eudes's father Robert, the late Baron de Larnay. Robert, in a fit of remorse that coincided with a tardy devoutness, had demanded that his daughter be recognised, and even Eudes, who would not gain from such an official recognition of parenthood, had complied. And so the old Baron Robert de Larnay had quickly married the adolescent girl off to his old drinking, feasting and fighting companion Hugues de Souarcy, a childless widower, but, above all, his most loyal vassal. He had settled a small dowry on Agnès, but her astonishing beauty and extreme youth had been enough to conquer the heart of her future spouse. For her part she had accepted with good grace this marriage that conferred upon her a certain status, but more importantly placed her beyond her half-brother's reach. But Hugues had died without producing a son and now, at twenty-five, the position in which she found herself was hardly better than when she had lived in her father's house. Naturally, she received a dower[3] from her husband's estate, though it was barely enough for her to run her household. It represented only a third of the few remaining properties Hugues had not squandered, comprising the Manoir de Souarcy and its adjoining land, as well as an expanse of arid grey terrain known as La Haute-Gravière where only thistles and nettles grew. However, her dower was far from safe, for if, as she feared, Eudes was able to show that her conduct as a widow was inappropriate, she would be dispossessed in accordance with an old Normandy custom stipulating: 'A loose-living woman forfeits her dower.' At the cost of interminable wars, the province of Normandy had remained in the realm for the past hundred years, but it conserved its customs and fiercely asserted the right to a 'Norman Charter' that enshrined its traditional privileges. These did not favour women, and if Agnès's half-brother achieved his ends, there would be only three ways for her to escape destitution: the convent – which would mean leaving her daughter in Eudes's predatory hands; remarriage, if he gave his consent – which he could withhold; and death – for she would never yield to him.

Mabile's sighs brought her back to reality.

'What a pity it is Wednesday, a fast day.[4] Were my master to stay until tomorrow he could enjoy our fine pheasants. Tonight he will have to make do with plain vegetable soup, no pork, spiced mushrooms and a dried fruit pudding.'

'There is no place for regrets of this kind in my house, Mabile. As for my brother, I am sure that, like the rest of us, he finds great solace in penitence,' Agnès retorted, her thoughts elsewhere.

'Oh yes, like the rest of us, Madame,' repeated the other woman, fearful her remark might be deemed sacrilegious.

A loud commotion emanating from the main courtyard put an end to Mabile's discomposure. Eudes had arrived. She hurried over to fetch the whip hanging behind the door that was used to calm the dogs, and rushed out squeaking with joy. The thought occurred to Agnès that her half-brother might enjoy in this lady's maid something more than a loyal servant. Perhaps the poor girl hoped Eudes would leave her with child, and deceived herself into thinking her bastard progeny would enjoy the same fate as Agnès and be recognised. She was mistaken. Eudes was not his father, Robert. Far from it, and yet the Baron had been no saint or even a man of honour. No, his son would sooner cast her out without a penny than suffer the slightest inconvenience. She would join the legions of dishonoured women who ended up in houses of ill repute, or worked on farms as day labourers in exchange for a meal and a tiny room in which to carry out their thankless chores.

Mathilde leapt up, scampering after Mabile to greet her uncle, who as a rule arrived bearing armfuls of rare and precious gifts. The Larnay wealth was among the most coveted in the Perche region. The family had had the good fortune to discover iron ore on their lands, which they exploited in the form of an opencast mine. The monarchy valued the ore – which was the envy of the English – and this manna had earned the feudal Baron a measure of royal patronage since King Philip IV the Fair* was eager to avoid any temptation on the part of the Larnay family to form an alliance with the age-old enemy. The kingdom of France had reached a partial accord with the English, but it was a volatile alliance on both sides, despite the planned union between Philip's daughter Isabelle and Edward II Plantagenet.[5]

Eudes, while not renowned for his intelligence, was no fool. Philip the Fair's limitless need for funds made him a difficult, even a dangerous sovereign. The Baron's approach was simple and had borne fruit: he would grovel and pledge his loyalty to the King by alluding indirectly to the demands and the offers of the English; in brief, he would show his allegiance, reassure him, while at the same time encouraging his generosity. It did not pay, however, to go too far; Philip and his counsellors had not hesitated to imprison Gui de Dampierre in order to rob him of Flanders, to confiscate the property of the Lombards and the Jews or even to order the abduction of Pope Boniface VIII* during his visit to Anagni.* Eudes was well aware that if he opposed the King or displeased him in the smallest way, it would not be long before he was discovered at the bottom of a ditch or stabbed to death by some providential vagabond.

Agnès stood up with a sigh, adjusting her belt and veil. A quiet voice made her jump:

'Take heart, Madame. He is no match for you.'

It was Clément. He was so good at making himself inconspicuous, invisible almost, that she had all but forgotten he was there.

'Do you believe that?'

'I know it. After all, he is only a dangerous fool.'

'Dangerous, indeed – dangerous and powerful.'

'More powerful than you, but less so than others.'

And with these words he slipped through a small postern door leading to the servants' garderobe.[6]

What a strange child, she thought, making her way towards the hubbub outside. Was he capable of reading her thoughts?

Eudes's voice boomed out. He was shouting orders, bullying this person and showering abuse on that. The moment Agnès appeared in the courtyard, the expression of loathing and irritation on her brother's face was replaced by a smile. He walked over to her with open arms and cried out:

'Madame, you grow more radiant every day! Those mastiffs of yours are wild animals. You must set aside a pair of males for me from the next litter.'

'What a pleasure to see you, brother. Indeed, they are fierce towards strangers, but loyal and gentle with their masters and the herds. I trust your household is thriving. And how is your good lady wife, my sister Apolline?'

'Big with child, as is her custom. If only she could manage to produce a son! And how she stinks of garlic, sweet Jesus! She pollutes the air from dawn till dusk. Her physic maintains that taking brews and baths made from the revolting bulb will produce a male. So she swallows it, stews in it, spews it – in short, she makes my days a living hell, and as for my nights …'

'Let us pray that she will soon bear you a sturdy son, and me a handsome nephew,' interrupted Agnès.

She, too, opened her arms in order to seize the hands that threatened to close around her body. And then she quickly moved away under the pretext of giving orders to the farm hand, who was struggling to control Eudes's exhausted, nervous mount.

'Why don't you get off that horse!' Eudes barked at the page, who was nodding off astride his broad-chested gelding.

The young lad, barely twelve years old, leapt from the saddle as if he had been kicked.

'Good. Now get a move on! A pox on your sluggishness,' Eudes roared.

The terrified boy began seeing to the load weighing down his packhorse.

Acting the suzerain, Eudes led his sister into the vast dining hall – so cool even the worst heatwave could barely warm its walls. Mabile had laid the table and was leaning against the wall awaiting her orders, her head bowed and her hands clasped in front of her apron. Agnès noticed that she had taken the trouble to change her bonnet.

'Fetch me a ewer so I may rinse my hands,' Eudes ordered, without so much as a glance in her direction.

As soon as the girl had gone, he asked Agnès:

'Does she please you, my lamb?'

'Indeed, brother, she is obedient and hard-working. Although I suspect she misses serving in your household.'

'What of it! Her opinion doesn't interest me. Good God, I'm ravenous! Well, my beauty. What news from your part of the world?'

'Not a great deal, to be sure, brother. We had four new piglets this spring, and so far the rye and barley crops are flourishing. We expect a good yield, if the continual rain of the past few years stays away. When I think that less than fifteen years ago they were harvesting strawberries in Alsace in January! But I mustn't bore you with my farmer's complaints. Your niece,' she pointed to Mathilde, 'has been bursting with eagerness to see you again.'

He turned towards the little girl, who had been vainly attempting to attract his attention with smiles and sighs.

'How pretty she is, with that little face and those honey-blonde curls. And those big dreamy eyes! What passions you will soon provoke, my beloved.'

The overjoyed girl gave a polite curtsey. Her uncle continued:

'She is made in your image, Agnès.'

'On the contrary, I think she resembles you when you were a child – much to my pleasure. Although you and I, it is true, might have been mistaken for twins had it not been for your superior strength.'

She was lying deliberately. They had never borne the slightest resemblance to one another – except for the colour of their coppery golden hair. Eudes was stocky, with heavy features, a square jaw, an overly pointed nose, and his skinny lips resembled a gash when they were not uttering some bawdy word or insult.

All of a sudden his face grew sullen, and she wondered if she had gone too far. His eyes still riveted on his half-sister, he said to the girl in a soft voice:

'How would you like to do me a good turn, my angel?'

'Nothing would please me more, uncle.'

'Run and find out what has become of that good-for-nothing page. He's taking a long time to unload his horse and bring me what I requested.'

Mathilde turned and hurried out to the courtyard. Eudes continued solemnly:

'Were it not for your goodness, Agnès, I would have resented the distress your arrival into this world caused my mother. What a slight, what an insult for such a pious, irreproachable woman.'

Agnès was glad of the remark, for she feared he had seen through her charade. Indeed, at every visit he managed to recall in the most obvious way his generosity as a boy, forgetting how he had snubbed and mistreated her until Baron Robert demanded that she be regarded as a young lady. Strangely, after her mother had died, when Agnès was barely three years old, Baroness Clémence had grown tremendously attached to this child of an adulterous union. It had amused her to show the girl how to read and write, to teach her Latin and the rudiments of arithmetic and philosophy, as well as her own two great passions: sewing and astronomy.

'Your mother was my good angel, Eudes. I can never thank her enough in my prayers for the kindness she showed me. Her memory is alive in my heart and a constant comfort.'

Tears welled up in her eyes, spontaneous tears for once that were a sign of true affection and grief.

'Forgive my brutishness, my beauty! I am well aware of your devotion to my mother. At times I behave like an oaf, pray forgive me.'

She forced a smile:

'No, brother. You are always good.'

Persuaded of her gratitude and respect for him, he changed the subject:

'And what of that little rascal who is always hiding behind your skirts. What is his name? He has not made an appearance yet.'

Agnès knew instantly that he was referring to Clément, but pretended she was racking her brains in order to give herself time to decide what attitude she should adopt.

'A little rascal, you say?'

'You know. The orphan whom your kindness compelled you to take into your household.'

'Do you mean Clément?'

'Indeed. What a shame he isn't a girl. We could have given him to the sisters at Clairets Abbey* as an offering to God[7] and spared you the extra mouth to feed.'

As overlord, Eudes had the authority to do this if he wished, and Agnès would have no say in the matter.

'Clément is no trouble to me, brother. He is content with little and has a gentle, quiet nature. I rarely see him, but at times his presence amuses me.' Convinced that her brother's aim was to gratify her at little cost to himself, she added, 'I confess that I would miss him. He accompanies me on my rounds of the estate and its neighbouring communes.'

'Indeed, too gentle and too puny to make a soldier out of him. He could become a friar, perhaps, in a few years' time.'

She must on no account openly oppose Eudes. He was one of those fools who dug in their heels at the slightest resistance, immediately manoeuvring others into a position of defeat. It was their customary way of convincing themselves of their power.

Agnès continued in the same measured tone with a hint of feigned uncertainty:

'If he proves competent enough, my intention is to make him my apothecary or physic. I shall be much in need of one. Learning fascinates him, and he already knows all about the medicinal herbs. But he is young yet. We shall discuss it when the time comes, brother, for I know you to be an able judge where people are concerned.'

Children are credited with an infallible instinct. Mathilde was worrying proof of the contrary. Having first tasted the fruits and sweetmeats, she sat at her uncle's feet chattering away, delighted each time he kissed her hair or slipped his fingers down the collar of her tunic to caress the nape of her neck. Her uncle's accounts of his hunting exploits and his travels fascinated her. She devoured him with her eyes, an enchanted smile spreading across her pretty face. Agnès thought that she must soon explain her uncle's shameful nature to her. But how? Mathilde adored Eudes. She regarded him as so powerful, so radiant; in short, so wonderful. He brought within the thick cold grey walls of the Manoir de Souarcy the promise of a life of easy grandeur that intoxicated her daughter to the point of clouding her judgement. Agnès could not blame her. What did she know of the ways of the world, this little girl who in less than a year would become a woman? She had only ever known the pressures of farm life: the mud of stables and sties, the worry of the harvests, the coarse clothing and the fear of famine and illness.

An unbearable thought struck Agnès with full force. Eudes would repeat with his niece what he had attempted with his half-sister when she was barely eight, given half the chance. The extent to which he was in thrall to his incestuous passion terrified Agnès. There were plenty of peasants and maids for him to mount, some of whom were flattered by the interest their master showed in their charms, while others – the majority – simply resigned themselves. After all, they had already suffered the father and grandfather before him.

Pleading the lateness of the hour, Agnès ordered her daughter to be put to bed. Where was Clément? She had not seen him since Eudes de Larnay's arrival.

Clairets Forest, May 1304

The massive torso bore down on him. A solid wall of rage. It seemed to the novice as though he had been standing for an eternity contemplating the perfect musculature rippling beneath the silky black skin slick with sweat. And yet the horse had only advanced a few paces towards him. The voice rang out again:

'The letter. Where is the letter? Give it to me and I will spare your life.'

The hand holding the reins tapered off into a set of long gleaming metal talons. The novice was able to make out a pair of straps attaching the lethal glove to the wrist. He thought he saw blood on the metal tips.

His panting breath resounded in his ears. The clawed hand moved upwards, perhaps in a gesture of conciliation. The novice watched each infinitesimal movement as though it were fractured through a prism. The action had been swift and yet the hand appeared to be endlessly repeating the same gesture. He closed his eyes for a split second, hoping to drive away the image. His head was reeling, and a terrible thirst caused his tongue to stick to the roof of his mouth.

'Give me the letter. You will live.'

From what dark depths did this voice emanate? It belonged to no ordinary mortal.

The novice turned his head, weighing up his chances of escape. Nearby, a thick clump of trees and shrubs shimmered in the setting sun. Their swaying branches were too tight for a horse to pass through. He made a dash for it. Careering like a madman, he nearly fell over twice and had to clutch the overhead branches to steady himself. His wheezing breath rose from his throat in loud gasps. He resisted the urge to collapse on the forest floor and lie there sobbing, waiting for his pursuer to catch up with him. Further to his right, the shrill echo of a magpie's startled chatter pierced the young man's eardrums. He ran on. A few more yards. Up ahead in a clearing, a tall bramble patch had colonised every inch of space. If he managed to hide there his pursuer might lose his trail. He leapt into the middle of the hellish undergrowth.

He clasped his hand over his mouth to stifle the cry that threatened to choke him. The blood throbbed in his throat, his ears and his temples.

There, motionless, silent, barely breathing. The brambles snagged his arms and legs and clung to his face. He watched their hooked claws creeping towards him. They quivered, stretching out and slackening, poised to tear into his flesh. They dug into his skin, twisting in order to snare their prey.

He tried hard to convince himself brambles were inanimate, yet they moved.

The night was crimson red when it fell. Even the trees turned crimson. The grass, the moss further off, the brambles, the mist, everything was tinged with crimson.

A terrible pain pulsed through his limbs as though he were being scorched by a flameless fire.

A faint noise. A noise like swirling water. If only he could put his hands over his ears to stop the rushing sound in his head. But he could not. The brambles clung to him with redoubled spite. The sound of approaching hooves.

The letter. It must not be found. He had promised to guard it with his life.

He tried to pray but stumbled over the words of his entreaty. They ran through his mind again and again like some meaningless litany. He clenched his jaw and pulled his right arm free of the spines that were crucifying him. He felt his skin ripping under the plant's stubborn barbs. His whole hand had turned black. His fingers would barely move, and felt so numb all of a sudden that he found it difficult to push them inside his cape to seize the parchment.

The missive was brief. The hooves were drawing near. In a matter of seconds they would be upon him. He ripped up the small piece of paper and crammed the fragments into his mouth, chewing frantically in order to ingest what was written before the hooves appeared. When the novice finally managed to swallow and the ball moistened with saliva disappeared inside him, he had the impression that those few magnificent lines were ripping his throat apart.

Flat against the forest floor which was thick with blackberry bushes, all he could see at first were the black horse's front legs. And yet it seemed to him they were multiplying, that suddenly there were four, six, eight animal's legs.

He tried to stop his breathing – so loud it must be echoing through the forest.

'The letter. Give me the letter.'

The voice was cavernous, distorted, as though it were coming from the depths of the earth. Could it be the devil?

The throbbing pain from the remorseless brambles disappeared as if by magic. God had heard his prayer at last. The young man rose up, emerging from the barbed snarl, indifferent to the scratches and gashes lacerating his skin. Blood was pouring down his face and from his hands, which he held out before him, red against the crimson night. Beads of it formed along the veins of his forearms as far as his elbows then vanished as quickly as they had come.

'The letter!' ordered the booming voice, resounding in his head.

He gazed down at his feet clad in sandals. They were so swollen he could no longer see the leather straps beneath the black blistered flesh.

He had sworn to guard the letter with his life. Was it not a crime then to have eaten it? He had given his word. Now he must give his life. He looked back at the ocean of brambles he had foolishly believed would be his salvation, and tried to judge its height. It stirred with a curious breathing motion, the blackberry branches rising, falling, rising again. Making the most of a long exhalation, he leapt over the hostile mass and ran in a straight line.

It felt as if he had been running for hours, or a few seconds, when the sound of galloping hooves caught up with him. He opened his lips wide and gulped a mouthful of air. The blood rushed to his throat and he burst into laughter. He was laughing so hard that he had to stop to catch his breath. He bent over and only then did he notice the long spike sticking out of his chest.

How did the broad spear come to be there? Who had run him through?

The young man slumped to his knees. A river of red flowed down his stomach and thighs and was soaked up by the crimson grass.

The horse pulled up a yard in front of the novice, and its rider, dressed in a long, hooded cape, dismounted. The spectre removed the lance swiftly and wiped its bloody shaft on the grass. He knelt down and searched the friar, cursing angrily as he did so.

Where was the letter?

The figure leapt up furiously and aimed a violent kick at the dying man. He was seized by a murderous rage just as the dried, shrivelled lips of the young man opened one last time to breathe:

'Amen.'

His head fell back.

Five long shiny metal claws approached the dead man's face and the spectre regretted only one thing: that his victim could no longer feel the pitiless destruction they were about to unleash upon his flesh.

Supper was a lengthy affair. The table manners of Agnès's half-brother revolted her. Had he never heard of the eminent Parisian theologian Hugues de Saint-Victor, who over half a century before had explained the rules of table etiquette? In his work he specified that one should not 'eat with one's fingers but with a spoon, nor wipe one's hands on one's clothes, nor place half-eaten food or detritus from between one's teeth on one's plate'. Eudes gorged himself noisily, chewed with his mouth open and used his sleeve to wipe away the flecks of soup on his face. He belched profusely as he finished off the last crumbs of the fruit pudding. Sated by the supper Mabile had managed to make delicious despite the lack of meat – forbidden on this fast day – Eudes said all of a sudden:

'And now … Gifts for my lamb and her little beloved. Send for Mathilde.'

'She is surely sleeping, brother.'

'Then let her be woken. I wish to perceive her joy.' Agnès obeyed, curbing her irritation.

A few moments later, the girl, her clothes thrown on in haste, came into the vast hall, her eyes glassy with sleep and with desire.

Eudes walked over to the big wooden box covered with hessian, which the page had carried in earlier. He relished carefully untying the ropes as his niece's expectancy mounted. At last he pulled out an earthenware flask, declaring enticingly:

'Naturally, for your toilet I have brought vinegar from Modena, ladies. They say its dark hue turns the skin pale and silky as a dew-covered petal. The finest Italian ladies use it in abundance.'

'You spoil us, brother.'

'And what of it? This is a mere trifle. Let us move on to more serious matters. Ah! What do I see next in my box ... five ells[+] of Genovese silk ...'

It was a gift worthy of a princess. Agnès had to remind herself what lay behind her half-brother's extravagance in order not to run over and feel the saffron-coloured fabric. But she could not stop herself from crying out:

'What finery! My God! Whatever shall we use it for? Why, I would be afraid to spoil it with some clumsy gesture.'

'Just imagine, Madame, that the dream of all silk is to caress your skin.'

The intensity of the look he gave her made her lower her eyes. He continued, however, in the same playful tone:

'And what might this heavy crimson velvet pouch contain? What could give off such a heady fragrance? Do you know what it is, Mademoiselle?' he teased, leaning towards his gaping niece.

'I admit I do not, uncle.'

'Well, let us open it then.'

He walked over to the table and spread out the blend of aniseed, coriander, fennel, ginger, juniper, almond, walnut and hazelnut, which the wealthy liked to sample before going to bed to freshen their breath and aid their digestion.

'*Épices de chambre*,' breathed the girl in an admiring, mesmerised voice.

'Correct. And for my beloved what have we in our treasure trove? For I do believe your birthday is fast approaching, is it not, pretty young lady?'

Choked with emotion, the excited Mathilde pranced around her uncle, twittering:

'In a few weeks' time, uncle.'

'Perfect! Then I shall be the first to congratulate you, and you'll not object to my haste, will you?'

'Oh no, uncle!'

'Now then, what have we here that might make a birthday gift worthy of a young princess? Ah! A silver and turquoise filigree brooch fashioned by Flemish silversmiths. And from Constantinople a mother-of-pearl comb that will make her even prettier and the moon grow green with envy ...'

The ecstatic child hardly dared touch the piece of jewellery shaped like a long pin. Her lower lip trembled as if she were about to burst into tears before such beauty, and Agnès thought again how the simplicity of their lives would soon become a burden to her daughter. But how would she explain to this girl, who was still a child, that in a few years' time her charming uncle would see in his half-niece a new source of pleasure. Agnès knew that she would stop at nothing to avoid it. He would never touch her daughter's soft skin with his filthy paws. Fortunately, as a boy, Clément was safe from such desires – and a lot more besides. Rumours concerning the strange tastes of other lords had reached Souarcy, but Eudes only liked girls, very young girls.

'And lastly, this!' he declaimed histrionically, as he pulled from the saddlebag a sack made of hide and fashioned in the shape of a long finger. He undid the thin piece of cord and took out a greyish phial.

Mathilde let out a cry of joy:

'Oh my lady mother! Sweet salt! Oh, how wonderful! I have never seen any before. May I taste it?'

'Presently. Show a little restraint, now, Mathilde! Take my

daughter back to her room, will you, Mabile? It is late and she has already stayed up far too long.'

Before reluctantly following the servant, the little girl politely took her leave, first of her uncle, who kissed her hair, and then of her mother.

'Well, brother, I admit to being no less impressed than my daughter. They say that Mahaut d'Artois, Comtesse de Bourgogne, is so partial to the stuff that she recently purchased fifteen bars of it at the Lagny fair.'

'It is true.'

'Yet I thought her poor. Sweet salt is said to be worth more than gold.'

'The woman pleads poverty loudly while possessing great wealth. At two gold crowns and five pennies the pound, fifteen bars, each weighing twenty pounds, represents a small fortune. Have you ever tasted sweet salt, Agnès? The Arabs call it saccharon.'[8]

'No. I only know that it is sap collected from a bamboo cane.'

'Then let us rectify the situation at once. Here, lick this, my dear. You will be amazed by the spice. It is so smooth and combines well with pastries and beverages.'

He lifted a long grey finger up to her lips and a wave of revulsion that was difficult to control caused the young woman's eyelids to close.

The evening stretched on. The stiff posture Agnès had obliged herself to maintain since her half-brother's arrival, in order to discourage any familiarity on his part, was taking its toll on her shoulders. Her head was spinning from listening to Eudes's endless stories, the sole aim of which was to show him in a good light. Without warning he exclaimed:

'Is it true what they tell me, Madame, that you have built bee yards[9] for the wild swarms where your land borders Souarcy Forest?'

For a while she had only been half listening to him, and his deceptively casual question almost threw her:

'You have been correctly informed, brother. In accordance with common practice we hollowed out some old tree stumps with a red-hot iron, installing crossed sticks before depositing the wild colonies.'

'But raising bees and harvesting honey is a man's work!'

'I have someone to assist me.' Eudes's eyes burned with curiosity.

'Have you seen the king of the colony yet?'[10]

'I confess I have not. The other bees guard him bravely and fiercely. Indeed, the idea of producing honey came to me when one of my farm hands was badly stung while helping himself to a free meal in the forest.'

'Such petty theft is considered to be poaching and is punishable by death. I know that you are a sensitive soul, and it is a charming attribute of womanhood. All the same, you could at least have ordered his hands to be cut off.'

'What use would I have for a farm hand with no hands?'

He responded to her remark with a hollow-sounding laugh, and she had the impression that he was trying to catch her out. Vassals were obliged to hand over two-thirds of their honey and a third of their wax to their lord – a levy Agnès had neglected to pay since she set up her bee yards two years before.

'Let me sample this nectar, then, my beauty.'

'Sadly, brother, we are still novices. Our very first harvest, last year, was a great disappointment. The continual rains turned the honey, making it unfit to eat. That is why I sent you none – for fear of making you and your servants ill. We fed it to our pigs, who tolerated it. On top of which I managed clumsily to spill one of the two pails. This year's harvest only yielded three pounds of poor quality – barely good enough to flavour the wine dregs. Let us hope that the harvest will be better this summer, and that I shall have the pleasure of sharing it with you and your household,' she said, feigning a sigh of despair before continuing, 'Oh, my sweet brother Eudes, I do not know how we would survive without your continued goodwill. The soil at Souarcy is poor. Imagine, I have only been able to replace half our draught animals with plough horses – oxen being so slow and clumsy. These bee yards should allow us to supplement our meagre everyday fare. Hugues, my dear departed husband, didn't … Well, he wasn't …'

'He was just a senile old man.'

'As you will soon be,' she muttered under her breath, and lowered her head as though out of embarrassment.

'That was an unwise decision of my father's if ever there was one. Marrying you to an old man of fifty, whose only claim to glory was a rash of battle scars! War does not make a man, it betrays his true nature – striking down the coward who hitherto employed a wealth of cunning to escape the slightest wound.'

'My father believed he was acting in my interests, Eudes.'

Since the beginning of their exchange she had attempted to adjust her speech, to emphasise their blood relationship – which he was at great pains to keep out of his own discourse, always addressing her as 'my beauty', 'my Agnès', 'my lamb', and occasionally as 'Madame'.

Nonetheless, Eudes's hesitation was palpable. Agnès cultivated it as best she could, in the knowledge that her only salvation lay in this final reticence. As long as he doubted his half-sister's awareness, he would continue to paw at the ground without daring to take the last guilty leap. On the other hand, the day he discovered she was wise to his deplorable lechery … Well, she did not know how else she could try to stop him.

She stood up from the bench and with a smile offered him her hand.

'Let us pray together to the Holy Virgin, brother. Nothing would give me greater pleasure, besides your presence here tonight. It would make Brother Bernard, my new chaplain, so happy to see us kneeling side by side. And afterwards you must rest. I regret being the motive for your undertaking such a long journey.'

He did not notice that she was taking leave of him, and was obliged reluctantly to do as she said.

When at last the following morning after terce[+] she watched Eudes and his page disappear across a field, Agnès felt exhausted and her head was spinning. She decided to make an inspection of the outlying buildings, more as a way of dispelling her continual unrest than out of any real necessity. Mabile, who was staring mournfully down the empty track, mistook Agnès's mood and remarked in a sorrowful voice:

'Such a short visit!'

Her face was pale and drawn, and Agnès reflected that for Eudes and his servant the night must have seemed even shorter.

'Yes indeed, Mabile, and yet how pleasant while it lasted,' she lied with such ease that she felt an almost superstitious fear creeping through her. Were lying and cheating really that simple despite all the Gospel's teachings? Undoubtedly – or at least when they were the only existing form of self-defence.

'How right you are, Madame.'

Only then did Agnès notice the strip of dark-purple muslin

draped over the girl's shoulders. She had not seen it before. Was it payment for services rendered or for favours granted?

'Let Mathilde sleep. She was up so late. Clément will accompany me – if and when he reappears.'

She hadn't seen the child since the previous evening. Was this coincidence or guile? Whatever the case, he was wise to keep away from Eudes's prying eyes.

'I am right behind you, Madame.'

She turned towards the soft voice, amused and at the same time intrigued. She had not heard him arrive. Clément would come and go, disappearing for days at a time without anyone knowing where he was, only to reappear suddenly as if by magic. She really should order him to stay by her side, for the surrounding forest was an unsafe place, especially for one so young, and indeed Agnès was constantly afraid that someone might come upon him bathing in a pond or a river. On the other hand, Clément was cautious, and his independence inspired Agnès – perhaps because she herself felt spied upon, trapped.

He followed noiselessly a few steps behind her, flanked by the two guard dogs, and only drew closer when Agnès, confident that they were out of earshot of the inquisitive Mabile, enquired gently:

'Where do your roamings take you?'

'I do not roam, Madame, I watch, I learn.'

'Whom do you watch? What do you learn?'

'You. Many things – thanks to the sisters at Clairets Abbey. And thanks to you,' he added.

She looked down at him. His strange blue-green almond-shaped eyes stared back at her gravely, and with a flicker of suspicion. She said in a hushed voice:

'Clairets Abbey is so far from here. Oh, I don't know whether it was right of me to insist that you attend lessons there. It is almost a league away – too far for a child.'

'Half that if you go through the forest.'

'I don't like to think of you in that forest'

'The forest is my friend. It teaches me many things.'

'Clairets Forest is … Well, they say it is sometimes visited by creatures, evil creatures.'

'By fairies and werewolves? Tall stories, Madame.'

'You mean you don't believe in werewolves?'

'No more than I believe in fairies.'

'And why not?'

'Because if they existed and were so powerful, Madame, at worst they would have already killed or eaten us and at best made our daily lives a hell.'

He smiled, and for the first time it occurred to Agnès that he only ever allowed himself to express amusement or joy with her. Clément and Mathilde's relationship was restricted to a good-natured selflessness on his part and an ill-tempered arrogance on hers. It was true that her daughter considered him a sort of privileged servant, and on no account would she have lowered herself by treating him as an equal.

'Upon my word, you have quite convinced me. And I am greatly relieved for I would have hated to come face to face with a werewolf,' she exclaimed jovially and then, growing serious again, she added in a worried voice, 'Will you be careful about what we have discussed, Clément? No one must know. Your life, and mine, depends on it.'

'I know that, Madame. I have known it for a long time. You need have no fear.'

They continued their dialogue in silence.

The village of Souarcy was built on a small hill. The alleyways leading up to the manor were lined with dwellings that twisted and turned, making it difficult for the hay-carts to manoeuvre without damaging the roofs of the houses. The positioning of the higgledy-piggledy buildings was entirely random, and yet they appeared to be huddled together as though seeking warmth. Souarcy, like a good many other manors, had no right to hold weaponry. At the time it was built, the English threat weighed heavily over the region and defence was the only option – hence its raised position in the middle of a forest. Indeed, the thick outer walls, within which peasants, serfs and craftsmen dwelled, had resisted many an attack with calm impudence.

Agnès replied with a perfunctory smile to the greetings, bows and curtseys of those she encountered as she made her way up to the manor via the muddy pathways, slippery with yellow clay after the recent rains. She stopped at the dovecote, but did not draw any of her usual pleasure from it. Eudes and his possible machinations were constantly on her mind. Even so, the magnificent birds welcomed her with a torrent of gently excited warbling. She glanced at the large, puffed-up male whose proud strutting always brought a smile to her lips. Not today. She had baptised him Vigil – the Watchful One – because at first light he liked to perch on the ridge beam of the manor house, cooing and watching the day break. He was the only bird who had a name. Yet another gift from her half-brother, who had brought the animal from Normandy the year before to inject new blood into her dovecote. He stretched out his muscular dark-pink neck, flecked with mauve, and she favoured him with a brief caress before leaving.

It was only after she had returned to the great hall at the manor that she realised Clément had cleverly avoided answering her question. It was too late now. The boy had disappeared again, and she would have to wait to ask him to explain the nature of what was increasingly keeping him away from the manor.

Eudes, too, was exhausted. He had only slept for an hour between Mabile's thighs. The strumpet was unstinting when it came to taking her pleasure. Happily – since her engagement in Agnès's household had yielded precious little else of any interest to her master. Unable to trap the mistress, he had tupped the servant. Scant compensation for the handsome piece of silk and the morsel of sweet salt, which alone had cost a small fortune, but it would have to do for the time being.

God, how his half-sister detested him! In Agnès's eyes he was insufferably conceited, boorish and depraved. He had come to realise that she loathed him some years before when she believed herself finally rid of him thanks to her marriage. The passion, the corrupt desire he had conceived for her when she was just eight and he ten had changed into a consuming hatred. He would break her and she would grovel at his feet. She would submit to his incestuous desire – so repugnant to her that sometimes it made the colour drain from her face. He had once hoped to conquer her love and that it would be strong enough to make her commit the unpardonable sin, but this was no longer the case. Now he wanted her to submit, to beg him.

He took out his vicious ill humour on his page, who had fallen asleep and was threatening to topple forward onto his gelding's neck.

'Wake up! Why, anyone would think you were a maid! And if indeed you are a maid I know how to make a woman of you.'

The threat had the desired effect. The young boy sat bolt upright as if he had been whipped.

Yes, he would break her. Soon. At twenty-five she had lost none of her beauty, although she was no longer a girl. And anyway, she had given birth, and it was well known that pregnancy spoiled a woman's body, in particular her breasts – and he preferred them pert, as was the fashion at the time, like little rounded apples, their skin pale and translucent. Who was to say that Agnès's had not been ruined by purple stretch marks? Perhaps even her belly was withered. In contrast, Mathilde was so pretty, so slim and graceful, just like her mother had been at her age. And Mathilde adored her extravagant uncle. In a year's time she would come of age and be ripe for the taking.

The thought cheered him no end, and he gave a loud guffaw: two birds with one stone. The worst revenge he could imagine taking on Agnès was called Mathilde. He would caress the daughter and destroy the mother. Of course, she would not leave the way clear for him. Despite his general lack of respect towards the fairer sex, Eudes was forced to acknowledge his half-sister's intelligence. She would strike him with all her might. A pox on females! All the same, the challenge could be exciting.

Upon further reflection, this particular stone would kill not two birds but three, since the Larnay mine, which assured his wealth and relative political safety, would soon be exhausted. Certainly, the earth's depths contained more hidden riches, but to get at them would require deep mining and neither his finances nor the geological conditions were favourable. The clay soil would give way at the first attempt to dig.

'Agnès, my lamb,' he murmured through his clenched jaw, 'your end is near. Tears of blood, my precious beauty, tears of blood will run down your sweet cheeks.'

Yes, he had been worrying about the mine for some time now.

He decided to go there and check the progress of the iron-ore extraction.

'Bring him to me! Drag him here on his backside if you have to! He won't be needing it much longer,' bellowed Eudes de Larnay as he glowered at the tiny pile of iron ore at his feet, the meagre result of a whole week's mining.

The two serfs, heads bowed, had stepped back a few yards. The Baron's angry outbursts were well known, and could end in vicious blows, or worse.

They did not wait to be asked twice, and were only too glad to have such an excellent excuse to put the greatest possible distance between them and their master's fists. And in any case, that half-wit Jules, who was no better than they were, had done his fair share of swaggering since being promoted to overseer. He had become too big for his boots and now the boot was on the other foot.

The two men, exhausted by overwork and lack of sleep and nourishment, hurled themselves across the tiny arid plain towards the oak grove that stretched for leagues – almost as far as Authon-du-Perche.

Once they had reached the relative safety of the trees, they slowed down, stopping for a moment to catch their breath.

'Why have we come to the forest, Anguille? This isn't where Jules ran off when the master arrived,' said the older of the two men.

'I don't know, damn it. What does it matter? We had to run somewhere or we'd be the ones taking the beating.'

'Do you know where Jules went?'

'No, and I don't care,' snapped Anguille, 'but it makes no

odds, he won't get far. The master's mad as a drunken lord, and a nasty piece of work to boot.'

'What is it with that cursed mine? It's not for lack of digging. My legs and arms are well nigh dropping off.'

Anguille shrugged his shoulders before replying:

'His cursed mine's dried up, hasn't it? Jules told him, but it's no good, he won't listen. It's about as useless as a dead rat and not worth all the fuss. He can cry all he likes, he'll get nothing but dust from it now.'

'And to think it gave them bags of lovely gold for nigh on three generations. What a deadly blow for the master. He must be taking it hard!'

'Oh yes? Well, he'll be over it before it ever bothers me. Because, you see, that cursed mine might have given him bags of gold, but what has it ever given me, or us, except aching limbs, floggings and an empty belly? Come on, let's go deeper into the forest and have a little snooze. We'll tell him we couldn't find Jules.'

'But that's a lie.'

Anguille looked at him, flabbergasted by his naivety, and said reassuringly:

'Yes, but if you don't tell him, he won't know.'

Cyprus, May 1304

The confused nightmare. Francesco de Leone sat up with a start on his straw mattress, his shirt drenched in sweat. He concentrated on breathing slowly to try to calm his wildly beating heart. Above all he wanted to avoid going back to sleep for fear the dream would continue.

And yet the Knight Hospitaller of Justice and Grace[11] had lived so long with this fear that he often wondered if he would ever be rid of it. The nightmare was more like a bad dream that had no end and always began with the echo of footsteps – his footsteps – on a stone floor. He was walking along the ambulatory of a church, brushing the rood screen shielding the chancel, trying by the weak light filtering through the dome to study the shadows massed behind the columns. What church was this? The rotunda suggested the Holy Sepulchre in Jerusalem or even the bravura architecture of the dome of the Hagia Sophia in Constantinople. Or could it be the Santa Costanza in Rome, the church which he believed opened onto the Light? What did it matter? In his dream, he knew exactly what he was looking for within those colossal walls of pinkish stone. He tried to catch up with the silently moving figure, betrayed only by the slight rustle of fabric. It was the figure of a woman, a woman hiding. It was at this point in the dream that he realised he was chasing her and that the design of the church, centred on the chancel, was hindering him. The figure circled as he circled, always a few steps ahead of him as though anticipating his movements, staying on the outside of the ambulatory while he moved along on the inside.

Francesco de Leone's hand reached slowly for the pommel of his sword, even as an overwhelming love made his eyes fill with tears. Why was he chasing this woman? Who was she? Was she real?

He gave a loud sigh, exhausted but tense at the same time. Only old women believed dreams were premonitions. And yet he had dreamt of the deaths of his sister and his mother only to discover their corpses soon afterwards.

He looked up at the tiny arrow slit opening onto the sky. The fragrant Cypriot night had no calming effect on him. He had been to so many places, known so many people that he could barely remember the town where he was born. He was from nowhere and felt like a stranger in this vast citadel, reconquered, following the siege of Acre in 1291, after a fierce battle led by the Knights Templar* and the Hospitallers. Guillaume de Beaujeu, the Grand-Master of the Knights Templar, had lost his life and Jean de Villiers, Grand-Master of the Knights Hospitaller, had been a hair's breadth from succumbing to his wounds. Only seven Hospitallers and ten Templars had survived the siege and the ensuing battle that signalled the end of Christendom in the Orient.

Most of the Knights Templar had returned to the West. As for the Knights Hospitaller, their hurried retreat to Cyprus had taken place with the mild opposition of the ruler of the island, King Henri II of Lusignan, who had reluctantly allowed them to settle in the town of Limassol on the southern coast. The monarch was worried about what might soon become a state within a state – both orders being exempt from all authority save that of the Pope. Lusignan had imposed on them boundless restrictions. Thus, to a man, their number on the island must never exceed seventy knights plus their entourages. It was a clever way of curbing their expansion and, above all, their influence. The Holy Knights were forced to submit while they waited for more auspicious times. It mattered little. Cyprus was a mere step, a brief respite that would allow them to recover their strength and regroup before reconquering the Holy Land. For the birthplace of Our Lord must not remain in the hands of the infidels. Guillaume de Villaret, who in 1296 succeeded his brother as Grand-Master, had had a premonition, and his attention was now turned to Rhodes, a fresh refuge for his order.

Francesco de Leone experienced a frisson of elation and joy when he imagined advancing towards the Holy Sepulchre, raised on the site where Joseph of Arimathea's garden had once stood. It was in the crypt beneath the church that Constantine's mother had discovered the cross.

He would fall to his knees on the flagstones, warm from the fierce desert sun outside. He envisaged the tip of his out-stretched hand brushing the strap of the sandal. He was ready to lay down his life with devotion and infinite humility for this deed; it was the Knight's supreme sacrifice.

The time had not yet arrived. Hours, days, months, even years, lay ahead. So many things must come to pass before then. Had he lost his way? Was his faith no longer entirely pure? Was he not beginning to enjoy the scheming of the powerful, which he was supposed to thwart?

He stood up. Despite his relative youth he felt as if he were a thousand years old. The human heart held few mysteries for him; it had afforded him some rare but dazzling moments of wonder and a great many more of despair, even disgust. To love man in Christ's image seemed to him at times an impossible ideal. And yet he would do well to conceal this chink in his faith. All the more so as man was not his mission; his mission, his many missions were Him. It was the indescribable joy of sacrifice that sustained Francesco de Leone during his darkest hours.

He moved noiselessly through the wing containing the cells and dormitory. Reaching the outside, he slipped on his sandals before crossing to the centre of a vast courtyard where the building housing the hospital was located.

He briskly descended the steps leading to the morgue beneath the infirmary. It was in this cramped cellar that bodies were laid out awaiting burial, their decomposition accelerated by the sweltering heat. On that particular morning, it was empty – not that the Knight would have been disturbed by the sight of a corpse. He had seen so many dead bodies, had advanced among them, stepping over them and occasionally turning one to search for a familiar face, blood up to his ankles. At the far end of the cellar a small postern door led to the carp pond chiselled out of the granite rock. This fish farm, inspired by a thousand-year-old Chinese tradition, provided additional food for the residents of the citadel and represented an economy since the carp lived on chicken excrement. His ablutions in the icy water of the deep pond, and the carp – rendered blind by years of darkness – brushing against his calves, did nothing to dislodge the profound unease he had felt since he awoke that morning.

By the time he entered the chapel to join the prior, who also occupied the position of Grand-Commander, dawn was just breaking.

Arnaud de Viancourt, a small, slim man with light-grey hair and an ageless face, turned to him smiling, and folded his hands across his black monk's habit.

'Let us go outside, brother, and make the most of these few hours of relative coolness,' he suggested.

Francesco de Leone nodded, certain that the early-morning

air was not the reason for the frail man's proposition. He was afraid of the spies Lusignan had placed everywhere, perhaps even within their order.

The two men walked for a while, their heads bowed and the hoods of their cloaks raised. Leone followed Arnaud de Viancourt to the great stone wall. His relationship with Guillaume de Villaret, their current Grand-Master, was founded upon the loyalty that bound the two men, as well as their intellectual complementarity. And yet the prior was unaware that this mutual trust had its limits; Guillaume de Villaret was well acquainted with the fears, hopes and motives of his Grand-Commander – as was his nephew and likely successor, Foulques de Villaret – but the reverse was not true.

Arnaud de Viancourt stopped walking and looked around carefully to make sure they were alone.

'Listen to the cicadas, brother. Like us they wake at dawn. What wonderful stubbornness they possess, do they not? But are they aware of why they sing? Surely not. Cicadas do not question their lot.'

'Then I am a cicada.'

'Like all of us here.'

Francesco waited. The prior was given to these preambles, to speaking in metaphors. Arnaud de Viancourt's mind made him think of a gigantic universal chessboard whose pieces were constantly moving and never obeyed the same rules. He wove such a complex web and it was easy to lose sight of the individual threads. Then suddenly each element would fall into place to form a perfect whole.

The prior said in an almost detached voice, as though he were thinking aloud:

'Our late lamented Holy Father Boniface VIII had the makings of an emperor. He dreamed of installing a papal theocracy, a Christian empire united under one sole power ...'

The veiled criticism was not lost on Francesco. Boniface had ruled with a rod of iron and been little disposed to dialogue, and his intransigence had won him many critics even within the Church.

'... His successor Nicolas Boccasini, our Pope Benoît XI,* is quite unlike him. No doubt his election surprised him more than anyone. Should I confess, brother, that we fear for his life? He wisely pardoned Philip the Fair for attempting to murder his predecessor.'

The idea that Benoît's life might be threatened filled the Knight with silent dread. The new Pope's purity of vision, his spiritualism even, was a cornerstone of the century-old combat which Leone had devoted himself to. He waited, however, for the other man to continue. The prior proceeded with customary caution:

'It ... It has been brought to our attention that Benoît intended to excommunicate Guillaume de Nogaret,* the monarch's ubiquitous shadow, who only played an accidental part in that abomination, although rumour has it Nogaret insulted Boniface. Be that as it may, Benoît must be seen to respond, to hold somebody to account. Complete absolution would undermine the Pope's already wavering authority.' He sighed before continuing. 'King Philip is no fool and he won't stop there. He needs a compliant pope and will have him elected if necessary. He will no longer tolerate any forces of opposition that might interfere with his plans. If our fears are justified and the Pope's succession is imminent, we could find ourselves on very uncertain, not to say dangerous, ground. We are no less in the firing line than the Knights Templar. I need not go on – you know as well as I.'

Francesco de Leone gazed up at the sky. The last stars were fading. Was the newly elected Pope's life really in danger? The prior digressed:

'Are they not miraculous? We might fear they will fade forever, and yet each evening they return to us, piercing the blackest night.'

Arnaud de Viancourt glanced at the taciturn Knight. The man never ceased to amaze him. Leone could have become one of the pillars of the Italian-speaking world – as admiral of the Hospitaller fleet or even a Grand-Master of their order. The noble blood that flowed in his veins, his bravery and his intelligence predisposed him to it. And yet he had refused these honours, these burdensome responsibilities. Why? Certainly not for fear of not measuring up to the task, even less so out of immaturity. Perhaps it was simply pride, a gentle pure sort of pride that made him long to give his life for his faith. An implacable, terrible pride that convinced him that he alone was capable of following his mission through to the end.

The old man observed his fellow Knight once more. He was tall, his features delicate but well defined. His honey-blond hair and dark blue eyes betrayed his northern Italian origins. The shapely sensuality of his lips might have suggested a carnal nature, and yet the prior was in no doubt as to his complete chastity – imperative in their order. What most astonished him was the extraordinary versatility of his brilliant mind, a strength that sometimes frightened him. Locked behind that lofty, pale brow was a world to which no one possessed the keys.

Leone was filled with foreboding. What would become of his

quest without the private, not to say secret, backing of the Pope? He sensed that the drawn-out silence of his superior required a response.

'Are your suspicions about this ... threat to our Holy Father related to the names Nogaret or Philip?'

'It is hard to tell the difference between the two. The critics abound: no one knows who governs France, Philip or his counsellors Nogaret, Pons d'Aumelas, Enguerran de Marigny, to name but a few. Do not be misled by my words. Philip is a stubborn, hard-hearted man and well known for his ruthlessness. Even so, to answer your question: no, King Philip is too convinced of his legitimacy to stoop to commit murder against God's representative on earth. We believe he will do as he did with Boniface and demand his removal from office. As for Nogaret – I doubt it. He is a man of faith and of the law. Moreover, were he to conceive such a plot without the endorsement of his monarch, he would be forced to commit – or have someone commit – a devious abhorrent form of murder, and I do not see him as a poisoner. However ...' Arnaud de Viancourt accentuated his pause with a slight nervous gesture of his hand '... a zealous follower might interpret and carry out their desires.'

'It wouldn't be the first time,' avowed Leone, feeling a frisson of horror at the idea.

'Hmm ...'

'Should we stay close to the Pope, then, in order to safeguard his life? I would willingly defend it with my own.'

As he spoke, the Knight was certain that the prior had been leading up to something else. The palpable sorrow in the man's eyes as he stared at Leone told him he had not been mistaken.

'My friend, my brother, you must know how difficult, nay, impossible it is to prevent this horror, and do we still have time?

Of course Benoît's life is our first priority. As we speak, two of our brave brothers are at his side, protecting him with their constant vigilance, tracking the would-be poisoners. However, if … If he were to pass away … In our grief we must not forget the future …'

Leone finished the sentence for him, pronouncing the painful words he knew nevertheless to be true:

'… which we must already begin forging if we are to prevent the destruction of Christendom.'

These words applied equally to the sacred mission to which he had committed himself body and soul, and about which Arnaud de Viancourt knew nothing. About which no one must know.

'The future, indeed. Benoît's succession – if our desperate attempts of the last few weeks to prevent it fail.'

'Are we hoping that an intervention on our part might influence events?'

'Hope? There is always hope, brother. Hope is our main strength. But hope is not enough in this instance. We must be certain that King Philip IV's plan fails. If his counsellors succeed, as I fear they will, in electing a puppet pope to the Vatican, they will be free to attack those whom they cannot control as they would wish – that is to say, the Order of the Knights Templar and our own, since we are considered to be the Pope's personal guard, a wealthy guard – and you know as well as I do of the King's need for money.'

'In which case the Templars are first in the line of fire,' observed Leone. 'Their extreme power has become their failing. The wealth that passes through their hands incites greed in others. Their system of depositing and transferring funds from one side of the world to the other has greatly facilitated this. Crusaders and pilgrims to the Holy Land need no longer live in fear of being robbed. Additionally, they receive a stream of donations and alms from all over Christendom.'

'We benefit from it as much as they, and I must remind you that we are almost certainly as wealthy,' corrected Arnaud de Viancourt.

'True, but the Templars are censured for their arrogance, their privileges, their wealth, even for being idle and uncharitable, whereas we are spared such criticism. There is no better way to fuel a fire than with jealousy and envy.'

'That is no reason to think, or more precisely to make others think, that this money has yielded such profits that they are now sitting on a veritable fortune. Have you ever asked yourself, Francesco, why Philip the Fair withdrew the administration of the royal finances from the Paris Templars in 1295 and entrusted it to the Italian moneylenders?'

'It was simpler for him to cancel his debt to the moneylenders by arresting them and confiscating their assets. The same strategy would have proved more risky if used against the Templars.'

'Precisely. And yet strangely enough two years ago the King granted the same Templars the right to collect taxes. Is it not a contradiction?'

'A measure which, when added to the rumours already circulating about the Templars, provoked the anger of the people.' The scattered elements of the prior's discourse had come together in Leone's mind, and he continued, 'So this is part of a long-term strategy thought up by the King in order to discredit the Templars permanently.'

'Stoking the fire as you said just now.'

The prior's words trailed off in a sigh. The prospect of the fate that awaited them had troubled him for so long now. Francesco de Leone finished his train of thought for him:

'And so the fire is already blazing. A conflagration would suit the King of France's purposes very well, and the other monarchs of Europe will not be displeased by the prospect of strengthening their power with regard to the Church. The defeat at Acre will only serve to kindle the flames. Their reasoning will be simple: why so much wealth and power for these military orders that lose us the Holy Land? In other words we cannot expect any help from outside. None will be forthcoming unless the other monarchs smell Philip the Fair's possible defeat, in which case they would flock to the Pope's side.'

'What a curious monologue-for-two our discussion is turning out to be, brother,' observed the prior. 'Is it possible that we have foreseen the future since we refer to it in the same terms?' A sudden sadness caused his pale features to stiffen. 'I am old, Francesco. Every day I count the tasks I am no longer able to undertake. All the years of war, crusades, death and blood ... All the years of obedience and self-denial. To what end?'

'Do you doubt your commitment, the sincerity of our order, of our mission, or worse still of your faith?'

'Nay, brother, certainly I do not doubt our order or my faith. I doubt only myself, my failing strength and ability. At times I feel like a frightened old woman whose only recourse is to tears.'

'Self-doubt, when mastered, is a friend to all men except fools and simpletons. Self-doubt is the resounding proof that we are but an infinitesimal, troubled part of the divine understanding. We are aware of our failings, yet we progress.'

'You are still young.'

'Not so young any more. I shall be twenty-six this coming March.'

'I am fifty-seven and nearing my end. It will be a glorious reward, I believe. I shall at last enter the Light. Until then my task is to continue to fight with you as my magnificent warrior, Francesco. Our enemies will use any means, including ignoble ones. It is a secret war, but a merciless one. And it has already begun.'

Leone sensed the prior's hesitation. What was he holding back? Knowing that a direct question would be awkward, he tried to curb his impatience.

'Are we to prevent Benoît's murder and the election of a pope favourable to Philip?'

Arnaud de Viancourt looked down, as though searching for the right words, before replying:

'What you do not yet know, brother, is that the old idea advocated twelve years ago by Pope Nicholas IV in his encyclical Dura nimis, of uniting the military orders, primarily those of the Templars and Hospitallers, is still alive.'

'Yet our relations with the Templars are … strained,' Leone argued.

Viancourt hesitated before deciding to keep quiet about the pace of negotiations between their Grand-Master, the Pope and the King of France. The union would benefit the Hospitallers who would take control of the other orders. A confrontation with the Templars, who would not willingly give up their autonomy, was imminent, all the more so as Jacques de Molay, the Templars' Grand-Master, was a traditionalist. An outstanding soldier and man of faith, he was weakened by his political naivety and blinkered by pride.

'Strained … That is putting it mildly. Philip the Fair is a fervent advocate of this union.'

Leone raised his eyebrows.

'His position is most surprising. A single order under the Pope's authority would represent an even greater threat to him.'

61

'That is true. However, the situation would be reversed if the union took place under his authority. Philip plans to name one of his sons Grand-Master of the newly constituted order.'

'The Pope will never agree to it.'

'The question is whether he will be in a position to refuse,' the prior clarified.

'And so we return to the problem of preventing the election of a pope favourable to Philip,' murmured Leone.

'Indeed. But do we have the right to influence the history of Christendom? The question plagues me.'

'Do we have the choice?' the Knight corrected gently.

'I am afraid the coming years will provide us with little room for manoeuvre. Therefore, no, we do not have the choice.'

The prior became engrossed in the study of a tuft of wild grass that had pushed its roots between two large blocks of stone. He murmured softly:

'The sheer tenacity of life. What a supreme miracle.'

He continued in a firmer voice:

'How should I put this? A fortuitous and unwitting intermediary will ... assist us against his will.'

The prior cleared his throat. Leone looked enquiringly at Arnaud de Viancourt, sensing that what he was about to say vexed him. He was not mistaken.

'Good God, even his name is ... difficult for me to pronounce.' He sighed before confessing, 'This intermediary is none other than Giotto Capella, one of the best-known Lombardy moneylenders of the Place de Paris.'

Leone grew faint and his eyes closed. He tried to protest but Viancourt interrupted:

'No. There is nothing you can say that I do not already know. I also know that time cannot heal all wounds. I spent days searching for another solution, in vain. Capella will never escape his tainted past. It is our trump card.'

Leone propped himself against the wall of broad, rough-hewn stones. He was overwhelmed by his emotions and struggling with his hatred. In truth he had been fighting it for so long now it had become like an unwanted companion he had learnt over the years to silence and control. And yet he knew if he freed himself, if he rid his soul of the loathing he felt for Capella, he would be one step closer to the Light. In a faltering voice he said:

'Blackmail? What if Capella is a reformed man, what if he simply acted out of cowardice …? One needs to have experienced terrible fear in order to forgive a coward. I was so young then, but now …'

Arnaud de Viancourt replied in a despondent voice:

'Brother, what purity of soul you possess. Many men would have been incapable …' He stopped himself, deeming it unacceptable to add to the pain Leone was clearly already suffering. 'Why should Capella help us in return for nothing when we have so little that interests him, and the King so much? I doubt it and it grieves me. Do men change unless they are compelled to? You may judge for yourself, brother. I know you to be a formidable judge of men's souls. You will soon perceive how much he has changed, or simply how willing he is to oblige. I hope for our sake – and for his too – that you will deem the letter we have prepared for him superfluous. I sincerely hope you find the solace of forgiveness – forgetting is human, forgiving is divine. If such is the case, you may destroy the missive. Otherwise … I regret inflicting this ordeal on you but you must leave for France straight away. I have prepared letters of introduction as well as a leave of absence[12] of unspecified duration. You will stay in our commanderies as and when required. You will find all the comfort and spiritual succour you need there. Giotto Capella should enable you to come within reach of our most redoubtable enemy, Guillaume de Nogaret. If we are right and Nogaret is already looking for a replacement pope, he will need money, a great deal of money. We suspect that the French cardinals are among the candidates of the King's Counsellor. They are licentious and extravagant and will not pass up this opportunity to fill their purses. To begin with your task will consist in identifying the most likely candidate, for there are already several lining up. At best a name, or at worst two, Francesco. It is our only chance of intervening before it is too late.'

So everything had long been decided. The prior's uncertainty and regrets were doubtless sincere, but he and the Grand-Master had already woven their web.

A clamour of contrasting emotions raged inside Francesco de Leone. An incredible feeling of hope overlaid his hatred for Capella.

Arville-en-Perche, France, site of one of the Templars' most important commanderies. The place where for months he had despaired of arriving, the place where another door, surely the decisive one, would open for him. His throat was dry, and he limited himself to a brief remark:

'They say Guillaume de Nogaret is a dangerous man.'

'He is. And all the more so as he possesses one of the most brilliant minds I have ever known. Remember, he is the worthy successor of Pierre Flote and, like him, a jurist and staunch advocate of the supremacy of the monarchy's power over that of the French clergy. We must under no circumstances allow a schism to occur in the Church, or any part of it to break away from the authority of the Pope. If this religious and political controversy were to assume greater proportions, the result would be catastrophic.'

'For the monarchy's power would become a divine right. Philip would rule directly through God, making him the highest authority in the realm.'

The prior nodded. He had spent entire nights devising strategies to defend against the coming avalanche, only at dawn to reject every last one as hopeless. The only remaining solution was to anticipate and prevent Philip from putting an end to the supreme authority of the Church over all the monarchs of Christendom.

Leone had regained some of his composure. He felt far away from the island sanctuary. He was already there, in the one place where his quest could continue.

'What practical information can you provide that will help me to ...' he began, when Arnaud de Viancourt interrupted him:

'We are groping in the dark, brother. Any conjecture on my part would be a dangerous imprudence.'

'And my weapons, my powers?'

The prior appeared to hesitate and then, in a clipped tone that left the Knight unperturbed, he replied:

'The choice is yours, provided they serve Christ, the Pope and ... our order.'

Had he been in any doubt, this declaration would have made it clear. Like the other orders, the Knights Hospitaller were strictly hierarchical and individual initiatives were strongly discouraged. The free rein given him was easy to interpret: the order was facing the most ruinous crisis it had known since its formation almost two centuries earlier.

'Will my mission be recorded?'

'You are not afraid, are you, Francesco? I cannot believe it. No. You know how suspicious we are of written records. That is why we only recently felt the need to have one of our own, Guillaume de Saint-Estène, copy out our founding texts. Few written transcripts of our rules exist and they must never find their way outside the order or be copied, as you know. You are not afraid, are you?' the prior repeated.

'No,' murmured Francesco de Leone and smiled. His first smile that early morning.

He knew that true fear would come later. What he felt now was an intense pressure crushing him, and he had to stop himself from slumping to his knees on the dust-covered ground to pray or perhaps even to cry out.

The last hours of daylight lingered in the west. Francesco de Leone had worked like a slave the whole day long, missing both meals as part of a private fast. He had helped care for 'our lords the sick' – one of the duties of the Order of the Hospitallers that distinguished it from the other military orders – as well as providing training in the use of arms for some of the recently admitted novices. The heat and physical exhaustion had offered him a vague respite.

Might Benoît die? Might everything fall into place now? After four long years of a quest that had been as discreet and unrelenting as it had been fruitless, might a political threat lead him to a doorway hitherto hidden? The reason for his journey was admittedly this difficult mission. And yet the coincidence seemed too great for it to be entirely accidental. A sign. He had waited so long for the Sign. He was going to France, to the country where the Ineffable Trace had re-emerged and with full powers granted to him by the prior and consequently by the

Grand-Master himself. He was going to discover there at last, perhaps, the meaning of the Light that had immersed him for a fleeting and divine moment at the heart of the Santa Costanza in Rome.

A ripple of anxiety coursed through him like a fever. What if it were only another illusion, another deadly disappointment? Would he have the strength to go on?

That choice was not his to make either.

Hoc quicumque stolam sanguine proluit, absergit maculas; et roseum decus, quo fiat similis protinus Angelis.[13]

Night was slowly falling. The clamour in the streets had gradually died down. It was almost supper time. The cloaked figure stepped over a pile of debris blocking the central drain and turned right into Rue du Cygne.

The foul acrid smell drifting on the breeze gave a better indication of the tavern's location than any sign. It was one of those establishments where workers and craftsmen from the guilds gathered in the evenings – in this case the tanners' and leatherworkers' guild. While some fiery preachers described them as 'dens of iniquity' that encouraged sinful behaviour, the truth was far more benign. They were drinking places with a family atmosphere: people settled most of their deals and differences there and stopped for a welcome rest surrounded by a friendly din.

The cloaked figure paused in front of the door. Laughter and cries echoed from inside. He had deliberately arrived late so that the customers' curiosity would not be roused by seeing a solitary figure seated at a table. The person he was meeting would then already be waiting inside. He drew his hood down over his forehead and, clasping the sides of his heavy cloak, which was far too warm for such a sultry evening, he pushed open the door.

Two steps. Two steps were all it took. An ocean; a universe. A gulf separating innocence from almost certain damnation. And yet innocence can be a burden and above all rarely profitable. Innocence affords private satisfaction; money and power simple recompense.

The cloaked figure descended the first step and then the second.

Except perhaps for a welcoming smile from one woman sitting at a table, his entrance elicited little response from the tavern's regular customers.

Calmly crossing the trodden earth floor strewn with straw, the cloaked figure approached a table towards the back of the room, which was plunged into darkness. The man he was meeting had snuffed out the oil lamp in front of him.

The figure sat down. The hubbub of conversation around them was in full swing and would conveniently drown out the transaction that was about to take place.

The man was plump and jovial. He filled a second glass with wine and said in a hushed voice:

'I ordered the best. Since her husband passed away, the landlady has developed the regrettable habit of watering down the drink. It's only natural. She buys it for a few pennies a barrel from one of her nieces, a nun at Épernon. They say the abbey possesses some fine presses.'

Did he really believe that such harmless banter would detract from the enormity of the matter that had brought them there? And yet, the cloaked figure betrayed no irritation but remained silent, bolt upright, awaiting his next move.

At last, the man, a former barber-surgeon if what he said was true – that is a butcher[14] of beards and of human flesh – vexed by the silence of the person opposite, slid his fleshy hand across the table. Clasped in his palm between his hairy thumb and fingers was a phial wrapped in a thin strip of paper. A second hand wearing a thick brown leather glove reached out from under the cloak to take it, and at the same time set down a bulging purse, which the barber quickly pocketed. He explained in an almost piqued, slightly menacing voice:

'I've brought the instructions. It requires somewhat delicate handling. The aconite enters through the skin. It's slower but every bit as lethal as if it's swallowed.'

The cloaked figure stood up, not having uttered a single word, nor tasted a single drop of wine, which would have meant pulling back the hood of the cloak.

Two steps. Only two steps to climb. Back in that dimly lit room buzzing with relaxed conversation lay the past. It no longer bore any relation to the future.

The past had been inflicted, had imposed itself with all its cruel injustices. The future would be freely chosen. But first it must be fashioned.

Clairets Abbey, Perche, May 1304

The abbey of the Order of Bernadine Cistercians was generously patronised and exempt from duties, as well as enjoying the privilege of low, middle and high justice, borne out by the gibbet erected on the gallows site. The abbey had permission to harvest timber for fuel and building from the forests owned by the Comte de Chartres. In addition to these charitable contributions, the abbey owned land at Masle and Theil that brought in a sizeable annual income, not to mention the numerous donations from local burghers or nobles or even from the more affluent peasants who had been pouring in steadily for years. The abbey's dedication service[15] had been witnessed by a certain Guillaume, commander of the Knights Templar at Arville.

Éleusie de Beaufort, Abbess of Clairets since the advent of her widowhood five years earlier, set down the letter written on Italian paper,[16] which she had received only moments before in the strictest secrecy. Had she not been convinced by the seals protecting the letter, she would certainly have burnt it or else dismissed it as a blasphemous fraud.

She looked up at the exhausted messenger who stood in silence awaiting her reply. She could tell by the man's despondent expression that he knew the contents of the missive. She played for time:

'My brother in Christ, you must rest a few hours. Your journey will be a long one.'

'Time is running out, Abbess. I have no desire to rest and as for my needs, well, they must wait.'

71

She smiled at him sadly and corrected herself:

'Then let us say I request the favour of a few moments' reflection and contemplation.'

'I consent, but do not forget that time is running out.'

Éleusie de Beaufort walked over to a doorway concealed behind a hanging. She led the man up a carved stone staircase to a heavy padlocked door that hid from the eyes of the world, and her fellow nuns, her private library – one of the most prestigious and the most dangerous in all Christendom. The counts and bishops of Chartres, various scholars, not to mention a few kings, princes and even some knights, had for decades deposited there the works they brought back from all four corners of the world, some of them in languages the Abbess, despite her great learning, was unable to decipher. She was the secret guardian of this science, of these books – most of them forgotten by the heirs and descendants of their original donors – and at times she experienced a frisson of uneasiness when she touched their covers. For she knew, she had read in Latin, in French and in the little she was able to decipher of English, that some of these volumes contained unrepeatable secrets. The mysteries of the universe were explained in three or four of them – possibly more for she read no Greek (a language that was little known and even looked down upon at the time), Arabic or Egyptian, and even less Aramaic. These secrets must remain beyond the reach of men, and no higher authority, save that of the Holy Father, would convince her otherwise. Why, then, did she not simply destroy them, reduce them to ashes? She had lain awake many a night asking herself that question. She had even got up to go to the great hearth in the library with the intention of fuelling a sacrilegious fire, only to make her way back to bed incapable of carrying out her plan. Why? Because they contained knowledge, and knowledge, however unbelievable, was sacred.

The Abbess made the messenger as comfortable as she could before unbolting another door opening onto the corridor. Cautiously poking her head out to check that the coast was clear, she walked through and closed it behind her. She made her way swiftly towards the kitchen to fetch a ewer of water, some bread and cheese and perhaps a few slices of smoked bacon – enough to replenish the traveller after his exhausting journey. She hurried along the corridor, like a thief, hugging the walls, listening out for the slightest sound for fear of being surprised.

A jovial voice rang out behind her. She swung round, summoning up all her strength in order to greet Yolande de Fleury's words with a smile. The young sister worked in the granary and was accompanied by the granary's custodian, Sister Adèle de Vigneux. Yolande de Fleury was a small, plump woman whose perpetual good humour, it appeared, nothing could dampen. She enquired:

'Abbess, where are you going in such a hurry? Might we assist you in some task?'

'No, my dear children. I felt a sudden but persistent thirst – a result of my bookkeeping no doubt. A walk to the kitchens will stretch my legs.'

Éleusie watched the two women disappear round the corner at the end of the corridor. Naturally she trusted her nuns, even her novices, as well as the majority of the lay servants, who were offerings to God. She could no doubt have shared the burden of her secret with some of them: Jeanne d'Amblin, for example, the most loyal of all, intelligent and, despite having no great illusions about the world, an optimist. These qualities, coupled with her tenacity, had encouraged Éleusie to confer on her the challenging task of Extern Sister.[17] Adélaïde Condeau was no less of an ally.

She had been baptised thus after a cooper discovered her at the edge of a forest of that name. She was only a few weeks old, two or three at the most. The man was not glad of his discovery and took the infant to the abbey. He had no need of a baby girl but the famished newborn infant's cries had moved him. Despite her youth and impressionability, Adélaïde, too, was already showing evidence of great perseverance coupled with an unwavering faith. Blanche de Blinot, the most senior nun and her prioress and second in command, had long been her confidante. Blanche's advanced age was her greatest asset, for she forgot most of what she was told. Even Annelette Beaupré, the apothecary nun, for all her tetchiness and arrogance was someone upon whom she knew she could rely. On the other hand, she did not entirely trust Berthe de Marchiennes, the cellarer nun,[18] who already occupied that demanding post before Éleusie's arrival at the abbey. Berthe's resentment was palpable beneath the façade of her devoutness. Her lack of physical beauty and a dowry had left her no other option but the monastic life, although she would certainly have preferred the secular one.

No, absolutely not. A secret is best kept when it is shared with no one. And in any case what right had she to burden these good women with dangerous revelations that were difficult to bear? It would be selfish of her. No, none of the sisters must know of this man's presence. He would leave as he had arrived, like a troubling enigma.

In order to reach the kitchen, Éleusie decided to cut through the guest house[19] that was squeezed in between the hot-room and the storeroom. With the exception of Thibaude de Gartempe, the guest mistress, and possibly of Jeanne d'Amblin, neither of whom were cloistered, she ran little risk of bumping into anyone at that hour. She hadn't noticed the small figure pressed behind one of the pillars beside the schoolroom door. Clément paused, ashamed at having hidden instinctively. He was disconcerted by the Abbess's behaviour. Why such caution, such furtiveness in her own convent?

Back in her study Éleusie de Beaufort sat down behind her heavy oak table. She touched the letter with the tip of her finger. It still bore the two crease marks where it had been folded, and looked inoffensive lying there among the registers to whose pages the Abbess carefully consigned the details of their daily lives: the donations, the harvests, the number and quality of wine barrels in the cellar, the amount of timber felled, received or donated, the births and deaths in the pigeon-house, plus the weight of droppings, which were used as fertiliser, the visits to the sick, the deaths, the levies imposed, the ingredients of the nuns' meals or their new linen. Half an hour ago, the task had bored her; she had baulked at it and wondered what possible use the endless lists, over which she nevertheless took great care, might one day have. Half an hour ago, she was still unaware how much she would soon mourn the thankless task. In the insignificant space of that half-hour, her world had collapsed, and she had not even sensed the approaching cataclysm that would silently ravage the calm of her study.

She was choked by a terrible grief. She stood by helplessly as the sanctuary that had been her home for five years was devastated. All those images she had managed to suppress, or rather to eradicate. All those hideous waking nightmares. Would they come back to haunt her now? The incomprehensible, bloody, violent and terrifying scenes she was powerless to stop that pulsed through her imagination. At one point, she had thought she was losing her mind, or that a demon was tormenting her with visions of hell. She never knew when she might be visited by the terrifying hallucinations. For nights on end she had prayed to the Holy Virgin for some reprieve. Her prayer had been answered the moment she arrived at the convent. She had almost managed to rid herself even of the memory of them. Were they going to come back? She would rather die than endure them again.

A woman lay face down on the rack, the blood from the gashes on her back oozing to the floor. The woman was moaning. Her long fair hair was sticky with sweat and blood. A hand brushed against her martyred flesh, pouring a grey powder onto her wounds. The woman arched her back and went limp, fainting. Suddenly Éleusie could make out the pale face. It was she. Éleusie.

This vision in particular had haunted her all those years ago, night after night for months on end. Éleusie had decided to take her religious vows.

She had to keep telling herself that it was only a horrible memory, nothing more. She could feel her heart pounding against her chest. Reluctantly she picked up the letter and forced herself to calm down. She proceeded to read it for the tenth time:

Hoc quicumque stolam sanguine proluit, absergit maculas; et roseum decus, quo fiat similis protinus Angelis.

The thing she had been dreading for years had caught up with her that day.

How should she reply to this demand? Could she pretend not to know, not to understand? What foolishness! What did her own blood matter compared to the divine blood that cleansed all sins? Little or nothing.

She began to trace the curved letters of her reply, which she knew by heart. She had repeated them for hours on end like an exorcism, thinking, hoping she would never need to write them:

Amen. Miserere nostri. Dies illa, solvet saeclum in favilla.[20]

A cold sweat drenched the hem of her veil, making her shiver suddenly and drop her quill.

She picked it up again and continued writing:

Statim autem post tribulationem dierum illorum sol obscurabitur et luna non dabit lumen suum et stellae cadent de caelo et virtutes caelorum commovebuntur.[21]

Amen.

He was blinking from exhaustion. The filthy rags he wore made him feel nauseated. And yet the messenger was accustomed to this endless journeying, these arduous missions under various guises. Occasionally, he would sleep for leagues at a time face down on his horse's neck, allowing the animal's legs to decide his fate and his path. However, this time he had been obliged to travel incognito and in this impoverished countryside a horse would have been too conspicuous.

A surge of joy lifted his spirits. He was the go-between, the necessary tool, the link between the powerful of this earth, those who shaped the world for future generations. Without him their decisions would remain as mere wishes, mere hopes. He gave them life, shape and substance. He was the humble artisan of the future.

He was only a hundred yards outside the abbey enclosure when the soft sound of racing feet made him swing round. A figure in a white tunic was running towards him, a wicker basket joggling back and forth on one arm.

'Oh dear God!' she gasped. 'I should not be here, but you are a brother monk. Our Abbess ... Well, I came here on my own initiative. You are so exhausted. Why did you not spend the night in our guest house? We often receive visitors. Oh here I am chattering away like a jackdaw ... You see, I feel so ashamed. Take these ...'

She handed him the provisions she had prepared and, blushing, explained:

'I thought to myself, if our Reverend Mother received you, it was because she trusted you and you were a friend. I know her well. She has much work and many responsibilities. I knew she would have thought to feed you, but not to supply you with food for your journey.'

He smiled. She had been right. She looked rather frail and yet a remarkable strength radiated from her every gesture. The kindly sister gazing up at him had broken the rule of the cloister for his sake, and she was glowing proof that his exhaustion was deserving and that Christ lived in them both.

'Thank you, sister.'

'Adélaïde ... I am Sister Adélaïde, in charge of the kitchens and of meals. Hush! Do not thank me. You know I should not be here, and I wasn't told to come – it was a simple oversight. I wished to make amends, that is all. I deserve no thanks. And yet I am happy to offer you these humble provisions – this rye bread, black but very nourishing, a bottle of our own cider – you'll find it delicious – a goat's cheese, some fruit and a big slice of spice cake, which I made myself. They say it's very flavourful.' She laughed, before confessing awkwardly, 'I love to feed people, no doubt it is a failing. I don't know why, it just gives me pleasure.' Suddenly guilty, she stammered, 'Oh dear, I should not say such things …'

'Indeed you should. It is good to feed people, above all the needy. Thank you for your precious offerings, Sister Adélaïde.' Suddenly glad of this brief exchange, which had lightened his spirits before his gruelling journey, he added, 'And you have my word, this will remain strictly between us – like a little secret that unites us over distance.'

Overjoyed, she bit her bottom lip and then, frightened, said hastily:

'I must go back. I sense your path will be a long one, brother. Let it be safe from harm. My prayers will follow you. No, they will accompany you. Make a little place for me in yours.'

He leant towards her, planted a fraternal kiss on her anxious brow, and murmured:

'Amen.'

Clément felt confident. All was quiet. The nuns had retired to their cells after supper and compline.[+] Outside, a chorus of frogs croaked and the jays' raucous complaints ricocheted from nest to nest. Further to his right, the tireless garden dormice tunnelled furiously between the stones with their claws. They were such cautious creatures that it was rare to catch a glimpse of their little black masked faces. The slightest unfamiliar presence would silence them. Clément delighted in the treasure trail nature left for those who knew how to watch and listen. He had uncovered most of its secrets, and its dangers too.

Cautiously, he stretched a numb leg out of his hiding place in the large hollowed stone the herbalist used for soaking the leaves, rhizomes, and berries she collected. The air was rank with the smell of rotten foliage. It would be dark within an hour. He had time to eat something and to reflect.

What was to become of them? The two of them that was, for Mathilde's fate was of little concern to him. She was far too vain and foolish to worry about anything except her little breasts that were not budding as fast as she would like, her ribbons and hair combs. What would become of Agnès and him? A feeling of joy made his eyes brim with tears, for there were two of them, he was not alone. The Dame de Souarcy would never forsake him, even at risk to her own life. The certain knowledge that it was true wrenched his heart.

Crouching unseen behind the door to the main hall, he had witnessed the gruelling evening to which her half-brother had subjected her the day before. As usual she had outwitted him.

And yet the following day, just after the scoundrel had left, while they were doing their round of the outbuildings, he had sensed her uncertainty and understood her fears: how far was Eudes prepared to go? What would he stop at?

The answer to the second question was obvious and Agnès knew it as well as Clément. He would stop at fear, when he came face to face with a beast more ferocious than he.

They were so alone, so vulnerable. They had no beast to champion them, to come to their aid. For months now the child had struggled with his despair. He must find a way out, a solution. He cursed his youth and his physical frailty. He cursed the truth of his origins, which he was forced to conceal for both their sakes. Agnès had explained this to him as soon as she could, and he knew her fears were well founded.

Knowledge was a weapon, Agnès had explained, especially when confronted with an ignorant boor like Eudes. Knowledge. It was passed on, to some extent, by the schoolmistresses at Clairets. And so, two years earlier, his lady had allowed him to attend the few classes open to children of all ages from the rich burgher families and gentry from the surrounding countryside. These offered him scant intellectual nourishment since, thanks to Agnès, he had long ago learnt to read and write in French and Latin. He had vainly hoped he might learn about the sciences, about life in distant lands. In reality, most of the time was spent on the study of the Gospels and learning by rote the words of worthy Latin scholars such as Cicero, Suetonius and Seneca. Added to these limitations was the terror the schoolmistress,[22] Emma de Pathus, inspired in them all. Her permanent sullenness and readiness to raise her hand was enough to strike fear into the hearts of her young charges.

In the end, it mattered little. The goodly Bernardines were

unstinting in their efforts, zealously caring for some, educating others, settling discords, calming hostilities, accompanying the dying. Unlike some of the other orders, they could not be accused of indifference towards the world outside the abbey, or of profiting from the misfortunes of humble folk. It mattered little because Clément had learnt so many things. Each seed of knowledge sprouted another. Each new key to understanding he forged unlocked a bigger door than the last. He had also learnt not to ask questions the sisters were unable to answer, for he realised that his curiosity, which initially rewarded their pains, ended by perplexing and then troubling them. In truth it mattered little because he had become convinced that the abbey contained an intriguing mystery.

Why had he slipped behind the pillar? He had been waiting for the Latin mistress. Was it instinct? Or was it the strange behaviour of the figure in white? The Abbess had looked around furtively before hurriedly locking the small postern door she had just emerged from, and then darted down the corridor, like a thief.

A quick, discreet enquiry left him none the wiser. No one seemed to know where that door led. What was in the room on the other side? Was it a secret cell for some important prisoner? Perhaps it was a torture chamber? The child's fertile imagination ran away with him until he decided to solve the mystery himself. A roughly drawn map of the central part of the abbey helped him to determine that, if there were a secret chamber, it must be quite small, unless it contained a window – one of the ones that gave onto the interior garden that ran alongside the scriptorium and the dormitories. And if his modest topographical plan was at all accurate, it must be in the middle of the Abbess's chambers and study.

He had been burning with curiosity and impatience ever since. He had given a great deal of thought to the problem of how to remain within the abbey enclosure in order to pursue his secret inquiry and test his theories. In the end one solution imposed itself: the herbarium adjacent to the medicinal garden would give him shelter for a few hours while he waited for nightfall.

The full moon that night was Clément's unwitting accomplice. He left the herbarium, moving as silently as a ghost and blending in to the outer wall of the dormitory. He passed beneath the scriptorium windows, taller and broader than the rest in order to allow the copyists as much light as possible. He continued alongside the smaller windows of the steam room, the only part of the abbey that was heated in winter, and the place where the sick were tended and the ink stored overnight so it wouldn't freeze. Only a couple more yards to go. The young boy was breathless with anxiety, wondering what explanation he might give for being there in the middle of the night if he were discovered, hardly daring to imagine the ensuing punishment. He slipped below the two small windows in the Abbess's study and below the two air vents cut into the stone wall of the circular room in her chamber containing the garderobe. The mystery chamber should be located somewhere between these two rooms. Clément retraced his steps and measured the distance in paces between Éleusie de Beaufort's chamber and her study. He estimated about twelve yards. Abbess or not, a nun's cell could not be that wide or spacious. The secret chamber, then, though much bigger than he had first calculated, must be windowless. The thought sent a shiver of fear and excitement down his spine. What if the room was an inquisitorial chamber? What if he discovered signs of torture there? No. There was no such thing as a female Inquisitor. He went back over the same patch, this time on his hands and knees, his nose to the ground. A cellar window, measuring approximately two yards long and a foot high, opened onto the ornamental flowerbeds at the base of the wall. Thick bars protected the window against intruders. Full-grown intruders, he supposed correctly, for they were widely enough spaced to allow a slim child to pass through. Relief gave way to panic. What should he do now? Curiosity prevailed over the many excellent reasons he could think of for turning back and leaving the abbey enclosure as quickly and, above all, as quietly as possible.

How far was the cellar window from the floor? A piece of gravel from the pathway bordering the flowerbeds served as a sounding device. Clément calculated from the clear and almost instantaneous impact it made on the ground that five feet at the very most lay between him and his objective. He was wrong.

Stretched out on his side, he struggled through the bars that dug into his flesh, holding his stomach in and exhaling as deeply as he could to make himself as thin as possible. Finally his chest squeezed through and he let himself fall to the floor. The length of time he was suspended in the void startled him. He landed like a dead weight and a searing pain almost made him cry out. His suffering soon gave way to panic. What if he had broken something? How would he find his way out of there? He gripped his rapidly swelling ankle, rotating it this way and that and forcing back the tears that pricked his eyes. It was a sprain, only a bad sprain. It would hurt but he would be able to walk.

He was encircled by thick blackness. A humid darkness in which wafts of dank air combined with a lingering sweet smell reminiscent of animal glue. The cool gloom of a cellar. He began to tremble with rage at himself. How could he have been so stupid, he who was so proud of his quick wits? How was he going to get out of there? He hadn't given it a thought. What a fool!

He waited a few moments for his eyes to become accustomed to that indoor gloom, denser than the darkness that had camouflaged him in the garden. A long table, like a work bench, covered in uneven heaps was the first thing he was able to make out. He limped towards it, his arms outstretched. Books. Piles of books on a table. Then, out of the gloom, the shape of a ladder. No. More like a small stepladder leaning against some shelves containing more books. A library. He was in a library. Over in the corner stretching up to the ceiling, a large indistinct shape loomed. He walked over to it, wincing from the pain in his ankle. It was a spiral staircase leading to another room, and below the steps were pinned pieces of fine leather, no doubt intended to repair the book bindings. He carefully climbed the stairs. The darkness seemed to grow less opaque the further up he went. Emerging on all fours into the room at the top, he slowly rose to his feet. He froze with astonishment. It was a vast library with a soaring ceiling and books covering every wall. Moonlight filtered through the horizontal arrow slits, ingeniously positioned more than four yards above ground level, which was why he had failed to notice them earlier. Their function was to allow both light and air to filter discreetly into the room. As though in a trance, he walked over to one of the bookcases and with reverential awe pulled out a few of the weighty volumes. The good condition they were in was proof of the care they received. Choked with emotion, Clément managed to read some of the titles. He sensed the world was opening up just for him. Everything he had always longed to discover, to learn, to know was here, within his grasp. Overcome, he murmured:

'My God! Could it be that the entire works of Claudius

Galen* are here? *De sanitate tuenda* ... And *De anatomicis administrationibus* ... And even *De usu partium corporis* ...'

The child's breathless voice trailed off.

He found a translation from the Latin by a certain Farag ben Salem of a book by Abu-Bakr-Mohammed-ibn-Zakariya al-Razi,* a name he had never heard of before. The work, *Al-Hawi*, or, in Latin, *Continens*, appeared to be on pharmacology but the feeble light of the moon hampered his ability to read.

Other books remained inaccessible to Clément, their strange-looking titles in foreign tongues guarding their secrets.

Was it Arabic, Greek or Hebrew? He did not know. So the room he had gone through to reach there was only a storeroom, or possibly a workshop. That would explain the smell of glue and the pieces of leather. Exhilarated, he studied the books for hours, losing all notion of time. The night sky filtering through the arrow slits became tinged with milky blue, finally alerting him that day was approaching.

With the help of the stepladder, Clément managed with great difficulty to climb back out through the cellar window. He could feel his ankle pounding – an immense throbbing pulse.

Porte Bucy, Paris, June 1304

The oppressive afternoon heat did not bother Francesco de Leone any more than the stench emanating from the mounds of refuse at the corner of every alleyway. On the other hand, the ceaseless activity of the human anthill made his head spin.

The city numbered over sixty thousand hearths, meaning a population of close on two hundred thousand souls. This buzzing populace was distributed on both sides of the river Seine, spanned by only two wooden bridges: the Grand Pont and the Petit Pont, which were recklessly over-constructed – the larger of the two accommodating a hundred and forty dwellings and a hundred shops, as well as the added weight of watermills. As a result, it was not unknown for flood waters to wash the bridges away as if they were clumps of straw.

The Knight slowly climbed Rue de Bucy, benignly refusing the advances of a famished-looking young woman with dark shadows under her eyes. He thought she must have come out of one of the steam rooms. It was common knowledge that the mixed public baths were also used for assignations of an amorous nature, whether of the clandestine or the remunerated variety. Sex was for sale all over Paris and there was no lack of customers. Carnal love was considered a minor sin so long as it had a price on it. It allowed men whose poverty inhibited them from marrying to satisfy their urgent needs, their desires. It also allowed starving girls, cast into the street because of an untimely pregnancy or by penniless parents, to survive, while at the same time saving married women from the lechery of the powerful.

At least these were a few of the glib arguments that acted as a balm for the consciences of some and the guilt of others. They did not persuade Francesco de Leone, and he was filled with a strange sadness. The oldest profession in the world, practised by women who were increasingly excluded from any others, was spreading in the city. At this rate they would soon be able to count their options on one hand: born to wealth, married, nuns or prostitutes. In the latter case they would end up eaten away by tuberculosis or intestinal diseases, or even slashed to ribbons by some casual client. Who cared what became of these spectres? Not the powers that be, not the Church, certainly not their families.

The girl kept her eyes fixed on him. She was intimidated by his appearance yet driven by hunger and fear of destitution. He paused to study her.

He was chasing that woman, always the same one, in the ambulatory of that church, always the same place. Did he want to kill her or was he trying to save her from some unseen enemy? He had prayed for the second theory to be the true one. And yet he remained unable to convince himself that it was.

The eternal misery of women, their astonishing frailty. His mother and infant sister, their throats slit like lambs, left to rot in the blazing sun, their wounds crawling with flies. He closed his eyes for a moment. When he opened them again, the girl was smiling at him, the pathetic smile of a poor unwanted creature looking for money for her supper and a bed for the night. There was nothing seductive or alluring about those sickly-looking lips. And yet, though powerless to seduce, she still attempted to persuade him.

He took five silver pennies from his purse, a fortune for a pauper, and walked over to her:

'Eat and rest a while, sister.'

She stared at the coins he had placed in the palm of her hand and shook her head.

When she looked up at him, her pale cheeks were streaked.

'I ... Come, I'm sweet and gentle, and I'm not sick, I promise ... I ...'

'Hush, rest.'

'But ... How may I ...'

'Pray for me.'

He turned on his heel and walked away quickly, leaving her weeping, overcome with relief and despair. For her and for his mother and sister, for all women who had no man to protect them, for Christ and his immense love for women, a love that had so long been scorned by miserable buffoons. Sinners, sinners disguised as practitioners of the faith.

Giotto Capella. Long ago in a land where the sun scorched the earth, the Knight would have given his life to slay this man. Arnaud de Viancourt knew nearly all there was to know of Francesco de Leone's childhood and had hesitated before pronouncing the name of their 'unwitting intermediary'. When he had finally uttered it and awaited his brother's response, he had evoked the threat that was hanging over them in order to justify imposing on him such a difficult task.

The handsome white stone house, completed only months before, dominated Rue de Bucy. It belonged to Giotto Capella, a native of Crema, a small Lombard village to the south-east of Milan. His third-floor windows gave onto the Seine and the Louvre. It was the reason he had chosen the location: to be close to the heart of power and thus to the biggest borrowers, but also to Paris's natural frontier. For the disposition of the powerful towards moneylenders was a fickle one. A fact that the Lombards – the name given to Italian and Jewish moneylenders alike regardless of whether they were natives of that province – had had the recent misfortune to discover. In reality, the inconsistencies of the new century with regard to usury should have amused Giotto, who was not an uncultivated man but one for whom money was a means and, above all, an end and a passion. How could they as merchants be expected to lend money to strangers without making a profit? Nonsense! There was a good reason why usury had been outlawed. It allowed kings and noblemen to borrow money and then banish the usurers, confiscating their assets and brandishing religion as a justification. How many times had they had to listen to that convenient verse from the Gospel encouraging the lender to expect nothing in return? Thus the debtors rid themselves of creditors, interest and debt. What fools they were. For someone who knew how to negotiate, a debt was always repayable, whether against cash or against less obvious forms of payment.

Giotto Capella set down his glass of mulled wine, a rare treat he permitted himself regardless of the gout that seared his foot and was progressively immobilising him. The Knight Hospitaller had been waiting outside in his anteroom for some minutes. What did he want? The moneylender had felt uneasy the moment he agreed to the meeting. The Leones were one of the most eminent Italian families and had been in the service of the papacy for centuries. They were exceedingly wealthy, notwithstanding the vows of poverty taken by a number of their male offspring, which included Francesco. The Templars and Hospitallers were the type of complex and powerful entity it was preferable not to associate with. No prince, king or bishop could make them yield, so what chance had a moneylender! Even less so, as Leone was not there to ask for money. On this Giotto Capella would have staked his life. A pity, since money was so simple: it retained, restrained, and subjugated. What did he want, then? A favour, a mediator, the means with which to blackmail somebody? If Giotto Capella had had the courage, he would have turned the Knight of Christ away. But that was a luxury he could ill afford. Conflict with a military order would hamper his long-held ambition: to hold the post of Captain General of the Lombards of France by adroitly forcing out the current holder, Giorgio Zuccari – if necessary into his grave. For years he had been unable to abide Zuccari. A man given to preaching and impossible to catch at his own game, such was the loathsome integrity he showed towards his peers and, worse still, towards his debtors. Thus he applied to the letter Saint Louis's recommendation that interest should not exceed 33 per cent. Why, if there were people crazy or desperate enough to pay 45 per cent? After all, Capella did not force potential borrowers onto his premises!

This line of reasoning repeated a hundred times worked like a charm. It had the power to lift his spirits. His light-heartedness, however, was short-lived. What the devil did Leone want from him? Why hadn't he gone directly to Zuccari? His name and the fact that he was a Hospitaller permitted it, and the old moneylender would have welcomed him with open arms. A pox on inscrutable people!

His unease combined with a feeling of displeasure the moment Francesco de Leone walked into his study – a veritable Ali Baba's cave jam-packed with paintings, carved wooden boxes, furs and valuable pieces of porcelain from his latest seizures. God, the man was handsome, while he resembled an ugly toad, wizened and yellow-looking from the constant privations decreed by his physic in a clipped voice. Even his wife closed her eyes in disgust now, the rare times he stroked her thighs.

He stood up, holding out his hands, forcing himself to be gracious.

'Knight, you honour my humble dwelling.'

Leone immediately sensed Capella's hostility. He moved forward a few paces, responding to the perfunctory greeting only with a slight raising of his eyebrows. It occurred to Giotto that the man belonged to that select few before whom others knelt without them even noticing. His resentment mounted. He checked it, however, by enquiring:

'Would you accept a goblet of my best wine?'

'With pleasure. I do not doubt that it is excellent.'

The moneylender considered for a moment whether the seemingly anodyne remark contained a hidden reproach. What he really wanted was for the Knight to show that he was as greedy as his fellow man, but shielded by his name, his order, his piety. Then he could despise him freely, dismiss him with feigned indignation. He could already hear himself saying:

'What! And you a Knight Hospitaller, Monsieur! What a disgrace!'

All those nobles and prelates, those so-called dignitaries who had filed before him and whom he had flattered, reassured and encouraged in their vices, which were the source of his livelihood – the never-ending source. Most had abandoned themselves to the deadly sins of cupidity and covetousness, which had corrupted their souls, their hearts, even their speech. But the man before him possessed the calm confidence of the pure, and they were the worst – especially when they were intelligent and no longer knew fear.

The two men sat in deceptively companionable silence while

a maidservant fetched the wine. Leone took the measure of the man opposite him. A few seconds were sufficient for him to know that Capella remained what he had always been: an avaricious swindler who only refrained sometimes from committing the vilest acts out of cowardice. An image flashed through his mind of a repulsive, carnivorous beast lying in wait uneasily, ready to pounce on his enemy's throat at the slightest sign of weakness. The possibility of redemption was not distributed equally among men, for there were those who did not wish it.

Francesco took a sip of wine and set down the goblet, made ugly by an excess of chasing and inlaid precious stones. He reached beneath his heavy linen surcoat[23] for the Grand-Master's letter and handed it to Capella. After the Lombard had broken the seal and read the first few lines, everything around him started spinning. He murmured:

'My God ...'

He shot a glance at Leone, who signalled to him to continue reading.

It had never occurred to Capella that this blood-soaked memory from nearly fifteen years ago might one day come back to haunt him. He had paid dearly enough for it in every sense of the word.

A warm tear fell on his hand, followed by another. He let the sheet of vellum fall to the marble floor he had had brought over from his native Carrara at great expense.

Was he aware that he was crying? Leone could not be sure. Francesco de Leone waited. He knew the contents of the letter, of the blackmail note more precisely: any weapon, the prior had specified, himself having recourse to this strategy of extremes.

What did he care about the usurer's tears, or his memories? So many people had died because of him.

The other man whispered breathlessly:

'This is monstrous.'

'Why? Because it is the truth?'

Giotto Capella gave the Knight the look of a drowning man and spluttered:

'Why? Because it was so long ago ... Because I have suffered the torment of guilt, and of the worst kind: that which we inflict on ourselves. And because I have tried so hard to be worthy of forgiveness ...'

'You mean, to be forgotten. We have never forgotten and we have not forgiven. And as for the torments of guilt, why, I would laugh if I were a mere soldier. Who let the Mamelukes invade Acre more than a month into the siege? Sultan Al-Ashraf Khalil was champing at the bit outside the city walls with his seventy thousand men on horseback and his hundred and fifty foot soldiers from Egypt and Syria. The defence of the citadel of Saint-Jean was heroic: there were only fifteen thousand Christian soldiers inside the city walls. They fought like lions, outnumbered by fifteen to one. The Sultan's men identified the weak points in the enclosure and in groups of a thousand tunnelled into the sewers and the butchers' pit with remarkable precision.'

Leone paused to study the breathless man, who was gripping the edges of his writing table with both hands.

Capella made an attempt to justify himself in a barely audible voice:

'The negotiations had been successful. Al-Ashraf had agreed to the citadel being evacuated if the defenders left behind all their possessions.'

'Come now. King Henri would never have accepted such a complete, such a dishonourable surrender. What is more, the defenders of the citadel were soon able to judge for themselves how far they could trust the Sultan's word,' retorted Leone in a calm voice, fixing the usurer with his deep-blue eyes. 'On 15 May, the New Tower, donated by the Comtesse de Blois, collapsed, having been undermined by sappers. Al-Ashraf then promised to allow the conquered to evacuate, above all their women and children. But the Mamelukes were already in the central square desecrating the chapel and raping the women. What followed was a bloodbath. The Dominicans, Franciscans, Clarisses were massacred and the women and children were taken away to be sold as slaves. That was only the beginning of the destruction. Almost everyone was slain: my brother Hospitallers, the Knights Templar of Saint-Lazare and Saint-Thomas. Only a handful of cripples were left alive.'

'But it was inevitable,' Capella whined. 'Two years before – in the month of August, I believe – some peasants and Muslim merchants were attacked by Hugues de Sully's Italian crusaders in a marketplace. The merchants were forced to seek refuge in their inn, and ...'

'And who came to their aid?' Leone interrupted in a voice that was now openly contemptuous. 'The Knights Templar and Hospitaller!'

'It was a war. Wars are ...'

'No. It was an ambush. An ambush that was admirably thought out and therefore worth its weight in gold. Was it not, moneylender? As for that skirmish at the marketplace, it was nothing but a poor excuse. Anyone starting a war must always provide some kind of justification. But that is neither here nor there. Had the Mamelukes not known the precise location of the New Tower and the sewers, the work of the sappers would have been useless, or at least slowed down. We could have waited for reinforcements or, at worst, negotiated the evacuation of most of the people. How much did they pay, Giotto Capella, for the slaughter of fifteen thousand men and almost as many women and children?'

'They ... they beat me. They ... they threatened to castrate me. They were going to ... They were laughing ...' he stammered.

The usurer's eyes swept the room, as if he were expecting some miraculous intervention. Leone stared at him. The sly rat was using his last defence: pity.

Early June 1291. The centre of the battle had moved. The Sidon Fort was now under siege and would not hold out much longer. A young boy of twelve struggled against the hand clutching his shoulder, that of his Uncle Henri, and, freeing himself from the iron grip, ran towards the ruins of Acre. He tripped and fell then leapt to his feet, his hands sticky with blood.

The broad white steps were bathed in sunlight. The broad white steps of the chapel defiled by streaks of dried blood and a morass of human flesh. The broad steps swarming with bloated, feasting flies.

Some of the women had attempted to seek refuge in the chapel, to hide their children there. Underneath one of them, whose head, almost severed from the neck, was facing the sky, the young boy recognised a mass of flaxen hair. Flaxen hair congealed with blood. His sister's hair.

'How much, Capella? How much for my mother and seven-year-old sister, defiled, their throats slit, left to rot in the sun, ravaged by dogs so that I could no longer recognise them? How much for your soul?'

The other man's gaze settled at last on the Knight. The gaze of a dead man, a gaze from the past. In a voice he no longer recognised as his own, and suspecting he might never recover from this confession, he said:

'Five hundred gold pieces.'

'You are lying. I can always detect your feeble lies. It was a smaller sum, wasn't it?'

Faced with the other man's silence, the Knight persisted:

'Wasn't it? What did you think? That doubling or tripling the amount in gold would absolve you? That by multiplying the price of your treachery and greed they would somehow be legitimised? That everything in this world has a price? How much do you imagine a thousand pounds, or a hundred thousand, or ten million is worth in the eyes of God? Why, the same as a single penny.'

'Three hundred … And I only saw half of it. They broke their word. They spat in my face when I went to claim the balance.'

'The rascals!' said the Knight, mockingly.

He closed his eyes, tilted back his head, and, as though speaking to himself, repeated:

'A hundred and fifty gold pieces for all those corpses, for those two women … A hundred and fifty gold pieces, which allowed you to become a usurer. A tidy sum for a … what were you when you still had a soul?'

'A meat merchant.'

'Oh yes … That would explain your perfect knowledge of the sewers at Acre and of the butchers' pit.' Leone sighed, before continuing in a hushed voice, 'I know you and your kind so well that I sometimes feel I am enveloped by a rotten stench. It follows me everywhere, sticks to my skin, makes my stomach heave. I can sense you before I see you, before I hear you. I can smell you. The stale odour of your dead decaying souls suffocates me. Do you know the stench of a rotting soul? It is worse than any stinking carcass.'

The other man leapt up, suddenly oblivious to the stabbing pain in his foot. His face drained of blood, he moved towards the Hospitaller's armchair, and fell to his knees, wailing:

'Mercy, I beg you, mercy!'

'That is beyond me, and I regret it. For my own sake.'

Some minutes passed, punctuated by the kneeling man's sobs. A violent sadness shook Leone. How could a simple act of forgiveness cause his infinite love for Him to waver? What had he lost, what had he destroyed of his faith? He pulled himself up with the thought that he had not yet become the Light, that he was still drawing near, with such difficulty, so much effort, like a desperate ant, deranged and sickened by darkness.

One day. One day he would reach out and touch it at last, the Light he had only been able to glimpse in the nave at Santa Costanza. One day he would embrace it, he would breathe it in, be immersed in it and all his sins would be cleansed. He was drawing near, he could feel it. For so long the tireless ant he had become had crossed oceans, climbed mountains, braved every obstacle, nearly died a hundred deaths, seared by the desert sun, wasted by fever, swept away by storms. And yet each time he had picked himself up and continued towards the Light. He longed one day to die inside the Light, to dissolve and at last to be at peace.

The Ineffable Trace, the Unutterable Secret was within his reach, all that was necessary to attain it was to shed blood, his own blood.

Leone stood up, gently pushing aside the broken man.

'I await this meeting with Guillaume de Nogaret. You are,

after all, an official moneylender to the kingdom of France, and I am sure you will find an excellent reason to explain my presence here. And remember: at the slightest sign of treachery Philip the Fair will learn who was responsible for the slaughter at Acre. I shall remain in your house for the duration of this enterprise. Do not speak to me, usurer, about any other matter. I shall take my meals alone in the room you will provide for me in your residence. I want it ready within the hour. I am going outside to breathe the putrid smell of the streets. It must be more tolerable than the one you mask with incense in your chambers.'

He paused in the doorway without turning and addressed the shell of a man:

'Never lie to me. I know so much about you, Capella, so much that you do not know. Should you be tempted to betray me for a fat sum or simply out of fear, I swear before God that I shall punish your days and nights with torments such as you have only touched upon in your wildest imaginings.'

Clairets Abbey, Perche, June 1304

Every night for weeks Clément had been coming back, drawn almost in spite of himself by the treasures in the secret library that were hidden from the eyes of the world. After a few uneasy forays he had gradually gained in confidence. He would enter at nightfall and occasionally felt bold enough to stay for the whole of the following day. He lived on the provisions he pilfered from the kitchens at Souarcy – for he was becoming more and more distrustful of Mabile. Indeed, his initial, rather dormant mistrust had grown keener since Eudes de Larnay's last visit. Up until then, he had been content to spy upon the spy in order to protect Agnès, but now he was on the lookout for any suspicious activity. He had soon seen through the folly of his first plan: catching Mabile red-handed in order to give the Dame de Souarcy a legitimate excuse to turn her out was too obvious – too obvious but, above all, of little or no use. Why not instead catch the spy out at her own game? Why not plant a few harmless secrets for her to find? Then if Eudes tried to use them against his half-sister, it would be easy to discredit him in spite of his lineage and wealth, which gave him nevertheless a significant advantage. All Clément needed to do now was convince his mistress to agree to this subterfuge. He knew that his lady was beginning to glimpse an unpleasant truth.

Noble victories or dignified defeats are only possible when confronting a noble enemy. The weak can fight a powerful villain only with cunning and deceit. He was certain Agnès had understood this even though she had still not accepted it completely. Still, in one sense Eudes's villainy had done the

Dame de Souarcy a good turn; it had silenced her remaining scruples and remorse. Eudes was an evil beast and in order to defeat him any line of attack was permissible.

His nightly forays into the secret library at Clairets Abbey were part of this. To begin with, Clément had comforted himself with the idea that if the Abbess had a sudden wish to go in there, he could simply hide under the spiral staircase, behind the pieces of leather that formed an improvised curtain. His fears soon proved groundless. The Abbess rarely entered the library, to which she alone possessed the keys, and of whose existence only she was aware. The fact that it held so little appeal for Éleusie de Beaufort, who was renowned for her learning, had at first surprised the child. But he had gradually begun to understand why. A number of these works contained such revelations, such shocking secrets – some so upsetting they had reduced Clément to tears. To begin with he had doubted the veracity of the words that expressed them. But the evidence was so overwhelming it had finally convinced him. Thus the earth was not surrounded by a void, but by some intangible fluid within which coexisted elements and organisms so microscopic as to be invisible to the human eye. Thus the stone in toads' brains that protected against poison was a mere fable, as were unicorns. Thus comas, convulsions, trembling and headaches were not symptoms of demonic possession but of a malfunction in the brain – if one were to believe Abu Marwan Abd Al-Malik Ibn Zuhr, called Avenzoar in the West, one of the twelfth century's most eminent Arab doctors of Jewish origin. Thus it was not enough to spit three times in a toad's mouth in order not to conceive for a year. Thus, thus, thus …

Was Éleusie de Beaufort trying to hold back this tidal wave? Had she grown pale at the thought of the threat this science posed to all the stale dogmas and, more importantly, the power it gave to those who wielded it?

A single slim volume had absorbed him for almost a whole month. It was a Greek primer for Latinists. He had even been bold enough to borrow it for a few days in order to further his learning of that strange language, which seemed to him more and more essential to an understanding of the world.

He had then scoured the library's interminable shelves for a similar work that would allow him to penetrate the mysteries of Hebrew and Aramaic; for during his feverish research a sort of logic had soon become apparent, an indefinable conducting thread that led him from one work to another.

He was stunned upon carefully opening a small collection of aphorisms bound in a kind of coarse red silk. That same name. That same name written in ink at the top of the first page in the last three books he had deciphered. He had discovered the connecting thread. Eustache de Rioux, Knight Hospitaller. Was the man dead? Had he bequeathed his books directly to Clairets Abbey or through a legatee? What was it that had drawn Clément to the works in his collection those past few days?

A sudden impulse made him go back to the shelf where he had found the book. One by one he pulled out the adjacent volumes, glancing inside them before replacing them. At last he found what he had been looking for. The large book was bound in roughly tanned leather of an unpleasant dark-purple hue that still gave off the sour smell of suint. There was no sign of any title, even on the title page, only the name of its former owner, like a code: Eustache de Rioux. From the diagrams that filled the first few pages Clément supposed it was a textbook on astronomy or astrology. The subsequent pages astonished him:

in them appeared the signs of the zodiac, some accompanied by a profusion of arrows pointing to complicated calculations and annotations penned by two distinct hands. One set of writing was even and graceful, though rushed, the other more squat. It was not so much a book as a personal notebook. Did it belong to the Knight de Rioux, and to another whose name did not appear in its pages? A sentence written in italics caught his attention:

Et tunc parabit signum Filii hominis.[24]

Another arrow pointed from this proclamation to the following page. What he discovered there left him utterly bewildered.

An ecliptic circle featuring only three of the zodiac signs – Capricorn, Aries and Virgo – was covered in the jottings and crossings-out of someone searching for answers. Comments ending in question marks bore out the impression of uncertainty. Others seemed only to be reminders for the author, or authors.

The Moon will eclipse the Sun on the day of his birth. The place of his birth is still unknown. Revisit the words of the Viking, a bondi, a trader in walrus tusks, amber and furs chanced upon in Constantinople.

Five women and at the centre a sixth.

Capricorn in the first decan and Virgo in the third being variable and the consanguinity of Aries in any decan too great.

The initial calculations were incorrect, failing to take into account the error relating to the year of birth of the Saviour. It is a fortunate blunder for it gives us a little more time.

These comments had been penned by the more graceful hand – visibly at ease with a quill pen. But to whom did they refer? This *Filii hominis*, the Son of Man, Christ? If so, then the first sentence made no sense at all, and the third even less so. More time to do what? And who was meant by 'we'? The two authors? As for the astrological reference, it was too abstruse. What was the 'consanguinity' of a sign? Who were the women referred to?

Clément raised his head towards the arrow slits. Outside, the sun was setting. He had not shown his face at the manor since the previous day, and Agnès would be worried. It was almost vespers. He could slip away while they were holding the service and go back.

He paused. He had a strong urge to take the notebook he had found back to Souarcy and study it at his leisure. But his good sense quickly dissuaded him, all the more so as the volume was unwieldy. So be it, he would return to the library after matins[+] and pick up where he had left off.

He stood up and snuffed out his little oil lamp, the benefits of which were that it smoked less than a torch and there were enough of them at the manor for one missing to go unnoticed, unlike the tallow lamps or candles, which were costly and therefore included in the kitchen inventory. He walked down to the storeroom.

Vatican Palace, Rome, June 1304

Cardinal Honorius Benedetti marvelled at the relief provided by the magnificent fan made of fine strips of mother-of-pearl. It had been given to him one morning, following a long and wakeful night, by a rosy-cheeked young lady from Jumièges – a pleasant souvenir over twenty years old. One of the few remaining from his brief secular life before it was touched by grace, leaving him changed and at the same time disoriented. The only son of a wealthy burgher from Verona, he had been companionable and a lover of the fair sex. Few of his qualities predisposed him to the cloth, least of all his penchant for the material things in life, at any rate when these proved pleasurable. Nevertheless, his rise through the religious hierarchy had been vertiginous. He had been helped by a towering intellect, a vast knowledge and, as he freely admitted, by simple cunning. And, no less, by a certain appetite for power – or rather for the possibilities it offered to those who knew how to manipulate it.

The sweat was streaming down Honorius Benedetti's face. For days now the city had been in the grip of an unbearable heatwave that seemed determined never to loosen its hold. The young Dominican sitting opposite him was surprised by his visible discomfort. Archbishop Benedetti was a small, slender, almost frail man, and it was difficult to imagine where he stored all the fluid that was drenching his silky grey hair and rolling down his forehead.

The prelate cast his eye over the nervous young friar whose hands trembled slightly as they lay stretched out on his knees. This was not the first accusation of cruelty and physical abuse

105

involving an Inquisitor to be brought before him. Not long ago, Robert le Bougre* had caused them a good deal of trouble and disgrace. The then Pope, Gregory IX, had lost sleep over the horrors uncovered during the investigation ordered by the Church. Naturally he recalled only too well his own error of judgement, for he had seen in that repentant former Cathar* a valuable 'rooter-out' of heretics.

'Brother Bartolomeo,' continued the Cardinal, 'what you have told me about the young Inquisitor Nicolas Florin puts me in a very awkward position.'

'Believe me, Your Eminence, I regret it deeply,' the novice apologised.

'If the Church, drawing on our late lamented Gregory IX's constitution *Excommunicamus*, decided to recruit her Inquisitors from the Dominican and, to a lesser extent, from the Franciscan orders, it is undoubtedly owing to their excellent knowledge of theology, but also to their humility and compassion. We have always viewed torture as the very last means of obtaining a confession and thus saving the soul of the accused. To have recourse to it from the outset of a trial is ... The expression "unacceptable" that you used just now will do. For indeed, there exists a – how should I say? – a scale of penalties and punishments which can, which must be applied beforehand, whether in the form of a pilgrimage – with or without the burden of the Cross – a public beating or a fine.'

Brother Bartolomeo stifled a sigh of relief. So he had not been mistaken. The prelate measured up to his reputation for wisdom and intelligence. And yet, having finally been ushered into the study of the Pope's private secretary, after a three-hour-long wait in the stuffy atmosphere of the anteroom, he had felt suddenly apprehensive. How would the Cardinal respond to his accusations? And was he, Bartolomeo, clear in his heart, and in his conscience, about the true nature of what had motivated his request for this interview? Was it a noble desire for justice or was there something more shameful involved: denunciation of a feared brother? For it was hopeless to try to deceive himself: Brother Nicolas Florin terrified him. It was strange how this angelic-faced young man appeared to take a sinister delight in brutalising, torturing and mutilating. He plunged his hands into the raw, screaming flesh without even a ripple of displeasure creasing his handsome brow or clouding his expression.

'Naturally, Your Eminence, since our only duty is to achieve repentance,' ventured Bartolomeo.

'Hmm …'

More than anything Honorius Benedetti feared a disastrous repetition of the Robert le Bougre affair. A silent rage mingled with his political concern. The fools! Innocent III had laid down the rules governing the inquisitorial process in his papal bull *Vergentis in senium*. His aim had not been to exterminate individuals but to eradicate heresies that threatened the foundations of the Church, holding up, among others, the example of Christ's poverty which – judging by the vast landed wealth of nearly all the monasteries – was not held in high esteem. As for Innocent IV, he had removed the final obstacle by permitting, from 1252 onwards, the use of torture in his papal bull *Ad extirpanda*.

Torturers. Inept, base torturers. Honorius Benedetti did not know whether he felt more angry or sad. And yet, if he were honest, he too had accepted the bizarre notion that love of the Saviour could, at times, be imposed by means of coercion or even extreme violence. He had felt absolved by the fact that a pope had opened the way before him. Ultimately, was not the boundless joy of having saved a soul, of having returned it to the bosom of Christ, what counted?

This young Bartolomeo and his love for his fellow man had placed him in a difficult situation, for he could no longer feign ignorance. What a fool to have received him! He should have left him mouldering in the anteroom. He might have ended up leaving, bored or annoyed. No, he was not the type to grow tired or impatient. His little mouth withered from the heat, the courage visible in his demeanour – even as his eyes were full of fear – his faltering but determined voice, all pointed to the doggedness of the pure and, in some way, evoked Archbishop Honorius Benedetti's own distant youth. There was only one way out: punishment or absolution. Absolution would be tantamount to endorsing an unacceptable cruelty and would fuel growing criticism among thinkers throughout Europe. It would provide Philip IV of France with a rod to break their backs, even though the monarch himself had not hesitated to resort to the methods of the Inquisition* in the past. It would be – and here the childishness of this last reasoning almost brought a smile to his lips – to disappoint the young man sitting opposite him, who believed in the possibility of governing without ever being content to compromise one's faith. So what about punishment? The prelate would be only too pleased to fight this Nicolas Florin, to make him choke on the power that had corrupted him, perhaps to demand his excommunication. And yet by sacrificing one diseased member of the flock he risked bringing disgrace upon all the Dominicans and the few Franciscans who had been named Inquisitors, and consequently upon the papacy itself. And the path from disgrace to rebellion was frequently a short one.

These were such troubled, such volatile times. The slightest scandal would be blown out of all proportion by the King of

France, and other monarchs, who were just waiting for such an opportunity.

Just then, one of the innumerable chamberlains that haunted the papal palace crept silently into his study and, bending down towards his ear, informed him in a whisper that his next visitor had arrived. He thanked the man more effusively than was his custom. At last, the excuse he had been waiting for to rid himself of the novice.

'Brother Bartolomeo, someone is waiting to see me.'

The other man leapt to his feet, blushing. The Cardinal reassured him with a gesture and continued:

'I am obliged to you, my son. I am unable, you understand, to reach any decision regarding the fate of Nicolas Florin on my own. However, I assure you that His Holiness will no more tolerate such monstrosities than I. They go against our faith and are a discredit to us all. Go in peace. Justice will soon be done.'

Bartolomeo left the vast chamber as though he were floating on air. How foolish he had been to harbour so many doubts and fears! His daily tormentor, the man who hounded, humiliated and tempted him, would soon darken his days, and his nights, no more. The butcher of humble folk would vanish like a bad dream.

He smiled feebly at the hooded figure waiting in the anteroom. It was only once he was outside, striding across the vast square with the euphoria of the triumphant, that it occurred to him that the person must have been very hot wearing all those clothes.

The mist enveloping Clément was so thick and close to the ground that he could barely see where he was putting his feet. Mists were common in that part of the country. Agnès found them poetic. She maintained that the swirls that clung to the wild grasses and bushes softened the too-sharp outlines of things. But today this veil was heavy with the scent of death.

The swarm of frenzied flies crawled over the evil-smelling carcass. A piece of half-torn flesh hanging from the cheek almost touched the ground, and moved to the rhythm of the tiny beetles boring below the cheekbone. The upper thigh and buttocks had been gnawed down to the bone.

The child let the small crossbow Agnès insisted he carry for his protection in the forest fall to his feet. He took another step forward, trying with difficulty to suppress the little gulps that brought an acid saliva into his mouth.

It was a man – a serf, no doubt, judging from his filthy rags, stained with viscid fluids and dried blood. He was lying on his side, his face turned up to the sky, his eye sockets staring towards the setting sun. The blackened leathery skin, mostly that on his hands and forearms, looked charred as if it had been exposed to naked flames. Had the man been attacked? Had he defended himself? Had he been set alight and then robbed? Of what? Beggars like him carried nothing of any value. Even so, Clément glanced around at the undergrowth and the bushes. There was no sign of any fire. Another step forward, then another. When he was less than a yard from the man, he forced himself to smell the air. The lingering odour of decaying flesh made his stomach heave. And yet he could detect no smell of burnt wood or smoke. The child recoiled suddenly, clasping his hand to his mouth. He was not afraid. The dead, unlike the living, were without guile and harmless. Moreover, what was spread out before him on the forest floor bore no resemblance to the descriptions he had read of plague victims.

Lying a few yards from the corpse at Clément's feet was a peasant's walking stick. He picked it up and examined it. It looked like the branch of a young ash, and had the pale milky hue of freshly carved wood. It bore no traces of blood. One detail surprised him: the pointed metal tip meant to strengthen it and give it more hold on the ground. What serf would have laboured to add such a feature when he could carve as many walking sticks as he wanted? Clément pointed the metal tip at the corpse and, aiming at the hand, he poked it. The wrist broke away partially and the forefinger dropped to the floor.

How long had the body being lying in this tiny clearing over half a league from the nearest dwelling? It was difficult to tell, especially given the state of the shrivelled brown skin. Then again he saw no sign of any bluebottles, although it was the season for them. He circled the pitiful remains and crouched a few feet away. Through a tear in the linen shirt he glimpsed a large blister covering the small of the back that was filled with a yellowy liquid. Aiming again with the end of the stick, he burst it, and turned his head just in time to avoid vomiting on his breeches. A small sea of maggots tumbled from the wound cavity. The bluebottles had had the time to lay their eggs, and the warm weather had favoured the larvae's development. The man must have been dead for at least three weeks.

Clément rose to his feet – in a sudden hurry to continue on his way. There was nothing more anyone could do for this poor wretch. The child had decided not to tell a living soul about his discovery, hardly eager to have to go all that way back just to show the bailiffs. He was struck by something odd. The man had mid-length hair, almost certainly light chestnut – though it was hard to tell with all the detritus, mud and parasites sticking to it. And yet, the tiny tonsure on his crown was still visible. The hair had grown back, but not enough to hide the trace of the barber's knife. Who might he have been? A cleric? Or perhaps one of those scholars who requested the tonsure as a sign of devotion and repentance?

His curiosity proved stronger than the queasiness he felt from his proximity to the stinking remains. He removed the crusts of bread and the plants from his shoulder bag, and thrust his right hand inside. Using the improvised glove for protection, he pulled aside the evil-smelling rags covering the man's body. Sweat poured down the child's face and ran into his eyes, and yet the nausea of the past few minutes had given way to exhilaration, to the extent that the putrid odour no longer affected him so strongly. He fought off the insects – exasperated by the disruption of their feast – driving them away with his gloved hand, and proceeded to inspect every inch of the corpse. Why would the man be wearing rags if he was a scholar? And if he was a friar, then where was his habit? Had he been travelling on foot? Where had he come from? What had caused his death? Had he perished in the clearing, or had somebody left him there after partially burning him somewhere else? Unfortunately, it was impossible for him to judge from the state of the hands, which were shrivelled up like pieces of old leather, whether the corpse had been a scholar or a peasant. Nothing, no object or any other particular feature, besides the tonsure, gave him any clues. Had he been robbed? If so, was it before or after he died? The obvious thought occurred to him that the hair on the man's head, and the body hair clinging to the flesh on his forearms and on his chest ravaged by vermin, though soiled with putrefaction, was intact. There was no sign of any singeing on the torn clothes hanging in shreds, which meant the man had not been set alight, for they would have caught fire before the skin could be attacked by the searing flames.

Clément struggled to roll the massive corpse onto its back and was almost propelled backwards by its weight. He peeled off the large piece of cloth adhering to the skin on the abdomen. The viscera were heaving with bloodless maggots. It was then that he noticed in the narrow strip of flattened grass where the man had been lying on his side a tiny hole no bigger than the size of a coin in the forest floor. It looked as though somebody had pushed their finger into the ground. Clément scraped carefully. Hidden beneath an inch or so of loose leaves and earth lay a wax seal. He cleaned the wax medallion and examined it closely. His mouth went dry. It was the ring of the fisherman! The papal seal. He was certain, having already come across it in the secret library at Clairets Abbey. But who was this man? An emissary of the Pope in disguise? Had he tried to bury the seal so that no one would find it? But what had become of the private missive the seal protected? Had he delivered it to Clairets Abbey – the only religious order of any importance in the vicinity? The child cast his gaze over the area immediately surrounding the tiny opening. What was that mark about a foot away? It looked like a letter of the alphabet. He leant closer and blew on the dried earth. There was a curved stroke like the beginning of the letter *M* or *N* or even a capital *B* or *D*. No. There was a tiny bar lower down – an *E* perhaps? No. There was no question: it was an *A*. Without knowing what motivated his gesture, he brushed the earth with his fingers, rubbing out all trace of the letter. He spent a moment longer filling in the hole that had shown him where to find the seal.

What did the *A* mean? Was it a surname? A Christian name? The name of the man's murderer? Or of a loved one who must be found and warned? Had the dead man left a sign for whoever found him? If this were the case, then he had indeed died in the clearing, and his death had been slow enough to enable him to hide the seal and to scratch the letter.

Clément silenced the clamour of questions racing through his mind. He must leave this place, and quickly. If the messenger was really as important as he seemed, then they were most likely searching for him already – or at least for the letter he had been carrying. The bailiffs were capable of anything to please their superior and the Comte d'Authon – not to mention the Pope. Anything, even roasting an innocent boy, provided it meant being left in peace.

Clément put the seal into his shoulder bag and hurried away.

In a flurry of rustling fabric, a figure darted behind the pillars in the little chapel. Brother Bernard was dining with Agnès and there was only a short time between courses.

Mabile was not displeased with herself. Agnès de Souarcy had expressed her wish to thank the good chaplain and the servant had prepared a proper feast – a six-course meal, no less. Following an hors d'oeuvre of fresh fruit, whose acidity was supposed to act as an aid to digestion, there was a broth made of almond milk. For the third course the servant had plumped for roasted quail spiced with a black pepper sauce. That insufferable Agnès de Souarcy was such a stickler for table manners that the baby fowl should keep her busy for a while. Brother Bernard would no doubt follow her example, thus allowing Mabile time to move onto the attack. The chaplain was young and attractive and his tonsure gave him an air of perpetual surprise and joviality. Mabile would gladly have let herself be seduced. Thus far, her judicious attempts in that direction had ended in failure. Was he harbouring shameful feelings towards Agnès de Souarcy? The thought made Mabile's mouth water. Eudes de Larnay would be happy to learn of it; and out of gratitude he would show her a little affection and, above all, generosity. Suddenly the girl became gloomy. Happy? Undoubtedly not. Satisfied, yes, but incensed with rage. At times he frightened her. Often. His loathing was so great it consumed him. Agnès and everything relating to her was like a knife piercing his entrails. He hounded her yet derived no pleasure from plotting his revenge. Even so, Mabile helped him, or, better still, she anticipated his murderous desires. She did not know exactly why. For love of her master? Certainly not. She yearned for him to lie on her belly, to possess her like he would a strumpet or a lady, according to his whim. And she liked it when occasionally, after their love-making and before drifting off to sleep, he would murmur: 'Agnès, my sweet.' So he was not thinking of her? How wrong he was! For she was his only Agnès and he would have to content himself with her. Mabile blinked back the tears of rage welling up in her eyes. One day. One day she would have obtained enough money from her master to be able to leave him behind without a single regret. She would go to the city and set herself up as a gold embroiderer. She was patient and clever. Ultimately … Mabile rather liked the fiction of Agnès's fondness for her chaplain, for not only would it harm Agnès's reputation, it would also wound her master. Mabile's bitterness was instantly replaced by a malicious glee.

The register in which the births and deaths at the manor were recorded would be in the sacristy. Mabile made her way straight there. She was trembling with rage. She enjoyed being the architect of Agnès's doom. It was a salve to the terrible envy that consumed her. In her view, as long as the natural order of things required that the serfs laboured while the master undertook to protect them, defectors like Agnès were intolerable. She had escaped her lot through marriage. A bastard. Agnès was nothing but a bastard, the daughter of a lady's maid just like her, Mabile. Why Agnès? If old Comte Robert hadn't begun to fear the wrath of heaven as he neared his end, he would never have recognised her. He had sowed enough wild oats in the hovels and farms on his estate. Why Agnès? Why should Mabile, born of a sacred union and into conditions that were enviable to many, seeing as her father was a dyer from Nogent-le-Rotrou, obtain less than a bastard – albeit a noble one? The hatred she felt for the Dame de Souarcy made her head spin at times. Regardless of whether he paid for her daily treachery, she would still have served Eudes de Larnay.

The bulky register was resting on a wooden lectern. Mabile hurriedly leafed through it until she came to the year 1294, the year that little good-for-nothing Clément, who spied on her so brazenly, was born. She searched through the columns filled in by the clumsy hand of the previous chaplain, who, judging from the fine lettering in the remainder of the register, had passed away at midnight on 26 January 1295. Mabile recalled that deadly winter when she had still been just a child. Finally her finger paused beside the entry she had been looking for: Clément, born posthumously to Sybille on the night of 28 December 1294.

She must hurry. The quail would not keep them busy forever. She should be back in the kitchen helping Adeline serve the desserts: a traditional goat's-milk blancmange followed by black nougat made from boiling honey and adding last year's walnuts and spices. To round off the meal she had prepared some hippocras, a mixture of red and white wine sweetened with honey and spiced with cinnamon and ginger.

She closed the register and hurried to the kitchens, declaring to the gaping-mouthed Adeline that the warm evening had made her sleepy and she had felt a sudden need to take the air.

'Only, they finished the third course and I didn't know what to do,' the young girl protested feebly.

'Serve the dessert on a fine trencher and pour the hippocras into the decanter to let it breathe, you fool! And remember Madame Agnès likes everyone to have their own trencher. This isn't a pauper's house, you know. I'm tired of having to tell you the same thing over and over again!' Mabile scolded.

Adeline lowered her head. She was so used to the other woman's reproaches that she barely registered them.

The conversation was flowing easily in the great hall. Mabile studied the distance between her mistress and the chaplain and wondered whether the gap hadn't closed a little. Agnès looked relaxed. And yet during her half-brother's visit her discomfort had been palpable. Mabile listened closely in the hope of overhearing some compromising snatch of conversation, but there was nothing in their exchange that would have been of any interest to Eudes.

'I scarcely see how castration could be a cure for leprosy, hernias and gout,' argued Agnès. 'They are such different afflictions, and it is well known that the wretched patients who were subjected to the operation in the leper hospital at Chartagne in the Mortagne region are none the better for it.'

'I am no expert in medical science, Madame, though I believe it is related to the similarity between the humours of the afflictions.'

Brother Bernard's perpetual good humour disposed him towards the pleasant things in life and so he turned from the gout and leprosy sufferers to enthuse once more about the quails he had just eaten.

Mabile returned to the kitchens. For some minutes her thoughts had been occupied by a nagging question. Why did the surname of this Sybille, her mistress's lady's maid, not figure in the register? Had she not received a Christian burial? Her grave was marked with a cross and had been dug at the edge of the plot reserved for the servants, which adjoined the cemetery where the lords of the manor, their wives and their descendants were buried. A few Souarcys lay buried beneath the chapel flagstones, but the limited space had necessitated the clearing of three hundred square yards of forest a good hundred yards from the chapel. Irrespective of her hostility towards Agnès, Mabile acknowledged that the Souarcys had always treated their servants' mortal remains with dignity. Not like a lot of others who would dump them in common graves unless a family member came to claim them. In point of fact, Eudes de Larnay showed no such compassion where his servants were concerned. She shook her head in irritation. What use had she for the Dame de Souarcy's kindness? It had nothing to do with her mission. Another thought flashed through her mind. The boundary where Clément's mother's remains lay; was it consecrated ground? She must try to find out. Sybille's having been a mother out of wedlock did not surprise Mabile. It was a common risk for girls in service. They found themselves inopportunely with child and their choice was clear: abortion, frequently followed by the mother's death, or, if the master was decent, a pregnancy carried to full term in secret. However, it did not explain why Clément was only registered under his Christian name? Who were his godparents? Without their presence a baptism would have been unthinkable. Their Christian names and surnames should be recorded in the register beside the child's. This baptism seemed to her altogether too clandestine for it to be completely orthodox.

Clément waited for a few moments, listening out just to make sure. Her snooping in the chapel having been successful, Mabile would not return again tonight. He crawled out of his hiding place in the honeysuckle bush. A cold sweat had drenched his shirt. It did not take a genius to guess what the fiendish woman had been trying to find out. So he was right and she did know how to read. He was annoyed with himself for not having anticipated this new piece of cunning. He should have taken the register of births

119

and deaths even without telling Agnès, for she would doubtless disapprove of any act that deprived Souarcy of its history.

He knew it. Eudes de Larnay was baring his teeth. His jaws were exposed, preparing to snap at their defenceless flesh.

The weather was so beautiful, so mild. From time to time Agnès caught a glimpse of the cloudless blue sky through an opening in the leaves. The boat was bobbing gently downstream. She lay with her head to the stern. She was alone, in sweet solitude. Her right hand caressed the calm surface of the water. A sudden eddy rocked the flimsy vessel. She sat up and looked around at the waves rippling out from the boat. What was it? A surprise current? A vast aquatic beast? Menacing? The shaking grew more violent and the boat jibbed, lurching dangerously from side to side. She wanted to cry out for help but no sound came from her throat. Suddenly she was aware of a small insistent voice whispering in her ear:

'Madame, Madame, I beg you, wake up, but do not make a sound.'

Agnès sat up in bed. Clément was staring at her, his head framed by the canopy curtains. Agnès's relief was short-lived and she demanded in a whisper:

'What are you doing in my chambers? What time is it?'

'It is after matins, Madame, but not yet dawn.'

'What are you doing here?' she repeated.

'I waited until Mabile and the other servants were asleep. While you were dining with Brother Bernard she stole into the chapel in order to look through the register.'

Agnès, wide awake now, concluded:

'So we know for certain that she can read.'

'Enough to perform her misdeeds.'

'What do you suppose? I'll wager she was searching for details about your birth or of Sybille's death.'

'I am convinced of it too.'

'What could she learn from reading those lines?' Agnès reflected out loud.

'I went over them again after she had left to try to imagine where her wickedness might be leading. I am registered under my Christian name only, and there is no mention of my god-father or godmother. As for Sybille, I may remind you, Madame, that her death is not recorded. She was a heretic and refused the sacraments of our Holy Church.'

'Hush! Do not utter that word. It is over. Gisèle was your godmother, and as for your godfather, it was too much of a risk. The only person we might have trusted was my previous chaplain, but he was dying and passed away shortly afterwards. What is more, it would have meant confessing to him, which was impossible. And so Gisèle and I decided to enter no surname at all since only one would have been more harmful. At the very worst, had an examination of the register been ordered, we could have claimed it was the error of an enfeebled hand and a mind already clouded by death.'

'So my baptism isn't ... It's as though I had never been baptised, isn't it?' asked Clément in a soft trembling voice.

Her blue-grey eyes gazed into those of the child, and she gestured to him to sit down beside her.

'God is our only true judge, Clément. Men, whoever they may be, are merely His tireless interpreters. What conceited fool can claim to know the sum of His desires, His designs, His truth? They are impenetrable and we can only glimpse them.'

Her own words troubled her. They had been intended to comfort the child. And yet, up until that moment none of her attempts to describe her tentative search for the true path to God had seemed so sincere. Was she seriously mistaken, was this blasphemy?

'Is that what you truly think, Madame?'

She replied unfalteringly: 'It shocks me and yet it is truly what I believe. Your baptism delivered you into the arms of God, Clément. Two women, Gisèle and I, bore you there with open hearts.'

The child sighed and leant against her. A few seconds later he asked:

'What are we going to do about the spy, Madame?'

'How does she plan to warn my brother, for he is the instigator of this sinister scheme? Larnay is far from here. The journey would take her two days on foot. Could Eudes have employed someone else to carry messages to him?'

'I doubt it very much, Madame. Eudes may be a fool but even he must realise that the more accomplices he has, the greater the risk of his secret being discovered.'

'You are right. So how does she inform him? He seldom comes to Souarcy, God be praised.'

'I shall find out, I promise. Rest now, Madame, I will return to my lair.'

Clément had made a little place for himself under the eaves. He had chosen the location with great care. He had built a ladder flimsy enough to deter any adult from climbing up. It gave him easy access from the end of the passageway that led to his mistress's anteroom and chamber. In this way he could see anyone approaching. Another advantage was a tiny window that ventilated the eaves, and allowed him, with the aid of a rope, to come and go without the servants seeing him.

A tall brown angel. Brother Nicolas Florin paused suddenly. The tonsure had not made this young man ugly; on the contrary it lengthened his pale brow, giving him the appearance of a proud chimera.

Brother Bartolomeo de Florence was standing on his right, his eyes lowered towards his clasped hands.

Nicolas murmured in his strangely soft yet cavernous voice:

'I am at a loss to understand why they are sending me north when I proved so useful to them here in the South during the riots last August that unleashed bloodshed and destruction on our good city. I took part in foiling the devilish plot of that depraved Franciscan, the execrable Bernard Délicieux.* Never was a name more ill suited. No, I honestly do not understand, unless they mean to honour me. Yet my instinct tells me the inverse is true.'

With a willowy hand Nicolas raised the resolutely lowered chin of his victim.

'What is your opinion, sweet brother?' he repeated, fixing Bartolomeo's eyes with his soft dark gaze.

The novice's throat was dry. He had prayed night and day for a miracle powerful enough to rid him of his tormentor, and now he dreaded the consequences. However much he reproached himself, repeated to himself *ad nauseam* that he had nothing to be afraid of, that the order for the transfer was signed by Cardinal Benedetti with no more mention of his name than of the true reason for the relocation, he remained uneasy. Nicolas and his insatiable desire for power, his appetite for inflicting pain, everything about this excessively beautiful, cunning creature terrified him.

The naive young Dominican had soon realised that faith was not the driving force behind his cell companion. For certain ambitious offspring of low birth, entry into the orders had always been a useful tool.

Bartolomeo had gathered from Nicolas's circumspect confessions that his father had been a lay illuminator to Charles d'Évreux, the Comte d'Étampes. Although as a child he showed little interest in the task of colouring and lettering, his lively mind had, with the aid of the Comte's splendid library, soaked up a fair amount of knowledge. He had been pampered and spoiled by an ageing mother for whom this late gift of a child was compensation for the years of suspicion about her ability to conceive. Added to the poor woman's humiliation was fear, for she exercised the profession of midwife to the ladies-in-waiting of Madame Marie d'Espagne, daughter of Ferdinand II and wife of the Comte.

One day, when they were praying side by side, Nicolas had whispered in Bartolomeo's ear in a voice that had made him tremble:

'The world is ours if we know how to take it.'

One night, as Bartolomeo lay sleeping in the cool darkness of their cell he thought he heard the words:

'Flesh is not earned, and only the feeble-minded share it. Flesh should be taken, snatched.'

Nicolas's excesses had begun soon after he arrived in the town of the four mendicant convents,* which at the time boasted ten thousand inhabitants. Bartolomeo was convinced that they had contributed to the hatred the populace felt towards them and to their uprising against the royal and religious authorities.

One particular memory wrung the young Dominican's heart. That poor girl Raimonde, who was touched in the head, and claimed to be visited at night by spirits. Encouraged by Nicolas, who preyed on her like a cat preys on a mouse, she attempted to demonstrate her powers, which she professed came from the Virgin. She stubbornly repeated incantations she claimed were capable of piercing rats and field mice. Despite the fact that her efforts ended in failure, Nicolas managed to make her admit responsibility for the death of a neighbour carried off by a mysterious summer fever, as well as for some cows miscarrying. The young Inquisitor's case was weak, and yet he proved her guilt, arguing that the Virgin could not transmit a lethal power, even one used only against harmful rodents. The devil alone could do that in exchange for a soul. The poor mad girl's insides hung from the rack. Her suffering had been interminable. Nicolas stared with satisfaction at the blood flowing from her entrails into the underground chamber's central drain, dug out for the purpose. Bartolomeo had fled the Viscount's Palace, loathing himself for his cowardice.

In reality, the young man was too rational to be able to turn a blind eye. He radiated faith, and love for his fellow man. He might have found the inner strength to rebel and even, why not, to defeat Nicolas. But a sort of evil curse of his own design prevented him. His excitement when Nicolas's hand brushed against his arm. His unpardonable urge to justify what was simple debauchery and cruelty on the part of his cell companion. Bartolomeo loved Nicolas with a love that was anything but fraternal. He loved him and he hated him. He would gladly die and at the same time live for his next smile. Naturally, Bartolomeo was aware that monks practised sodomy, as they did concubinage. Not he. Not he who dreamt of angels as others dream of girls or finery.

The beautiful demon must go, he must vanish for evermore.

'I am talking to you, Bartolomeo. What do you think?'

The novice mustered all his strength to reply in a steady voice:

'I see in it only a sign of approval. Surely it is not a reprimand, much less a punishment.'

'But you will miss me, will you not?' Nicolas taunted him.

'Yes …'

He spoke the truth and it made him want to weep with rage, and sorrow too. The firm belief that his morbid fascination for Nicolas would be the only insurmountable ordeal he must endure devastated him.

The brambles and the long grass still trapped the early-morning mist. It was as if the earth, jealous of the sky, had formed its own clouds. Gilbert used to be afraid of it. Everybody said it was the breath of spirits, some of whom were so resentful of their fate that they would lure you into their limbo. But his good fairy had told him that was just nonsense and stories to make little children do as they were told. Mist came from the forest floor when it was full of water and the heat made it rise. That was all. Gilbert had found this explanation very reassuring and had felt suddenly superior to all the fools taken in by a lot of tall tales. For his good fairy was always right.

Gilbert chuckled with glee. His shoulder bag was already full to bursting with morels. The autumn rains and forest fires the previous year had been favourable. He would keep one large handful for himself to cook in the embers the way he liked. All the rest would go to his good fairy. For he was certain she was a fairy. One of those fairies who have grown accustomed to human ways and who make their lives more beautiful and sweet.

With the underneath of his sleeve, he wiped away the saliva running down his chin. He was jubilant.

She adored the morels he picked for her each spring. Oh! He could already imagine her feeling the weight of them in her beautiful pale hands and declaring:

'Why, Gilbert, they look even bigger than last year's crop! Where do you manage to find such marvels?'

He wouldn't tell her. And yet he was prepared to do anything to please her. But he was no fool; if he showed her his secret places for picking morels, ceps and chanterelles, he would have no more lovely gifts to bring her. And that would be sad because then she wouldn't give him that happy smile any more. Just like the magnificent wild trout he caught with his bare hands in the icy waters of the river Huisne. Gilbert swelled with pride: only he knew where to find the tiny creeks that held the biggest fish. What is more, he took great pains when going there to make sure nobody was following him, looking back and listening out. If he stood still where the current was weakest he could almost pluck them from the water like fruit. Every Friday he brought a pair for his good fairy to brighten up her fast days.

His mood changed abruptly, and he became sullen. Of course he would give his life for his good fairy. And yet he was so afraid of death since he had lain in bed with it for two days and three nights. He could have sworn that open-eyed death was staring at him even while he slept. It didn't smell too bad though because of the cold. It was in winter; he forgot which year. A cruel winter when many people died, even at the manor, even the old chaplain and his good fairy's maidservant, the one who was with child. He remembered that the Dame de Souarcy had allowed hunting on her land because he had caught some rabbits. At first, he had lain close to open-eyed death, hoping in vain for some warmth. He had been too young at the time to know that dead people suck up all the heat. When they, the others, finally noticed them, death and him, they dragged open-eyed death away and flung her on top of a pile of other bodies on a cart. One of the others had said:

'What'll we do with the idiot now the old woman's gone? He's just another mouth to feed. I think we should leave him at the edge of the forest to fend for himself.'

A woman who was standing apart from the others protested as a matter of form:

'It's not Christian! He's too young. He'll perish in no time.'

'He has no sense in his head so it's not as bad as if it were one of us.'

'I say it's not Christian,' the woman had insisted before walking away.

The nine-year-old Gilbert had watched them, hardly understanding what they were scheming, only sensing that his chances of survival were waning as his quivering mother, sprawled on top of a pile of other corpses, was drawn away on a rattling ox-cart.

Blanche, the tanner's wife, renowned for her piety and good sense, had declared:

'Mariette's right. It isn't Christian. He's still a child.'

'He's a dirty little cat-killer,' replied the man, who was in a hurry to despatch Gilbert to a better world, preferably one where he wouldn't need feeding.

True, he had skinned a couple of the neighbours' cats. But it wasn't as if they were dogs, and anyway it was so he could line his clogs with their pelts. It was wrong of him to be sure. It was wrong to harm the predators of the field mice that ravaged the grain stocks, except if they were black. He could kill any number of those, for safety, for they were liable to turn into hosts of the devil.

Blanche had shot the man an angry look that had all but made him recoil. She replied in a sharp voice:

'I think I shall bring the subject of our disaccord before our lady. I feel sure that she will see it my way.'

The man had lowered his head. He, too, felt sure.

And so it was. Agnès had ordered the simpleton to be brought before her, and had warned that anyone unjustly beating, harming or punishing the boy in any way would have her to answer to.

129

Gilbert the simpleton had grown in size and strength under the protection of the manor, but his mind was still that of a child. Like a child he sought his good fairy's affection, growing gentle and meek when she stroked his hair or spoke softly to him. And like a child a wild temper could flare up in him when he feared for his good fairy or for himself. His colossal strength had not only protected the Dame de Souarcy but had also discouraged any attempts on the part of the villagers to taunt or mistreat him.

For some time, the one they so often called the idiot had been alerted by a strange premonition: the season of the beast was drawing near. It would soon be upon them. Occasionally, when night fell, Gilbert would be thrown into a panic, unable to imagine what form this beast would take. And yet he could feel it, he could smell it coming. His fear never left him and compelled him to remain by Clément's side, even though he disliked the boy, envying him his privileged position close to Agnès. But Clément loved the good fairy, too, with a love that was true and pure, and the simpleton knew this. Clément had the brains which Gilbert lacked but in contrast possessed none of Gilbert's extraordinary physical strength. Together they could become their lady's knight in shining armour. Together they could fight off many dangers, perhaps even the beast itself.

The troubled mood that had overtaken him a few minutes before gave way to a burst of renewed confidence. He would pick a few more morels and then gather the medicinal herbs his fairy had requested. He knew so many plants and herbs with miraculous powers. Some healed burns while others could kill an ox. The trouble was he didn't know their names. He recognised them by their pleasant aroma or their nauseating stench, or by their flowers or the shape of their leaves. The previous winter, he had cured his lady's cough with a few simple decoctions. As soon as he had picked enough he would go back. He was already feeling hungry.

He knew exactly where to find a nice crop, just beyond that bit of undergrowth that looked so much bigger than last year. He lay on his belly beside the tangle of brambles and bindweed and slid his hand between the nasty thorns. What was that touching his fingers? It felt like cloth. What was it doing there in the middle of his good fairy's mushrooms? The snarl of weeds was so dense that he couldn't make out much, just a vague outline almost the size of a stag, except that stags didn't wear clothes. Gilbert pulled his sleeves down to protect his hands and tugged at the wild brambles until he had cleared a sort of tunnel through which he was able to crawl towards the shape.

Closed-eyed death. It wasn't staring at him for there were no eyes – only two puffy slits. Inches from the soft mass that had once been a face, the simpleton was breathless with terror. He crawled backwards, twisting like a snake and whimpering, his mouth closed. Fear clouded the few brain cells he possessed. He tried to stand up, the thorns from the blackberry bush spiking the flesh on his shoulders, arms and legs.

He ran like a madman towards the village, panting and clasping his bag of mushrooms to his belly. A single sentence kept racing through his head: the beast was here, the beast was upon them.

The corpse, or what remained of it, lay on a plank resting on two trestles in the hay barn at the Manoir de Souarcy. Agnès had sent three farm hands with a cart to bring it back. Clément had taken advantage of the general commotion to go in and take a look undisturbed. It was true that the state it was in was hardly an enticement to onlookers.

It was a man, in his thirties, fairly tall and well built. There was

131

no sign of any tonsure to suggest he might be a friar. Clément did not trouble to go through the dead man's pockets, certain that the farm hands would have filched anything of value he might have been carrying, and then scattered the rest to make it look as if a thief had arrived there first.

The man had not been dead long, three or four days probably, judging by the state of the flesh that bore almost no signs of decomposition. In addition, the smell he gave off was still tolerable. On the other hand, it looked as though some animal had attacked him, unleashing itself on his face until it was unrecognisable, an exposed mass of mutilated flesh. Such a sustained attack by a carnivorous animal on one part of the body was inconceivable. The face is not the fleshiest part of the body – far from it. Predators and carrion feeders go for the buttocks, thighs, belly and arms, leaving the bony parts covered in skin or a thin layer of flesh for the insects or other small scroungers.

Were his deductions the result of his previous encounter with the corpse in Clairets Forest, or of the science he had been devouring over the past few weeks? Doubtless both. In any event the corpse made no impression on Clément and he walked over to it unflinchingly.

He lifted the tattered shirt hanging from the man's chest with the tip of his forefinger in order to examine the abdomen. The greenish hue had not yet spread over the entire stomach, although blisters filled with foul-smelling gases – a sign of putrefaction – were beginning to appear on the skin, bearing out Clément's first speculation as to the time of death. He walked around the table so that he was standing directly behind the man's head. It looked as though a set of talons had ripped into his face, slashing his brow, cheeks and neck so savagely that even a close friend would have difficulty recognising him. He found one detail puzzling. How would an animal have gone about maiming its prey in this way? The direction of the wound was obvious from the way the slashes on the right cheek were neater by the nose and clogged with skin and flesh towards the ear. Examining the wounds on the left cheek, he noticed that the inverse was true. So this hypothetical creature must have lashed at one ear with its claws and ripped the flesh towards the nose and then done the opposite on the other side of the face. It couldn't be the result of a single movement of the claws slashing from right to left because the nose was intact. Another detail caught his attention. He had read, in the introduction to a work by a renowned eleventh-century Iranian doctor called Avicenna, that wounds inflicted post mortem were easily identifiable. They neither bled nor showed signs of inflammation. Exactly like those the man presented. The bloodless edges of the elongated contusions ravaging the victim's face cried out their truth to those who knew how to listen. The man had been attacked after he was dead.

The sound of a man's heavy gait accompanied by a lighter step, which Clément immediately recognised as Agnès's, interrupted his reflections. He dived behind some bales of straw stacked at the far end of the barn.

That man's death was not the work of any animal. His wounds had been inflicted post mortem in order to conceal his identity or divert suspicion. As for his attacker, the boy would have sworn it was a beast of the two-legged variety that drank from a cup.

The footsteps drew closer and then came to a halt. The silence was broken by the sound of heavy and increasingly irregular breathing. Clément deduced from it that the man was examining the corpse. A rustic accent declared:

'Confound it! It takes an angry beast to rip a fellow to shreds like that. Well then ... I'll go and inform my master. He has to see this for himself.'

So the man worked for Monge de Brineux, Chief Bailiff of Comte Artus d'Authon. The boy heard the Dame de Souarcy give a deep sigh. He could sense her anxiety as soon as she spoke. She was counting on the man's stupidity and his agitation to attempt one last ploy. If she succeeded in convincing him, there was a good chance the investigation would end there.

'Since it is the work of an animal, it seems unnecessary to trouble Monsieur de Brineux and make him come all the way here. However, you are right and I shall order my men to track it down. It must be killed without delay. Follow me to the kitchens. A goblet of our wine will refresh you.'

'Hmm ... An animal. With all due respect, Madame, I'm not so sure. An animal would have eaten more of him than that.'

A heavy sense of foreboding warned Clément that their troubles had begun, and he blamed himself for his lack of foresight.

When Clément returned to the manor that morning, following another night of feverish reading and discovery, he was alerted by an unusual commotion in the courtyard. Three geldings, nearly the size of ceremonial horses, were tied to the wall-rings of the barn, and a few yards away a bay palfrey pawed the ground, snorting nervously. Clément studied the magnificent steed. It was rare in these parts to see one so fine. The exertion of galloping had left white streaks down its neck and sides. It had come a long way, and at speed. Who might ride such an animal and be accompanied by three others?

Clément slipped through the kitchens and down the passageway leading past the garderobe until he reached the small postern door the servants used to enter the great hall. He pressed himself against it in the hope of discovering who was visiting Agnès so early in the morning. He heard his lady reply:

'What can I say, my Lord Bailiff? Up until your arrival I knew nothing of these mysterious deaths, as you have described them. One of my servants was out picking mushrooms and discovered this poor wretch in a thicket.'

Monge de Brineux, Comte Artus d'Authon's Chief Bailiff, Clément thought.

'And yet, rumours spread fast, Madame. Had they honestly not reached you?'

'Indeed not. We are very isolated here. Four victims in two months, and all of them friars, you say?'

'Three out of the four — we know precious little about the man in your barn except that he met an identical fate ...'

'Were all their faces slashed in that way?'

'All but the second victim, an emissary of the Pope, like the first. As you can imagine, his death has caused great upset in Rome. However, it is the first two deaths that are proving to be a real puzzle. It would seem both men were burnt, or at least that is what their black shrivelled skin leads us to believe. And yet their clothes show no sign of having been exposed to flames. Were they undressed before being tortured and then dressed again? It seems improbable.'

So there was another corpse before the one he had found in the clearing, Clément deduced. And his clothes bore no trace of having been destroyed by fire, any more than his hair or body hair.

'We were unable to find the message he was carrying. The Abbess of Clairets admits she wrote it, while not wishing to disclose the contents to us. According to her, the two other friars never reached the abbey. And as for the man lying in your barn, the brief description we gave her stirred no memory. So far we know next to nothing about any of them.'

'And yet you maintain they are friars.'

'That is correct.'

'How can you be so sure?'

'A detail that concerns only those charged with the investigation,' replied the Bailiff in a polite but firm voice.

The tonsure, Clément thought instantly.

Agnès understood the warning. She remained silent for a few moments. When she spoke again, her changed tone alarmed the child pressed up against the other side of the door. It was sharper, almost imperious.

'What are you implying, my Lord Bailiff?'

'Whatever do you mean, Madame?'

'I have a curious feeling that you are being evasive.'

The ensuing silence made Clément uneasy. Monge de Brineux was a powerful man. His office and his authority came directly from the very influential Comte Artus d'Authon. A childhood friend of King Philip, the Comte had had the good sense to refuse the royal favours he knew to be fickle, and devote himself to the running of his estate. The attention he paid to his affairs had enabled him to preserve his friendship with the monarch, who mistook Artus's political circumspection for dignified disinterest, while making his little county one of the richest and most peaceable in France. Clément reassured himself; Agnès's perceptiveness was equalled only by her intelligence. She must have taken the measure of her interlocutor before adopting such a strategy.

'Whatever do you mean, Madame?' he repeated.

'Come now, Monsieur, have the good grace not to under-estimate me. You and I both know that no animal is responsible for what happened to that poor wretch. I have not seen the others but your presence here is proof enough. At least three of these men were slain, and their slayer, or slayers, attempted to mask the crime by savagely clawing their victims' faces.'

By clumsily clawing their faces, Clément corrected from his spy hole.

There was another, briefer silence before Monsieur de Brineux confessed:

'I had indeed reached the same conclusion.'

'So why this urgent visit? For surely you did not ride all this way with three of your men simply to examine a mutilated body decomposing in a barn. In what way are these murders connected with Souarcy and its mistress? Come now, the truth, Monsieur.'

'The truth is …' The Bailiff paused. 'The truth, Madame, is

that we found a letter scratched in the ground under the bodies of two of the victims. My men are presently combing the thicket your man Gilbert showed us to make sure there is … no letter.'

My God! The *A* in the ground under the Pope's emissary, which he had instinctively brushed away with his hand.

'A letter? What sort of letter?' asked Agnès.

'A letter of the alphabet. An *A*.'

'An *A*? I see … *A* as in "Agnès"?'

'Indeed, or as in any number of words or Christian names, I grant you.'

He was cut short by an incongruous laugh. The Dame de Souarcy quickly pulled herself together before adding:

'Plenty indeed – why, I could give you thirty without even having to think about it! Well, Monsieur? Do you really see me running through the forest armed with a claw and attacking men twice as heavy as I, if the size of the one lying in my outbuilding is anything to judge by? Moreover, you must suppose that my victims know me well enough to know my Christian name and do not hesitate to use it to incriminate me. If the situation were not so serious, your suppositions would be purely grotesque. Lastly, and if I may be permitted to say so, I would be most foolish to have proceeded in this way.'

'I do not understand what you mean.'

'And yet it is very simple. Now, let us just suppose that for some unknown reason I am a bloodthirsty monster. I do not know why, but I kill men. And I try to make my crimes look like the work of a wild beast. A bear perhaps; they are to be found in our forests. Would I really be so foolish as to simulate an attack by setting about the face and nothing else, not even the clothes? Why, any serf or huntsman would see through it immediately. Even your half-witted sergeant was not fooled! A five-year-old child could see that this was no animal. And this leads to my question: is the killer a simpleton, or much cleverer than you imagine?'

'What are you insinuating, Madame?'

'I insinuate nothing; I suggest. I suggest that this evil criminal wanted, on the contrary, to draw attention to these murders. In fact, do you not find it strange that all four were discovered within such a short time? Two months, did you say? Many, I am sure, who are tossed into ravines, buried in caves, weighted down and thrown into rivers for the fish to colonise, or reduced to ashes will never be found. You must confess that the connecting threads in this case are glaringly obvious.'

Clément could not see the smile that played across the Bailiff's lips. The man was astonished, not by a woman displaying the kind of intelligence and quick wits he wished more of his men possessed – after all his own wife Julienne was his most valuable counsellor – but that she did not hesitate to contradict him openly.

He rose to take his leave, remarking in an amused voice:

'You would delight my master, the Comte d'Authon, Madame. He has reached the same conclusion as you. The fact remains that we have four bodies on our hands, three of whom are friars – who knows, perhaps even four – and a persistently recurring letter that may have been scratched by the victims or by their aggressor.'

His smile faded and his pursed lips betrayed his perplexity.

'There is one other detail I hesitated to mention ...'

He pulled a tiny pale-blue square of cloth from his leather shoulder bag and unfolded it before her.

'Do you recognise this linen handkerchief, Madame? It bears your initial in the corner.'

Mabile, or even Eudes himself. Clément was convinced.

Agnès's half-brother could have taken the handkerchief during his last visit. The timing was not impossible.

'Indeed I do, it belongs to me,' declared Agnès.

'We found it hanging from a low branch, two yards from the second victim.'

'So in addition to being bloodthirsty and extremely foolish I must also be very careless to run through the woods with a linen handkerchief in one hand and a set of claws in the other! What a flattering picture you paint of me, Monsieur.'

'No, Madame, to be sure, I would be a fool myself to suggest such a thing,' Monge de Brineux chaffed. 'I must set off again. The journey to Authon is a long one. Believe me, this meeting has been more of a pleasure than I anticipated. I take my leave of you, Madame. Pray do not trouble yourself ... I can find my own way to my horse.'

Clément listened to the Bailiff's footsteps walking off towards the main door that opened onto the courtyard. The footsteps halted.

'Madame. I confess I am still unsure of the facts. But if what you say is true, then I strongly recommend you to be on your guard.'

A few seconds later, Clément emerged from his hiding place and approached Agnès.

'You were listening?'

'Yes, Madame.'

'What do you think of all this?'

'It worries me. The Bailiff is right – we must be doubly vigilant.'

'Do you think Eudes might be behind this plot?'

'If so, I doubt he is the instigator. He is better suited to spying on you in your home. He has no head for strategy.'

'Someone who has might be guiding him. Moreover, how did my handkerchief find its way into the forest?'

'Mabile?'

'Why not? She is cunning, and I think she nurses some kind of hatred towards us – the hatred of the weak who prefer attacking other prey rather than risk being caught in the jaws of the predator.'

'I was intrigued, not to say alarmed, by the turn you gave to that ... conversation, Madame.'

She looked at him and grinned.

'Do you mean to say, assertive ... Confrontational?'

'That's right.'

'You see, Clément, by dint of being subjugated by them, women learn to recognise the tracks men leave behind them – similar to wild game. You will understand it better as you get older.'

'And what species might he be?'

'Hmm ... a young boar in his prime perhaps.'

'They are lean and muscular and prefer scaring off to attacking.'

'But when they attack, nothing can survive their charge. Monge de Brineux was testing me. It became clear after only a few sentences. I do not know why. What I do know is that nothing I said to him came as a surprise. It remains to be seen what his true motive for coming here was. Furthermore, I could not allow him to sense my apprehension.'

'They say the Comte d'Authon is very powerful.'

'Indeed, he is.'

'Your half-brother is a feudal baron and his vassal.'

'As I am my brother's, which makes of me the Comte's under-vassal.'

'Have you ever met him?'

'I remember a tall young man, serious and reserved, who came to pay the late Baron Robert a visit once. That is all. I was still a girl.'

'Madame, could you not demand his direct protection?'

'You know as well as I that a liege lord will not intervene directly in the affairs of another liege lord's vassal, except in cases of injustice or wrong judgement and we have not reached that stage yet. Artus d'Authon will not involve himself in a family dispute at the risk of sparking a political row that could prove injurious to him. Eudes is admittedly only a member of the lower nobility, but he holds an important trump card: his iron mines.'

'You mean, his iron mine, his last, which they say is almost exhausted,' corrected Clément.

'He extracts enough ore from it to keep the King happy. Clément …'

'Yes, Madame?'

'I do not like to involve you in such schemes, but …'

He understood at once what was troubling her and informed her:

'Since her visit to the chapel, Mabile has not been out for quite some time and has encountered no one likely to take messages to your brother.'

She reached out her hand, and he closed his eyes as he laid his cheek in her palm.

Towards the middle of the afternoon a second visitor did little to lift Agnès's spirits. Jeanne d'Amblin from Clairets Abbey was making her monthly rounds. Usually, Agnès found the jolly Extern Sister delightful. Her ready supply of stories and harmless gossip about her encounters with the wealthy burghers, merchants and farmers or even with the local nobility amused the younger woman. The nun brought her news of the outside world, its births, marriages, deaths, pregnancies and its harvests. Today, however, the good sister's unease was palpable. They sat in the little anteroom outside Agnès's quarters, furnished with a small round table and two chairs. Agnès's veil fluttered in a gentle current of air and she looked up at the high window. Several of the diamond-shaped panes were broken. By birds? When? She only ever passed through this tiny room, never stopping to sit there unless a lady visitor came, which was rare. What a day it had been! Glass was so costly and difficult to come by. The few glazed windows at the manor were the only reminder of Hugues's extravagant tastes. When winter came, the rest would be stopped up with hemp or hides. How would she find the money to pay for the missing panes? Presently ... She made an effort to attend to her visitor.

'Would you accept a cup of hippocras?'

'I never refuse good hippocras, and the one you make here is among the best.'

'You flatter me.'

The nun's smile lacked conviction, and she went straight to the point:

'I hurried here as soon as I learnt of the Bailiff's visit.'

'News travels fast,' observed Agnès.

'Not really. Monge de Brineux stopped off at Clairets Abbey on his way. Just after lauds.'[+]

'And why did he go to the abbey before dawn?'

'He desired a meeting with our Abbess. That is how we knew he was setting off afterwards for Souarcy. I can tell you precious little else. The Abbess asked me to come here to make sure that you were safe and sound – which I would have done anyway had her thoughts not anticipated my own,' Jeanne d'Amblin added.

'What wicked murders, for they are murders, are they not?'

'Everything would suggest it.'

'Wicked,' repeated the nun, clasping the large wooden crucifix hanging round her neck. 'Friars ... Sister Adélaïde was right. This matter of the tonsures is so mysterious ... I mean, why did those three friars, if not four, let their hair grow?'

'So as to blend in, to go unnoticed, I suppose.'

'Hmm ... A convincing theory. At least it seems fitting in the case of the second victim, the papal emissary who met with our Abbess. She was terribly upset after he left. Naturally, it was only much later that we connected her distress with his visit, since we knew nothing of his mission.'

'What became of the missive he was carrying?' Agnès asked, even though thanks to the Bailiff she already knew the answer.

'Vanished into thin air. Our Abbess is worried sick about it. She refuses to disclose the contents and, knowing her as I do, I am certain she has every good reason.'

'And did the other victims ...'

'... No, they did not visit us, if that's what you were going to ask. Few men besides the chaplain and the young pupils are allowed within our walls, otherwise it would be difficult for us to be so sure. The state of their faces made any identification virtually impossible.'

She paused, and looked at Agnès with a grave expression on her face before continuing:

'Something terrible is being hatched, I can sense it. And I am not the only one. Thibaude de Gartempe, our guest mistress, is anxious too. And others. Even Yolande de Fleury, who never seems upset by anything. Our Abbess's desperate silence contributes to our concern. For it is desperate. She has retreated into herself in order to protect us, her girls, from what I do not know. We are afraid, Madame …'

Agnès did not doubt it. An unshakeable gloom seemed to have clouded the Extern Sister's usually bright happy face. She continued:

'I am afraid of an unknown entity whose form I cannot make out … It feels as if a deadly fog were about to engulf us, as if an evil beast were approaching by stealth. You will think me raving like some mad superstitious old woman.'

'No, indeed. You have described my own instinct. I too dread … I know not what.'

This was only half true. She had in some measure identified her fear: Eudes. And yet, like the nun, Agnès sensed something far more terrifying was secretly preparing to strike them and with great force.

Jeanne d'Amblin appeared to pause before deciding to speak:

'I did not only come here today to see how you were, but also to … how should I say …? Well, we were wondering whether my Seigneur de Brineux had confided in you … some detail, anything that might help us to see more clearly, to have some idea, to console our Abbess, perhaps even to help her, to save other wretched victims?'

'No, and to be very honest I had the impression that he, like us, is groping in the dark.'

Shortly after the Extern Sister had left, Agnès resolved to take her mind off things by going to see if Vigil had come back from his latest jaunt. He had the habit of disappearing for a day at a time but always returned to the pigeon-house in the evening to guard his females. She had not seen him the previous evening, and a vague concern for the cocky bird added to the dark mood that never left her. Some huntsmen were quick to take aim and had few scruples.

Vigil was neither in the pigeon-house nor perched on the rooftop of the manor. The angry and unexpected peck she received from one of his mates as she tried to stroke it seemed to her a bad omen.

In response to the pressure of his rider's leg the magnificent stallion came to a halt, statuesque. His immaculate black coat gleamed with sweat. He breathed without a single tremor of his powerful neck muscles, aware that the archer on his back was flexing his Turkish bow, made of two ox-horns joined by a metal spring.

The three-foot-long fletched arrow whistled through the air. It would have continued its flight for a hundred yards or so had it not struck the target, whose wings spread out in shock and pain as it plummeted in a swirl of feathers towards the archer. The rider swiftly dismounted and stooped to pick up the bird. The arrow had run it through, piercing the breast and exiting behind the wing joint. The huntsman's gloved hand paused an inch from the handsome pinkish-purple neck, now bloodied bright red. One of its sturdy feet was ringed; the other had a message attached. The huntsman pursed his lips in an expression of displeasure. He had shot a carrier pigeon – a superb animal whose loss the rightful owner would regret. What a fine haul! He would be obliged to compensate the lord or convent that owned the pigeon, despite having shot it down on his own land. A second infuriating thought occurred to him: his eyesight was waning. He who had been capable of following a falcon during the hunt without ever losing sight of it would soon be unable to tell the difference between a pigeon and a common pheasant! The silent devastation wrought by age. He became more aware by the day of its undermining effect. He would soon be forty-three. True, he was still a long way from old age, having only just passed the forty-year threshold signalling the end of youth. And yet, his joints would grumble after a day spent in the saddle, and he no longer had the urge to sleep out in all weathers. If he were to believe *The Four Ages of Man*, the treatise written forty years before by a lord of Novara, he still had a few good years before he entered old age. Artus d'Authon slipped off his right glove and pinched the skin on the back of his hand. Weathered from decades spent outside and leathery from handling weapons, it had grown more slack and seemed to want to come away in places from the flesh underneath. As for his wrist, it had lost some of its musculature.

'A pox on the years,' he muttered between his teeth.

The years had passed so quickly and yet he had been so terribly bored throughout, one day running into the next so that in the end he was barely able to tell them apart.

Born under the reign of Louis IX, he had grown up during that of Philip III, the Bold, under whom his father served as supreme commander of the French armies for some years before dying prematurely. He was nine years old at the birth of Philip, who would later become the fourth monarch to bear that name. He had initiated the young future king into the art of hunting and handling a bow. The inflexibility, the severity of the man, who would later be given the sobriquet 'the Fair', were already apparent. Artus was convinced that he would make a good king if he received good counsel, but a king he would prefer to admire from afar. Thus he had declined the honour of taking up the onerous post filled by his father, which would have been conferred on him owing to his friendship with the monarch, but also because its bestowal had become almost hereditary. Artus had then ridden halfway around the world, fighting wherever fortune or his fervour took him until he reached the Holy Land.

It had brought him some subtle surprises, a few furious rages and a fair share of wounds that flared up in stormy weather. He had defended causes with both his brain and his brawn, but none had convinced him sufficiently for him to embrace any one completely. He had returned to France without having experienced the hoped-for transformation and had sunk back into the repetitive tedium of every day seeming the same.

Thereafter, the running of his small county had taken up all his time. His father's fascination with royal politics had led to its neglect, and it fell to Artus to put his house in order, to bring to heel, with more or less recourse to force, the lower nobility who were at each other's throats over the systematic carving-up of land that was not theirs. Widowed at thirty-two, he had all but forgotten the features of his ghostly wife who had died bearing him a son. Little Gauzelin had inherited his mother's frailty and, too weak to live, had died aged four. A father's grief had turned into a destructive animal rage. He had stormed the castle for weeks on end, sending the servants scattering for cover like mice whenever they heard the madman approach. Two deaths. Two pointless deaths and no heir. Only a terrible loneliness and regret for what had not been.

He pulled himself together. If he let his thoughts go down that bitter path again, the day – yet another day – would be irrevocably ruined.

He picked up the pigeon and examined the ring, pausing before he removed the long arrow implanted in the still warm flesh. A capital *S* was followed by a small *y*. Souarcy. The animal was the property of the young widow, Eudes de Larnay's half-sister, born of an adulterous liaison. He could not remember ever having met her, though Brineux had described her briefly and with a roguish glint in his eye.

A few days earlier, when his Chief Bailiff, Monge de Brineux, returned from his inquiries, Artus had asked him:

'And what of the cornered doe you ran down?'

'If she's a cornered doe, then I'm a newly hatched gosling. The lady was not ruffled in the slightest by my visit – either that or she's a brilliant actress. That woman is more like a lynx than a doe. She's cautious, bold, clever and patient. She lures her prey into her territory by feigning sleep. As for the hunters, she plays with them, pretending to show herself while in reality protecting her young, covering her rear and preparing her escape.'

'Do you believe she is involved in these murders?'

'No, my Lord.'

'You seem very sure.'

'I can read men's souls.'

'Those of women are harder to decipher, my friend, especially,' the Comte added with a half-smile, 'when they are lynxes.'

'Goodness me, yes! She was fearful but not because of any guilt. Her show of arrogance was intended to convince me of the contrary. In my opinion she has nothing to do with these murders. And so the question we must now ask is glaringly obvious: how did her handkerchief come to be in those bushes? Somebody placed it there, but who? With the aim of implicating her, but why? I have gathered some reliable information. She possesses no great fortune; on the contrary. Souarcy is nothing but a large farm and rather less splendid than most of those belonging to our wealthy farmers in and around Authon. Moreover, the manor and its land are part of her dower. She owns nothing in her own right. If as a widow she were to lose the usufruct of the property, it would revert to her half-brother, until her only child, Mathilde, Hugues de Souarcy's heir, comes of age. Having said this, the property in question would hardly be enough to attract the wealthy Eudes de Larnay, even though he scatters his fortune and that of his wife to the four winds.'

Eudes de Larnay. The mere thought of his vassal's name put Artus in a bad mood again. Eudes the rat. Beneath his bulky physique and his virile, seductive exterior he was a coward and a vile scavenger. Any man who beat the women he bedded was not worthy of being called a man. This at least was the wretched reputation of the feudal Baron as it had reached Artus's ears.

He paused for a moment, stroking with his forefinger the tiny roll of paper wrapped round the dead bird's leg. No. This message had been sent by the Dame de Souarcy or was intended for her, and it would be unseemly of him to read it without her permission.

'Let us go and take a look for ourselves, Ogier, my beauty,' he declared to the destrier, who pricked up his ears on hearing his name.

Artus d'Authon pulled out the arrow and made himself look at the blood that dripped from it. He remounted and gently squeezed the flanks of his horse, who took off towards the north. After all, it was as good a way as any to end a new day and he had to confess that Monge had excited his curiosity.

The Comte did not entirely trust his Bailiff's enraptured description of the lady. Brineux felt a mixture of affection and admiration towards women, which his marriage to a very quick-witted mischievous member of the burgher class from Alençon had done nothing to allay. Julienne might not have been the most beautiful girl in Perche, despite her pretty face and attractive figure, but she was incontestably the most entertaining, and had made him and Monge laugh many times with her gift for mimicry that bordered on genius. The way she impersonated Comte Artus right under his nose, frowning solemnly and lowering her pensive brow, crossing her hands behind her back and stooping as she walked, as though embarrassed by her great height, had the man himself in stitches, but he would never have accepted this playful mockery from any other.

It was a three-hour ride to Souarcy – a little less if he kept up a good pace. Madame de Souarcy could not refuse her liege lord lodging for the night, should he require it. As soon as he had satisfied his curiosity he would return home.

A farm hand, overcome by panic on hearing his name, had spluttered directions to the forest where he would find the lady of the manor.

Ogier walked at a slow pace, sensing his rider's hesitancy in the slackening of the reins and the bit.

'It's not too late to turn back,' Artus d'Authon muttered, as though seeking his horse's approval. 'What a ridiculous fool to have come here at all. No matter. We shall finish what we have begun, so be it!'

Ogier lengthened his step.

A good thirty yards away, a blanket of smoke caught his attention. Two men, one tall and heavily built, the other slender, were gesticulating in its midst. Two serfs, judging from their short tunics, tied at the waist with a wide leather strap, and their thick linen breeches. The two men both wore gloves and a peculiar bonnet on their heads with a fine veil bunched at the neck.

Artus was alerted by his horse's sudden jumpiness. Why was a swarm of wild bees coming towards them? Hives. The two serfs were smoking out hives. He pulled up short and made Ogier walk back a few paces before dismounting and continuing alone on foot.

He was only a few yards from the two servants, yet they were seemingly so absorbed in their task that they did not notice his arrival. No doubt the strange protective garb they wore made it difficult to hear.

'Hey there!' he cried, alerting them to his presence while driving away the surrounding bees with a gloved hand.

The slender figure turned a veiled head towards him and a youthful, boyish voice spoke in a brusque tone that surprised the Comte:

'Stand back, Monsieur, they are angry.'

'Are they defending their honey?'

'No, their king, and with a ferocity and self-sacrifice that would be the envy of many a soldier,' replied the sharp voice.

'Stand back, I tell you. Their sting is fierce.'

Artus obeyed. This was no boy but a woman, and a very comely one at that, in spite of her outlandish costume. So Agnès de Souarcy had of necessity become a beekeeper. Monge de Brineux was right, the lynx was brave, for those bees when they attacked could prove lethal.

A good ten minutes elapsed, during which he did not take his eyes off her, studying each of her precise, agile movements, admiring how calm she stayed in order not to alarm the bees, listening to the patient way she instructed her farm hand, who towered above her like a giant. Artus felt half amused, half embarrassed. It would doubtless grieve her to be caught wearing breeches, though these were certainly far better suited to collecting honey than a robe. Even so, the wearing of men's clothes by women, for any reason, was strongly censured, although the doughty Eleanor of Aquitaine had done so in her day.

At last it appeared the two beekeepers had finished with the hives. They made their way towards him, the farm hand carefully carrying two pails brimming with the amber crop while the Dame de Souarcy loosened her protective veil, revealing two strawberry-blonde braids, which unfurled on either side of her pretty head.

As she walked up she addressed him blandly: 'They will

calm down now and rejoin their king.' Then her tone changed suddenly, became scathing. 'You surprised me wearing unsightly and improper clothing, Monsieur. It would surely have been more appropriate for you to have sent one of my servants to announce your arrival and to have waited until I returned to the manor.'

He had seldom seen a woman so completely beautiful right up to her high, pale brow with the hairline set slightly back, according to the fashion of the time. He opened his mouth to utter the apology he had prepared but she cut across him:

'Souarcy is only a farm, I'll grant you. However, I insist on a modicum of good manners and couth behaviour! Your name, Monsieur?'

Good gracious, the woman's temper was beginning to unsettle him, and he a warrior and huntsman and one of the most redoubtable swordsmen in the kingdom of France. In truth he was quite unaccustomed to being snapped at like this. He recovered his poise and declared in a calm voice:

'Artus, Comte d'Authon, Seigneur de Masle, Béthonvilliers, Luigny, Thiron and Bonnetable, at your service, Madame.'

A shiver ran down Agnès's spine. The one man she ought never to have snubbed, much less offended. Admittedly, she had always doubted he would intervene on her behalf, and yet this powerful figure in the shadows had become like a magic spell she could never invoke for fear it might not work. Her inaccessible lucky charm. Indeed, this was the main reason why she had always refused to call upon him or his justice. If, as she feared, he were to turn her away, then she would be completely helpless, alone against Eudes and no longer able to delude herself into believing that some miracle might save her. And yet now more than ever she needed to believe it.

She closed her eyes and breathed a sigh, her face white as a sheet.

'Are you unwell, Madame?' he enquired, concerned, and offered her his hand.

'It is nothing, just the heat and my fatigue.' She collected herself and continued, 'And the Seigneur de Souarcy. You forgot Souarcy.'

'Souarcy is under the protection of Baron de Larnay, Madame.'

'And he is your vassal.'

'Indeed.'

Agnès gave a polite if belated curtsey encumbered by her peasant's outfit.

'You are right to mention it Madame; I have behaved like an oaf … Are you finished with the bees?'

'Gilbert will see that they return to the hives. They like him. He is a gentle good soul. Would you be so kind, Gilbert?'

'Oh yes, my good lady, I shall fetch the honey and the wax, too, don't you worry.'

'You look weary, Madame. Pray let Ogier take you back to the manor. Allow me.'

He stooped, clasping his fingers to make a foothold for her. She was dainty and lithe, and mounted with a natural ease, sitting astride the saddle. Despite the inappropriateness of this position for a lady he found her fascinating. She was undaunted by his destrier, which was an awkward animal with anyone but its master. She sat admirably well on the huge black stallion, and horse and rider made an astonishingly handsome pair. Artus was beginning to think Monge had been right. He was reluctant now to mention the pigeon he had killed earlier, afraid of spoiling this singular moment.

Too soon for his liking, for he had been savouring their silent walk, they reached the courtyard of the manor. Agnès did not wait for his helping hand but slid from the saddle down Ogier's motionless flank.

Mabile had come running and the pale look on her face convinced Agnès that she was right in believing this man a godsend. The girl gave a deep curtsey. So she had already seen him at her master's residence.

'Pray excuse me, Monsieur, while I change. Mabile will fetch you some refreshments and a bowl of fresh fruit.'

'I have something to show you, Madame,' he began in a faltering voice, tapping the leather game bag that was attached to his saddle, 'something I regret with all my heart.'

'Some wild game?'

'A terrible blunder.'

He pulled out the pigeon, stiff now, its silky throat stained with a layer of dried blood.

'Vigil …'

'He is yours, then.'

'Indeed,' Agnès murmured, fighting back the tears that veiled her eyes.

'Madame, I am truly regretful. He was flying through one of my forests, I took aim and …'

Mabile made a mad rush for the animal, crying:

'I'll take him, Madame, don't …'

'Stop!'

The order resounded. Agnès had seen the message round the animal's leg.

'Leave it. I will deal with it.'

The girl retreated under Comte d'Authon's baffled gaze.

Agnès understood from her darting eyes and trembling lip that she was the author of the message, but she managed to keep her composure.

Her lucky charm. This man had already made a small miracle happen, for she was certain the message was addressed to Eudes. Now she knew how the plotters communicated: thanks to the beautiful trained bird, a generous gift from her half-brother. Her sadness at Vigil's loss quickly faded and she turned, smiling, to face the person who had no notion of the enormity of the good turn he had just done her.

'I am … an oaf. Pray believe me, Madame. I mistook it for a small pheasant. It was flying quite high and …'

'Do not mention it, Monsieur. Your blunder saddens me for I was fond of the bird, but … not everyone would have shown your consideration by returning the animal to me. Pray excuse me a few moments. I shall rejoin you shortly.'

She clutched Vigil and went up to her chamber. Before entering she called out from the bottom of the rickety ladder.

'Clément! I need your help.'

'I'm coming, Madame.'

She heard a quiet patter of feet and a face peered through the trapdoor opening.

'Vigil!'

'Yes. Come down. He's carrying a message.'

'So he was their messenger!'

'The huntsman is no other than Comte d'Authon. He is waiting for me in the great hall. Hurry.'

The child hurled himself down the ladder and joined her in her chamber. She briefly explained the unexpected encounter, which she dared not as yet consider a timely one. He listened with a smile on his lips that was betrayed by the gravity in his blue-green eyes.

'Change out of your clothes, Madame. I will remove the message from the bird's leg.'

Agnès paused. She had only a few minutes left in which to dress. What should she wear? Not the ceremonial robe she had fashioned from the sumptuous piece of silk Eudes had given her. Finery was not sufficient to charm this man. And charm him she must, her life depended on it. It was something at which she excelled and yet today she felt hindered by an unusual apprehensiveness.

'It is written in code, Madame. Each number stands for a letter, except for these Roman numerals – they probably represent real numbers. It doesn't need a genius to work out what they stand for: XXVIII – XII – MCCXCIV: 1294, the date of my birth. Mabile was sending him the information she found in the chapel register. The message might contain other clues that throw light on their plan.'

She turned towards Clément, who, out of a sense of modesty, was looking in the other direction over at the narrow window in the stone wall of her closet.

'Will you be able to decipher its secrets? You must, Clément.'

'I shall do my utmost. It is common to use a reference book and the few there are at Souarcy would mostly be inaccessible to the servants. My first choice would be the translation into French of the psalter you gave them. My only worry is that the two plotters might have been cleverer than we supposed. You see, the accomplices agree on a page and then number all the letters on that page. The ingenuity consists in beginning a few letters or lines into the page instead of with the first letter of the first line. It makes the job of decoding far more laborious and time-consuming.'

'Where did you obtain all this knowledge?'

'From books, Madame – they contain many marvels.'

'Indeed, but they are difficult to come by, and I was unaware that our modest library possessed so many treasures.'

'May I leave you to finish dressing, Madame?'

'You may, but do not vanish as is your custom.'

'Not tonight, Madame. I shall be watching over you.'

She stifled a smile. And yet what would she do without him, without his vigilance and his intelligence, which she saw new facets of every day?

Before leaving the room he whirled round and said in a hushed voice:

'And what type of game do you think this one is, Madame? A stag?'

'He is certainly strong and noble enough, but no, he possesses far more cunning. The stag runs until he hears the sound of the mort and then bravely but foolishly turns before charging. This one weighs up, thinks ahead. He knows when to renounce strategy in favour of strength, never the other way round. No. Not a stag, a fox, perhaps.'

'Hmm … A worthy animal, though almost impossible to tame.'

He closed behind him the heavy, studded door.

The pale-grey robe she wore for mass would do perfectly. She covered her braids with a long fine veil fixed at her crown by a small darker-grey turban. The fluid contours of the robe enhanced her graceful figure and made her look taller, which was acceptable given the height of her guest. She had matched the elegant austerity of her clothes to her perception of him. She chewed a pinch of *épices de chambre* to scent her breath, and put a drop of the belladonna Eudes had brought from Italy the year before in the corner of her eye. She had used the contents of the little phial studded with grey pearls and miniature turquoises but once, to see the effect it had. The eyes seemed to dissolve, becoming strangely deeper, like two languid pools.

Agnès walked back via the kitchens where she knew she would find Mathilde. The little girl was greedily watching Adeline and Mabile prepare the food.

'My lady daughter, the Comte d'Authon, an important man, has honoured us with his presence. I would like you to make an excellent impression, and then to take your leave without needing to be asked.'

'The Comte d'Authon here, Madame?'

'Indeed, it is no small surprise.'

'But … my dress is old and ugly and …'

'It is perfect. Besides, neither of our dresses could compete with those of the ladies in our lord's entourage, and so we must content ourselves with being dignified, which is a woman's best finery. Go and comb your hair and come back down at once.'

When Agnès rejoined the Comte in the great hall, he was sitting on one of the sideboards playing with the dogs.

'Fine beasts, Madame.'

'They are fearsome guard dogs … Or at least they were until your arrival.'

He smiled at the mild compliment and replied:

'Animals seem to warm to me. No doubt it is on account of my good manners.'

She offered no apology for her earlier rebuke. It would be a mistake, for he would instantly detect her servility. The simple fawning she used so abundantly with Eudes would never work on this man. On the contrary, it would almost certainly repulse him.

A moment later, Mathilde made her entrance as agreed. She was struggling to catch her breath from running, but walked with a calm, measured step towards her liege lord.

'Monsieur,' she began, curtseying gracefully, 'your presence within our walls is a rare pleasure indeed. And the honour you confer upon us brightens our humble dwelling.'

He went over to her, suppressing a good-natured chuckle.

'You are utterly charming, Mademoiselle. As for pleasures and honours, believe me, they are all mine. Had I known that two of the most precious pearls in Perche lodged here at the manor, I should not have delayed so long in coming. It is an unforgivable oversight on my part.'

The little girl's face flushed with joy at the immense flattery, and she took her leave, curtseying again.

'Your daughter is delightful, Madame. How old is she?'

'She is twelve. I try to teach her refinement. I hope she may enjoy a more … a more sumptuous life than the running of Souarcy.'

'To which you have nonetheless devoted yourself.'

'Mathilde was not born between two beds in the servants' quarters, albeit the servant in question was a lady's maid.'

Artus knew of the Dame de Souarcy's illegitimate birth. It disconcerted him that she would flaunt it until he realised that by making light of it she was defending herself against gossip or, worse still, ridicule. She really was a fine lynx. And she pleased him greatly.

The dinner began on a note of delightful banter, notwithstanding the miserable expression Mabile wore as she served the

162

cretonnée of new peas, freshly picked; the creamy soup thickened with egg yolk beaten in warm milk looked appetising.

Artus perceived that the lady was cultured, lively and intelligent and had a facility for repartee rare in a woman of her social standing.

When he complimented her on her composure earlier in the middle of a swarm of unfriendly bees, she told him of her first harvest with a playful look:

'… A column of bees was coming towards me. I shrieked and in a moment of foolish panic threw the pail of honey at them, half believing that if I gave it back they would leave me alone. Nay! I was obliged to hitch up my dress and run as fast as my legs would carry me back to the manor. You should have seen me in my crooked turban with my veil half torn off. I even lost a shoe. One of the fierce sentinels flew under my skirts and stung me – well, above my knee, and hence the breeches. In short, I made an utter fool of myself. Thankfully Gilbert was the only witness to my pitiable retreat. He bravely drove back the bees, thrashing his arms in the air like an angry goose to protect me. He came back covered in swellings and running a temperature.'

Artus burst out laughing as he pictured the scene. How long since he had laughed like that and, above all, in the company of a woman?

His mind grew troubled by a memory. The small frightened face of the frail young woman he had married when he was nearing his thirtieth birthday. Madeleine, the only child of the d'Omoy family, was eighteen, a perfectly decent age for becoming a wife and mother. And yet she still played with dolls. Her weeping mother and her father, who would have gladly continued treating her as a child for a few more years if he had not needed to secure a commercial transaction with the Comte, agreed to her

163

marriage to Artus. Normandy and its ports, which supplied large areas of the hinterland via an extensive network of waterways, was vital to the flourishing of Artus d'Authon's commerce, all the more so since the region was equally rich in iron ore. As for Huchald d'Omoy, an impoverished yet distinguished nobleman, the Comte d'Authon's gold would allow him to regild the family crest, tarnished following a series of ruinous investments. The young Madeleine d'Omoy sealed their contract. Anyone might have thought she had been abducted by a barbarian. For her their marriage began as a betrayal then turned into an ordeal when she realised that the physical distance separating her from her parents meant she would rarely see them. Artus could picture her now languishing in the room she almost never left, sitting on a chair under one of the arrow slits staring up at the sky, watching out for he knew not what. If he enquired, she would invariably turn her ashen face towards him, forcing a smile, and reply:

'The birds, Monsieur.'

'You would glimpse them more easily from the garden. It is warm outside, Madame.'

'No doubt it is, Monsieur, but I am cold.' She stayed where she was.

His visits to his wife's bedroom became more infrequent. He felt unwelcome there, and had it not been for his need of an heir he would doubtless have ceased inconveniencing Madeleine with his presence. He had never felt any desire for her. That skinny angular body, which he hardly dared touch for fear it might break, inspired a sort of pity in him that had gradually become mingled with repulsion.

The birth had been a nightmare. For hours on end he had listened to her groans from the lobby of her chamber.

Immediately after the delivery she had nearly succumbed to a haemorrhage that all but drained her weak blood. Despite the attentions she received from the physic and the midwife, which appeared partially to revive her, she doubtless had little will to live and three weeks after Gauzelin's birth, without a last word or even a gesture, her frail existence was snuffed out like a candle.

He surprised himself casting furtive glances at Agnès. She was strikingly beautiful and graced her speech with elegant gestures. Underneath all this refinement he was sure she possessed a rare strength of mind. Hugues de Souarcy had been a fortunate man when he married her at Robert de Larnay's request – she much less so. Not that Hugues was a bad man – on the contrary – but he was a coarse man whose rough edges had hardly been refined by wars and the tireless frequenting of taverns. Moreover, he was already quite advanced in years when they married. How old had she been then, thirteen, fourteen perhaps?

They talked of this and that, making each other laugh and jumping from one subject to another in an atmosphere of humorous repartee. She paused, concluding:

'With their *Roman de la Rose** Messieurs de Lorris and de Meung left me, how should I say … disappointed. The beginning and the end were so different. I found parts of the first story conventional, not to say over-indulgent, while the second, the satire on "feminine etiquette" by Ami et la Vieille, grated on my nerves.'

'The second author was a Parisian scholar and not always successful in avoiding the pitfalls of his education – which he was fond of parading – or of his milieu, or indeed those of farce itself.'

'In contrast, I confess to being extremely partial to the ballads

165

and fables of Madame Marie de France.* What wisdom, what finesse! The way she makes the animals speak as though they were humans.'

Artus could not resist seizing the opportunity.

'I, too, admire the lady's finesse and use of language. And what did you think of the poem entitled *Yonec*?'

Agnès immediately understood the reference. In that enchanting poem – the pretext for a discourse on true love – a woman who has married against her will prays to heaven to send her a sweet lover. Her wish is granted and the lover arrives in the form of a bird which turns into a prince.

She took her time responding, lowering her gaze towards the snail, herb and onion pâté which, enthralled as she was by their conversation, she had hardly tasted. He reproached himself for her silence:

'The term uncouth would seem perfectly suited to me this evening. Pray forgive my tasteless question, Madame.'

'Why, Monsieur? Indeed, my Seigneur Hugues was not the husband of a young girl's dreams, but he was courteous and respectful towards his wife. Besides, I did not dream. Dreams were a luxury I was scarcely permitted.'

'More's the pity, Madame.'

'Indeed.'

The acute sadness his idiotic question had caused the young woman wounded him.

'I feel I have behaved like an insensitive oaf.'

'No, for, with all due respect, I would not have allowed that. Hugues was my life raft – I believe that is the name sailors give it, and he was no less dependable. I was thirteen years of age. My mother had left this world when I was still a child and as for the Baroness, God rest her good soul, she was more interested in astronomy than matchmaking. In brief, I knew nothing of the role of wife … nothing of the duties involved.'

'Some of which can be pleasurable.'

'So I believe. In any event, Hugues never lost his patience with me. His only failing in my eyes was that he allowed Souarcy to go to rack and ruin. He was no farmer, even less an administrator, he was a soldier. Most of the land had turned into a wilderness and parts of it had become barren.'

'Why did you not seek your brother's protection after your husband's death? Life at Larnay would surely have been less arduous for a young widow and her child.'

Agnès's face froze, and her pursed lips spoke louder than any words. He quickly changed the subject. Now he knew the answer to the question he had been asking himself all evening.

'The snail pâté is divine.'

He sensed the effort she needed to make in order to return to polite conversation and he was overcome by a strange tenderness.

'Is it not? The little animals are very partial to the baby lettuce we grow here. It gives them a sweet flavour, which we bring out with sautéed onion. And what they don't eat we use in soups or salads.'

Next, Mabile served roast rack of wild boar in a glistening sauce made of verjuice, wine, ginger, cinnamon and clove, served with broad bean purée and stewed apple. As soon as the servant had returned to the kitchen Artus declared:

'That girl is peculiar.'

She is afraid I might find out the meaning of the message Vigil was carrying, that is why she is peculiar, thought Agnès. She fixed the Comte's dark eyes with her grey-blue gaze and said:

'A gift from my half-brother Eudes.'

It was clear to him from her voice that it was one she would have gladly refused and that she mistrusted the girl.

The dinner continued. Agnès put the conversation back on a pleasant light-hearted footing. Their amusing exchanges were once again punctuated by repartee, learned observations and poetic quotations. Not that the Comte's earlier seriousness had annoyed the lady; on the contrary it had allowed her to let him glimpse the aversion she felt for her half-brother. She had said nothing to compromise herself, and if the Comte were on friendly terms with Eudes, she could always maintain that he had misinterpreted her mood. The cause would once again be attributed to the fickle nature of women's disposition.

Having achieved her aim of gratifying him with her company and her conversation, Agnès now studied him properly for the first time. He towered above her by a head and a half, though she was tall for a woman. He had dark hair and dark eyes – rare in a region where men tended to have light-chestnut or blond hair and blue eyes. He wore his hair shoulder-length, as was the fashion among the powerful. It was wavy and flecked with grey. He had a good, straight nose, and a chin that revealed authority, and intolerance, too. He moved with rare elegance for a man with such a muscular build. His brow was deeply furrowed, weathered from years of riding. A fine specimen indeed.

'You are examining me, Madame,' a deep voice said, not without a hint of satisfaction.

Agnès's cheeks flushed and she dissembled:

'You have a hearty appetite. It is a pleasure to receive you in my home.'

'Believe me, the pleasure is all mine.'

She detected an amused sparkle in his eye.

All at once, the Comte's smile faded, and he instinctively raised his hand to tell her to be quiet. He strained his ear in the direction of the postern door.

Agnès swallowed hard. Clément.

Artus d'Authon rose to his feet and crept cat-like over to the door. What should she do? Feign a sudden attack of coughing? Warn the child by crying out: 'What is it, Monsieur!' in a loud voice? No. The Comte would see through the ruse and the evening had been going too well to risk ruining everything now.

He pulled hard on the door, and Clément toppled into the room like a sack of potatoes. He hauled him up sharply by the ear.

'What are you doing here? Were you spying on us?'

'No, Monsieur. No, no ...'

Clément shot Agnès an alarmed look. Artus would be within his rights to flog the hide off him if he saw fit. He was trapped. The Dame de Souarcy thought quickly.

'Come over here, Clément, my dear.'

'Is he one of your servants?'

'The very best. He is my protector. He was keeping a watch on you to make sure his lady was in no danger.'

'He is a little on the small side to offer much protection.'

'Indeed, but he is brave.'

'And what would you have done, my boy, had my wicked intention been to pounce on your lady?'

Clément pulled out the carving knife he carried on him at all times, and declared in a solemn voice:

'Why, I would have killed you, Monsieur.'

The Comte burst out laughing and, amidst gasps of merriment, declared:

'Do you know, young man, I believe you capable of it! Now off to bed with you; nothing untoward will happen to your mistress, upon my honour.'

Clément stared at Agnès, who nodded in agreement. He vanished as if by magic.

'You stir passionate loyalties, Madame.'

'He is still a child.'

'A child who would have stabbed me to death if necessary, I am sure of it.'

A bewildering thought flashed through his mind. This woman was worth risking life and limb to protect.

Just then Mabile entered the room, her eyes bright with curiosity.

'A thousand pardons. I thought you might be in need of assistance, Madame.'

'No. We are waiting for the third course,' Agnès replied curtly. The girl bowed her head, slowly enough for the Dame de Souarcy to be able to glimpse the spite in her eyes.

The dessert of fruit and nut rissoles soon appeared. Mabile's face wore a more friendly expression. Even so, Agnès would have to put a stop to this girl and the façade they had been keeping up for months, and the thought worried her. Up until then, she had been able to manipulate Eudes by pretending she admired and trusted him. The incident with the pigeon had undermined this strategy, which, however dishonest, had succeeded over the years. The secret battle between her and her half-brother was about to burst out into the open and she was unprepared. She would be defeated. She had acted rashly and foolishly by demanding the carrier pigeon be returned to her. Restraining herself would have enabled her to keep up the pretence of not knowing Eudes's true intentions a little longer. Comte Artus's miraculous arrival and the obvious pleasure he had derived from their evening together only increased her anger with herself. With a little more time she might have gained in him an important ally. Her reckless anger towards the girl had spoiled everything. Agnès silenced her anxieties.

The last course was a thick cherry cream with wine, served on crêpes.

'You have treated me to a veritable banquet, Madame.'

'A modest one for a nobleman of your standing.'

He was surprised by this formal courtesy coming from her lips, but understood when he looked up and saw the servant now waiting on them. It was no longer the sullen, miserable-looking woman from before but a rather ungainly, stocky young girl.

'Adeline, you will prepare the master bedroom in the South Wing for Seigneur d'Authon.'

The young girl mumbled her consent and curtseyed clumsily before scurrying from the room.

'She is not very bright, but she is trustworthy,' Agnès explained.

'Unlike Mabile, do you mean?'

Agnès responded with a vague smile.

'I regret having put you to so much trouble. I fear I have outstayed my welcome. I shall leave at dawn. Pray, grant me the favour of not troubling yourself to attend my departure. One of your farm hands can saddle my horse.'

'And I am obliged to you for the rare and all too brief entertainment your visit has brought me. The evenings here at Souarcy are long, and your presence has lifted the customary dullness that descends upon them.'

He stared at her, hoping that her glib speech was more than just a mark of exquisite politeness.

*

Less than an hour later, he was settled in what had been Hugues de Souarcy's chamber, which Adeline had gone to great pains to prepare – even starting a fire in the grate although the evening was mild. He walked over to the metal sconces in order to blow out the candles. Their sheer number attested to their having been lit in his honour. No small luxury for such a modest household, for even if her hives produced wax, Agnès probably sold it instead of using it. After removing his surcoat, he stretched out on the bed without taking the trouble to undress or even to take off his shoes, and lay with his eyes open, staring into the darkness.

Artus acknowledged his confusion. What had started as mere curiosity on his part had turned into something quite unexpected. He had even forgotten about the gruesome murders.

Clearly the lady pleased him greatly, and this type of attraction had become rare enough in his life for it to unsettle and surprise him. Was his life really so empty that the Dame de Souarcy could fill it this easily? His life, it was true, had become a wilderness. In reality, it had always been one – a wilderness full of obligations and interests, which helped him to forget the painfully slow passing of time. And now eight hours had just gone by in a flash. Over the course of a single evening, time had regained its urgency. This lady had cured Artus's boredom and, what was more, his expectation of boredom. Her victory had been a swift one and yet she suspected nothing.

He was mistaken. Agnès was fully aware of the gains she had made during the course of their dinner. And, although she felt triumphant, she was clear-sighted enough to realise that she had won only a simple battle and that the real war was yet to come.

After leaving instructions for the Comte to be woken, she went back up to her chamber, pretending not to notice Mabile's absence from the kitchens. Perhaps the evil creature had run to seek refuge with her former master? Nonsense! Not in the night and on foot.

The glow of an oil lamp made her pause at the top of the stone steps.

A voice whispered:

'Madame ...'

'Are you not asleep yet, Clément?'

'I was waiting for you.'

He went ahead of her into her room, which was sparsely lit by a few tallow lamps. The resin torches, which blackened the walls, were reserved for the long bare stone passageways or for the cavernous halls.

'Has something bad happened?' Agnès asked, after pushing the heavy door closed.

'You could say that. Somebody removed the pigeon and the message from your chamber this evening.'

'But you took it up to your attic with you,' objected the lady.

'Only while I copied out the message. Afterwards I rolled the strip of paper carefully round the bird's leg and replaced him in your quarters, on the dressing table.'

'You knew she would take it, didn't you? So that is where she went between courses.'

'I could have sworn it,' the boy retorted. 'Madame, we are not ready to confront the Baron head on. Mabile cannot be certain you saw the message or, even worse, that you suspect it comes from her. It suits her purposes not to know, to turn a blind eye. Otherwise she would be obliged to tell her master that their plan has failed, and he would not thank her for it. We need to gain more time in order to prepare for this fight, especially now after the Comte's unexpected visit.'

173

Agnès closed her eyes in relief, and bent down to embrace the child.

'What would I do if it weren't for you?'

'Were it not for you I would be dead, Madame; were it not for you I would die.'

'Then let us both do our utmost to stay alive, dear Clément.' She planted a kiss on the boy's forehead and watched him leave the room noiselessly, her eyes moist with tears.

She stood still for a few moments, struggling against the memory of years of sadness and privation, of loneliness and fear. She fought off, inch by inch, the stubborn desire to surrender, to abandon herself.

A sudden voice, a voice she knew as if it were her own, floated into her consciousness. A sweet, gentle, but firm voice whose words she had treasured, the voice of her good angel, the Baroness Clémence de Larnay. How could she have almost forgotten her own mother when Madame Clémence's every gesture, smile, frown or caress was imprinted on her body and soul? God only knew how much she had loved that woman, so much that there were times when she thought of her as her only mother because they had chosen each other. God only knew how bereft she had felt when the woman died.

Her eyes brimmed with burning tears and she heard herself murmur:

'Madame, I miss you so very much.'

Agnès let herself be engulfed by all the years of lessons, laughter, secrets and affection they had shared. Madame Clémence had insisted the little girl choose a constellation for them. Agnès had taken a long time deciding between Virgo, Orion, the Plough and countless others, plumping finally for Cygnus, which shone so bright in early September. It was Madame Clémence who had read and re-read the ballads of Madame Marie de France to her. How they had both relished the poem *Lanval*, about a brave knight to whom a fairy promised her love on condition that he kept it secret. The Baroness had taught her how to play chess, roguishly warning her: 'I confess to cheating. However, for love of you I shall try to play fairly for the first few games.'

Had Madame Clémence been happy? Perhaps, during the first few years of her marriage, though Agnès could not know for sure. In fact, it was their mutual loneliness that had first brought them together. The loneliness of a beautiful lady declining in years, whose husband and son appeared to treat her like a piece of furniture, addressing her with frosty politeness, and of a little girl terrified by the thought of being abandoned after her mother's death, tormented by Eudes, who had dinned it into her that she would do well to obey him if she did not want to find herself out on the street. Deep down, Agnès realised that she had always been afraid, except when Madame Clémence's presence had given her the courage to keep going, to face her fears.

She recalled a long-forgotten scene. What had happened exactly? No doubt Baron Robert had returned to Larnay after one of his amorous encounters, the worse for drink and reeking of the female sex. He had charged into his wife's chamber without taking the trouble to knock, intent on gratifying one last urge. Agnès was sitting at Madame Clémence's feet being read a story. At her husband's rude drunken entrance the Baroness stood up. He muttered a few words that caused Madame Clémence's face to turn pale, but which the little girl did not understand.

Agnès could still hear the cold, sharp voice ringing in her ears: 'Leave here this instant, Monsieur!'

The Baron had staggered over to his wife, his hand raised as though to slap her. Instead of backing away or crying out she had moved towards him and, seizing him by his coat collar, had growled:

'You do not scare me, Monsieur! Do not forget who I am or where I come from! Who do you think you are, you pig? Go and mount your whores if it pleases you and leave us in peace. I do not wish to see your face until you are sober and penitent. I command you to leave here at once, you uncouth drunkard!'

Agnès remembered seeing the Baron visibly recoil, his shoulders hunched, his drunken red face turning a greyish-green. He had opened his mouth, but no sound had come. The Baroness stared at him, unflinching, standing her ground.

He had done as she asked, or more precisely, as she commanded, muttering feebly for a man of his pride: 'You've gone too far!'

As soon as the door to her quarters had closed, Madame Clémence had been seized by a fit of trembling. She had explained to the alarmed and confused Agnès in a voice that was once more gentle:

'The only way to bring a dog to heel is to growl more fiercely than he, to raise your ears and tail and bare your teeth.'

'And then he won't go for your throat?'

Madame Clémence had smiled and stroked Agnès's hair. 'In most cases he will back down, though sometimes he will attack, and when that happens you must fight.'

'Even if you are afraid he might bite you?'

'Fear will not save you from being bitten, my dear. On the contrary.'

To fight.

Up until then, Agnès had always tried to avoid conflict by outwitting her enemy, by using her guile. For years the strategy had seemed to work. Though not entirely, for she now found herself in an even more dangerous position than the one she had been in before her marriage or just after Hugues's death.

Guile? That was what she had always told herself. But why not admit it: she had no guile; she was simply afraid. She had comforted herself with the thought that as a woman it was more appropriate, more becoming, to take a defensive position. But vultures such as Eudes made no exceptions for women. On the contrary, women inflamed their thirst for blood because they counted on a woman's weakness and fear to provide them with a swift and painless victory.

To fight. There would be no more evasion, no more pretence.

It was her turn to attack and she would show no more mercy than her enemy.

The iron mine, Eudes's mine, which rumour had it was almost exhausted. Her half-brother and his ancestors before him had built the Larnay fortune on it and, more importantly, had received the self-interested benevolence of the monarchs they served. What if King Philip were to learn that the deposit was nearly depleted? Unquestionably the small favours its owner enjoyed would soon dry up, too. Eudes would be alone and defenceless. Artus d'Authon would once more be his all-powerful liege lord, and Artus liked Agnès, she knew. It is easy to observe when emotion takes a sincere man by surprise. No more guile, she had said. But there was nothing wrong with her using her feminine wiles. They were a weapon, one of the few that a woman was still permitted to wield.

To growl more fiercely, to raise her ears and tail, and bare her teeth. And above all to be ready to leap at her enemy's throat. To prevail.

How would she reach the King? The answer was simple: anonymously. The only intermediary the Dame de Souarcy could think of was Monsieur de Nogaret, of whom it was said he watched over the interests of the kingdom as if his own life depended on it.

She felt a sudden release and let her body slowly slide to the floor. She let out a long and peaceful sigh:

'Thank you, my angel, thank you, Clémence.'

It was not yet daybreak when Artus climbed back into the saddle the following morning. There was no reason for him to leave so early other than an irrational fear of meeting again, so soon, the woman who had robbed him of his sleep. For he had lain awake the whole of that short night, smiling one minute as he recalled her almost girlish hilarity, troubled the next by his strange infatuation.

A regular popinjay! He chuckled at the image of himself, a man over forty years of age behaving like a foolish lovesick youth! What a miracle! What a delightful miracle!

He sat up straight, trying his best to put on a sombre face in keeping with his reputation.

A few moments later he was riding across country, intoxicated by the powerful supple speed of Ogier, who was refreshed after his night's rest. A sudden anxious thought sobered him: what if he were making a mistake? What if she were a mere illusion and not the ideal woman he had, until then, never allowed himself to believe in?

He slowed his horse to a walk, troubled by the notion.

A hundred yards on he was smiling again as he recalled her account of her first honey harvest that had ended in a farcical failure.

The riotous flurry of emotions startled him. Zounds! Could he be falling in love? So soon? The attraction was clear, at least as far as he was concerned. However, attraction of the senses was, in everyone's opinion, commonplace and arbitrary enough for it not to cause him any great concern. But love and love's pains … In all honesty he could not say he had ever experienced them.

A sudden fit of laughter threw him onto the pommel of his saddle and against Ogier's neck. The horse gave a friendly shake of its mane.

Rue de Bucy, Paris, July 1304

In the implacable calm of that early evening, the echo of feet on a stone floor. Francesco de Leone strained his ears to hear where the sound was coming from, only to realise all of a sudden that the footsteps were his.

He was walking along the ambulatory of the church. His sleeveless black coat flapped around his calves, occasionally brushing the rood screen shielding the chancel. A large white crucifix with eight branches fused together in pairs was sewn onto the garment, above his heart.

How long had he been advancing in this way? For a while no doubt, as his eyes were accustomed to the semi-darkness. He tried by the weak light filtering through the dome to study the shadows that mocked him. They seemed to be flowing between the pillars, lapping at the base of the walls, slipping between the balustrades. What church was this? What did it matter? It was not very big and yet he had been turning in it for so many hours he knew every last one of the massive stones whose ochre hue appeared tinged with pink in the gloom.

He tried to catch up with the silently moving figure, betrayed only by the faint rustle of fabric, of heavy silk. It was the figure of a woman, a woman hiding. A proud figure, almost as tall as he. Suddenly he noticed the woman's long hair. So long it reached below her knees, merging in a wave with her silk dress.

A stabbing pain made him breathe in sharply. And yet the cold that reigned within those walls was biting. His breath condensed in the air, moistening his lips.

He was chasing the woman. She was not fleeing, only keeping

the distance between them. She circled as he circled, always a few steps ahead of him as though anticipating his movements, staying on the outside of the ambulatory while he moved along on the inside.

He paused. A single step and then she stopped. He heard the sound of calm slow breathing, but he might have imagined it. As he moved off again so did his shadow.

Francesco de Leone's hand reached slowly for the pommel of his sword, even as an overwhelming love made his eyes fill with tears. He looked in disbelief at his hand clutching the metal pommel. Had he aged? Great bulging veins protruded under the pale skin, which was covered in a mesh of fine wrinkles.

Why was he chasing this woman? Who was she? Was she real? Did he wish to kill her?

Francesco de Leone woke up with a start, his face bathed in sweat. His heart was beating so fast it almost hurt and he was breathless. He lifted his arm and turned his hand. It was long and broad without being heavy. A layer of silky, pale flesh covered the subtle bluish maze of veins.

He sat on the edge of the canopied bed in the chamber Capella had allocated to him, struggling against the debilitating dizziness.

The dream, the nightmare, was becoming clearer. Leone was nearing his goal. The dream was the future, he was certain of that now.

He had to get out of there, to take advantage of the dawn and wander through the city streets. That chamber, that house oppressed him. The lingering stagnant odour choked him.

Giotto Capella was worried sick. Over the years he had developed a genuine aversion to honesty. This was not in his case because of any particular liking for vice; it was more out of superstition. Honesty had come to be equated in his mind with weakness, and to be weak was to be humiliated.

What could this handsome Knight from an eminent family possibly know of humiliation? Capella resented him bitterly. Not because of his noble birth or because he chose to disregard the privileges of such a birth, not even because of his implacable judgement of the betrayal at Acre. What did he think? That Giotto was such a fool that he had not weighed up his crime when he made his transaction with the enemy? Three hundred gold pieces for so many men, women and children, for so many screams, for so much blood? He had accepted the deal and been cheated. No. Capella resented him for having brought right into his study the proof that no memory can ever be entirely laid to rest. For in the end the usurer had managed to accommodate his. It was true that from time to time they would seep into his brain, above all at night. And yet these infiltrations had gradually become less frequent. Giotto owed his easy conscience to a convenient theory he had invented for himself: after all, who could say that reinforcements would have arrived in time to save the citadel at Acre? What is more, someone else might have revealed the plans of the sewers if he hadn't. They would have died anyway in the end. And so the usurer had cleared his conscience by convincing himself that the massacre had been inevitable, and that he was one guilty party among a host of other potential ones. Now, thanks to the Hospitaller who had never known fear, the white walls at Acre never left his thoughts. Now, honesty was beating a pathway to his door accompanied by its ruinous counterpart: clarity. Now, here he was telling himself that but for his crime thirty thousand souls would still be alive.

In reality, as much as he hated Leone, his petty predator's

instinct told him that this was not a man upon whom he could wreak revenge. He must be killed outright, and Giotto was too much of a coward to do that.

Before the arrival of Monsieur de Nogaret's envoy that afternoon he had entertained the foolish hope that some miracle, some sleight of hand might remove this troublesome guest from his midst. Each time he heard the man leave, as he had that early morning, he prayed he would never return. Countless people met their deaths in that city every day so why not the Knight Hospitaller? Giotto Capella knew this was foolish wishful thinking. There was another, less remote possibility: if he were to do nothing, why, the Knight would never meet Guillaume de Nogaret and might end up leaving. He could once again apply his favourite dictum: 'Always put off until tomorrow what people ask you to do today.' It had brought him fortune and riches up until then, but he was mindful that it might let him down now.

Capella's world, which he had worked so hard to build, was being trampled under the Knight's feet. In the space of a few days he had lost his appetite for life; even the lure of easy profit no longer filled him with feverish excitement. Why not admit it, since Leone was forcing him to be honest: it was not remorse that was demoralising him so much as the fear of his faults being imminently made public. A fault confessed is half redressed. Poppycock! Only those you succeed in burying never come back to haunt you.

Dressed in his nightclothes and a flannel nightcap, Giotto Capella was worried sick, plunged into despair for the past few minutes by the thought that his fear of reprisal prevented him from striking back. This impossibility had taken away his appetite for his supper and he was livid. Monsieur de Nogaret's messenger had left discreetly a few hours earlier and Leone could not have seen him sneaking out of the service entrance to the building. Monsieur de Nogaret had requested Giotto's presence two days later. The matter could only relate to money. King Philip did not baulk at borrowing vast sums of money even if it meant later on having to expel the moneylenders in order to avoid repaying the debts of the realm. If that meant money could be made by practising a barely concealed usury on, among others, the King's barons, then all the better. Since the man had left, Capella had been dragging his feet. What if he went to the meeting alone and warned his Seigneur de Nogaret of the Knight's extraordinary request? After all, what did one more betrayal matter? And yet the memory of the Knight's silences dissuaded him. Silences reveal a great deal more than words. And those of this man declared that he belonged to that race of wolves whom God's love has convinced to watch over His flock. A wolf possessed of a terrifying purity.

A nervous servant girl entered, stammering unintelligibly:

'I ... I ... he wouldn't listen, master, it's not my fault ...'

Francesco de Leone appeared behind the girl, and dismissed her with a gesture. He studied Giotto Capella's apparel. A man in a nightshirt and nightcap will give less resistance than the same man fully dressed. No. The Knight expected no opposition from the Lombard usurer. His threats had already turned Capella's face even more sallow. Would he carry them out if it proved necessary? He might. Only those capable of pity were deserving of it and this man had not hesitated to profit from the massacre of men, women and children.

'When do you plan to arrange my meeting with Nogaret, Lombard?' he asked, without troubling to greet his recalcitrant host.

The coincidence was too great and Capella understood that

the Knight had seen the messenger sent by the King's Counsellor.

'I was waiting for the right moment.'

'And?'

'It has arrived.'

'When did you mean to inform me?'

'Tomorrow morning.'

'Why the delay?'

The Knight's calm voice alarmed Giotto, who protested in a rasping whine:

'What were you expecting?'

'From you? The worst.'

'Foul lies!'

'Take heed, usurer. I have killed many men who caused me no harm. You, I shall turn over. The King's executioners have an enthusiasm for torture that inspires … respect.'

The apparent irony of this last remark worried the usurer, who made a show of his sincerity, explaining:

'We shall undoubtedly be received by Guillaume de Plaisians. Do you know him?'

'Only by reputation and not very well. He was Nogaret's student at Montpellier, I believe, and then a judge at the royal court in that city before becoming seneschal at Beaucaire.'

'Make no mistake, he is Seigneur de Nogaret's *éminence grise*. He began working with him last year as a jurist under direct orders to the King. In this case the expression "right-hand man" would be inexact for no one knows whether Nogaret or Plaisians is the brains behind any reform. The two men are equally brilliant, but Nogaret is no speaker, while the other will harangue a crowd until it no longer knows whether it is coming or going, and then make it perform a volte-face. I still remember his extraordinary and fearsome diatribe against Boniface VIII. Their physical appearance is as dissimilar as their talent for oratory. Guillaume de Plaisians is a handsome fellow. In brief, he is no less of a man to be reckoned with than my Seigneur de Nogaret.'

A doubt flashed through Francesco de Leone's mind. Why had the prior Arnaud de Viancourt not mentioned Nogaret's *éminence grise* as Capella referred to him?

The pitch-black stallion pawed the ground while its rider, a shadowy figure wrapped in a brown woollen cloak, scanned the gloomy forest in search of his prey. A shiny metal claw on the end of his right hand gripped the reins. The ghostly figure sat up in his saddle and gave a grunt of disgust. This time, the fools had chosen a slip of a girl as a messenger. Did they really think she stood more of a chance than the men they had sacrificed up until then? The fools. And yet, having tracked her for more than half an hour, the ghostly slayer's contempt was gradually giving way to impatience, even to a sense of unease. The young girl moved swiftly and noiselessly. How could she not be exhausted? Where was she hiding, in which piece of undergrowth? Why had she not given in to her panic like the others before her? For they had not all been poisoned to the point of delirium. Why did she not make a run for it in a pathetic attempt to flee?

The figure tensed his calf muscles against the horse's flanks. The animal shifted restlessly, sensing the doubt creeping into the mind of its master.

What had brought this girl to Arville? Was her mission related to the Templar commandery? Hitherto all papal messages had passed through Clairets Abbey. The ghostly figure began to grow angry. He hated straying from his habitual hunting ground. He tried to calm himself by imagining what effect killing his first female would have on him. Would her face register the same expression of terror when she saw the metal claw? Would a woman's flesh tear more easily than a man's? Let it be done. Night was falling and the journey back was a long one.

The robed phantom scoured the brambles, shrubs and thickets. All the scheming, lies and murders he had been forced to tolerate and then to accept. For he did not revel in them, that was not his vice. Killing brought him neither pleasure nor displeasure. At best it was a hazard of the job, and at worst an unavoidable part of his mission, and if there was no other way …

The years of bitter disappointment, humiliation and needless hardship had placed his life on its present course. The exhilarating feeling of no longer being an insignificant person among others had achieved the rest. For the first time his existence had meaning, was becoming pivotal, and little did it matter in the end what cause he served. For the first time, he was no longer the victim of power but the one wielding it.

Lying flat on the forest floor some twenty yards from the horse's hooves, concealed under a mass of ferns, Esquive watched her pursuer, who had begun tracking her before she was able to deliver the message she was carrying. She had known of the dangers involved when she accepted the mission. Why had they chosen novices as messengers before sending her? The idea of taking a life was so alien to them that they preferred to sacrifice their own. Not she, who was a redoubtable swordswoman thanks to her father. The archangel Hospitaller would also have known how to fight the phantom and his pitch-black stallion, but he was still so far away. What did he remember of their meeting years before? Very little no doubt – at least with regard to her.

Esquive concentrated all her attention on the horse once more as it nervously sidestepped a few paces then came to a standstill. The evil phantom was growing anxious and communicating his alarm to the horse.

In spite of her faith, the strength of mind she had inherited from her father, and her immeasurable love for the archangel of Cyprus, Esquive had been seized with dread when she first caught sight of the enormous black stallion rising out of the evening mist. The animal had hurled itself at her and the spectre had raised his hideous gloved hand.

She had fled, her suppleness and speed giving her a head start. She had dug herself down into the earth and remained there motionless, like a root, in order to catch her breath and recover her presence of mind.

She could not allow herself to die now. She was less important than the information she was carrying. What then? Then God would decide. Death mattered little to her for she would be taking her archangel of flesh and blood with her.

At first the phantom saw only two pale amber pools, two almost yellow pools. Two immense eyes. Then a mane of long dark wavy hair. Finally a tiny heart-shaped mouth and skin as pale as moonlight. The command rang out even as a slender hand drew a short sword from a belted scabbard.

'Dismount. Dismount and fight.'

This unexpected reversal of fortune gave the phantom cause to hesitate. The young girl continued in a startlingly deep voice:

'Do you want my life? Come and take it. It will cost you dearly.'

What was happening? Nothing had gone according to plan. What came next was so unexpected it caught the phantom off guard. The girl hurled herself at the horse, brandishing her sword, and thrust the sharp blade into the powerful chest of the animal, which whinnied in pain and surprise and threw its rider, rigid with shock.

A fierce joy made Esquive's strange eyes shine even brighter. She smiled, stepped back a few paces, and stood with her legs apart, ready to fight.

The phantom heaved himself up. Fear. The fear he had believed he could make vanish forever pervaded him again. That dreadful fear of death, of suffering, of being nothing again. He removed his glove, which felt ridiculous now, and tentatively drew his dagger. He knew how to fight, of course, but the girl's posture informed him he was dealing with an expert swordswoman.

He cast a desperate glance around him, choked by the self-loathing which up until a few minutes before he had believed himself rid of. He was a miserable coward, a weakling who had become drunk on the power of others, mistaking it for his own.

He hated the girl. She was responsible for resuscitating his past. She would pay for it; she would pay for his self-loathing. One day, he would take pleasure in killing her, in hearing her scream, then whimper, then die. One day. Soon.

Esquive sensed her enemy was about to flee. She hesitated a fraction of a second too long between her anger, her desire to slay the one who had killed so many of their own, and the over-arching importance of her mission. Did the phantom notice?

He bolted towards the big black stallion that had come to a halt a few dozen yards away, not quickly enough though to avoid the broad blade thudding into his right shoulder. The pain made him cry out, but fear and loathing drove him on. He heaved himself into the saddle with his left hand, and horse and rider vanished into the dark night of the forest.

The first days of July had brought with them a sweltering heat even more terrible than the one people had endured in June. The air seemed so rarefied that breathing it in required an effort. No breeze stirred to offer even a moment's reprieve.

Cardinal Benedetti had been overcome by the merciless heat. He had dozed off at his desk, his forehead resting on his left hand, his nose on the beautiful mother-of-pearl fan.

The figure paused and strained his ears. He was carrying a small basket, the arch of which was decorated with a white ribbon. The anteroom was empty, it being lunchtime, and the Archbishop's breathing was calm and regular. The figure glanced at the half-empty goblet of macerated sage and thyme, which it was the Cardinal's custom to drink every afternoon as a remedy against bloating and wind. The taste was unpleasant enough to mask the bitterness of the dose of powdered opium administered in order to induce extreme drowsiness.

Without a sound, without even stirring the air, the figure walked behind the desk inlaid with ivory, mother-of-pearl and turquoise. A gloved hand lifted a tapestry, which depicted a shy diaphanous Virgin surrounded by hovering angels, and concealed a low passageway between two thick walls. At the far end was the Pope's council chamber.

The figure stooped and crossed the ten yards separating him from the conclusion of his mission.

The vast chamber was empty, as predicted. Benoît XI had not yet returned from his midday meal. He was not known for his vices, with the exception of his fondness for food, especially anything that reminded him of the pleasant years he had spent as Bishop of Ostia.

The figure moved forward, crossing the luxurious carpet with its purple and gold motif that covered almost the entire expanse of marble floor. The consular table evoked the Last Supper and was dominated by the heavily ornate papal chair perched on a white dais in the centre. As he set down the basket directly opposite it on the table he grimaced from the pain he still felt in his shoulder. Figs. Splendid, perfectly ripe figs. Nicolas Boccasini had been very partial to them before he became Benoît.

The afternoon meeting began late as a result of Benedetti needing to be roused. His face had a sickly pallor and his head was swimming. As for his garbled speech, it shocked the others coming from the lips of a man renowned for his oratory skills. Nevertheless, the Pope listened attentively to his Cardinal's counsel. Honorius was undoubtedly the only friend who had remained true since his election. He was all the more grateful because the prelate had made no secret of his admiration for Boniface VIII. Benoît was ready to admit that he possessed neither the authority nor the Olympian nature of his predecessor, nor did this man whose eyes filled with tears at the evocation of Christ's torment or Mary's flight share the same imperial vision for the Church. And so the Cardinal's unfailing support, at first invaluable to him, he now cherished.

The Pope was uneasy. Guillaume de Nogaret's excommunication would greatly displease the King of France. And yet he had to show his authority. A failure to administer punishment would betray his fear of the ruthless monarch, and might further undermine their political influence. Honorius Benedetti had persuaded him that a direct attack on Philip the Fair could prove suicidal. Nogaret, on the other hand, made a good scapegoat.

Benoît listened to each of his counsellors in turn as he ate his figs. His discomfort was such that they seemed unusually bitter and he did not derive his customary pleasure from them.

They left Rue de Bucy shortly after none.

The Knight Hospitaller Francesco de Leone, his head bowed, followed two steps behind Giotto Capella as a mark of subordination.

The construction work on the Île de la Cité palace requested by Saint Louis having not yet commenced, all the state powers were housed under the roof of the forbidding Louvre citadel, located just outside the city walls near the Saint-Honoré gate. They crowded as best they could into what remained the simple keep built by Philip II Augustus to centralise the Ministry of Justice, the Courts and the Exchequer.

They proceeded down Rue Saint-Jacques, which took them as far as the Petit Pont, and from there crossed Île de la Cité until they reached the Grand Pont, still known as the Pont au Change, which opened onto Rue Saint-Denis. Then they turned left, crossing to the Right Bank and backtracking in order to arrive at the Great Louvre Tower. A motley crowd of merchants, fishermen from the Seine, passers-by, beggars, women of easy virtue and street urchins jostled, called out and hurled abuse at one another in the maze of narrow streets filled with the stench of refuse. Metal-beaters[25] and millers blocked the alleyways with their handcarts, arguing over who had arrived first and therefore had right of way.

Giotto complained – more out of habit than because he hoped to engage his silent companion in conversation:

'Look at these encumbrances! It is growing steadily worse! Will they ever get around to widening these bridges? The Louvre is but a few hundred yards from Rue de Bucy as the crow flies, and yet we have walked thrice that distance.'

The Knight was content to retort in a good-natured voice:

'Are there not boatmen who ferry passengers and goods between the Louvre and the Tour de Nesle?'

Capella glanced at him with a hangdog expression before admitting:

'Yes ... but they take your money.'

'Is avarice to be counted among your vices, then? And there was I thinking that the frugal meals you have been sending up to me were a sign of your consideration for my health.'

Capella was not about to pay for two crossings on top of everything else! The pain of his gout was throbbing in his foot and in his calf up to the knee, but it couldn't be helped, they would have to walk slowly.

The usher's pompous expression betrayed the satisfaction he derived from his lowly position. They waited in Monsieur de Nogaret's anteroom for a good half-hour in stony silence.

Finally they were shown in. Leone found himself face to face with their gravest enemy, for this could not be the same Guillaume de Plaisians whom Giotto had described as a handsome fellow. The man of at least thirty years of age who was seated behind the long cluttered table that served as a desk was small, almost puny-looking. He wore a fine indigo felt bonnet that covered his head and ears, sharpening an already emaciated face, out of which stared two intense eyes rendered almost repulsive by their lack of eyelashes. Despite the vogue of the period for extravagant and ostentatious dress, and the fashion for shorter men's clothes, Nogaret had adhered to the long austere jurist's robe. Over it he wore a sleeveless coat open down the front, whose only embellishment was a fur trim.[26] A fire blazed in the hearth and Leone wondered whether Nogaret might not be doing them the kindness of suffering from some serious ailment.

'Pray, have a seat, Giotto, my good friend,' Guillaume de Nogaret bade him.

Francesco remained standing, as befitted a moneylender's clerk. Finally, the jurist appeared to notice him and, without so much as a glance in his direction, enquired:

'Who is your companion?'

'My nephew, the son of my dearly departed brother.'

'I did not know you had a brother.'

'Who does not, my Lord? Francesco. Francesco Capella. We have every reason to be proud of our nephew ...'

Nogaret, who found polite conversation tedious and who was not renowned for his drawing-room manners, listened with a forced smile. The thirty thousand pounds he was hoping to borrow from the usurer were worth a small amount of indulgence.

'... for three years he was chamberlain to our dearly departed Holy Father, Boniface ...'

A spark of interest lit up the strange staring eyes.

'... and then a scandal involving a woman – a brawl. In brief, a fall from grace.'

'When was this?'

'Not long before the death of our beloved Pope – God rest his soul.'

Nogaret nodded, adding in a bitter voice:

'If indeed His judgement will wash away so many sins.'

Nogaret was a man of faith, a rigorous faith that had made him loathe Boniface, whom he considered unworthy of the greatness of the Church. Unlike his predecessor Pierre Flote, who was intent on ridding the monarchy once and for all of the continual interference of the Pope's authority, Nogaret's aim was to allow the King to provide the Church with a faultless representative of God on earth. Leone knew of his role in the great religious disputes that had shaken France. Nogaret had subsequently abandoned the corridors of power and come out into the light of day. Most notably, the year before he had made a virulent speech denouncing Boniface VIII's 'crimes'. In other words, he was paving the way for the King's future pope, no doubt with Plaisians's assistance.

The names of one or two cardinals who had already been approached, that was what the prior and the Grand-Master needed in order to be able to intervene.

Nogaret's animosity towards Boniface had not diminished with the latter's death. The insult the supreme head of the Church had publicly hurled at him, referring to him explicitly as the 'son of a Cathar', still rankled. On learning of the Pope's death the Counsellor had simply murmured:

'Let him meet his Judge.'

Nogaret had not finished with the man whom he considered at best an appalling disgrace and at worst an emissary of the devil, hellbent on destroying the Church.

For the first time he studied the silent young man whose unassuming manner pleased him.

'Be seated … Francesco, is it?'

'It is, my Lord.'

'It was a great honour and a privilege to serve the Pope. And yet you threw it away – and for the sake of a girl, moreover.'

'A young lady – that is, almost.'

'How gallant! Very well, a young lady, then. And what do you recall most about the time you spent in that prestigious service?'

He had hooked the big fish. The prior had been right. Despite his intelligence, Nogaret was a zealot. He was zealous about the State, his king and the law. Zeal drives men but it also blinds them.

'Many things, my Lord,' Leone sighed.

'And yet this abundance hardly gives you reason to rejoice.' 'It is only that His Extreme Holiness was ... Well. The love of our Lord should impose itself without ...'

A smile played across Nogaret's thin lips. He had taken the bait. How much did this usurer's nephew really know? Even if it were only sordid malicious gossip, he would feel gratified and confirmed in his loathing of Boniface. All the more so as chamberlains poked their noses everywhere, trading secrets of the chamber pot and the garderobe where some left evidence of the affairs of state: the evil-smelling colic of a great man could herald an impending succession. Turning once again to Giotto, he asked:

'And so your nephew will take up the torch of your profession?'

'Oh no, my Lord, regrettably he has no interest in business, and I doubt he has any head for it. Indeed, I am on the lookout among my prestigious connections for someone who would be willing to take him on. He is extremely intelligent, fluent in five languages, not counting Latin, and the unfortunate matter of the lady has chastened him enormously – why, anyone would think him a friar. He is highly trustworthy and knows that in our profession silence is golden.'

'Interesting ... As a kindly gesture towards you, my friend Giotto, I might be prepared to try him out.'

'What an honour. What a great honour. How thoughtful, how generous ... I would never have expected ...'

'It is because I value our agreeable and rewarding association, Giotto.'

Leone feigned boundless gratitude, going down on one knee, his head bowed, his hand on his heart.

'Very well ... I shall expect you tomorrow at prime[+] and we shall pray together. I know no better way of meeting than through prayer.'

At last Nogaret could broach the subject that most concerned him. A new loan, of thirty thousand pounds no less! Plaisians had calculated as precisely as he could. This was the amount they needed to fund the countless meetings with the French cardinals, and to pay the various intermediaries – not to mention the 'gifts' the majority of prelates would expect in return for renouncing their own greed for supreme power in favour of a single candidate: that of Philip. As for the King, he had no fixed preference. It mattered little to him who was elected as long as the man did not meddle in France's affairs. The monarch was willing to support and finance anyone who could guarantee this.

Neither Giotto nor Leone was taken in by the Counsellor's justification for the loan: to prepare a fresh crusade in order to reconquer the Holy Land. Philip had far too much on his hands with Flanders and the Languedoc to be able to deploy his troops elsewhere. However, it was only polite to applaud any new project of this sort and Giotto did not breach the rule.

'And what terms will you grant us, my Lord? For, while the sum is not vast, it is by no means insignificant.'

'The interest rate set by Saint Louis.' Giotto had expected as much.

'And repayment?'

'Two years.'

'Really? Only, it is a long time and I am not sure my lenders will ...'

'Eighteen months, that is my final offer.'

'Very good, my Lord, very good.'

Moments later they were walking out of the Great Louvre Tower. Giotto rubbed his hands together.

'So are you satisfied, Knight? You have your position.'

'Don't expect any gratitude from me, moneylender. As for my mood, it is no concern of yours. Incidentally, I shall be staying on at your house.'

Capella pursed his lips. He had imagined that he was finally rid of this presence, which he rarely encountered but which he could feel even in the cold air that crept over his skin. He pretended to be unworried and asked:

'And what did you think of this loan? The pretext of the crusade is very clever. It can be adapted to suit any circumstance. Thirty thousand pounds is a substantial sum but hardly enough to send an army of crusaders halfway across the world. Our friend Nogaret has other things in mind.'

'What could it possibly matter to you? You have been paid, have you not?'

'On the contrary, it matters a great deal to me. To read the minds of the powerful is to anticipate their needs and ward off their blows. We poor defenceless moneylenders are always expecting to receive the boot by way of thanks. Such is life.'

'I am choked with tears.'

The snub did not fluster the spiteful rat, who persisted:

'So what did you think?'

'I found it extremely interesting for reasons you perhaps have not yet fully grasped.'

'And what might they be?' demanded Capella.

'You have just betrayed Monsieur de Nogaret. You have set a trap for him, and if he comes to learn of it … you would do well to die fast.'

It was so glaringly obvious that it had not even occurred to Giotto. His usual cunning and shrewdness had failed to alert him to the fact that by escaping one danger he was exposing himself to another, even greater one.

Ten minutes after they had left, the usher showed a slim figure wrapped in a heavy cloak into Guillaume de Nogaret's office.

'Well?'

'We are nearing our objective, my Lord. Everything is in readiness in keeping with your wishes.'

'Good. Carry on with your work. You will be rewarded for your pains, as agreed. The strictest secrecy is essential.'

'Discretion is my profession and my passion.'

A sudden misgiving made Nogaret ask:

'What do you think of our affairs?'

'What I think depends on how much you pay me, my Lord. Consequently your affairs are of a most noble nature.'

Sext[+] had just finished when Comte Artus d'Authon dismounted in the interior courtyard of the Château de Larnay. He had instantly thought of Agnès, of her illegitimate childhood spent within those walls.

The ferment caused by his arrival might have amused him under different circumstances. However, he had spent the last few days since his encounter with the Dame de Souarcy in a state of tension, and his resulting moodiness was only made worse by the half-hour wait he had just been subjected to.

A matronly woman hurried towards him in a panic, fanning herself with her apron.

'My Lord, my Lord ...' she stammered, almost kneeling before him. 'My master is away, you see. Oh dear God!' she howled as if the end of the world had come.

Artus was aware that Eudes de Larnay's business took him to Paris at the end of every month. Indeed, it was what had compelled the Comte to travel the fifteen leagues between Authon and his vassal's chateau.

'Might his good lady wife be ailing?'

The woman understood the reproach and clumsily explained.

'Nay, nay, she enjoys good health, given she has nearly reached full term, that is, praise be to God. Since she learnt of your arrival she has been preparing to receive you properly. She was asleep and ... Oh, but I am a chattering old fool ... Pray follow me, my Lord. My lady will join you at once.'

Artus could picture the charming, feather-brained woman, whose customary silence concealed a lack of intelligence, fretting in her room, cursing her husband's absence and wondering what she should say, not say, avoid or offer in order not to earn Eudes's wrath upon his return.

At last Apolline de Larnay stepped into the room, preceded by a pungent smell of garlic. Her pregnancy had not been in evidence the last time Artus saw her and her appearance disconcerted him. She was not one of those women who radiate health when they are with child. Her usually delightful face was spoiled by a grey pallor and the rings under her eyes had a purplish hue. He offered her his hand so that she would not be obliged to curtsey, and greeted her with an untruth:

'Madame, you look radiant.'

'And you are too kind, Monsieur,' she rejoined, demonstrating that she was not taken in by his flattery. 'My husband is ...'

'... away, so I have been told. It is unfortunate.'

'Do you have some urgent business to discuss?'

'Urgent would be putting it too strongly. Let us say I wished to speak to him about a project I have devised.'

Something about her had changed. The pretty little vacuous creature he had once known seemed filled with sorrow.

'Eudes's ... My husband's affairs take up so much of his time that I have seen him only once in a month.'

'Mining is a complicated business.'

She lifted her gaze towards him and he sensed she was fighting back her tears. Yet she replied:

'Indeed, it is the reason he gives.' Then pulling herself together, she added, 'I am failing in all my duties. You must have found the heat oppressive on your journey. A bowl of cider will quench your thirst.'

'With pleasure.'

She gave the command while he took a seat on one of the

benches at the main table. She sat facing him, her body turned sideways to accommodate her rounded belly. An awkward silence followed, which he was the first to break:

'Did you know that I met your sister-in-law, the Dame de Souarcy, recently?'

At the mention of her name the little grey woman's face lit up.

'Agnès ... and how is she?'

'She seemed in fine health.'

'And Mathilde? It must be five years since I saw her last.'

'She has turned into a charming and very pretty young lady.'

'Just like her mother. Madame Agnès was always a great beauty and I regret that all those years ago she refused my husband's offer to come and live here at the chateau with her daughter. Life at Souarcy is so precarious and difficult for a widow with no experience of farming. We would have been sisters and I would have had company – and of the best kind, for she is so full of life, so lovely.'

'It would have been a perfect solution for all. So why did she refuse?'

Apolline de Larnay's eyes misted over. She was such a bad liar that he sensed all the sadness she was trying to conceal.

'I do not know why ... Perhaps out of an attachment to her estate.'

His suspicion was confirmed: Eudes de Larnay's reasons for offering protection to his half-sister bordered on the profane. Up until then, the feudal Baron's self-conceit and cowardice, his boorishness towards women had simply angered Artus, but now his exasperation was replaced with the revulsion that such perversions inspired in him.[27]

Sweet Apolline's gentle frivolity had been reduced to ashes –

grey like herself. This, too, was Eudes's doing. The realisation filled the Comte with an indefinable sorrow, and he felt angry at himself for having manoeuvred this young woman he had once considered rather foolish into revealing her half-secrets.

As he took his leave of her he experienced for the first time a feeling of tenderness towards her and counselled:

'Take good care of yourself, Madame. The child you bear is precious.'

She murmured a response:

'Do you think so, Monsieur?'

The journey back to Authon did nothing to dispel his unease. It was growing dark when he joined his Chief Bailiff, Monge de Brineux, who was waiting for him in the library.

The modest-sized room with the rotunda was one of Artus's favourite places. It contained a fine collection of books he had brought back from his restless wanderings across the world. He felt on his own ground there, surrounded by memories the details of which had paled over time. All the people he had encountered, all the names he had uttered, all the places he had passed through, and in the end so few attachments.

Monge was drinking fruit wine and gorging himself on quince and honey conserve. When Artus entered, he rose to his feet, declaring:

'Oh, Monsieur, you have saved me from my own gluttony.'

'Must you eat those confections by the handful?'

'Their sweetness calms me.'

'Tell me the bad news, then.'

The Comte's perceptiveness hardly surprised Monge de Brineux, but the grave expression he wore troubled him.

'Is something worrying you, my Lord?'

'The question would be more apt in the plural. I am completely in the dark. Come along, Brineux, out with it.'

'One of my sergeants rode over here in a great hurry at midday. Another disfigured corpse has been found close to the edge of Clairets Forest. This one appears to have been killed recently.'

'Another friar?'

'It would seem.'

'Near the forest's edge, you say?'

'Yes, my Lord. The killer has been very careless.'

'Or very cunning,' suggested Artus. 'In this way he could be sure his victim would be found relatively quickly. Was there a letter *A* near the body?'

'Yes, right beside the corpse's leg, scratched in the ground.'

'What else?'

'For the moment that is all I know. I have given the order to make a thorough search of the surrounding area,' the Bailiff explained.

Monge de Brineux hesitated to pick up their earlier conversation. His admiration and liking for the Comte did not make of him a close friend, or even a companion. In fact there were few who could boast such a degree of intimacy with Artus. His lord was remote in a way that, while not hostile, discouraged familiarity. However, Monge knew the man to be just and good. He continued:

'Did your meeting with the Dame de Souarcy bear out my description of her?'

'Indeed. I do not see her as a bloodthirsty criminal. She is learned, excellent company and undoubtedly a pious woman.'

'And do you not find the young widow very beautiful?'

No sooner had Monge uttered these words than he cursed his

indiscretion. The Comte would immediately see what he was hinting at. What followed proved him right. Artus glanced up at him and Monge detected a flicker of irony in those dark eyes.

'I do indeed. You wouldn't be playing at matchmaking, would you, Brineux?'

The Bailiff remained silent but beneath his stubble his face turned bright red.

'Come, Brineux, don't pull such a face! I am touched by your concern for me. Marriage agrees with you so well, my friend, that you hear the sound of wedding bells everywhere. Have no fear. Sooner or later I shall produce an heir, like my father before me.'

It was largely Julienne who was to blame for Monge's recent propensity to wish marriage on anyone whose happiness was dear to his heart. The Comte had been a widower for many years and had no direct heir, his wife had argued one evening. How sad it was to see a man of his distinction grow old alone, without the love of a woman, she had insisted. Monge had tempered his wife's redoubtable zeal for matchmaking with the observation:

'It all depends on the lady.'

'I did not mean …' Brineux stuttered rather ashamedly.

'Do you really think that Madame Agnès is one of those fine ladies one mounts in the antechamber? It is true that we have both enjoyed the favours of a few of those ourselves.'

'I think I had better take my leave of you now, my Lord, before I dig myself deeper and make even more of a fool of myself.'

'I am teasing you, my friend. On the contrary, I bid you stay. I need you to help me gain a clearer understanding. Nothing seems to make any sense in this affair.'

Monge sat down opposite Artus. The Bailiff could tell his lord was lost in thought from the way his eyes stared into space and from his tensed jaw and rigid posture. He waited. He was accustomed to these moments when Artus became immersed in deep reflection.

A few minutes elapsed in complete silence before the Comte emerged from the furthest reaches of his mind and said:

'It makes no sense whichever way you look at it.'

'What do you mean?'

'We agree on one point, Brineux, which is that Agnès de Souarcy played no part in these killings.'

'As she so ably made me see, I cannot imagine her running through the undergrowth armed with a claw, intent on slashing the faces of a few unfortunate friars – except perhaps in a fit of homicidal madness or temporary possession. Besides, these men – especially the last one – are twice the lady's weight.'

'If we include this last killing, four of the victims, it would seem, traced the letter *A* before they died, and a linen handkerchief belonging to the lady was found near one of them. Somebody is trying to implicate her, then.'

'I had reached the same conclusion.'

'Before posing the fundamental questions, namely who and why, let us consider the killer's intelligence.'

'Whoever it is must be a fool,' Brineux retorted.

'It seems likely, for there are far more convincing ways of incriminating Agnès de Souarcy – unless, and this is what I am beginning to fear, we have understood nothing of these murders and have been mistaken right from the very start of your investigation.'

'I do not follow.'

'I am a little lost myself, Brineux. What if it has never been the villain's intention to point us in the direction of the Manoir de Souarcy? What if the letter *A* means something entirely different?'

'And the linen handkerchief, have you forgotten about that?'

'Yes, you are right. There is still the question of the linen handkerchief,' admitted the Comte.

After a brief silence, Artus d'Authon continued:

'I wish to ask you a rather delicate question – or rather an extremely indelicate one.'

'I am at your service, Monsieur.'

'I would prefer you to answer me as a friend.'

'I should be honoured.'

'Are you aware of any stories, any malicious gossip concerning Eudes de Larnay's relationship with his half-sister?'

Artus understood from the way his Bailiff pursed his lips that some rumour had indeed reached his ears.

'Larnay is not a very pleasant man.'

'It comes as no surprise,' admitted the Comte.

'I mean to a degree that offends the ear. His ill treatment of his wife is infamous. The poor woman is more cuckolded than an Eastern queen. They tell me he thinks nothing of entertaining strumpets in the very chambers of the chateau. And that some of these women of easy virtue have been discovered brutally beaten after their encounters with him. None has been willing to recount their story to my men for fear of reprisals.'

'And what about his sister?'

'It would appear that Eudes de Larnay has a very loose notion of kinship and blood relationship. He showers the lady with lavish gifts ...'

'Which she accepts?'

'She would be foolish to refuse. I heard he even gave her sweet salt.'

'Goodness me! The man treats her like a princess!' remarked the Comte.

'Or an expensive prostitute.'

'Do you think that they … I mean that she …'

'I admit having entertained the idea up until I met her – after all Larnay may be rotten inside, but he is still an attractive man. No. I do not believe that she would rub herself against that miserable brute. Other facts concur.'

'And what are they?'

Artus d'Authon realised at that very moment that it was not only necessary but vital for him to be certain of Agnès's indifference towards her brother, and if possible her detestation of him.

'Agnès de Souarcy has always refused her half-brother's "hospitality", despite the true affection and compassion she feels for her sister-in-law, Madame Apolline. She goes out of her way to avoid meeting him. In addition, one of Eudes's mother's – the late Baroness de Larnay's – ladies-in-waiting confided that Agnès instantly accepted the first offer of marriage as a way of escaping from her brother's predatory instincts. Fate would have it that Hugues died prematurely, killed by an injured stag, delivering her once more into Eudes's clutches.'

'A fine catch, that Hugues de Souarcy, to be sure!'

'It was no doubt preferable in the lady's eyes to wed him than be bedded by her wicked brother.'

'How do you know all this?'

'I am your Bailiff, my Lord. It is my task, my duty and my privilege to keep my "big ears" – as Julienne calls them – open in order to serve you.'

'And I am grateful to you for it.'

Clément had spent the last few days trying to decipher the coded message he had copied out. He had gone through every possible combination, varying the pattern, beginning with the first word of each psalm, then realigning his transcription by moving along a few words or lines. But to no avail. He had a nagging suspicion: what if he was wrong and Mabile had used a different book? But if so, which one? The few there were at Souarcy were mostly in Latin, and Clément was sure Mabile had no notion of that language reserved for erudite people. Given that piety was hardly the servant's main virtue, she could have chosen something more suited to her, a work in French that would be more easily accessible. Where was she hiding it? Agnès was keeping the scoundrel occupied as they had planned earlier that morning.

When Clément walked into the kitchen, Adeline was sweeping the ashes out of the big hearth.

'I'm looking for Mabile,' he lied,

'She's with our lady.'

'Well, in that case I'll keep you company while I wait for her. Chatting lightens chores.'

'That's very true.'

'You work hard and our lady is pleased with you.'

Adeline looked up, blushing.

'She's a good person.'

'Yes, she is. Unlike … Well, sometimes I have the feeling Mabile isn't very nice to you.'

The girl's usually flaccid lips puckered.

'She's a nasty piece of work.'

'To be sure.'

Adeline became emboldened, adding:

'She's like a boil on the backside, she is! Only I tell you one thing and that is you can prick a boil and it'll stop hurting. She thinks she's so high and mighty, with all her simpering … Just because she's being …'

Adeline froze suddenly and her eyes darted anxiously towards Clément. She had spoken out of turn and felt afraid suddenly of Mabile's possible retribution.

'Just because she's being tupped by her former master it doesn't give her the right to lord it over the rest of us,' Clément concluded to make the girl feel at ease. 'This will be our secret.'

Adeline's broad face lit up with a smile of relief and she nodded.

'What's more, she puts on airs and graces just because she can read a little,' Clément continued.

'Yes. Well, I don't need to read to know how to prepare a dish. Whereas she … She's always got her nose stuck in that meat recipe book of hers just to show off. She is a good cook, mind you, it's just that …'

'So she uses a meat recipe book, does she!' exclaimed Clément. 'And there I was thinking she knew it all herself …'

'No, she cheats!' affirmed Adeline. 'But not me. It's all in here, in my head, not in some book!'

'Well! I'd be interested to know if that's where she got the recipe for the sauce she made to go with the rack of wild boar, which so impressed the Comte d'Authon. For if she copied it from someone, then the compliments shouldn't go to her.'

'That's the honest truth,' agreed Adeline, pleased with herself.

'Only she never lets that recipe book out of her sight in case anyone discovers her deception. She hides it in her room!'

'By Jove she doesn't!'

'She does,' Adeline assured him, puffed up by a sudden sense of her own importance, and with a glint in her eye she added:

'But I know where she keeps it.'

'I *thought* you were a crafty one!'

'I am, too. It's under her mattress.'

Clément stayed chatting with the girl for a while longer and then stood up to leave.

The door had scarcely closed behind him before he raced upstairs to the servants' quarters. He only had a few minutes left before Agnès would be forced to release Mabile, who was surely astonished by the sudden interest her mistress was showing in her.

He immediately found the recipe book hidden where Adeline had told him. There was some writing on the first page: 'Copied from Monsieur Debray, chef to his most gracious and powerful majesty Sire Louis VIII, the Lion King.'

The boy paused. Should he replace the book and wait until Mabile was absent again in order to compare it with the text of the message, or should he take it? Time was running out and he chose the second solution. If Mabile noticed it was gone before he had a chance to return it, she would no doubt accuse Adeline. Agnès would then need to protect the poor girl from the servant's wrath.

He climbed silently back up to his eaves and set to work at once. He must be quick. The conflict was steadily becoming clearer. He must return to the secret library at Clairets Abbey to try to throw light on another mystery: the notebook of the Knight Eustache de Rioux.

Vatican Palace, Rome, July 1304

Cardinal Honorius Benedetti was deathly pale. Although he found the heat so insufferable, he was chilled to the bone.

Nicolas Boccasini, Benoît XI, lay gasping as he clutched the prelate's fingers with his clammy hand.

The front of his white robe was disappearing under the blood-streaked vomit. All night long he had been racked by griping pains, leaving him exhausted by the early morning. Arnaud de Villeneuve* – one of the century's most eminent doctors, whose ideas were a little too reformist for the Inquisition's liking – had not left his bedside. His diagnosis had been immediate: the Pope was dying from poisoning and no antidote other than prayer could save him. Thus, without holding out much hope they had tried fumigating with incense, praying, and Monsieur de Villeneuve had been against bleeding, whose ineffectiveness in cases of poisoning was well known since the time of Monsieur Galen.

Benoît made a feeble but impatient gesture signalling that he wished to be left alone with his Cardinal. Before he left the dying Pope's chambers, Villeneuve turned to the prelate and murmured in a voice trembling with emotion:

'Your Eminence will have understood the nature of yesterday's mysterious drowsiness.'

Honorius looked at him, puzzled. The practitioner continued:

'You were drugged and, judging from your disorientation and encumbered speech in the afternoon, I would wager it was with opium powder. Somebody needed you out of the way in order to reach His Holiness.'

Honorius closed his eyes and crossed himself.

'There was nothing you could have done, Your Eminence. These accursed poisoners always achieve their ends. I regret it from the very depths of my soul.'

Arnaud de Villeneuve then left the two men to their final exchange.

Benoît had heard nothing of this monologue. Death was in his chamber and deserved his full attention in the company of the only friend he had found in this palace that was too vast, too onerous.

The room was filled with a strange sickly-sweet odour – the odour of the dying man's breath. His end was approaching and with it a miraculous release.

'My brother ...'

The voice was so frail that Honorius was obliged to bend over the Holy Father, fighting off the tears he had been holding back for hours.

'Your Holiness ...'

Benoît shook his head in frustration.

'No ... brother ...'

'My brother?'

A smile played across the dying man's cracked lips:

'Yes, your brother. That is all I wished to be ... Do not suffer. It was inevitable and I have no fear. Bless me, my brother, my friend. The figs ... What day is it today?'

'The seventh of July.'

Soon after the extreme unction performed by his friend and confidant, the Pope sank into a coma punctuated by delirium.

'... the almond trees at Ostia, how wonderful they were ... Every year a little girl would offer me a basketful ... I was so fond of them ... She must be a mother now ... I join You, my

Lord … It was a mistake … I tried to do my best, to foresee as best I could … The Light, behold the Light, It bathes me … Unto God, gentle brother.'

Nicolas Boccasini's hand gripped Honorius's fingers then suddenly relaxed, leaving the Cardinal cold and alone in the world.

There was a last sigh.

Eternal sorrow, infinite tears. Choking with sobs, Honorius Benedetti fell forward until his brow was resting on the large red stain soiling the deceased Pope's chest.

He trembled for a long moment against the torso of his dead brother before managing to stand up to go and notify the people crammed into the anteroom where a deathly hush reigned.

Dawn was breaking, pushing back the night. Clément had not slept for two days. His head was spinning with exhaustion, or was it the euphoria of success?

A thought suddenly occurred to him that tempered his complacency. The poisonous snake! In those few lines he had transcribed from the message Vigil was carrying when he was pierced by an arrow was all the hatred and jealousy in the world. The venom was concealed in one of Mabile's famously delicious recipes for broad bean purée.

Place the beans on the heat and bring them to the boil, then drain the water from the pot and add fresh water to cover the beans, salt according to taste …

Eudes and Mabile had made no effort of imagination, beginning their code with the first letter of the first line.

The deciphered text made Clément shudder with horror. Following the details of his birth, his lack of a surname, godmother and godfather, were the wicked words:

Chaplain Bernard bewitched by Agnès. Sharing a bed?

The evil scoundrel. She was lying shamelessly in order to please her master. Another more likely reason suddenly occurred to Clément. She was lying in order to hurt him, and also to take revenge. Eudes's deep-rooted hatred of his half-sister was so confused, so mixed up with his unrequited love and unsatisfied desire. He wanted Agnès to grovel even as he continued to believe that, were it not for their blood ties, she would have loved him more than anyone. Mabile was aware of this. Her hatred was keen and merciless, like the blade of a knife.

Clément waited another hour before stealing down to his mistress's chamber to inform her of his discovery.

Seated on her bed, the lady studied him. A flush of anger had gradually replaced the pallor on her face when she learnt the contents of the message.

'I'll unmask her and throw her out on her ear. I'll give her a good thrashing!'

'I understand your anger, Madame, but it would be a mistake.'

'She accuses me of …'

'Of sharing your chaplain's bed, indeed.'

'It is a crime, not a mere error of judgement.'

'I am well aware of that.'

'Do you realise what would become of me if anyone were to give credence to this monstrous calumny?'

'You would lose your dower.'

'And more than that! Brother Bernard is not a man, he is a priest. I would be dragged before the courts, accused of demonically driving a man of God to commit the sin of sensual pleasure. In short, of being a succubus. And you know what fate is reserved for them.'

'The stake.'

'After everything else.'

She fell silent for a few moments before continuing:

'Eudes is expecting this message. How many more has he received from the loyal Vigil since he offered him to me? No matter. The pigeon is dead and we have no way of replacing Mabile's original note. Worse still, I cannot even rid myself of her without rousing my half-brother's suspicions. What am I to do, Clément?'

'Kill her,' he proposed, with great solemnity. Agnès looked at him aghast:

'What are you saying?'

'I can kill her. It is simple; there are so many plants I could use. I would not be guilty of committing a capital sin since she is not a human being but a snake.'

'Have you lost your senses? I forbid it. Killing is only justified when one's life is threatened.'

'She is a threat to us. She threatens your life, and therefore mine.'

'No. You will not taint your soul. Do you hear me? It is an order. If anyone is to send that witch to her damnation, it should be me.'

Clément lowered his head and murmured:

'I refuse. I refuse to let you be damned. I will obey you, Madame, as I always obey, just to please you.'

Damnation? She had lived with the possibility for so long that she had ended up no longer fearing it.

'Clément. There must be some other defence against his evil. I need precise information about the state of Monsieur de Larnay's mines. I will give the order to saddle a horse for you. Our draught animals do not go very fast, but the journey will be less tiring for you and its imposing physique will deter brigands.'

They were running short of time.

Returning to her room that evening, Mabile discovered sooner than expected that her recipe book was missing. She charged to the end of the passageway leading to the servants' quarters, and burst into Adeline's chamber like a fury. The evil woman set upon Adeline's sleeping form, tearing at her hair and punching her.

The portly girl tried to scream, but a brutal hand clamped itself over her mouth and she felt the tip of a knife pricking her neck and a voice growled in her ear:

'Where is it, pig? Where's my recipe book? Give it to me now! If you cry out, I'll skin you alive. Do you hear me?'

'I haven't got it, I haven't got it, I swear on the Gospel! I didn't take it,' squealed Adeline.

'Who did then? Quick, out with it, you ugly cow, my patience is wearing thin.'

'It must've been Clément. He was asking me where you kept it – the recipe book, I mean! So I told him, I did.'

'A pox on that sneak of a boy!'

Mabile's thoughts were racing. She had been careless. They had certainly found the message meant for Eudes de Larnay – contrary to what she had believed so as to put her mind at rest. No doubt knowing that she would try to recover the dead pigeon, that loathsome dwarf had placed it in the Dame de Souarcy's chamber for her to find. The missing recipe book showed he had discovered the nature of the code and probably already deciphered it.

She must leave the manor. Agnès had sufficient reason to demand her punishment.

Why did that miserable bastard always triumph? And why did Clément love her so much that he was prepared to risk Mabile's vengeance? And Gilbert? And the others? Why?

A sudden calm came over Mabile. Up until then she thought she had hated the Dame de Souarcy, but she hadn't. She had been content merely to hurt her. True hatred, the hatred that destroys everything, was only just beginning. It drove her and nothing could withstand it. It eclipsed all fear, all remorse.

Adeline was still sobbing as the tip of the knife pulled away from her neck.

'Listen to me carefully, you little fool! I'm going back to my room. If I so much as hear you move before dawn or raise the alarm, you're dead. Do you understand? Wet the bed if you have to, but I don't want to hear a sound!'

The girl nodded her head frantically.

Mabile left the tiny chamber. She only had a few hours' head start to put a distance between her and Agnès de Souarcy's men.

Agnès was not surprised to learn the news of Mabile's disappearance. Even less so was Clément, to whom Adeline had confessed, her face puffy from crying.

'May she be torn apart by bears,' Clément began, as they stood in the hay barn where the corpse that the Bailiff's men had brought back had lain.

'They, too, are wary of snakes.'

'Are you thinking of sending some men after her, Madame?'

'She has several hours' head start and they won't catch up with her on our draught horses. And even if they did find her, what would I do with her? Remember, she is my half-brother's property. I would be obliged to hand her over in order for him to mete out justice.'

'Indeed, we would do better to let her roam in the forest. Adeline said she must have left in a great hurry. She took very little food with her and even less water and clothing. Who knows …?'

'Do not hope for miracles, Clément.'

'Then the war is at our gates.'

Agnès ran her fingers through the child's hair, and murmured in a voice so weary it startled him:

'You have summed up our situation admirably. Leave me now, I need to think.'

He appeared to hesitate, but did as she had asked.

Agnès climbed the stairs to her quarters, her limbs weighed down by an immeasurable fatigue. No sooner had she closed the door than the façade of self-control she had kept up for Clément's sake fell away. If Mabile managed to spread her poisonous lies, Eudes would believe them or pretend to give them credence. If her half-brother then concluded that the irregularities in the chapel register regarding Clément's birth and Sybille's death were designed to conceal Sybille's heresy, Agnès was lost. Her supposed crimes would be brought before the Inquisition. Choked with sobs, she slumped to her knees on the stone floor.

What would she do – what could she do? Her mind was flooded with questions, each more insoluble than the last.

What would become of Clément? He would be handed over to the Baron de Larnay – unless she managed to convince him to flee. He would never leave without her – she would force him. Above all, he must not suspect the danger Agnès faced, or he would cling to her in the hope of saving her, forgetting about his youth, the circumstances of his birth and what he knew he must conceal.

And what of Mathilde? Mathilde must be protected – but where could she send her? The Abbess of Clairets might take her in for a while. But if Agnès were accused of having incited a priest to commit concubinage, she would be stripped of her dower and her parental rights …

A garbled prayer came from her lips:

'I beg you, Lord! Do not punish them for my sins. Do what You will with me, only spare them for they are innocent.'

How long did she cry like that? She had no idea. She fought against the exhaustion that made her eyelids heavy.

Fear will not save you from being bitten, my dear, on the contrary.

Agnès's fury roused her and she castigated herself.

Stop this at once!

Stand up! Who do you think you are, grovelling like this! If you falter, they will pounce on you and rip you to shreds like the hounds their quarry.

If you falter, they will take Clément and Mathilde, your name and your estate. Think of what they will do to Clément.

If you falter, you will have deserved your fate and you will be responsible for what befalls the child.

Growl more fiercely, raise your ears and tail, and bare your teeth to ward off the dangers that threaten you.

Fight.

Nicolas Florin, the Inquisitor, had swapped his robe for breeches, a chemise, a fustian doublet[28] and a rather old-fashioned long dark-grey tunic that would help him to go unnoticed. A taupe-coloured cowl, the pointed end of which was wrapped round his neck, concealed the tonsure that would have drawn attention to him the moment he entered the tavern on Rue du Croc. There were few customers seated at the tables that early afternoon.

He identified the man who had requested the meeting by his affluent appearance, and walked over to his table. The man greeted him without a smile and invited him to sit down, beginning as soon as the innkeeper had served them another jug of wine.

'As my messenger told you yesterday, this is a delicate matter and requires the utmost discretion.'

'I understand,' Nicolas nodded, sipping his wine.

Something struck his knee under the table. He grasped hold of it. A nice full purse, as agreed.

'There is a hundred pounds, and a hundred more will follow when the trial is over,' affirmed Eudes de Larnay in a murmur.

'I am interested to know how you came to me.'

'There are only three appointed Inquisitors in the Alençon region.'

'This does not explain how you ruled out the other two candidates.'

'It hardly matters,' retorted Eudes, uneasily. 'What matters is that the information I was given turns out to be correct. However, if you are not interested in the ... affair, we shall let it rest,' he concluded weakly.

Nicolas was not fooled. The other man needed him or he would never have risked arranging such a meeting. And he was not about to let go of two hundred pounds – a small fortune. He agreed wholeheartedly:

'Indeed, you are right. Let us return to business.'

Eudes took what he hoped was a discreet gulp of air, before commencing the little speech he had rehearsed a dozen times.

'My half-sister Madame Agnès de Souarcy is a wanton woman of loose morals. As for her devotion to the Holy Mother Church ... the least I can say is that it lacks conviction ...'

Nicolas did not believe a word of Larnay's preamble. He had become very gifted at detecting liars and, aided by his own extraordinary talent for deception, was clever at discovering other people's motives. What a fool the Baron was! Did he really believe Nicolas needed a good reason for dragging somebody before an inquisitorial court? Money more than sufficed. As for evidence and witnesses, he was perfectly capable of providing or procuring these himself. Yes, the wine was good and Baron de Larnay was the first real client on a list he trusted would be long and lucrative. There was no shortage of impatient heirs, vengeful or jealous vassals, or even ambitious or bankrupt merchants. It was worth spending a little of his time listening to this man spout his nonsense.

'She indulges in carnal relations with a man of God, whom she has no doubt led astray through witchcraft. The man in question is her young chaplain – a certain Brother Bernard. The poor fool is so in her thrall that he has betrayed his faith. Moreover, for some years she has carried on unspeakable dealings with a simpleton who is as faithful to her as a dog.'

Well, well. Here was somebody who might help him. His patience had been rewarded.

'Really? And what is the nature of these dealings?'

'Potions, poisons and philtres in exchange for her favours.'

'Do you have any evidence or witnesses to support this charge?'

'The testimony of a very devout person who lived in Agnès de Souarcy's household, and I'll wager we can find others.'

'I do not doubt it. Demonology is becoming more and more bound up with the pursuit of heretics. It is understandable – for what is the worship of demons if not the supreme form of heresy, an unforgivable offence against God?'

Eudes, who was uninterested in these finer points, continued:

'A number of friars have met their deaths under strange and terrible circumstances near to her estate.'

'Indeed! But is murder not a matter for the high justice of Seigneur d'Authon and his Bailiff ?'

'They have made precious little progress since the bodies were discovered.'

'Are you suggesting that this lady might have cast a spell on Comte Artus and Monsieur de Brineux?'

'The possibility cannot be ruled out – though it would be difficult to bring the matter to light given the rank and reputation of the two men.'

'Indeed.'

Since his arrival at Alençon, Nicolas, who was a judicious manipulator, had spent part of his time familiarising himself with the powerful people of the region. It was out of the question for him to make an enemy of the Comte d'Authon, a friend to the King, and this reticence applied equally to Monge de Brineux. He continued his enquiry:

'Madame de Souarcy, then, enjoys the backing of influential men even if she obtains it by demonic means?' asked Nicolas Florin in a hushed voice.

Eudes realised he had made a tactical error. But his desire to drag Agnès through the mud blinded him. He tried to reassure the Inquisitor, correcting himself over-emphatically:

'She is only another of my father's bastard offspring. Why did he have to recognise her so late in life?'

His violent outburst caused some heads in the tavern to turn. He lowered his voice:

'She has almost no property of her own, and I doubt whether Comte Artus and Monsieur de Brineux would defend her if she were found guilty of witchcraft. They are pious men of honour.' Eudes paused suddenly. He had for some moments had a niggling suspicion, but his thinking was clouded by resentment and emotion.

'Pray continue,' urged Nicolas.

The Inquisitor's soft voice made Eudes uneasy. However, he kept going:

'The final and, no doubt, most serious charge, my Lord Inquisitor, is that Agnès de Souarcy once offered her protection to a heretic and with such zeal that one wonders whether she herself did not espouse the same theories. Moreover, she brought up the woman's posthumous son whose devotion to her is such that he would lay down his life.'

A greedy smile formed on the Inquisitor's exquisite lips.

'The facts, for pity's sake ... you are keeping me in suspense.' The sentence terminated in a sigh.

'In the chapel register there is no surname entered for the child, Clément, or his mother, Sybille, for whom no funeral mass was held. Nor is there any mention of the name and status of the child's godparents. Notwithstanding the cross planted on her tomb, Sybille was buried just outside the consecrated ground reserved for the servants of the manor.'

'That is extremely interesting,' Nicolas observed. Heresy remained the ideal grounds for accusation. The charges of witchcraft or demonic possession, which were more difficult to substantiate, suddenly seemed incidental.

Nicolas continued:

'In accordance with your wishes the lady will be tried for heresy and complicity in heresy. Do you wish her confession to be ... drawn out?'

At first, Eudes did not understand the precise meaning of the words. And then it struck him with full force and the blood fled from his face:

'Let us be clear ... it is out of the question for ... for her ...' His voice had become so choked that Nicolas was obliged to lean over. '... Flogging will be sufficient. I want her to be afraid, to believe she is lost. I want her whipped until her pretty back and belly turn black and blue. I want her estate and her dower to be confiscated according to the law and to revert to her daughter, who will become my ward. I do not want her to die. I do not want her maimed or disfigured. The two hundred pounds are contingent upon this.'

The pronouncement dampened Nicolas's enthusiasm. The affair was already losing its appeal for him. He comforted himself with the thought that he would soon have plenty of other toys to play with. It was better to take the money – the cornerstone of his fortune.

'Everything will be done according to your wishes, Monsieur.'

'Let us part company now. It is better for us not to be seen together.'

He wanted to be alone, away from the seductive presence he found so disquieting.

Nicolas stood up and took his leave with a radiant smile.

The nagging doubt the Baron had begun to feel earlier was growing stronger. Something was not right – something was very wrong. He placed his hands on his temples then swigged down the rest of his wine.

How had it come to this? True, he wanted Agnès to grovel and beg. He wanted to terrify her and make her swallow the contempt she felt for him. He wanted her dower. But at such a cost?

Was it he or Mabile who had first thought of delivering her into the hands of the Inquisition? He could no longer be sure.

Mabile had told him of her encounter with a friar who had refused to let her see his face and whose few words had been disguised by his thick woollen cowl. Was it this monk she had barely glimpsed who had suggested the name Nicolas Florin and the plot that was beginning to make Eudes increasingly uneasy?

Mathilde hurled her dress to the floor at the foot of the bed.
'What's all this now, young miss?' bleated Adeline,
rushing to pick up the discarded garment.

'Out, you fool! Out of my room at once! That oafish girl will
be the death of me!'

Adeline did not wait to be asked twice, fleeing the chamber of
her young mistress whose tantrums she knew from experience to
be fearful. Mathilde had already slapped her on several occasions,
and without the slightest compunction had one day thrown a
hairbrush in her face.

Mathilde was seething. She felt she could burst into tears at
any moment. Rags were what she was forced to wear. What good
was it everybody thinking her pretty if she was made ugly by
shapeless tatters? She couldn't even bring herself to wear the
beautiful hair comb her dear Uncle Eudes had given her, it would
have clashed so horribly with the few unfashionable shoddy
garments she possessed. Her sweet uncle ... at least he treated
her like a young lady.

All that filth, the insufferable smells, the dirty uncouth farm
hands she was forced to mix with ... Life at the manor was an
ordeal. Only that beggar, the conceited Clément, could endure it.
What a half-breed he was. And he had the impudence to stick his
nose in the air when she gave him orders, as if he only received
them from the Dame de Souarcy, her mother.

Madame – her mother. How did Agnès de Souarcy put up with
this life? What a disgrace to have to watch her go and collect
honey dressed as a man, worse still, as a serf. How degrading to

be reduced to counting newborn piglets like a common peasant. True ladies did not deign to perform such tasks. Her mother's hands would soon be as rough as those of a farm hand!

Why had her mother not accepted Baron de Larnay's generous offer of going to live at his chateau? The two of them would have enjoyed a life befitting their position. Her Uncle Eudes gave myriad parties where beautiful ladies and gallant knights mingled. He even hired troubadours to delight his guests during meals made up of delicacies and exotic dishes. There was dancing and merriment to the music of *chifonies*,[29] *chevrettes*[30] and *citoles*,[31] and the subject of love was discussed openly, though chivalrously.

No, Agnès de Souarcy had flatly refused, thus depriving her daughter of the happiness that was her birthright.

The young girl was filled with bitterness. Thanks to her mother, she would never wear magnificent furs and sumptuous robes. Thanks to her obstinacy, that life of sophistication would forever remain a mystery. Thanks again to her stupid resolve, her daughter Mathilde would no doubt also be deprived of the kind of marriage to which she aspired.

Her eyes became moist with tears and she trembled at the thought of the future that awaited her in that miserable pigsty, Souarcy. A peasant's life spent rummaging in the soil with her bare hands for food, and dressing like a beggar to go and collect honey! What misery! She did not deserve such a fate. She hurled herself onto the bed in despair. The life she had been forced to put up with for years was a dishonour. Just because the mother was prepared to wither and die because of some inexplicable pride, it did not mean the daughter had to share the same fate.

Her sorrow gave way to rage.

Mathilde was born within the sanctity of marriage, and of

noble blood – the Larnays' on her grandfather Robert's side and the Souarcys' on her father's.

She did not intend to fade away within Souarcy's damp, grey walls. She refused to count pigeons' eggs as if her life depended upon it. She would not stoop to bartering cords of wood for a few yards of linen. Never. Not like her mother.

As for Clément, Mathilde couldn't care less what became of him. He could die with his good lady if he wished. She had had enough of his superiority all these years!

Clément was overwhelmed by an almost painful anguish. Each passing hour weighed on him like a curse. Agnès's silence had not fooled him. He knew that if Eudes chose to believe in an unpardonable liaison between the Dame de Souarcy and her chaplain and if he guessed the truth about Sybille, he could request the intervention of one of the Inquisitors at Alençon.

The boy shuddered.

Clément recalled the scene as if it were yesterday. He was five years old. Gisèle, the nursemaid who looked after him, had taken him one evening to his lady's chamber before putting him to bed. For a long moment, the two women, whom he knew were very close, looked questioningly at one another. Agnès had murmured:

'Do you not think it is premature?'

And Gisèle had retorted:

'We cannot delay any longer. It is too dangerous. All the more so since she suspects the truth, even though she doesn't understand. I watch her closely and I know.'

At the time Clément had wondered who the two women were talking about.

'But she is still so young ... I'm afraid that ...'

The nursemaid cut across her in a firm voice:

'There is no place for such fears now. Think what would happen if anyone discovered our secret.'

Agnès de Souarcy had begun with a sigh. She had told him what it was he needed to know about his birth in order to understand that only complete secrecy could save them. At the tender age of fifteen, his mother, Sybille Chalis, had been seduced by the evangelical purity of the Waldensian Church. She had run away from her family, wealthy burghers from the Dauphiné region, in order to join her brothers and sisters in hiding and to be ordained a priest. Their tiny congregation had been denounced, but the young girl had just managed to escape. She hid, travelling by night, hardly knowing where she was headed, begging for bread in exchange for a few hours' labour. It was only a matter of time before disaster struck in the form of two drunken brutes who raped and beat her and left her for dead. Sybille already knew she was pregnant by the time she arrived at the manor one evening. Agnès took her in, oblivious to the fact that in doing so she was harbouring a heretic. But even had the young woman revealed the truth about her faith, the Dame de Souarcy would not have ordered her men to throw her out. Agnès had paused briefly before relating what for Clément had been the worst: his mother could not tolerate the idea of her soul being trapped in a defiled body and had let herself die of starvation and cold during the deadly winter of 1294.

Sensing that her mistress was unable to go on, Gisèle had concluded:

'She pushed you from her womb as she lay dying – that was on 28 December.'

Clément was overcome, great tears rolled down his cheeks. He could see from Agnès's staring eyes that she was reliving those nightmarish scenes. She had stroked his brow with a trembling hand before continuing in a choked voice:

'Clément, you are not a boy. That is why we insisted you never bathe with the servants' children and that you stayed away from them and did not join in their games.'

He – she – already suspected, having noticed that his body had more in common with those of little girls.

'But ... why?' he had stammered.

'Because I could not have kept a motherless girl in my service, and you would have become one of the many offerings to God who end up in convents. Eudes de Larnay would have demanded it and I would have been in no position to refuse.' At this point Agnès had closed her eyes for a brief moment and when she spoke again her voice was firmer: 'Orphans of low birth have no other choice but to enter servitude – or worse, but you are still too young for that. They have no access to knowledge and their lives are harsh. I wanted to spare you. If my brother and his breed were to learn your true sex ... That can wait. What you need to realise now, dear Clément, is that nobody must ever discover the truth about you. Never ... Well ... the day might dawn when ... Your fate would be cruel. Do you see?'

Afterwards he – she – had cried all night long, wondering whether the mother he had so often imagined, so often pictured as a beautiful star or a gentle ray of sunshine had also wished him dead before he was born. What use was a life so worthless that even his mother had rejected it? The question had haunted him for weeks before he had had the courage to put it to his lady. She had gazed into his eyes, tilting her head to one side so that her veil brushed her waist, and smiled such a beautiful, desperate smile:

'Your life is terribly precious to me, Clément ... Clémence. I swear on my soul.'

He had Agnès. His whole life depended on his lady. After all, she fed him and protected him like a mother. He knew she loved him. And he adored her.

As for the rest – this inversion of his sex – it hardly mattered to him in the end. His lady was right. A low-born girl, the orphan of a heretic mother, was nothing or worse than nothing. He would continue thinking of himself as a boy for his own and Agnès's protection. And besides, a boy's life was so much more exciting than that of a girl.

Clément wiped away the tears that had wet his lips and chin with his sleeve. Enough! Enough memories! The past was over. He must devote himself to the future. He must concentrate on living even as so many dangers were stacking up against them.

Why, whence the need he felt to penetrate the mystery of the diary belonging to the Knight Eustache de Rioux and his co-author? How might the crossings-out, question marks, blind searchings of these men, who were perhaps dead, help them – Agnès and him? And yet he was driven on by an instinct he found difficult to analyse. This astrology and astronomy, these mathematical calculations, furious or fervent jottings and hinted-at secrets were a nonsense to him:

> *The Moon will eclipse the Sun on the day of his birth. The place of his birth is still unknown. Revisit the words of the Viking, a bondi trader in walrus tusks, amber and furs chanced upon in Constantinople.*

What were these words? Where did they come from?

> *Five women and at the centre a sixth.*

A geometrical shape? A metaphor? What?

> *Capricorn in the first decan and Virgo in the third being variable and the consanguinity of Aries in any decan too great.*

Was this a reference to a past or future birth, and if so, whose? And what did 'consanguinity' mean in relation to a zodiac sign?

The initial calculations were incorrect, failing to take into account the error relating to the year of birth of the Saviour. It is a fortunate blunder for it gives us a little more time.

Could some error have been made concerning the date of Christ's birth? And more time for what? Clément leafed through the long notebook, fighting back his feelings of frustration and despair.

He must read it through from the beginning, pushing aside his impatience and his looming sense of panic.

What was the drawing with a line through it which he had been struggling for hours to comprehend? It was shaped like some sort of disc. In the margins on either side of it were columns of Roman numerals, preceded by some initials and symbols. The same sequence of letters – *E*, *Su*, *Me*, *Ma*, *V*, *J*, *Sa*, *GE1*, *GE2*, *As* – reappeared in various places next to the signs of the zodiac. It did not take a genius to work out that some of these initials referred to the planets – except for *GE1*, *GE2* and *As*, which meant nothing to him.[32] As for the Roman numerals, they represented the different astrological houses. Clément compared the two columns depicting astral or birth charts. They were almost identical except for the two planets Jupiter and Saturn. In one column they were in Pisces and Capricorn respectively and in the other in Sagittarius and Pisces. Capricorn. That was between 22 December and 20 January. Had it not been for the gravity of the situation the coincidence might have amused him. He was born on the night of 28 December.

The first time he had examined the scored-through drawing he had been devastated by the writing below it:

Equatoire[33] carried out in accordance with the measurements of the Arab mathematician Ibn as-Samh originated from the illogicality defended by Ptolemy. The figures obtained thus are unusable since the Earth is not stationary! Therefore they were all mistaken.

God in heaven! Was such an aberration possible? How could the Earth be anything but stationary? And if so, where was it going?

The Greek astronomer and mathematician Ptolemy had affirmed that the universe was finite and flat and that the Earth was at its centre, fixed. The nearest planet to Earth was the Moon, followed in an almost straight line by Mars, Venus and the Sun. Everyone recognised the truth of this system – in particular the Church, and thus the schoolmistresses at the convent praised its importance. How, then, could Eustache de Rioux and his fellow author describe it as illogical? And yet the Knight – or whichever of the two wrote in a bolder, less flowing script – had reiterated at the bottom of the page:

It was necessary to do all the calculations again using Vallombroso's theory, which we did.

Clément could find no other mention of this Vallombroso, despite having trawled through the notebook several times.

On the back of the sketch that had given rise to Monsieur de Rioux's (or his co-author's) rage was a sentence they had been so keen to obliterate they had scraped away the letters with a knife. The paper still bore the marks, and Clément had carefully examined it, holding the page up to the oil lamp to see whether the light might expose its secrets. He had been able to make out some speech marks framing the scratched-out letters. So it was a quotation. The ink that had seeped into the layers of pulp revealed a few letters, but not enough to give any real clue as to the meaning of the words: 'b…me…re…au…per…t.' Below the sentence was another drawing, of a rose in full bloom.

Were these the words of the Viking merchant which the Knight had earlier quoted?

Clément discovered something he had missed on his first reading of the journal: the bold script disappeared completely a few pages on, where some strange drawings the size and shape of almonds in the form of a cross had been traced by a fine hand. The words 'Freya's cross' at the top of the page provided no clue, since Clément did not know who or what Freya was. At the centre of each almond was one of the indecipherable cuneiform letters he had already come across in other works. These strange signs were transcriptions of ancient languages. Each had an arrow pointing from it to a strange word.

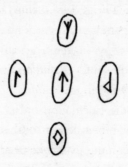

The almond on the left branch was called – or signified – 'Upright-Lagu' and the one on the far right 'Reversed-Thorn'. The almond at the centre of the cross was described as 'Upright-

Tyr' and the one on the top branch 'Upright-Eolh'. The bottom branch was given as 'Reversed-Ing'. Although the actual names meant nothing to Clément, the alternation of 'upright' and 'reversed' was implicit: it was some sort of prophesy, since fortune tellers used similar terms for their cards.

Clément paused. He could memorise the letters and their corresponding names, as well as the two charts. However, he sensed that their precision was of paramount importance and was afraid of making a mistake when trying to reproduce them back in his eaves. He felt a strong temptation to go over to the lectern and make use of the hollow quill pen and ink pot standing there. He did not resist for long, promising himself he would take great care not to move anything, and above all to leave nothing behind that might draw attention to his intrusion. All he needed now was a piece of paper. He searched the library in vain. Paper was a luxury that was kept carefully locked away in cabinets. He struggled for a few seconds with a thought that kept going through his head. Why not tear out one of the last two pages of the diary – blank because the co-author's notes stopped before the end of the notebook? The gesture seemed to him so sacrilegious that it took him three attempts to pluck up the courage.

Satisfied with his copy, he removed all trace of his labours, cleaning the tube of the quill pen and his fingers with a corner of his tunic moistened with saliva.

In order to turn the calculation on its head and discover a date that would show him whether these combinations referred to a birth or a forthcoming event, he needed to find out which system the Knight and his companion had used – in other words: Vallombroso's theory. As for the cuneiform letters, their meaning must be recorded somewhere.

The child spent the last remaining hours of darkness consulting every manual on physics, astronomy and astrology and every glossary in the library, without finding anything resembling that name or that shed light on the symbols in the almonds.

Vallombroso, Vallombroso ... He resumed the search. It was the small hours of the morning before he came across what he considered to be a sign from God. He had stumbled upon a copy of Gui Faucoi's[34] *Consultationes ad inquisitores haereticae pravitatis*, accompanied by a slim manual detailing a series of blood-curdling procedures.

Reading them left him beyond all rage, filled with dread.

Louvre Palace, Paris, July 1304

Guillaume de Nogaret had been awake all night since learning of Benoît XI's demise. He had spent hours weighing up the pros and cons, tossing and turning in his bed as he imagined the worst possible consequences for the kingdom of France. He was choked with rage at the idea that somebody could have stooped so low as to poison the Pope. Not that he had held the Holy Father in particularly high esteem. However, as a lover of the law, Nogaret required that all matters be settled by it. And the law served equally to depose a pope, making it unnecessary to kill him.

This murder was a personal and political calamity. Everybody knew that Benoît XI had decided to excommunicate him in order to punish Philip the Fair for his attempt to force out Boniface VIII. Had this excommunication come to pass, it would have deeply injured Nogaret, who was an extremely religious man, and cast a long shadow over his future political career. In other words he had better reasons than anyone for instigating this poisoning. As the hours slipped by before dawn, his concern for the future of the kingdom eclipsed any fears he might have about his own.

Nogaret and Plaisians were not yet prepared. They had begun spinning their web, advancing their pawns across the papal chessboard. They had counted on a few years of relative respite during Benoît's pontificate, which they hoped would be brief. Not as brief as this, however.

It was barely four o'clock in the morning when, sleep

resolutely refusing to come, he decided to rise from his bed and pray before getting down to some work.

Francesco de Leone, known as Capella for reasons of his espionage mission, was already busy checking registers when Nogaret opened the door to his office. The Counsellor hesitated between feeling irritation at not being able to enjoy a few hours of solitude, and contentment at having engaged such a diligent secretary. The latter prevailed – perhaps because he felt the need to engage in pleasant conversation.

'You are an early riser, Francesco.'

'No, it is the work, my Lord, it seems to pile up overnight as if by magic.'

The reply elicited a weak smile from Nogaret, who nodded:

'It often seems so.'

'My Lord …' Francesco paused with consummate skill. 'What are we to think of the appalling demise of our Pope?'

'Who do you mean by "we"? "We" the State, or "we" you and I?'

'Are not "you" and "the State" one and the same?'

The flattery was too subtle for Nogaret to perceive. On the contrary, the remark pleased him to the point of lifting his troubled mood a little. He responded with an already lighter sigh:

'Not now, not any more. You see, Francesco, I do not know what to think. Naturally, the threat of being excommunicated worried me, even though I understood that it was Benoît's way of affirming his authority over that of the kingdom of France.' Suddenly it seemed essential to Guillaume de Nogaret to be clear on one point – perhaps because he realised that the man he had just taken into his employ possessed a keen intellect and deserved to be treated as his equal. 'You should know that I swear before

God I played no part in the attempt on Boniface's life at Anagni. I went there to give him a summons to appear before the next ecumenical council. I was in the wrong place at the wrong time. We had a strong chance of removing that unworthy Pope by means of a religious tribunal. Any intervention by force was therefore superfluous.'

Leone studied him in silence for a moment then declared in a slow and sincere voice:

'I believe you, my Lord.'

He was certain that this powerful man was speaking the truth, he who recognised a lie as plainly as the nose on his own face.

Nogaret was filled with a disproportionate sense of relief, and it surprised him. After all, Francesco Capella was a mere secretary and the nephew of one of the most predatory usurers of the Place de Paris; what did it matter to him what the man thought? He went on:

'In answer to your question … This premature death could turn out to be an untimely setback. We are unprepared to take action behind the scenes, unless we can delay the election of a new pope.'

'How would you achieve that?'

'By relying on man's basest instincts, which the vast majority of our cardinals have not been spared. Namely cupidity, envy, jealousy and a thirst for power.'

Francesco estimated he had discovered enough for one day, and was afraid of rousing Nogaret's suspicions with more questions. He changed the subject:

'I have been checking the register of court accounts while I waited for you, and …'

Leone made a play of pausing awkwardly.

'And what? Come on, speak up, Francesco.'

'Well … Monsieur de Marigny's accounts are … how should I put it? Well … Large sums of money have been credited to him without any mention of what they have been used for.'

'There are three Marignys: the King's Head Chamberlain, Enguerran, who is well placed in court and close to the Queen, Joan of Navarre; his brother Jean, Bishop of Beauvais, and Philippe, the King's clerk and Bishop of Cambrai. To which do you refer?'

'To the latter in particular. As for Charles de Valois,* he is a bottomless pit!'

Nogaret, frowning at this remark, explained:

'The King's only brother is beyond reproach. Our sovereign is at times blinded by the affection he feels for him. That is the way it is and we have no choice but to accept it. His Royal Highness Charles is very generous with other people's money. We must tolerate it while deftly alerting our sovereign.'

Leone was surprised that Nogaret did not demand details of expenditure carried out in Philippe de Marigny's name. He continued bluntly:

'Monsieur de Marigny, Philippe, spent ten thousand pounds of Treasury money in less than six months. That is no small sum! His letters of withdrawal were drafted by Monsieur Enguerran and countersigned by the King and there is nowhere any mention of how the money was to be used.'

'If the King countersigned them, then it is no concern of ours,' retorted the Counsellor drily.

Leone blinked deferentially by way of assent and returned to his work.

What had this money the King approved been destined for? The withdrawals had begun six months ago – some time before Benoît XI's death. Moreover, Nogaret had been obliged to call upon Giotto Capella to raise the necessary funds in order to manipulate the next papal election. The money granted to Philippe de Marigny must have been meant for some other mission, secret enough to warrant it being unaccounted for in the Treasury register. Guillaume de Nogaret's brusque response was proof that he knew about it.

Nearly an hour passed. Leone did not glance up from his work. The task the King's Counsellor had given him, though tedious, was undemanding and his mind was occupied elsewhere. Soon, he sensed, soon he would have completed his mission in this place. But Arnaud de Viancourt, the prior of the commandery at Cyprus, need not know straight away. Under the guise of continuing his investigation Francesco could stay in France in order to reach the end of his own quest. And then what? Then the world would no longer be what it was now. There would be an end to hypocrisy, scheming and guile. The idols would fall … He must first reach the commandery at Arville, the property of the Knights Templar. They would be reluctant to offer their help to a Knight Hospitaller, at least the sort of help Leone badly needed.

Guillaume de Nogaret cleared his throat. The Knight looked up from the rows of figures he had been examining since his arrival.

'Let us rest for a moment, Francesco. Your uncle told the truth, you speak French admirably well.'

'There is no merit in it, my Lord. My mother was French.' Leone quickly changed the subject. 'Your task would indeed appear to be vexing you.'

'My head is spinning from these marriage contracts. Every contingency must be covered, even – above all – the unforeseeable.'

'What marriage is this, if I may be so bold as to ask?'

'It is no great mystery. His Royal Highness Philippe, Comte de Poitou and our King's second son, is to wed Madame Jeanne de Bourgogne, daughter of Othon IV, Comte de Bourgogne, and of Comtesse Mahaut d'Artois. The county of Artois is a permanently troublesome area. And that of Burgundy – well! In brief, allowance must be made for every eventuality: deaths, births, marriages, annulments, sterility ... I tell you, my head is spinning.'

Sensing that Monsieur de Nogaret regretted his earlier ill temper, the Knight gave him a look of commiseration and waited for what would come next. It did not take long.

'It is so gloomy within these cheerless walls of the Louvre citadel. Do you not yearn for the Rome light and the splendour of the papal palace?'

'The early-morning light in Rome ... is an utter marvel.' Leone's enchanted smile faded. 'Naturally, I long for it ... But I do not miss the years I spent in Boniface's service.'

The Counsellor tried to feign indifference and began smoothing down his quill pen. The man was a useless liar and dissembler, thought Leone, and berated himself; he must be careful not to take a liking to Nogaret. Nogaret was the enemy and he should not forget it. Nogaret tried, rather unsuccessfully, to pretend no more than polite interest.

'Is that so? And yet, though it was an honorary function, it was not without material benefits.'

'Indeed.'

Leone was brilliant at feigning discretion, drawing the Counsellor out even further.

'Now it is I who fear being too bold, Francesco. However, I am greatly satisfied with your work and I believe this to be the start of a long and fruitful association. It is therefore my ... fatherly concern that makes me suspect there was some other reason for your departure than this … lady.'

Leone stared at him wide-eyed, as though stunned by the man's perceptiveness.

'Indeed …' he repeated.

'I would not wish to …'

'My Lord … if a king considers your honour and devotion worthy of his friendship, it would be madness for a humble clerk such as I not to put my trust in you. It is simply that … it is such a difficult thing to confide. For we are speaking in confidence, are we not?'

'You have my word,' Nogaret assured him with complete sincerity.

If what the secretary revealed proved important, he could always divulge his confidences without naming his source – thus keeping his promise.

'Well, you see, my Seigneur de Nogaret, there were so many falsehoods, conspiracies, undesirable connections under Boniface's reign. The papacy was not enough for him, he wanted to be emperor.'

Nogaret was convinced of the truth of this, largely because the loathing he felt for the deceased Pope blinded him at times. All the same, hearing it from the mouth of a chamberlain, and moreover an Italian, who had served Boniface for years, was a great comfort to him.

'Did it offend you?'

'It did … though I fear my reasons will displease you.'

'If it is the case, then I shall tell you and we will avoid any future exchanges of ideas. Pray continue.'

'The kingdom of souls, the defence of our faith and the purity of our devotion to God – all these things, in my view, come under the domain of the Holy Father's authority and wisdom. On the other hand, the construction, administration and protection of the State are the responsibility of the king or emperor. Boniface refused to accept this.'

Nogaret was growing increasingly pleased at having taken on Giotto Capella's nephew. He agreed:

'We share your feelings. But you spoke, too, of undesirable connections and conspiracies …'

'Oh yes …'

Nogaret champed at the bit, waiting for the other man to continue, not rushing him for fear he might close up. Francesco de Leone, meanwhile, was desperately trying to think up some convincing lie. For a lie to be convincing it must be simple, rooted in reality and, above all, pleasing to the listener.

'The Bishop of Pamiers, Bernard Saisset* … exiled by King Philip after he plotted against him …'

'Yes? What about him?'

'Saisset lacked finesse. He was reckless and easily manipulated.'

Nogaret froze with astonishment:

'Do you mean to say that Boniface was behind Saisset's mutiny against the King, and not the other way round, as we have always supposed?'

'Just so. I was present at one of the Pope's meetings with the Bishop. Saisset was a puppet. All that was necessary in order for him to charge was a red rag.'

'Gentle Jesus,' murmured Nogaret.

A few moments of silence elapsed before the Counsellor continued:

'And … these rumours that reached my ears …'

Francesco waited. He knew what Nogaret was referring to, but the question was a delicate one, and the man opposite him weighed each word before uttering it, for the accusation was serious:

'These … how should I say … shocking rumours about Boniface, or one of his acolytes, resorting to witchcraft in order to reinforce his power?'

This slanderous rumour had indeed circulated. Leone had never given it any credence. He had encountered many fake witches and bogus magicians, in many different countries and cultures, and none had succeeded in demonstrating powers that stood up under the scrutiny of logic and science. On the other hand, he knew the origin of this evil rumour that had cast a further slur on the previous Pope's character. He wondered briefly whether the best approach would not be to agree whole-heartedly with the Counsellor. The man's intelligence in theoretical matters was keen, but he was naive where the occult universe was concerned. Leone's instinct, as well as the necessity of convincing Nogaret of his absolute sincerity in order to gain his friendship, dissuaded him:

'Frankly, I never witnessed such things nor had any reason to suspect them. May I let you into a secret?'

'Naturally, it will be safe with me.'

'I replaced in His Holy Father's service a certain Gachelin Humeau. He was … how may I describe him in the simplest terms? Let us say that he had a very peculiar notion of the meaning of duty, honour and gratitude. Humeau was a parasite, a sneak thief, a spy who enjoyed unearthing people's secrets and selling them to the highest bidder. He was caught red-handed stealing manuscripts from the Pope's private library. His fall from grace was swift and justly deserved. Gachelin Humeau disappeared, but not before avenging himself in the way he knew best by slandering Boniface and his cardinals.'

The story was partly true, though the actual events had taken place not four but five years before.

Gachelin Humeau had decided to supplement the remuneration he received in his position as chamberlain by purloining, sometimes to order, diverse objects of value – above all, rare manuscripts of whose existence nobody but the Pope and his cardinals knew. A discreet inventory of the library's contents revealed that fifteen books were missing, five of which, it turned out, were unique copies. The works whose loss was immeasurable included a parchment written in Archimedes'* hand, which Humeau claimed contained astonishing advances in mathematics, a terrifying work on necromancy, the mere mention of which caused Humeau to cross himself, and a treatise on astronomy with the rather undistinguished title *Vallombroso's Theory*. The thief maintained that the contents of this last book, if they became known, would shake the entire universe to its foundations. Gachelin Humeau escaped arrest – fearing, and rightly so, that the Inquisition would force him to confess where he had hidden his priceless and redoubtable booty. He had then traded them in the utmost secrecy for a not inconsiderable sum that allowed him to envisage a future free from care. One of his customers had been none other than the Knight Francesco de Leone himself, who had ordered two works, for which he paid a small fortune. And it was thus he discovered where to resume his quest. The manuscripts, with their alarming and wonderful revelations, were now in a safe place. Before vanishing forever, Humeau had wished to spread his venom, further tarnishing the Pope's reputation.

*

Nogaret took in the words of his secretary before declaring:

'I am grateful for your honesty, Francesco. It is entirely appropriate and, rest assured, I appreciate it.'

Nogaret, because he believed his secretary had taken him into his confidence, felt relieved to be able to do the same. The position of King's Counsellor was a lonely, hazardous one. It warmed his heart to have found in this young man seated before him an unexpected friend.

Francesco de Leone immersed himself once more in the tedious inventories. Nogaret would be attending the King's Council that afternoon. This would provide him with a few hours in which to discover some clue as to the identity of the French cardinals whom the Counsellor was trying to persuade or buy.

For the past few days Leone had been acutely aware that time was running short. Evil, dark forces were at work, toiling relentlessly. He had never doubted their tenacity or savagery but now their imminence was growing apparent. The Darkness was approaching to engulf the emerging Light. The Darkness would resort to any weapon or artifice, however base, in order to perpetuate the shadows it fed upon.

He needed to reach the Templar commandery at Arville as soon as possible. He was not so foolish as to believe that he would discover the key to the Light within its walls, but he knew that concealed within those foundations and flagstones was the instrument necessary to forge it.

Ensconced in the little office the Inquisition had provided him with, Nicolas Florin was radiant. Recalling his anxiety at leaving Carcassonne, he felt annoyed at his 'girlish fright', as he called it. He realised now that even the young Dominican Bartolomeo, whom he thought he might be a little sorry to leave behind, bored him to death with all his timidity. How predictable the little friar was! Nicolas had wanted to see whether he could seduce him. It had proved so easy that he had instantly wearied of his victory. Seduction was a weapon and, as with any weapon, it was advisable to test its reliability and effectiveness on a variety of targets. In spite of his habit, Bartolomeo was easy to penetrate, he put up little resistance. A none too intelligent, awkward virgin summed him up to perfection. Undeserving prey for Nicolas. It is true that, in Carcassonne, Nicolas had not been spoiled for choice. He had been surrounded by sententious old fogies, monks embalmed in their dignity and their ridiculous doctrinaire squabbling. What did he care whether Francesco Bernadone – who after a life of poverty and devotion to Christ would take the name of Francis of Assisi – had emptied his father's warehouses in order to pay for the restoration of San Damiano? His father had ended by disinheriting him – a fact Nicolas considered wholly appropriate. As for the endless controversy over whether Saint Martin of Tours had offered all or only half his coat to a beggar whom he identified as the Saviour – he was sick to death of hearing about it. Of course this pedantic quibbling had but one aim: to separate the advocates of the poverty of Christ and his disciples, and consequently of the Church, from their virulent opponents who were legion. Nicolas could not have cared less. If he had been born to riches, he would have laboured to protect his wealth and would never have been tempted by religion. He was poor but his Inquisitor's robes and position would help him to make this poverty provisional.

An image flashed through his mind. His mother enamoured of her only son. She had been so clever at delivering the offspring of Madame d'Espagne's ladies-in-waiting, and yet so foolish. What had become of her after he left? What did it matter? And his father, that timid scholar and lover of pretty historiated vignettes[35] and initial letters[36] ornamented with tracery,[37] his fingers stained with brightly coloured inks and powdered gold. He would mix cuttlefish and oak gall with egg white and powdered clove,[38] failing to remember that the Comte for whom he was ruining his eyesight preferred war and women's bellies to manuscripts. Lackeys! That was all they both were. Nicolas's perfect features, as well as his talent for duplicity, had earned him the favours of many ladies and a few lords. His intelligence would soon place him high above them all. No one could stop him and he would no longer need to grovel to anyone. Even the great lords of the realm trembled before the Inquisition. Only one master, the Pope, and he was far away.

The power of terror. He already enjoyed it and would exploit it to the full.

The tidy recompense torture brought – the death he could mete out as he saw fit. It was so easy to accuse someone of heresy or possession. So easy to force someone to confess to crimes he, Nicolas, had invented. There was no need even for an executioner, he dispensed with them and completed the job himself. A few moments in the interrogation chamber with him. Nothing more. Nicolas had confirmed it again and again. If the accused was wealthy, an agreement could be reached. If not, he died, and his terror, his pain were compensation for Nicolas. In both cases he won. The thought made him sigh with pleasure.

What a perfect model, that Robert le Bougre. A tidal wave of screams, blood, strewn viscera, crushed feet, put-out eyes, torn flesh. Fifty deaths in a few months – victims of his brief stays at Châlons-sur-Marne, Péronne, Douai and Lille. The great pyre of Saint-Aimé: a hundred and eighty-three 'pure', or so they claimed, Cathars burnt to cinders in a few hours.

Poor tiresome Bartolomeo. He would never experience greatness – even less the joy it procures.

He must now devote himself to the matter of Agnès de Souarcy, recently brought before him together with a first handsome payment. He would receive the second after her disgrace. Why not her death? But the Baron who had sought his services had insisted the young widow must not die, either on the rack or at the stake. And as far as torture was concerned he was to be as restrained as possible; the more 'benevolent' nature of the abuse inflicted on women compared to men made this possible.[39] This was all Nicolas needed in order to understand that he was dealing with an incestuous lover seeking retribution – one, moreover, who had been spurned.

A woman, a lady, how pleasurable. How stirring they were when they squirmed with terror! Especially this one, whom he had heard tell was ravishingly beautiful.

What a disappointment! No matter. After all, he had been handsomely rewarded. Some other brainless victim would serve to vent his frustration. There was no lack of people falsely accused.

The evidence the Baron had provided as justification for an inquisitorial examination was a little unclear and so Nicolas had decided to furnish his own. Heresy was the most suitable charge. He knew all the necessary ruses for these trials. None of the accused, even those who were innocent as newborn lambs, escaped his clutches.

He stretched his arms out contentedly and fell back in his chair, closing his eyes, and then, sensing another presence, instinctively opened them again.

The figure, wrapped in a brown cloak of coarse wool with a cowl drawn over its eyes, was standing motionless in front of him. He had heard no one enter his study. Nicolas's good humour was eclipsed by a sudden rage. Who dared to enter unannounced? Who had the gall to disregard his importance and his position in this way?

He rose, and was about to scold the intruder when a gloved hand emerged from a sleeve and handed him a small scroll of paper.

He was overcome by a series of conflicting emotions as he read the contents: astonishment, fear, avidity and finally intense joy.

The figure waited in silence.

'What am I to think of this?' murmured Nicolas, his voice trembling with delight.

A deep voice, disguised by the thick cowl concealing the face, said tersely:

'She must die. Three hundred pounds in exchange for a life, it is more than enough.'

Nicolas was tempted by the idea of a little blackmail in order to raise the fee:

'Only …'

'Three hundred pounds or your life, decide quickly.'

The coldness in the voice of the person standing before him convinced him the threat was real.

'Madame de Souarcy will die.'

'You are a sensible man. You will stay at Clairets Abbey during the period of grace. Thus you will be closer to your new … toy. No order is rich or powerful enough to oppose the actions of a Grand Inquisitor and the good nuns will do as they are told. Thus you will find yourself only a few leagues away from your prey, the sweet Agnès.'

The news of Apolline de Larnay's death during childbirth did not surprise Artus d'Authon, although he was more affected by it than he had imagined he would be. Death was already visible in the grey woman's eyes when he last saw her. And in her belly. The newborn baby, another girl, had outlived her mother by only a few hours. No one expected their loss to upset the feudal Baron unduly.

The death of this creature, whom he had once despised, stirred in him a strange sadness, the sadness of senseless waste.

He surprised himself contemplating Apolline's life. She was one of those women who live only through their desire to be loved by the one they love. Eudes was neither her beloved nor had he ever loved her. And so she had remained locked inside herself, observing the passing of the years, emerging only on rare occasions – as when he had visited her two weeks before.

What on earth was the matter with him? Why did everything seem so painful to him of late? After the devastation caused by the death of his son, he had managed to make a life for himself that was relatively dull yet almost devoid of pain. True, he had never been one of those cheerful light-hearted fellows who are well liked in society. And yet since Gauzelin's death nothing had come near to hurting him. So what was happening to him now? Why did Madame Apolline's unjust end affect him so much? Countless women died in childbirth. He had discovered in himself recently an edginess and sensitivity he was unaware he possessed.

That woman … A smile appeared on his lips for the first time that bleak day, which had been heralded by one equally gloomy. He urged himself to think clearly – it would save time. He admitted that he had not stopped thinking about her since he left Souarcy. He was visited by images of her at night or in the middle of a meeting with his tenant farmers or during a hunt – causing him to miss his mark. When he calculated the difference between their ages, he was shocked to discover that he was nearly twenty years her senior, and yet her deceased husband had been more than thirty years older than her. And besides, a man's age was of little consequence since his role was to provide for, honour and protect in exchange for love, obedience and a fecundity that would last his lifetime. Yes, but she was a widow, and the status of a widowed noblewoman with a child was without question one of the most favourable any lady could enjoy. If she possessed no fortune of her own, at least she would enjoy a dower, since it was unthinkable that a woman who had fulfilled her duties as both wife and mother could be left to fend for herself. Without a father or husband such a woman became mistress of her own destiny. This fortuitous status explained why many a noblewomen or burgher had no wish to remarry. Did Agnès de Souarcy subscribe to this way of thinking? He had no way of knowing. And anyway, who was to say she found him attractive or even simply agreeable?

After he had finished posing these troubling and unanswerable questions a black mood replaced the nervousness that was preventing him from finding any peace.

He brought his fist down on the table, almost upsetting the ink pot in the shape of a ship's hull.

A strumpet was what he needed. Attractive and glad to accept the money he offered her. A girl who would provoke no interest in him. A moment of paid pleasure, meaningless and unmemorable. He had already grown tired of the idea before taking it any further. He did not want a girl.

The announcement of Monge de Brineux interrupted his troubled thoughts.

'We have made some progress regarding the fifth and last victim.'

'Have you determined his identity?'

'Not as yet. However, he must have died a terrible death.'

'How so?'

'He almost certainly died from internal bleeding.'

'What proof have you?'

'The inside of his mouth was full of very fine cuts.[40] In my opinion the victim was given food containing crushed glass. By the time he realised, it was too late. The poor devil bled to death internally.'

'It is a method they use to kill wild animals in some countries. A truly terrible way to die. What of the other victims? Have you made any progress?'

'It is very slow. I sought the advice of a medical theologian at the Sorbonne.'

'And?'

'An awful lot of science and very little assistance.'

'I see. And what was his opinion?'

'Only that the victims died violently.'

'An inspired conclusion! He has solved the mystery for us!' said Artus sardonically. 'You would have done as well to seek the advice of my doctor, Joseph.'

'The problem with those people is that they never leave their amphitheatres, and they keep as far away as possible from their patients, or the corpses they are entrusted with, for fear of being contaminated. They are content to learn by rote and trot out what others discovered over a thousand years ago. They can quote Latin at you until your head is spinning, but if it is treatment you want for a boil or a corn on your foot …'

'We shall reach the bottom of this, Brineux, I assure you.'

'Yes, but when? How? At least four of the victims were friars. One was an emissary of our Holy Father Benoît XI who has just died, poisoned. This affair, which might have remained a local act of villainy, is taking on the proportions of a political incident. We must make progress, and quickly.'

For several days now Artus had feared this. The last thing the delicate situation between the French monarchy and the papacy needed was a papal emissary discovered burnt to death without any trace of fire.

Éleusie de Beaufort listened calmly to the young Dominican who had been announced earlier. The Extern Sister, Jeanne d'Amblin, her usually beaming face wearing an ominous expression of solemnity, had brought him to her study.

In common with her, Jeanne d'Amblin, Yolande de Fleury, Annelette Beaupré, the apothecary nun, and, in particular, Hedwige du Thilay, the treasurer nun,[41] whose uncle by marriage had perished in the slaughter at Carcassonne, were sufficiently intelligent women to be able to articulate, on occasion and in veiled terms, their disapproval of Rome's chosen methods for defending the purity of the faith. Doubtless others shared their reservations – Adélaïde or even Blanche de Blinot during her moments of lucidity – but they were more reticent. Éleusie found herself regretting, however, that the majority of her girls did not.

Indeed, despite her unquestioning faith and her obedience, the alarming evolution of the Inquisition upset the Abbess. Saving the souls of those who have strayed so that they might rejoin God's flock was of the utmost importance, and yet it remained inconceivable to her that friars should resort to torture and death in the name of Christ's love and tolerance. Naturally, they had no blood on their hands since those condemned were surrendered to the secular authorities for them to carry out the death sentence; but this expedient hypocrisy did not reassure her, especially now that a certain number of Grand Inquisitors presided over the torture sessions.

She recalled the courageous, nearly century-old warning Hilaire de Poitiers had given upon meeting Auxence de Milan:

I ask you who would call yourselves bishops: how did the Apostles ensure the purity of the Gospels? What powers did they depend upon in order to spread Christ's teachings? ... Alas, today ... the Church uses imprisonment and exile to force people to believe what once they believed in the face of imprisonment and exile.

Even so, these Dominicans and Franciscans had full powers and could exercise them over everybody, and that included her.

How handsome and radiant he was, this Brother Nicolas Florin. The ease with which he had requested that the convent extend him its hospitality for a month pointed to an order beneath the polite formalities. Strangely, no sooner had he entered her study than the Abbess had been seized by an almost uncontrollable feeling of revulsion. This had surprised her – she who was always so distrustful of instinctive responses. And yet there was something about this young man, although she could not put her finger on what it was, which alarmed her.

'You are compiling information for an inquiry, you say?'

'That is correct, Abbess. I would normally be accompanied by two brothers, but the urgency ...'

'I do not believe I can recall a single case of heresy in Perche, my son.'

'And what of sorcery and demonic possession, for I assume you must have had your share of succubi and incubi?'

'Who has not?'

He gave her an angelic smile, agreeing in a soft pained voice:

'A sad but true admission. Doubtless you understand that I cannot reveal to you the identity of the person I am investigating. You also know that our methods are wholly compassionate and just. I will duly inform the person concerned of their month's grace. If within this time they do not denounce themselves, their interrogation will commence. If, on the other hand, they confess to their sins, they will almost certainly be pardoned and their identity kept a secret in order to spare them the condemnation of their … neighbours.'

He clasped his beautiful long hands together and prayed that Agnès would maintain her innocence. If what he had heard about her was true, there was every chance that she would. And, if not, then he was prepared. He would simply claim that she had retracted her confession, relapsed heretics being considered the worst kind. None escaped the flames. Agnès de Souarcy's word counted for nothing against that of a Grand Inquisitor. The feudal Baron who merely wished to terrorise and disgrace his half-sister was in for a nasty surprise. Nicolas felt drunk on his own duplicity. He was powerful enough now to challenge and overrule the orders of a baron.

'It requires at least two witnesses to bring an accusation,' Éleusie de Beaufort insisted.

'Oh, I would not even be here if I did not have more than that. There again, as you know, our aim is above all to protect. And so our witnesses and their depositions remain a secret. We wish to spare them any possible reprisals.'

A dark-haired angel, his face tilted slightly towards his shoulder, his brow illuminated by an almost unearthly glow that reminded Éleusie of the light that shone through the mullioned windows in the abbey's Notre-Dame church. The long eyelashes curling towards the brow veiled with a bluish transparency the bottomless gaze, the gaze of death.

*

A mask. Raw red beneath the pale skin eaten away by vermin. Festering flesh, strips of greenish skin, viscous foul-smelling fluids. Liquefied cheeks, hollowed eye-sockets, rotting gums. Reddish carapaces, a mass of legs, hungry mouths and tenacious claws burrowing into flesh. The stench of rotting carcasses. A piercing shriek lifted the empty thorax and the ribcage gnawed by unforgiving teeth. A rat scuttled out, its snout red with blood. The beast was upon them.

Éleusie de Beaufort gripped the edge of her great desk with both hands, suppressing the scream she felt rising in her throat. A voice spoke to her from far away:

'Is anything the matter, Abbess?'

'A dizzy spell, nothing more,' she managed to reply before adding, 'You are welcome, my son. Pray excuse me for a few moments. It must be the heat ...'

He took his leave at once, and Éleusie remained standing alone in the middle of the vast study whose edges were beginning to recede.

They had come back. The infernal visions. There was nowhere she could seek protection from them now.

He was so young and handsome, so radiant, that Agnès foolishly thought he must be benevolent. When Adeline had come to announce in a stammering voice the arrival of a lord monk from Alençon who was waiting for her in the great hall, dressed in a beige cloak and a black robe, she had known immediately. She had paused briefly: it was too late to turn back now.

He was standing waiting, his hands clasped around his big wooden crucifix.

'Monsieur?'

'Brother Nicolas … I am attached to the headquarters of the Inquisition at Alençon.'

She raised her eyebrows, feigning surprise, struggling to calm her pounding heart. He smiled at her and it occurred to her that he had the most moving smile she had ever seen. Something resembling sadness seemed to well up in the Dominican's eyes, and he murmured in a pained voice:

'It has reached our ears, Madame my sister in Christ, that you once sheltered a heretic rather than surrender her to our justice. It has reached our ears that you brought up her posthumous son under circumstances that suggest the work of a demon.'

'You must be referring to a lady's maid by the name of Sybille who served me briefly before dying of weakness during childbirth. It was a deadly cold winter that year and claimed many lives.'

'Indeed, Madame. Everything points to her having been an escaped heretic.'

'Nonsense. They are the rumours of a jealous woman and I can even provide you with the name of your informant. I am a pious Christian ...'

He interrupted her with an elegant gesture of his hand.

'As your chaplain, Brother Bernard, would confirm?'

'The Abbess of Clairets as well as the Extern Sister, Jeanne d'Amblin, who is a frequent visitor here, would swear it before God.'

After a few days and some clever questioning at the abbey, Nicolas had arrived at the same conclusion. He had also resolved to put aside the charge of carnal relations with a man of God. He would use it only as a last resort. He moved on:

'We have not yet arrived at the trial stage, still less at the verdict. This is the time of grace, my sister.' He closed his eyes and his angelic face stiffened with pain. 'Confess. Confess and repent, Madame, for the Church is good and just and watches over you. The Church will pardon you. Nobody will know I have been here and you will have washed your soul of all its impurities.'

The Church would pardon her, but she would be handed over to the secular authorities who would confiscate her dower, her daughter and Clément. She hesitated, doubting her ability to withstand an inquisitorial interrogation, and decided to try to gain a little time.

'My brother ... I know nothing about the atrocious crimes of which I stand accused. However, your robes and your office inspire me with trust. Have I let myself be deceived? Am I guilty of having been too trusting? I must search my soul for the answer. Be that as it may, Clément was brought up to respect and love the Holy Church and has no knowledge of the deplorable error of his mother's ways ... if such they were.'

Replacing his crucifix in the inside pocket of his surcoat, he walked towards her, arms outstretched, a satisfied smile on his lips.

> *A mask … Raw red … eaten away by vermin … Reddish carapaces, a mass of legs, hungry mouths and tenacious claws burrowing into flesh. The stench of rotting carcasses … the ribcage gnawed by unforgiving teeth … A rat, its snout red with blood.*

The image was so real it made Agnès gasp. Where did they come from, these excruciating visions of death and suffering? The beast was before her. She stepped back.

Nicolas paused a few paces from Agnès, attempting to penetrate the mystery of the pretty face that suddenly looked so distraught. He had the fleeting impression that he had experienced this scene before, though he was unable to recall the precise circumstances. A feeling he had believed himself rid of forever made his throat go dry: fear. He stifled it and leapt at the chance to turn Agnès de Souarcy's strange reaction to his advantage.

'Have you strayed so far down the road to perdition that you fear the embrace of a man of God?'

'No,' she breathed in an almost inaudible voice.

This man was a personification of Evil. He loved Evil. She was certain of it, though she did not know how. And yet for the last few moments, since that horrific vision, she was no longer alone. A powerful shade was fighting beside her. More than one. She was filled with a strength she thought she had lost. She let herself be guided, replying boldly:

'No … I am taken aback by your assertion. Did Sybille deceive me? Did she take advantage of my kindness, my naivety? What a terrible thought. I am afraid that, if Clément were to learn the awful truth about his mother, it would destroy him,' she dissimulated with an ease imparted to her by the good shades.

They, too, compelled her with open arms towards this diabolical angel and made her clasp the shoulders of this man who repelled her in a gesture of love and trust.

He had not come here for her confession – he wanted her life, whispered the shades to Agnès, whose mind was now humming with voices that were not her own. Was one of them Clémence? Agnès could not tell.

As she relaxed her embrace the eyes staring back at her had become veiled with a kind of anger. The struggle threatened to be more prolonged than he had envisaged. If she confessed before the inquisitorial court that the lady's maid had been a heretic but insisted that her error had been made in good faith, the judges would be predisposed to leniency. She would be let off with a mere pilgrimage or, at worst, a few novenas. He could bid farewell to the Baron's hundred pounds – which he had had no intention of returning following the death of his half-sister, as well as the three hundred pledged to him by the mysterious messenger. He could say goodbye to his pleasure.

Then the anguish Nicolas had contrived to suppress returned, striking him with full force; his life was in danger should he fail. The cloaked figure had the power to show no mercy. Whereas before he had merely despised his future victim – his toy – now he was beginning to detest her.

No sooner had he left than Agnès slumped to her knees. She begged the voices to come back, for they had grown silent since the Inquisitor's departure.

Was she losing her mind? She prayed for what seemed like

hours. She was in the grip of a sort of delirium. At that very moment, she would have given anything for the voices to live in her again, to soothe her.

'My angel,' she sobbed quietly.

A sigh, like a caress, inside her head.

Clément found Agnès huddled on the stone floor in the main hall. A moment of sheer panic. He rushed to her side as it struck him she might be dead. She was sleeping. The child stroked the thick plaits coiled round his mistress's head and beseeched her:

'Madame! Pray wake up, Madame. What is the matter? Why …'

'Hush! He was here, and it was Evil who embraced me. You must leave here immediately, Clément.' Sensing a mounting protest, she added in a firm voice, 'It is an order and I will not accept any argument.' Softening all of a sudden, she continued, still seated on the floor, 'You must do as I say out of love for me. The inquisitorial procedure has begun.'

Clément's eyes grew wide with fright and he trembled:

'My God …'

'Hush and listen to me. Something extraordinary has occurred. Something so extraordinary that I hesitate to share it with you for I myself am so bewildered that I can barely gather my thoughts.'

'What was it, Madame?'

'A presence, or rather several presences … It is very difficult to describe. The realisation that I was being helped by some kind of benevolent force.'

'By God?'

'No. But whatever they might be they inspired me with a feeling of confidence, a strength that tells me I am able to defeat this evil being, this Inquisitor named Nicolas Florin. He is … a personification of the worst, Clément. How can I explain it to you? Eudes is wicked but this man is evil. You must disappear, for while you have been my strength all these years, now you are my biggest weakness. You know as well as I. If that man manages to persuade the superstitious fools he will appoint as judges that you are an incubus, your youth will be no protection, on the contrary. And if he finds out that we have concealed your true sex, the outcome will be even worse. His judgement will be implacable in their eyes for you are the child of a heretic. And then they will believe anything that monster tells them. You must leave, Clément. For my sake.'

'What about Mathilde?'

'I shall ask the Abbess of Clairets to take her in for a while.'

'But I can …' he tried to argue.

'I beg you, Clément! You can help me by leaving. Go quickly.'

'Would it really be helping you, Madame? Are you not just trying to protect me?'

'I am trying to protect us all.'

'But where will I go, Madame?'

Her immediate response was a despairing smile:

'Of course nobody will rush to our aid. The only person I could think of approaching for protection is Artus d'Authon and I do not know whether he will grant it to me on your behalf. If he refuses for fear of the consequences, flee, it does not matter where. Swear to me on your soul. Swear!'

He paused then yielded before her insistence:

'I swear.'

She clasped the child to her, and he buried his face in her rosemary-scented, silky hair. A terrible grief made him want to burst into tears, to cling on to his lady. He felt as if all his strength were being sucked out of him. Without her he was lost, without her he knew not which way to turn. For her he could do anything, of that he was certain. But the huge void that grew even as she spoke paralysed his body and crushed his spirit.

'Thank you, my sweet child. I shall write a letter for you to give the Comte. If he should refuse to hide you ... I have saved some gold coins, not many but enough for you to reach a port and sail to England – the only country that has not yielded to the temptation of the Inquisition. Go and saddle a horse and fetch some supplies and join me in my chamber.'

When she released him from her embrace, he felt he was dying there at her feet.

Did she sense it? She whispered in his ear:

'I am not afraid any more, Clément. I will prevail – for your sake and mine, for everyone's sake, and for the sake of the good shades. Never forget that you are always with me even though we are apart. Never forget that I am guided by love and when love fights it overcomes all. Never forget.'

'I will not forget, Madame. I love you so.'

'Prove it to me by not coming back until I have defeated this creature of darkness.'

In a few short years Clément would have grown into a young woman. The deception that had allowed Agnès to keep her by her side would be too difficult to maintain. What would be Clément's, Clémence's, reaction when she discovered the whole truth about her birth? The weighty secret shared by three women, two of whom were now dead.

In a few short years ... if God allowed them both to live.

As she watched the child leave, Agnès was surprised by how much he had grown in a few months. His breeches reached halfway up his legs and his heels were sticking out over the backs of his clogs. She felt absurdly cross with herself for not having noticed it before. Suddenly it seemed vital to her to remedy the situation before his departure – as though such a simple gesture were a clear link to the future, as though it were proof they would soon be reunited.

And what if she was deluding herself ? What if she was unable to survive an interrogation, to defeat that beautiful infernal creature? What if she never saw Clément again? What if she perished? What if Comte Artus was merely a pleasant façade concealing a coward? What if he sent Clément away or, worse still, delivered him into the hands of the Inquisition?

Stop! Stop this instant!

A month would pass, a month of grace. She had time to reflect, to prepare her defence, to think of other solutions. Clément had already helped her to do so one evening when he came back from one of his mysterious night-time forays.

A courage she had not expected to feel since the shades grew silent returned. She was no longer alone, even though she had chosen to send Clément away. She had not been lying to him. He was at this moment her greatest weakness. She felt capable of resisting anything except a threat to his young life. Now he was gone, out of harm's way, she could confront them. A strange thought occurred to her, a thought which up until a few days before she would never have had. She would show no mercy. Eudes had woven the web that was closing in on her. If she survived this ordeal, she would make him pay, ruthlessly. The time for forgiveness, for moderation was over.

She went to the kitchens and calmly ordered Adeline to find some clothes that would fit Clément and to pack a bundle of food for him, without satisfying the girl's silent curiosity.

Château d'Authon-du-Perche, August 1304

Torrential rain had threatened to ruin the harvest, which took place later in Perche than in Beauce. Everybody had pitched in, working night and day to beat the storms.

Artus had galvanised his troop of peasants and serfs, riding from one farm to another, scolding some, praising others. They had watched him roll up the sleeves of his fine linen tunic, pacify two enormous Perche horses harnessed to a cart and drive them to collect the harvested wheat. The women had marvelled at his physical strength and the men admired him for not shying away from such ignoble and punishing work. He had shared their meals of cider, coarse bread and bacon, and, like them, had collapsed onto the haystacks for an hour's rest and sworn like a soldier that 'this accursed weather won't get the better of me, by God!' They had worked for two whole days and nights without stopping.

Artus d'Authon had returned worn out, soaked to the skin, covered in grime and stinking. Before collapsing fully dressed onto the bed he had felt comforted by the fact that since morning he had hardly thought about her at all.

He slept through the night and most of the next day. When he awoke, Ronan, who had served his father, had drawn him a hot bath and was waiting armed with brush, soap and bath sheets.

'Those hay fleas have eaten you alive, my Lord,' observed the old man.

'In which case they must all be dead,' Artus joked. 'Careful, you evil tormentor, my eyes aren't dirty so don't put soap in them!'

'Forgive me, my Lord, you're covered in grime and, well, it's very stubborn grime.'

'It is the real sort, the sort that comes from the earth. I am hungry, Ronan, very hungry. Are you planning to torture me much longer with this brush?'

'There's still your hair to do, my Lord. I was leaving the best until last. A young boy arrived last night. He seemed exhausted.'

'Who?'

'His name is Clément, and he claims he had the honour of meeting you at his mistress's house.'

Artus d'Authon rose suddenly to his feet, causing a wave of soapy grey water to spill over the sides of the huge tub and soak the floorboards. He cried, almost shouted:

'What did you do with him? Is he still here?'

'Your hair, my Lord, your hair! I shall tell you the rest if you sit down quietly in the tub and let me clean that ... stuff on your head.'

Ronan had witnessed worse, first with the late Comte d'Authon and then with Artus, whom he had known since he was born.

'Don't speak to me like a nanny,' grumbled the Comte.

'Why not since that's what I am?'

'I was afraid you would say that.'

Artus adored Ronan. He embodied Artus's living memories – the most wonderful and most dreadful. He was the only one who had braved his master's murderous rage following the death of little Gauzelin. Without saying a word he had doggedly carried on taking Artus's supper up to his chamber, despite his master's threats if he continued. The only time Artus had ever begged for God's forgiveness was on account of Ronan, on account of the slap he had given his faithful servant that had sent him crashing to the floor. Ronan had picked himself up, the imprint of Artus's fingers reddening on his cheek. He had stared at the Comte, a terrible sadness in his eyes, and said:

'Until the morning, then, my Lord. I hope the night is kind to you.'

The following day an even more haggard-looking Artus had apologised, his head bowed in obediance. Ronan, his eyes brimming with tears, had walked over and embraced Artus for the first time since he was a child:

'My poor boy, my poor boy, it is a terrible injustice ... I beg you during this dreadful ordeal not to forget your goodness and generosity of spirit, for if you do then death will have triumphed on all fronts.'

It was no doubt thanks to that slap that Artus's rage had abated. He had continued along the path of life.

'Quick, tell me, what did you do with him?' Artus repeated, wincing as Ronan scrubbed his head hard enough to take the skin off.

'I put him in one of the outbuildings and gave him some food, a blanket and a straw mattress until I could find out what you wanted to do with him. One of the farm hands saw to his horse. The boy has a letter. He showed me the roll of parchment, but refused to give it to me. It is addressed to you and no one else. His story sounded true enough. I hope I did not act naively regarding the boy.'

'No. You did well. Gently does it – it's my hair, not a horse's mane.'

'It could easily be mistaken for one, my Lord.'

'So what about this Clément? What story was this?'

'His mistress ordered him to come here to you.' Ronan sighed before continuing, 'The boy's terrified, and I think I am right in saying that he did not wish to leave her side, only she commanded it. He is waiting for you.'

'Have you done with that brush yet? There we are. I'm as shiny as a new gold coin!'

'Talking of gold coins ...'

Ronan paused. His voice had a strange catch in it as he continued:

'He asked me how much the meal I gave him last night would cost. He explained that he had seven gold coins – his mistress's entire fortune, which she entrusted to him when he left. He said he did not wish to squander what she had worked so hard to save, and would prefer to eat only a little bread and soup. I had great difficulty trying to convince him that I was not an inn keeper and that he was your guest.'

Artus closed his eyes, pretending they were stinging from the soap. The heart he had believed lifeless skipped a beat. He was overwhelmed by a sweet pain raging in his breast. His life was so empty of love it felt as if he were discovering it anew: the boundless love Clément had for his lady, the love she felt for the brave boy, his own love for Agnès. Seven gold coins. The whole of her tiny fortune – barely the price of a handsome coat with a fur trim.

'Yes, yes, I've finished,' Ronan informed him. 'And yes, the boy is fed and rested and waiting for you, my Lord.'

Artus stepped out of his bath and, hopping about impatiently, allowed Ronan to dry him.

Artus walked up and down, hunched forward, his hands clasped behind his back. The large blue-green eyes followed his every movement. Clément had explained the situation in a few words. The Inquisition, Mabile's supposed revelations, the Dominican's visit, the time of grace dwindling like the grains of sand in an hourglass. He had sobbed when he related Agnès's fear that he would be arrested and tortured, and how she had made him swear on his soul to go away and not come back, to flee, leaving her to face the Inquisition alone. And then he had had to stop, for his tears drowned out his words – and he was so afraid for her. The Comte d'Authon walked over to his desk again and read Agnès's letter for the tenth time.

Monsieur,

Believe me when I tell you I regret the anguish I am about to cause you. Believe me also when I say that I am your humble and loyal under-vassal and that your decision will be mine.

I find myself at present in a dangerous and very delicate situation. It is my destiny to confront it and I am prepared – at least I hope I am. God will be my guide.

This is not the motive of my appeal, but I am indeed appealing to you. You know Clément. He has served me faithfully and is very dear to my heart. He is a pure and loyal soul and as such deserves protection.

When I understood that I must send him away for his own safety, is it not curious that only your name should come to my mind?

If you decide after hearing the boy that you cannot accept Clément into your household, I beg you, with all due obedience and respect, to let him go and to inform no one. I have given him seven gold coins, all that I possess.

He should be able to survive for some time on that sum. I
would be eternally grateful to you.

I am guilty of none of the monstrosities of which I stand
accused and Clément even less so. If I am right in thinking
I know the origin of this plot that threatens my life, I
have a vague feeling that it is no longer in the hands of
its perpetrator.

Whatever the case, Monsieur, rest assured that the
memory of your visit to Souarcy is the most agreeable one
I have had since I was widowed. In truth, and if I may be
so bold, I avow that I have not experienced such pleasant
moments since death took Madame Clémence from me –
may she rest in everlasting peace.

May God protect you, and may He protect Clément.
Your very sincere and obedient vassal,
Agnès de Souarcy.

The Comte was plunged into a maelstrom of conflicting emotions
that prevented him from speaking to this oddly slender boy, who
seemed so young, standing before him, his head held high, his
gaze steady even as he trembled with fear.

But why had she not sought his protection herself ? He could
have intervened, made this Inquisitor withdraw his accusations.
Admittedly they wielded great power, but it did not extend to
angering the King of France, and for her Artus was prepared to
lower himself to request the King to intervene. For her. Philip
would have understood. He was a great king and a man of honour
and of his word when the affairs of state were not in the balance.
And, moreover, he was not overly fond of the Church or of the
Inquisition, even if he used them as his needs dictated.

This woman bowled him over, exasperated him, humbled him, moved him in a way nobody else ever had. Her courage was equalled only by her reckless blindness.

Did she really believe she could fight a Grand Inquisitor alone? With what weapons?

No, she was not blind. She was as Monge had described her – a lynx. She was using guile, protecting her young, exposing her throat in order to distract her enemy momentarily.

Did she really believe she could turn on him, bury her teeth in his accursed flesh? She could not stand up to them. They had full powers and enjoyed complete immunity since each absolved the other of his sins whatever they might be.

What if she knew this? What if it was deliberate suicide? He was enough of a huntsman to know that female lynxes were capable of it, and when this happened he would stop the chase and let the animal go. Once, one had turned after fleeing a few paces and gazed at him with her yellow eyes before vanishing like a ghost into the thicket. Artus had been struck by the mysterious certainty that the animal had been acknowledging, perhaps even thanking him.

The predator Clément had described would never retract his claws and release his prey. Agnès stood no chance against him.

His fist struck the table and he cried out:

'No!'

Clément did not flinch.

'We must find a way out,' mumbled Artus. 'But how? We have no pope. Any petition, even from the King himself, would be lost in the Vatican's maze of officialdom, each in turn giving the excuse of there being no pontiff as a justification for doing nothing.'

Clément waited, motionless, expecting he knew not what from this man – a miracle perhaps. He suggested:

'Was not the King's brother, Monsieur Charles de Valois, awarded the county of Alençon last year?'

'Yes, he was.'

'The headquarters of the Inquisition to which Nicolas Florin is attached are at Alençon,' insisted the child.

'If I thought that an intervention by the royal family might help us, I would choose Philip, not our good Charles, who is not known for his political finesse. My boy … Comte d'Alençon or no, Charles can do nothing. The Inquisition takes orders from no one but the Pope.'

'And we have no pope,' repeated Clément.

His voice was quaking, and he bit his lip to stop himself from continuing, but Artus must have read his thoughts and bellowed:

'No! Cast that idea from your mind! She is not lost! I am not done thinking about it yet. Leave me now. I need peace in order to reflect and your deafening silence prevents me.'

Clément left without a sound.

Reflect.

The realisation he had just come to while he was speaking to the young boy with the blue-green eyes stunned him by its simplicity, its intensity. He would do anything to save her. It was accompanied by his increasing lucidity, cynicism even, as regards almost the entire religious apparatus. Faith was quickly set aside when power and money came into play. Artus knew that some Inquisitors could be bought, and this one was no exception to the rule since Eudes had clearly paid him for his services. All he needed to do, then, was to offer a higher price.

He would leave for Alençon the next day.

Artus was stunned by the young man's perfect beauty. The image Agnès and Clément had painted of him was by no means exaggerated. The Inquisitor's unctuousness was so predictable that under any other circumstances he might have found it amusing.

'Your visit is an honour for me, Monsieur, lowly monk that I am.'

'A lowly monk! You judge yourself too harshly, Monsieur.'

Nicolas resented this noble who put him at a secular level, denuding him of his religious aura. All the more so, since his polite phrase had permitted the Comte not to return the honour. He did not doubt that the Comte's choice of words had been deliberate.

During the journey there, Artus had mulled over the best way to tackle the Inquisitor. Should he broach his subject gradually or go straight to the point? His deep uneasiness, and the fact that he wanted above all to avoid giving the other man the impression he was unsure of himself, made him choose the second strategy.

'I understand you recently went to notify a lady – a friend of mine – of her time of grace, did you not?'

'Madame de Souarcy?'

Artus nodded. He sensed the Inquisitor's uncertainty. Nicolas cursed that fool Larnay who had assured him that the Comte d'Authon would not intervene in favour of the lady. He recalled the words, and the warning, of the figure in the dark cloak and quickly calmed down. What could the Comte do in the face of such power, even if he did enjoy the friendship of the King? He replied in a soft voice:

'I was unaware that Madame de Souarcy was a friend of yours, Monsieur.'

It occurred to Artus that had Agnès not opened his eyes to Nicolas Florin through Clément, he would almost certainly have considered him above suspicion. After all, if evil were not so deeply seductive, how did it win over so many adepts?

'She is.' Artus paused then continued, 'I do not doubt that you are a man of faith …'

A pair of blinking eyes responded.

'… and intelligence. The motive for Monsieur de Larnay's anger at his half-sister is not one with which a pious man of honour would wish to be associated. It is of a personal nature and … how should I say … reprehensible in the extreme.'

'What are you trying to tell me?' said the offended Florin, amused at his own duplicity.

'He failed to mention that aspect to you, and the true nature of his resentment.'

'Indeed!' agreed Nicolas, who had understood perfectly that Eudes was not motivated by religious zeal and the defence of the purity of the faith.

'In short, he has made you waste your precious time,' continued Artus, 'for which I insist on compensating you. Nobody is aware yet that an inquiry has been instigated against Madame de Souarcy. Therefore you may call a halt to it.'

Nicolas was enjoying himself greatly. Power. Power was finally his – the power to slap down the Comte, to send him packing. The power to be his superior. He gave a clumsy show of wounded indignation in order to make it clear to the other man that he was mocking him.

'Monsieur … I hardly dare believe that you are offering me money in order to … Do you imagine that I would have been to see Madame de Souarcy had I not been convinced of the legitimacy of her half-brother's suspicions concerning her? I am indeed a man of God. I have given Him my labour and my life.'

'How much?'

'Monsieur, I must ask you to leave here at once and never return. You have offended both me and the Church. Out of respect for your reputation I bid you, let it rest.'

Artus understood the implicit threat and, while it did not unduly alarm him, something else made him feel far more uneasy. What hidden power was protecting Nicolas Florin, making him feel so unassailable that he could allow himself the luxury of mocking a lord? Certainly not that cipher Eudes de Larnay.

He recalled Agnès's suspicion: something far darker and more fearsome was at work behind these accusations against her.

On the road back to Authon, Artus came to a decision.

If necessary, Nicolas Florin would die – an inconspicuous death that would have all the appearance of being an accident. He was clear in his mind that the annihilation of harmful vermin did not constitute a crime. His mouth set in a grimace. All the more so as he would afterwards turn the vermin's weapons against Agnès's enemies. He would loudly proclaim that God's judgement had intervened. That God had punished Nicolas for his inclemency and injustice. In His infinite wisdom and His magnificent goodness He had spared the innocent Agnès. While most people now had reservations regarding divine intervention, which had never once been proven during the many trials by ordeal,[42] none would dare contradict him.

Artus relaxed and Ogier shook his mane in harmony with his master's changed mood.

If necessary, he was prepared. Though he hoped a reversal of fortune would spare him from having to bloody his hands outside the field of honourable combat.

Louvre Palace, Paris, August 1304

The candlelight cast eerie shadows on the ugly walls of the office cluttered with registers. Monsieur de Nogaret certainly had an austere notion of comfort. There was little in the way of wall hangings to protect the occupants from the cold and damp. In fact there was only one that covered the large stones behind Nogaret's work table. Francesco de Leone kicked himself for not having thought of it before. Taking advantage of the absences of the King's Counsellor, he had searched for hours, finding nothing of any interest. And then, the previous evening, as he was preparing to go to bed after the meagre supper Giotto Capella had had sent up to him, an image flashed through his mind of a pack of dogs on a dark-blue background, their flanks hollow from exertion, their open mouths highlighted with red stitching.

He lifted the tapestry. Flush with the stone was a small metal plate. A padlocked safe set in the wall. Leone studied it. He had opened enough prison doors and safes considered foolproof by their inventors for this lock not to present any great difficulty. He pulled a fine metal rod out of his breeches and skilfully opened it within seconds. Even if his intrusion were discovered, which he doubted, he would be gone within a few hours, and Capella would have to deal with Nogaret's men. Inside the tiny space were scrolls of parchment and a bag bulging with what must have been gold pieces. A slim notebook bound in black calfskin caught his attention. The pages were covered in the Counsellor's narrow, hurried script. Francesco skimmed through it. The State secrets it contained, if divulged, would cause repercussions throughout the whole of Christendom. And so the holy crusade against the Albigensians had been a pretext to remove Raymond VI of Toulouse, recover the Languedoc and allow the lords of the North to carve out the southern fiefs as they wished. And so, despite the bitter defeat at Courtrai the previous year, King Philip's army was preparing for battle again in a few days' time in Flanders. He felt a painful wrench in his heart when he came across the rows of figures spread over several pages: an estimate of the fortunes of the Templars and the Order of the Hospitallers. So it was true: their suppression was planned. The Templars, who were wealthier, as well as more vulnerable, would be the first to go. Then it would be the turn of the Hospitallers.

There was a sound of footsteps close by. Francesco replaced the tapestry and unsheathed his dagger. They approached the door then died away along the corridor. He must hurry.

Underneath the rows of figures were a few brief comments dotted with questions marks:

> *Exemption from taxes granted to Templars? Will hopefully increase anger and resentment on the part of the populace.*
>
> *Association with heretics or demons? Secret dealings with the infidel? Sodomy? Perjury, blasphemy or idolatry? Human sacrifice, sacrifice of children?*

So the prior, Arnaud de Viancourt, had been right: exemption from taxes had only been granted to the Templars so as to precipitate their downfall. As for the rest, what did it mean? Were these authentic suspicions, or a list of imaginary and interchangeable charges for King Philip to make use of when the time came to justify an inquiry and a trial? The fate of the two great military orders was sealed. Arnaud de Viancourt and the Grand-Master had been right. When would sentence be passed?

Leone struggled with the anger and grief choking him and read on.

There were other sets of figures – a detailed inventory right down to the payment of a few pennies to spies in service, which accounted for some of Monsieur Philippe de Marigny's expenditure of Treasury money. Thus he learnt that Squire Thierry had received a hundred pennies for examining the contents of a cardinal's letters, and a launderer by the name of Ninon eighty for inspecting a prelate's bed linen in order to ascertain whether the man was ill before approaching him. Monsieur de Nogaret was a meticulous and prudent man. Finally he came across two names underlined in a list including four others that had been crossed out: Renaud de Cherlieu, Cardinal of Troyes, and Bertrand de Got,* Archbishop of Bordeaux.

The Knight replaced the notebook and closed the padlock.

He regretted not having more time to peruse the other documents. What did it matter in the end? Only one kingdom mattered to him, that of God. Men would continue to tear each other apart over stupidities blown out of all proportion. Soon the truth would be clear for all to see, and nobody would be able to pretend that it wasn't there any more simply by closing their eyes.

Francesco de Leone left the Louvre. The night was fortuitously dark. The stench in the streets, intensified by the seasonal heat, did not bother him any more than the odour emanating from the mass of humanity crowded into hovels.

He had a few minutes left in which to compose a coded letter to Arnaud de Viancourt. He must then deliver it to a priest friend at the Église Saint-Germain-l'Auxerrois who would make sure it reached Cyprus. The content was to the point and would make little sense to the uninitiated.

> *Dearest Cousin,*
>
> *My research into angelology is proceeding at a slower pace than I had anticipated and than you had hoped, despite the inestimable help provided by the writings of Augustine – above all the remarkable City of God. The second order[43] of Dominations, Virtues and Powers is extremely difficult to comprehend in its entirety and no less so the third order of Principalities, Archangels and Angels. Nevertheless, I persevere in earnest and hope that in my next missive I shall be able to inform you of important advances in my work.*
>
> *Your humble and indebted Guillaume.*

Arnaud de Viancourt would understand from this that Leone had discovered the names of six French prelates who enjoyed the King of France's backing, but that he needed more time to unearth the identity of those most likely to be elected pope. The Knight did not mention the catastrophic discovery of the planned demise of the Templar and Hospitaller orders. He must reflect more on the best form of counter-attack.

He left the little church[44] that stood near the Seine less than an hour later. The horse he had left with an ostler was waiting for him, together with his meagre baggage.

South to Perche, the commandery at Arville and Clairets Abbey. South to the Sign.

The tall figure scaled the walled enclosure around the abbey, placing its feet in the crevices as though it knew exactly where the mortar was worn away between the rough stones. It crept quietly along Notre-Dame church and made directly for the long building containing the Abbess's chambers and the nuns' dormitories.

Éleusie de Beaufort woke up with a start. She had had difficulty sleeping since the arrival of that creature she so feared and detested, and since the hallucination that had revealed to her his true nature. Nicolas Florin was, without doubt, an emanation of the Dark Forces. The Abbess had just drifted into sleep, although troubled by impenetrable nightmares, when a repetitive scratching at the window of her study, next to her bedchamber, had wrenched her back to consciousness. She pulled herself out of bed and walked unsteadily into the adjoining room. She paused, fearful. Who was that man out on the stone ledge? How had he contrived to be there? She saw him raise his hand and pull back his cowl to reveal his face.

'Jesus be praised …'

She hurried to open the window. The figure hopped nimbly into the room and took her in its arms.

'Aunt, how happy I am to see you again at last! Shall we go next door? Let me take a better look at you.'

'Francesco, you scared me out of my wits! I hope nobody saw you. The majority of my girls are not strictly cloistered.'

Her delight at seeing him and embracing him was so great she cried out:

'What joy! You seem to have grown even taller. Oh! I have so many things to tell you, so many dreadful things, so many riddles I hardly know where to begin.'

'The night is still young, aunt.'

'My God ... The emissary they found burnt to death but with no trace of any fire, my vanished letter, the Pope's death by poisoning, Agnès de Souarcy the object of an inquisitorial inquiry, falsely accused by someone, we suppose, for she is certainly innocent, the visions that have returned and are driving me mad, the Inquisitor, Nicolas Florin, who as he speaks to me changes into a repulsive flesh-eating insect. He has installed himself here in the abbey. You must on no account let him or any of my nuns see you. Little Mathilde de Souarcy is here and her uncle insists on taking her.' She let out a dry sob that caught in her throat, causing her to cough. 'Oh Francesco, Francesco, I thought I would never see you again and that all was lost. My nephew, my dear sweet nephew.'

A look of contentment flashed across Éleusie's pretty face, and she observed:

'You look more and more like your mother, my sister. Did you know she was the prettiest of us all? Pious, charming Claire. Her name could not have suited her more.'

Francesco had grown tense at the mention of another name. He led the Abbess into her bedchamber. The study windows overlooked the courtyard and they risked being seen.

'You say Agnès de Souarcy is threatened with an inquisitorial inquiry?'

'That evil man Florin refused to divulge her name when he arrived. It was Madame de Souarcy herself who confirmed it to me over two weeks ago now, when she came to implore me to look after her daughter. Our guest mistress, Thibaude de

Gartempe, has taken the girl under her wing, but Mathilde is proving unruly.'

'What more did Madame de Souarcy tell you?'

Éleusie sat down on the edge of her bed and clasped her hands together. She was shivering. A deadly cold coursed through her veins despite the heat of the past few days. She saw in it a sign of her impending demise. But this coming end did not worry her, for there was no end. She was more afraid of not having the time to help her nephew.

'She said very little. She was aware the Inquisitor was staying with us and was concerned lest she compromise my situation in relation to him. Nicolas Florin's foul odour pollutes the air and suffocates us – well, some of us anyway. Jeanne, our Extern Sister, has never been so long about her rounds and spends as little time in the abbey as possible. Annelette Beaupré, our apothecary nun, no longer leaves her herbarium, and gentle Adélaïde stays close to her pots and spit as if her life depended on it. As for my good Blanche, the silent reveries her age permits grow longer every day. There are plenty of others who let themselves be taken in by the perfect façade of that insidious creature. Indeed, he is so beautiful, so refined and so devout that I even wonder sometimes whether I am not losing my mind in suspecting the worst of him. He has the face of an angel. I dare not confide in my friends for fear of placing them in an awkward position. And besides, most of those whom I sense are on my side have no doubt found the right solution in fleeing. However, some of my girls surprise and worry me. Berthe de Marchiennes, our cellarer … I knew I should have got rid of her when I first arrived at Clairets. As for Emma de Pathus, the schoolmistress, her brother is a Dominican monk and an Inquisitor at Toulouse. I do not trust one inch these alleged purists who have never experienced doubt.'

Éleusie sighed, her eyes gazing off into he knew not what space before continuing:

'I shall not list all those of whom I am unsure: Thibaude de Gartempe and even the delightful Yolande de Fleury ... Did it take this creature coming into our midst for me to discover that I knew some of them only as a smile and a face? I am just beginning to reach an understanding of what lies in their hearts.'

She was straying from the point, but Francesco sensed her relief at being able to confide these secrets and waited.

She started suddenly, exclaiming:

'I have forgotten my duties as your second mother. Are you hungry?'

For a split second the Knight felt the immense burden he had been carrying for so long lighten. A wave of infinitesimal memories, warm and pleasant, washed over him from his Éleusie years, as he referred to them. The years that followed the horror.

Éleusie, sweet Éleusie, and her husband Henri de Beaufort had taken him in after the death of his father and the massacre of his mother and sister at Acre. Éleusie had brought him up with love and care, in place of Claire, whose memory she evoked daily in order that the child keep the image of his mother alive. Éleusie, who with her ceaseless love had contrived to soothe a little the terrible pain of the child he still was. He had clung to her and it was she no doubt who had saved him from developing a desire for vengeance. He owed her his soul. He owed her more than his life, and how good it felt to owe her so much.

'I am famished, for I have eaten nothing since I left Paris last night. But my stomach can wait. Speak to me of Agnès de Souarcy and the deaths of these messengers.'

Éleusie related what Agnès had told her and what she thought she had understood from her silences, and went on to tell of Eudes de Larnay and his destructive passion, Mathilde, Sybille and her heretical past, the repulsive role played by Mabile, and, above all, Clément and his devotion to his mistress, before concluding:

'As for the messengers, I received only one. As I explained to the Chief Bailiff, Monge de Brineux, the others never came to the abbey. Do you suppose they were on their way to see me when they encountered their killer? The thought torments me. For if so, then what became of the missives they were relaying from Benoît to me? Did they fall into the hands of our enemies? Is there some connection between their contents and the Pope's recent poisoning? What were their contents? Now that they have murdered our dear Holy Father we have no way of knowing. Day and night my mind is assailed by questions I am unable to find the answers to.'

Daylight was tentatively beginning to push back the darkness when they entered the secret library. They had both agreed on this hiding place, where he would be out of sight of the Inquisitor and the nuns and able to consult the rare manuscripts he had purchased from that crook, Gachelin Humeau.

Éleusie de Beaufort took advantage of the pre-dawn lull to go down to the kitchens and fetch some food for her nephew.

She then took an hour's sleep, free from nightmares, awakening just before lauds. The peace she felt filled her with wonder, like a sign. Death could come, she had fulfilled her duty. Francesco had returned.

What must be would be.

The light was fading when Leone awoke. He stretched and groaned, his body sore from the hardness of the flagstones, which was barely attenuated by the two hangings he had laid one on top of the other to form a mattress.

He was surprised to find a water jar and a wooden basin beside him. His aunt had attended to his toilet before going about her various tasks.

Leone immediately spotted the Knight Eustache de Rioux's distinguished notebook on top of some heavy volumes that filled one of the shelves. Eustache, his godfather in the order, who had guided his first steps as a Knight. Eustache, one of the seven Hospitallers who survived the siege of Acre.

A series of the kind of coincidences that only occur during the most terrible events had placed in the Knight de Rioux's hands the revelations which he had consigned to those pages. During the massive assault on the Temple Keep, Eustache, already twice wounded, sensed that all was lost and the slaughter was about to commence. He was ready to die in combat to defend the 'lambs', as he called them, and his faith. Death meant nothing to him since he had already sacrificed his life when he joined the Order of the Hospitallers. Enemy soldiers killing one another, whether they were friars or not, was for him part of the cycle of life. But not all these women and children … If he managed to save even a handful of them, then his life would not have been in vain; he offered it willingly in exchange for theirs. Accompanied by two Knights of the Order of the Templars, he had made one more attempt to break out, leading a flock of panic-stricken women and children into the tunnels that came out near the beaches – near to where the Frankish ships were anchored off the coast, unable to reach harbour due to rough seas. By then the Temple Keep, a veritable fortress made up of five towers and considered impregnable because it had resisted longer than the New Tower of Madame de Blois, had begun to collapse and a mass of rocks as high as a man had fallen, blocking all the exits. Eustache de Rioux had tried hopelessly to calm the twenty-odd women and thirty-odd children who had followed him. His warnings and prayers were drowned out by the cries of the children clinging to their mothers' skirts, and by the women's sobbing and occasional outbursts of hysteria. In every crowd there is always one man or woman who believes they know best, and whose incompetence and stupidity is matched only by their self-assurance. They are the ones who drive the herd over the cliff's edge to their death below. And that is what happened. Eustache de Rioux would never forget the tall, skinny woman whose name he never knew. She had exhorted the women to surrender, insisting they should trust the infidel soldiers to spare their lives. He had shouted at her, almost struck her. They had without exception followed her, dragging their children behind them. Eustache, beside himself with rage at the stupid woman, had refused to escort them back to the slaughter. In contrast, the two Knights Templar had gone after them, despite the certain knowledge that none of their little flock would escape. As if proof were needed, the older of the two had turned towards Eustache and handed him a notebook stained with his own blood, which he had been carrying under his surcoat next to his skin. In a hopeless but brave voice he had murmured:

'My brother ... the end is near. My whole life's research is contained within these pages. I owe much of it to the tireless efforts of a few other Templars. It was born of an encounter in the souks of Jerusalem with a Bedouin from whom I purchased a roll of papyrus written in Aramaic. It did not take me long to realise that I had in my possession one of the holiest texts in the whole of civilisation. I kept it hidden in a safe place – at one of our commanderies. A series of other events ensued, events so incredible they could not have been simple coincidences. They convinced me that I, that we, were not suffering from a delusion or some other form of insanity. Time is running out. This quest far outweighs me and must not be allowed to perish here with me. You are a man of God, of war and of honour. You will know what to do with it. My life has been directed by a higher force and I believe I was meant to give you this notebook on this day in this place and that none of it has been fortuitous. Live, my friend, I beg you. Live for the love of God and continue the sublime quest. Pray for those of us who are about to die.'

They had disappeared around a bend in the collapsed tunnel. The battle raged above. Cries mingled with the whistle of stones launched from catapults and the clash of blades and arrows raining down.

In the now deserted passage, Eustache collapsed to the damp earth floor, sobbing like a baby and clutching the thick notebook of worn leather. Why was he not up there with the others, fighting destiny alongside them? Why was he not sacrificing his life in a lost battle?

The Knight of Light and Grace Eustache de Rioux had survived and returned to Cyprus. As soon as he arrived on the island refuge, overwhelmed by the scope and complexity of the quest, Rioux had sought the man who must take up the burdensome torch with him and continue bearing it after him. A very young man, still almost an adolescent, had crossed his path by a curious route. Curious because from its very inception it was the tradition in the novice's family for the men to join the Order of the Templars. It was almost inevitable, therefore, that he would do likewise. And yet he had requested to join the Hospitallers. When Eustache asked him why this was, the young man had been at a loss to reply. Of course, he argued, the element of caring for the poor and sick had influenced him, but if he were to be honest, his choice had been guided by an intuition. Rioux had seen in this the sign that they should continue their path together.

They had copied out the notebook belonging to the Knight Templar who had died at Acre, and in an attempt to unlock its secrets had scoured the libraries of the world to try to penetrate its many mysteries. Some of these had gradually revealed themselves, though the majority had remained stubbornly hidden.

The Knight Eustache de Rioux had spent the last seven years of his life regretting by turns having not followed his two brothers and believing that the notebook was destined to be saved, and that some mysterious divine intervention had meant him to take possession of it. He was to suffer until the very end, like some ordeal, the burden of his life being spared at Acre.

When finally Rioux died in the Cypriot citadel, Leone had vowed to him that he would continue their quest to find the Light and would keep it secret until at last the Light burst forth.

Despite Leone's tireless efforts, at times he felt he had barely made any progress since his godfather's death. Except perhaps in the matter of the runes, which a Viking he ran into in Constantinople had explained to him.

Eustache and he had mistakenly thought they were Aramaic. They were not. The alphabet was known as futhark, and the Scandinavians had almost certainly adapted it from the Etruscan. These ancient letters gradually transcended their own meaning to become symbols, divinations. One evening, many years before, at a stall serving refreshing drinks made from the leaves of the chai tree, Leone had placed the strange cross upon a table before a merchant seafarer. The smile had vanished from the Viking's face. He had shaken his head and pursed his lips. Leone had urged him to speak and offered him money. The man had refused, muttering:

'No good. Witchcraft. Forbidden.'

'I need to understand the meaning of these symbols, pray, help me.'

'I not know all. That one Freya's cross.'

'Freya?'

'Freya twin sister Frey. Woman-god.'

'A goddess?'

The man had nodded and continued:

'She woman-god beauty and love ... love of flesh. She woman-god of war, like Tyr, he man-god. She lead warriors. Twin brother Frey. Other man-god, riches, fertility, land. Freya's cross to know if we win war.'

The sailor had but one desire: to leave the stall as quickly as possible. Leone had held him back by his sleeve and insisted:

'But what do the other symbols mean?'

'Not know. All forbidden.'

He had pulled away brusquely and disappeared into the colourful maze of the grand bazaar.

It had taken Leone more than a year to unravel the mystery of the almonds. He had had to wait for another of those unlikely coincidences, those improbable encounters the Knight Templar had evoked in the tunnel under Acre.

That morning, Francesco de Leone had been leaving on a mission to see Henri II of Lusignan. The hopes they had entertained of forcing the King of Cyprus to permit them to reinforce their numbers on the island had once again been dashed. He was approached by a small young girl dressed in rags, with long curly brown hair so tangled it resembled a clump of straw. Her head bowed, she silently held out a small grubby palm. Smiling, he placed a few small coins there – nothing much, enough to buy a little bread and cheese. Finally, when she looked up at him with her pale amber, almost yellow, eyes, Leone was astonished. The expression in them was so profound, so old for one of her years that he wondered whether she might not indeed be older than she looked. In a strikingly deep voice, she said to him:

'You are a good man. That is as it should be. I have been looking for you. I am told you possess a paper cross whose meaning you do not understand. I can help you.'

For a brief moment the Knight imagined he must be dreaming. How could this little beggar girl, one of many on the island, know about the mystery and address him as though she were a thousand-year-old woman? How could a Cypriot child decipher symbols belonging to an ancient alphabet known only to a handful of Vikings?

She led him, or, more precisely, he followed her, a few alleyways further along. She sat cross-legged on the floor behind a hut made of mud and straw. He did likewise.

Once again she held out her hand in silence. He took from his surcoat the piece of folded parchment he carried with him always. The small girl had spread it out on the ground and, hunched over, studied it.

A long moment passed before she looked up at him with her yellow eyes:

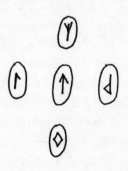

'Everything is written in this cross, brother. It is Freya's cross, but you already knew this. It is used to predict the outcome of a battle. And this is a battle. The left-hand branch signifies what is, what you inherit. It is Lagu, water. Water is inert yet sensitive and intuitive. Lagu is upright on your cross. You are lost, reality seems insurmountable to you. Listen to your soul and to your dreams. Long journeys are imminent. Keep in mind that you have been chosen, that you are a mere tool.'

Leone had taken a breath but the little girl had stopped him in a firm voice:

'Do not speak. It is pointless to ask me any questions. I am telling you what you must know. The rest will come from you. The right-hand branch signifies the obstacles you must overcome. It is negative. This sign is Thorn. Thorn is the warrior god of thunder and rain. He is strong and free of all immorality. But the rune is reversed. Beware of anger and revenge – they would spell doom for you. Do not trust advice, it will mostly mislead you. Your enemies are powerful and hidden. They hide behind the beauty of angels and have been hatching their plot for a long time, for a very long time. The top branch symbolises the help that will be given to you and which you must accept.' She paused for a moment before continuing, 'Are you aware, brother, that this is not one man's quest. It is an unbreakable chain. The rune Eolh is upright …'

The young girl's face broke into a beautiful smile and she said in a soft voice:

'I am glad. Eolh offers the most powerful protection you could enjoy. It is magical and so unpredictable that you will not recognise it when it appears. Do not fear being swayed by influences you do not understand. The lowest branch signifies what will happen in the near future. It is Ing and is reversed. Ing is the god of fertility and all its cycles. A task is nearing its end ... yet the outcome is not favourable to you. You have failed. You have made a mistake and must go back to the beginning ...' She had stared at him with her cat-like eyes before asking:

'What mistake have you made, brother? When? Where? You must find out very soon, time is running short. It has been running short for centuries.' She lifted her hand to silence the questions the Knight was burning to ask. 'Be quiet. I know nothing of the nature of the mistake, only that if you do not correct it very soon, the quest will reach an impasse. Nor do I know anything about the nature of the quest. I am, like you, a mere tool and my work will soon be done. Yours might never be. Ing reversed, then, means the period is unfavourable. Step back a little. Allow yourself time to repair the errors of judgement, whether yours or your predecessor's. The rune at the middle of the cross signifies the future outcome. Tyr upright. Tyr is the sacred lance, the just war. It stands for courage, honour and sacrifice. As a guarantee, Tyr left his hand in the mouth of the wolf Fenrir who threatened the world with destruction. The struggle will be long and fierce but crowned with victory. You will need to be loyal, just and, at times, merciless. Keep in mind that pity, like all else, must be merited. Do not waste it on those who show none. I do not know whether you will be present at this victory or whether it is reserved for the one who comes after you. The struggle is already more than a thousand years old. It has been hiding in the shadows for over twelve hundred years.'

For the past few minutes, Leone had by turns been reassured by this reading of the runes and worried that he understood even less than he had before his meeting with the little beggar girl. He had stammered:

'I implore you, speak to me of this struggle!'

'Did you not hear what I said? I know nothing. I have revealed all I know. My task was to interpret this cross.'

'Who entrusted you with it?' Leone had roared, his panic gaining the upper hand.

All of a sudden, the young girl's yellow gaze had fixed on a point behind him and he had turned his head. There had been nothing but a hill planted with olive groves, no menacing shadow. When he had turned back she had vanished, and only the imprint of her ragged dress on the dusty earth and the few coins he had given her proved he had not been dreaming.

He spent a whole week vainly searching for the girl in alleyways, peering inside stalls or churches, without ever glimpsing her frail figure.

Through a dogged effort Francesco de Leone had gradually understood the mistake they had all made from the very initiation of the chain, as the Cypriot beggar girl had referred to it. The two birth charts in the Templar Knight's notebook were false. The equatoire used to interpret them was an aberration derived from an obsolete astronomical theory.

The mathematician monk from an Italian monastery – the Vallombroso Monastery[45] – had discovered this truth and, fearing the consequences, hastened to conceal it. He had died soon afterwards in a crypt, having mysteriously fallen and cracked his skull open against a pillar. His notebook was never found. Until the day that the thief, Humeau, catering to the demands of his purchasers, had drawn up a small inventory of books in the Pope's private library. Leone had approached him as a buyer, bidding against another anonymous customer. Gachelin Humeau played the two off against each other, coaxing, using delaying tactics and, above all, pushing up the price. Which one should he sell to? He procrastinated. He wanted to please everybody, but after all business was business. With a movement so swift as to barely give the man time to blink, Leone had pulled his dagger, grabbed the scoundrel by the throat and, pressing the sharp blade against his neck, had announced in a clear, calm voice:

'How much for your life? Quick, name a price and then add it to the offer I just made. Is the other bid still higher?'

These were not empty threats and Humeau knew it. He had begrudgingly handed over the stolen work – for an exorbitant sum nonetheless.

Do not waste your pity on those who show none, the little girl had warned.

Leone was stupefied upon reading the treatise. There were other distant and invisible planets, whose existence had been proven by these calculations. Two giant stars,[46] named by their discoverer *GE1* and *GE2*, and an asteroid that was certainly smaller than the Moon but massive[47] nonetheless, which he had denominated As. A further shocking revelation affirmed that the Earth was not fixed at the centre of the firmament but turned around the Sun.

For weeks on end the Knight had busied himself with painstaking and complex calculations. He had been obliged to go back to the positions of the planets in the signs and houses of the zodiac in order to discover the dates of birth of two people, or two events, whose star charts were almost identical. His deductions were still incomplete, for he lacked the necessary data to calculate GE2's revolutions. However, he had reached a new stage in his clarifications that had allowed him to discover one date: the first decan of Capricorn, 25 December. Christmas Day. Agnès de Souarcy's birthday.

Ing, the rune indicating error, had been overcome. Leone was waiting for a sign that would allow him to complete his astral charts, and, more importantly, to understand their vital meaning. He was also waiting for his 'powerful, hidden' enemies to show themselves. He could sense them unseen in the shadows, ready to strike. They had already dealt one deadly blow, and Benoît XI had been felled by it, of that Leone was certain.

He walked over to one of the book cabinets and gave it a sharp push. The high shelves slid along invisible rails, revealing a flagstone that was wider and lighter than the others. A niche had been hollowed out below. There was the Vallombroso manuscript, carefully wrapped in a piece of linen coated in beeswax to protect it from damp and insects. Underneath was a second volume he had glanced through only once, the acid saliva of nausea rising up his gorge. He had purchased it from Humeau with the intention of destroying it, and then something had dissuaded him. It was a work of necromancy written by a certain Justus and filled with loathsome instructions whose aim was not to communicate with the dead, but to torment them, to enslave them, turning them into servants of the living. Leone felt a ripple of disgust each time he saw the cover, and yet he kept putting off the moment when he would consign it to the flames, reducing it to mere ashes.

He re-read the Vallombroso treatise on astronomy for the thousandth time, and for the thousandth time studied the annotations Eustache and he had written in the large notebook. It was then that a tiny detail caught his attention. He walked over to the wall where the high arrow slits afforded a little more light and took a closer look.

What was the faint smudge of ink that resembled a finger mark?

Behind him a rustling sound, elegant and feminine, made his heart skip a beat. No, it was not the unknown woman in the church from his dream, it was his aunt. He swivelled round.

'You made me jump, aunt. Have you consulted this notebook in my absence?'

'You know perfectly well how uneasy I feel about those hieroglyphs.'

'They are not hieroglyphs, they are secret runes.'

'They are forbidden by the Church.'

'Like many things.'

'Are you blaspheming, my nephew?'

'Blasphemy exists only against God, and I would rather die than allow it. What do you think would befall us if our quest became known?'

'I do not know … The purity of it would convince them and make them rejoice.'

'Do you really think so?'

'Why this sarcasm, nephew?'

He looked at her for a moment, bowing his head before replying:

'Do you really believe that those who wield such power and wealth would gladly let it slip through their fingers?'

'I still have hopes that the Light will impose itself of its own accord, Francesco.'

'How I envy you.'

'Benoît died on account of this Light, Francesco. And many more before him,' she reminded him in a sad voice.

'You are right. Forgive me, aunt.'

'You know I am incapable of being cross with you, my dear.'

He paused for a moment before enquiring:

'Are you absolutely certain that Madame de Souarcy was born on 25 December?'

She stifled a chuckle before replying:

'Do you think me an old fool, my sweet boy? I have told you repeatedly that she was born on Christmas Day. It is a significant enough date, despite its pagan origins,[48] for it to be remarked upon and remembered ... I came to make sure you have everything you need. I must leave you now – there are many things that require my attention. I shall see you presently, nephew.'

'Farewell, aunt.'

The Abbess gone, Leone trawled through the many notes he and Eustache had scribbled on the notebook's pages. All of a sudden his blood ran cold and for a moment he felt so dizzy he nearly lost his balance.

Somebody had torn out the last but one page of the notebook! A moment of sheer panic made his mind go blank. Somebody had consulted the notebook. But who? He was certain his aunt was telling the truth when she said she had not looked at it during his absence. Who then? One of the other nuns? Nobody else knew of the library's existence.

He had been mistaken. Ing, the rune signifying error, was not pointing to the erroneous astral charts, but to his unforgivable stupidity.

The last two deceptively blank pages contained the calculations and diagrams – the most secret notes of all.

Did the thief know this?

Since Nicolas Florin's arrival, Éleusie de Beaufort had tried her best to perform her usual tasks in the belief that her diligence would be a comfort to her girls. Were it not for this wish to carry on as though nothing in their lives had changed, she would have remained in her chambers despising her cowardice.

She was on her way to the steam room, walking unhurriedly, when her attention was caught by two figures standing side by side. Without really knowing why, the Abbess flattened herself against the wall behind one of the pillars holding up the vaulted ceiling, and watched the scene taking place twenty yards away. Her heart was pounding and she pressed her hand against her mouth, convinced that her quickened breathing could be heard at the other end of the abbey.

Florin. Florin was leaning over and whispering something to one of the sisters. The Inquisitor's back obscured the listener's identity. A few seconds passed, which seemed to her like an eternity. At last the two figures separated and the Inquisitor promptly disappeared down the right-hand corridor leading to the relics' chamber.

The person to whom he had been speaking remained motionless for a moment, and then appeared to make up her mind, turning towards the gardens.

It was Emma de Pathus, the schoolmistress.

Esquive d'Estouville put down the phoenix she had started embroidering many months before. The piece of linen cloth was fraying in places and covered in poor stitching that was coming loose. Needlework had always bored her, but it gave her the appearance of composure.

The young woman let out a sigh and her charming face became tense with frustration. It was such a long wait, and she was so eager to join her beautiful archangel, her Hospitaller. Her frustration was mixed with a curious happiness. To suffer a little each day for the one who would suffer so much. He did not know it yet and it was better that way.

When would she see him again, when would she permit herself to see him?

Esquive's lady's maid knocked at the door of the little room in the townhouse where she spent most of her time, when she was not handling weapons.

The maid was carrying a sumptuous cream-coloured dress over her arm.

'It's ready, Madame. I thought you'd want to see it straight away.'

'You were right, Hermione. Let us look at this marvel I have been waiting for three weeks to see.'

Hermione approached her, avoiding as always the young Comtesse's gaze, which made her so uneasy – those huge amber, almost yellow, eyes. The eyes of a little wild cat.

The bell for prime had sounded, but he would not be there. Nicolas Florin was in too much of a good mood to risk ruining it by inflicting a service upon himself. Thirty-one days, thirty-one days exactly. Thank God she had neither confessed to nor atoned for her sins. She was all his and nothing, no one, could save her now.

The armed escort had arrived the evening before and was just waiting for a sign from him. Agnès de Souarcy would be escorted in a few hours by carriage to the headquarters of the Inquisition at Alençon. Once inside its walls no one would hear her supplications or her screams, however loud.

He stretched with contentment as he lay on his bed trying to envisage Comte Artus's confusion. Soon, everybody would dread the new Inquisitor's power.

A momentary doubt clouded his optimism. The Abbess seemed to him changed of late, as though some unexpected certainty had all of a sudden allayed her fears. What of it! She might be an Abbess but she was only another female.

He gave a satisfied laugh. His female was so pretty, the one he had been coveting for a whole month now. He imagined her receiving him later, wringing her hands, wiping away her tears, her face pale and distraught with fear. Even though she had no idea to what extent her terror was justified.

A wave of voluptuousness washed over him, leaving him breathless with joy.

He would play for a long time, for a very long time. He closed his eyes as an explosion of pleasure wrenched his belly.

Agnès read one last time Clément's brief message, which Comte Artus had ordered his men-at-arms to bring, before casting it reluctantly into the hearth. She so wished she could have kept it with her.

The young woman had not been mistaken and Clément had taken great care with his words in case the missive fell into the wrong hands.

> *My dear Madame,*
>
> *I miss you so. I grow more anxious by the day. The Comte is very good to me and has allowed me access to his wonderful library. His doctor, a Jew from Bologna, who is not only a physic but a great scholar, is teaching me, among other things, about medicine.*
>
> *I am very worried, Madame. Since you will not allow me to come to you, I beg you to take the greatest care of yourself, in every possible way.*
>
> *Your life is mine.*
> *Your Clément.*

The Comte had also scribbled a few cryptic lines, intended only to be understood by the addressee.

> *Everything is being done to try to frustrate this dreadful deception. Everything. Take heart, Madame, you are dear to us.*
>
> *Your respectful, Artus, Comte d'Authon.*

*

Adeline burst into the great hall without troubling to knock. She was weeping and stammering:

'He's here … He's here, the black monk, the evil one.'

And she fled, as though her life, too, were in danger.

'Madame?'

'I was waiting for you, Monsieur.'

Agnès turned to face him, her back to the hearth. Florin's good mood faltered. She was not weeping. Nor was she wringing her hands in dread.

'I am ready. You may take me.'

'Have you nothing …'

She interrupted him sharply:

'I have nothing to confess. I have not sinned and I intend to prove it. Let us go, Monsieur, it is a long way to Alençon.'

Part Two:
The Breath of the Rose

Gentle Pye,
go to your brother,
with no pain.

On the road to Alençon, Perche, September 1304

Nicolas Florin was adamant that Agnès de Souarcy should be installed in the stout wooden wagon that gave the impression of a tomb on wheels. Minute arrow slits on each side allowed the occupants a limited view of the outside world. These were covered by leather curtains so that in the event of an attack no arrow could pierce the narrow openings. Four Perche horses were needed to draw the wagon.

The five men-at-arms requested by Nicolas Florin sat beside the driver or were jostled about on a cart trundling along behind. Agnès's belongings were contained in a small chest while, in an astonishing display of extravagance for an inquisitor, those of Nicolas filled an enormous trunk. An escort of five men-at-arms for one woman seemed an exaggerated precaution, but the Dominican was fond of such excesses. He saw them as visible proof of his newly acquired power.

His eyes were glued to Agnès, watching for the slightest sigh, the merest tensing of her jaw. Indeed, it was the reason he had given the order for her to travel with him in the wagon instead of in the cart. Did she regard the gesture as a mark of respect for her social status? Florin could not tell, and the thought had irritated him from the outset of their journey. Things were not going according to plan and had not been since the day of their first encounter when he had gone to notify her of the beginning of her period of grace. Did she really think she could get the better of him? Or that he would show her mercy? If this were the case, she would soon be disappointed. He lifted the leather flap and peered out at the sky. Night was falling. Since sext[+] they

315

had been advancing at the horses' slow but steady pace. She had not once raised her eyes from her hands clasped upon her lap, or uttered a single word, or even asked for water or a halt in order to relieve herself – something Nicolas would have been only too glad to agree to in the hope that she might be humiliated into wetting her shoes or the hem of her skirts in the presence of one of his guards.

A vague feeling of unease crept into the Grand Inquisitor's irritation. Had his victim received guarantees of protection? If so, from whom? From Comte Artus d'Authon or the Abbess of Clairets* or someone more highly placed? But who could be more powerful than the man behind the imposing figure who had paid him a visit at the Inquisition* headquarters in Alençon? No. He was behaving like a scared child. The bastard was adopting the haughty air of the sort of lady she aspired to be, nothing more.

She raised her blue-grey eyes from her hands, which were joined in prayer, and stared at Nicolas. He felt an unpleasant warmth suffusing his face and diverted his gaze, cursing himself as he did so. There was something peculiar about this woman – something he had not taken the time or had been unwilling to see. He tried now to analyse what he felt, but without much success. At times he had experienced the thrill of terrifying her, just as he did the others. But then all of a sudden another woman appeared, like a secret door leading to a mysterious underground passageway. And that other woman was not afraid of him. For some reason, Florin was quite sure that Agnès had no control over these transformations. Had he been an unthinking fanatic like some of his brothers, he would no doubt have seen it as proof of demonic possession. But Florin did not believe in the devil. And as for God, well, he had little time for Him. The pleasures life had to offer to those who knew how to take them were of greater concern to the Grand Inquisitor. Among the many he had condemned to death for sorcery or possession, Florin had never come across any convincing proof of the existence of miracle workers or witches.

His annoyance got the better of his cunning and he blurted out:

'As I am sure you are aware, Madame, the inquisitorial procedure* permits no other counsel than the accused himself.'

'Indeed.'

'Indeed?'

'I am aware of that particularity,' she said in a voice whose confident tone humiliated the inquisitor.

He stifled the anger welling up in him and the accompanying urge to slap her. He knew he should have held his tongue, but the desire to watch her face turn pale was too overpowering, and he continued, forcing himself to speak softly:

'It is not customary to reveal the identity of the witnesses for the prosecution, any more than the content of their accusations ... However, because you are a lady, I may grant you this privilege ...'

'I have no doubt that you will do all that is necessary and correct, Monsieur. If you do not mind, I should like to take a short nap. The long days ahead require me to be rested.'

She leaned her head against the back of the wooden bench and closed her eyes.

Florin's eyes filled with tears of rage, and he pursed his lips for fear he might utter an oath that would reveal his agitation to Agnès. He was vaguely consoled by the words of one of the most celebrated canonists: 'The aim of trying and sentencing the accused to death is not to save his soul but to uphold public morals and strike fear into the hearts of the people ... When an innocent refuses to confess, I resort to torture in order to send him to the stake.'[49]

Agnès had no wish to sleep. She was reflecting. Had she won a first victory in the long battle for which she was preparing herself? She sensed this man's puzzling hostility towards her and his exasperation.

Is it your still-innocent soul that protects me even now, Clément? Thanks to him Agnès knew that Florin was using the first of many tricks in the inquisitor's arsenal.

Many months before, on a July evening when it was nearly dark, Clément had returned in an excited state from one of his frequent forays. It was already late and Agnès had retired to her chambers. The young girl had scratched at her door and asked to see her for a moment.

No. She must never think of Clément other than as a boy or she risked making a blunder that would endanger both their lives. She must continue to refer to him only in the masculine.

The child had tapped at her door and asked to see her for a moment. He had stumbled upon a copy of *Consultationes ad inquisitores haereticae pravitatis*[50] by Gui Faucoi, who had been counsellor to Saint Louis before becoming Pope Clément IV. The treatise was accompanied by a slim volume, or, rather, a manual of blood-curdling procedures. He had stammered:

'M-Madame, Madame ... if only you knew ... they use trickery and deceit in order to obtain confessions, even false ones.'

An inscription at the head of the slender manual read:

'Everything should be done to ensure that the accused cannot proclaim his innocence so the sentence cannot be deemed unjust ...'[51]

'What an abomination,' she had murmured in disbelief. 'But

this is about trial by ordeal ... How is it possible? Where did you come across these works?'

The child had given a muddled explanation. He had mentioned a library and then skilfully evaded Agnès's questions.

'I see in it a sign from God, Madame. Knowing and anticipating your enemies' ploys means avoiding the traps they lay for you.'

He had described them to her: the technique of coercion and humiliation aimed at breaking down even the toughest resistance, the scheming, the manipulation of witnesses. The wretched victims were questioned on points of Christian doctrine. Their ignorance should have come as no surprise to anyone and yet was used as proof of their heresy. Clément had also listed the few possibilities of appeal at the disposition of the accused. As almost no one was made aware of them they were rarely invoked. It was possible, for example, to appeal to the Pope – though such appeals had every chance of being mislaid, often intentionally, unless an influential messenger delivered them directly to Rome. An objection to an inquisitor could be made on the grounds that he harboured a particular animosity towards the accused. However, the process was liable to miscarry since it required judgement, and very few judges were willing to risk getting on the wrong side of an inquisitor or a bishop associated with the Inquisition.

Clément had managed to dash any last hopes his lady might have entertained by adding that the majority of inquisitors, although they received a wage, rewarded themselves with the confiscated property of the condemned men and women. It was therefore against their interests for the latter to be found innocent, and wealthy victims, although more difficult targets, were desirable prey.

The knowledge Clément had acquired from some unknown

source had allowed Agnès to forge what she hoped would be her most reliable weapons when confronting Florin.

The inquisitors' initial ploy, then, was to swap the names of the witnesses and their accusations. Thus the first accusation would be attributed to the fifth witness, the second to the fourth, the third to the first, and so on … In this way the accused would appear clumsy in his defence against each informer. Cleverer still, they added the names of people who had never come forward as witnesses to the list of actual informers. But the subtlest, most convincing and preferred method was to ask the accused in a roundabout way whether he was aware of having any deadly enemies who might perjure themselves in order to bring about his downfall. If the accused failed to mention the most fervent of his accusers, their testimony was placed above suspicion since by his own admission they could not be fabrications. In each case the protection of witnesses was considered essential for the very good reason that 'without such a precaution, nobody would ever dare testify'.

Curiously, these revelations, which had so shaken her that night, now came to her aid. Had she believed that she was about to be dragged before impartial judges whose sole concerns were truth and faith, then her resolve would have been weakened. She would have searched inside herself for the failing that could justify such harsh punishment. Clément had helped her to understand the wicked nature of this farcical trial. Only a noble enemy deserves a fair fight.

Her thoughts had been wandering in this way for a while when Florin's voice almost made her jump. He thought he had woken her and this gave him further cause for alarm. How was she able to sleep at a time like this?

'Owing to the limited space at the Alençon headquarters, you will be subjected to *murus strictus* while you are in custody, unless that is ... the midwife attests that you are with child.'

'Perhaps you have forgotten that I have been a widow for many years. Is not *murus strictus* a severe punishment rather than a ... temporary accommodation?'

He seemed surprised that she would have knowledge of such things; the secrets of the Inquisition were jealously guarded in order to further demoralise the accused. The 'narrow wall' was simply a gloomy, damp dungeon the size of a cupboard where it was possible to chain prisoners to the walls.

'Madame ... we are not monsters!' he exclaimed with feigned indignation. 'You are allowed brief visits from members of your close family – at least before the beginning of ... the real interrogation.'

The torture, she thought. She tried to respond in an impassive voice:

'You are too kind, my lord.'

Agnès closed her eyes again in order to end the conversation, whose only aim was to frighten her. Her heart was pounding in her chest and it took a supreme effort of will for her to control her breathing. The only way she could control or stifle her mounting terror was by clinging to the thought that she had managed to place Mathilde and Clément out of harm's way.

Half an hour later, Florin shouted: 'Stop!' causing Agnès to start.

'We shall make a brief halt, Madame. Would you like to use the opportunity to stretch your legs?'

Despite her determination not to give in, she needed a moment to herself. After a second's hesitation she replied:

'Gladly.'

He leapt nimbly to the ground and refrained from offering to help her down. One of the guards hurried over and handed him a package, probably containing food and refreshment. The inquisitor studied her for a moment and asked:

'Do you require a little privacy, Madame?'

Stifling a sigh of relief, she accepted:

'Indeed, my Lord Inquisitor.'

'I think we all do. Hey, you over there, escort Madame.'

A big brute with a squashed face walked up to them. Agnès was on the verge of changing her mind, of saying that she preferred to wait until they reached Alençon. She was dissuaded by the smirk on Florin's face and the pain that had been searing her belly for hours. She spotted a thicket of bushes and walked over to it. The brute followed.

Once she was out of view of the others, she waited for the man to turn away, but his eyes were glued to her. His moist lips spread in a lecherous smile as she lifted her skirts. Agnès squatted, her anger eclipsing any embarrassment she might have felt, and stared straight at her escort. The man's smile dissolved and he lowered his gaze. This small victory comforted the young woman. It was a sign that she could prevail.

She did not remain outside enjoying a little more fresh air, but climbed straight back into the clumsy wagon. She could smell through the crack in the door the faintly acrid odour of bracken and the soothing forest air, heavy with humidity.

Florin glanced down at the hem of her dress as he sat down opposite her. Agnès fought back the urge to point out that she had not wet her gown. She had hitched up her skirts and if his man-at-arms had glimpsed her calf or her knee, then much good might it do him. She was beyond such foolish concerns, though at other times and in other places they would have seemed of the utmost importance to her.

When they finally reached Alençon, Agnès's lips were parched with thirst.

The wagon rattled over the cobbled courtyard of the Inquisition headquarters. Florin announced in a hushed voice:

'We have arrived, Madame. You must be exhausted after the long journey. I will show you without delay to what will be your ... lodgings over the coming weeks.'

Agnès was in no doubt as to his motives. He wanted to see the distress on her face, and she prepared for the worst – or so she thought.

Despite the enveloping gloom, the inquisitor strode confidently towards a small flight of steps leading up to a heavy door reinforced with struts. She followed, aware of two guards some yards behind her.

An icy cold pervaded the hallway. Florin ordered a few candles to be lit, and in the flickering light it occurred to Agnès that he resembled a beautiful vision of evil.

'Come along,' he chivvied, the excitement becoming evident in his voice.

They crossed the low-ceilinged room, which was devoid of any furniture except for a vast table of dark wood flanked by benches. Florin walked over to a door on the right of the enormous room.

Suddenly, a young man appeared as if from nowhere and stood at Agnès's side.

Florin declared in an alarmingly gentle voice:

'Why, Agnan, you look only half awake. Could it be that while

I was crossing hill and dale for the greater glory of the Church you were sleeping?'

Out of all the clerics, Nicolas had chosen Agnan to be his secretary because the young man's unredeemed ugliness suited him to perfection. Ugliness. What a splendid example of injustice. Agnan was the sweetest, gentlest creature, honest and pious, and yet those beady close-set eyes, that bony protruding nose and receding chin were deformities that inspired immediate mistrust in the onlooker. On the other hand, who would have believed that Nicolas's long slender frame, his gentle slanting eyes and full lips concealed a soul whose darkness would have struck fear into the heart of any lay executioner? And so Agnan suited Nicolas down to the ground, and moreover he was easily intimidated.

'Indeed not, my Lord Inquisitor. I have been busy assembling the various pieces of evidence for the forthcoming trial in order to further you in your task,' explained the other man timidly.

'Good.' Nicolas gestured towards Agnès without looking at her, and added: 'Madame de Souarcy is to be our guest.'

Agnan glanced nervously at the young woman then quickly lowered his head. And yet she could have sworn she saw a flicker of compassion in the secretary's eyes.

'Very good, run along now and keep up the good work.'

The other man bowed, stammering his agreement, and left with a rustle of his dowdy habit made of homespun wool.

One of the men-at-arms rushed to open the low door. A stone spiral staircase plunged into the murky blackness. The guard went ahead to light the way. As they descended into the cellars, the damp, acrid air caught in Agnès's throat and soon combined with the lingering odour of mud, excrement, pus and rotting flesh.

The staircase opened onto a floor of beaten earth that had

turned into sludge with the first rise in the water level of the river Sarthe. Agnès breathed through her mouth in an attempt to quell her feeling of nausea. Florin declared cheerfully:

'After a few days one grows accustomed to it and the stench is no longer noticeable.'

The underground chamber seemed vast; bigger, Agnès thought, than the surface area of the Inquisition headquarters. The supporting pillars were joined up by bars that demarcated the cells. They walked alongside the cages, which were too cramped for a man to stand up in. Occasionally, the flickering light from Florin's candle briefly illuminated an inert figure huddled in a corner, asleep perhaps, or dead.

'We are not accustomed to receiving ladies of your standing,' Florin said ironically. 'Although I am a monk, I am still a man of the world and as such have reserved one of the three individual cells for you.'

Agnès was perfectly aware that this gesture was not motivated by any consideration for her wellbeing. His aim was to deprive her of all contact – even with her fellow prisoners, who admittedly were in no position to offer her any solace. For the first time she found herself wondering whether he might not be afraid of her. Nonsense. What could he possibly fear from her?

The floor sloped gently downwards, and they passed beneath the vaulted ceiling and alongside the remaining cells enclosing the poor tortured, terrified souls. Agnès's shoes sank into the thick mud. They were certainly close to the river. A damp, unhealthy chill caused her to shiver, and the idea that she would soon be alone, shut in with this foul odour, undermined her resolve not to allow her fear to show. Strangely, even Florin's evil presence felt preferable to this void full of horrors that awaited her. All of a sudden something slippery gripped her ankle and she screamed.

A guard rushed over and, pulling her roughly to one side, stamped his heavy wooden clog onto a hand ... A bloodstained hand drooping through the bars of one of the cages. There was a wail, then whimpering ending in a sob.

'Madame ... there is no hope of salvation here. Die, Madame, die quickly.'

'What foolishness!' exclaimed Florin, and then in a voice that had regained all of its cheerfulness he warned the shadowy figure of a man hunched against the bars: 'Pray, but pray in silence; you have offended our ears enough with your griping!'

She remained motionless a few steps away from the cage, peering into the darkness that the candle flames struggled vainly to illuminate. Could those two blue openings surrounded by what looked like raw flesh be eyes? And was that gaping wound a mouth?

'Dear God ...' she groaned.

'He has forsaken us,' responded the feeble voice.

'Blasphemy!' Florin shrieked, pulling her by her coat sleeve. 'And he protests his innocence.'

A few yards further on they came to a door that could only be entered by bending double. It had no peephole. One of the guards drew back the bolt and stepped aside. The inquisitor walked in, followed by Agnès.

'Your chamber, Madame,' he announced cheerily, and then in a voice suddenly filled with loving sadness: 'Believe me, my child, there is nothing quite like peace and quiet for putting one's thoughts in order. I hope that you will have time in here to reflect, to see the error of your ways. My overriding desire is to help you return to the Lord's fold. I would give my life in return for saving your lost soul.'

The door slammed, the bolt grated. She was standing alone in total darkness. She began to walk tentatively, sliding one foot after the other. As soon as her leg touched the primitive bed she had been able to make out in the gloom, she collapsed on it in a heap.

She was gripped by a sudden panic, and it was all she could do to stop herself from screaming and hurling herself against the door, pummelling it with all her might, begging them to come back for her.

And what if they left her there to rot, dying of hunger and thirst? What if they waited until she went mad and then declared her possessed?

That man, that wretched soul who had grasped her ankle and implored her to die quickly. He knew. He knew that years of detention awaiting trial could turn into a lifetime on the pretext of further inquiries. He knew about privation, humiliation, weeks of torture. He had learned to live with the fear and certainty that few ever escaped the Inquisition's clutches.

Silence! He wants you to give up and let go of life. I order you to stand firm! Baronne de Larnay, Madame Clémence would not have given in. Stand firm!

If you plead guilty, you will languish here until death comes to claim you, and Mathilde and Clément will be doomed. They will endeavour to declare you a relapsed heretic – the most heinous of crimes in their eyes.

Remember, you will be shown no mercy, he will not be moved to pity. Stand firm!

Even as she admonished herself, she was struck by the terrible certainty that Florin was enjoying himself. However absurd the idea might seem, Florin was not driven by material gain, still less by faith. He took pleasure in torturing. He enjoyed causing suffering, lacerating and disembowelling. He rejoiced in making his victims scream. She was his latest toy.

An acid saliva rose in her mouth and she bent double as she cried out.

Clémence … Clémence, my angel, bless me with a miracle.

Show that you deserve the miracle by standing firm!

Château d'Authon-du-Perche, September 1304

J oseph, Artus d'Authon's old Jewish physician, masked his contentment. He felt flattered that young Clément possessed such a rare ability to learn and could express his awe so openly to him.

And yet it had taken all of the child's powers of persuasion and the Comte's insistence to convince him to take the boy on as an apprentice. The mere idea of having to explain, repeat, din the beauty of science into the young boy's head exhausted him.

Joseph had soon been surprised by how much Clément already knew. He had even lost his temper with the boy, ordering him to be silent when he mentioned certain medical facts known only to a small number of scholars – facts which, if openly talked about, ran the risk of provoking religious reprisals.

'But why lie when one possesses true knowledge that could prevent suffering and death?'

'Because knowledge is power, my child, and those who control knowledge have no wish to share power.'

'And will they always control it?'

'No, because knowledge is like water: you may try to cup it in your hands but it will always slip through your fingers.'

As the weeks went by, Joseph had allowed himself to become enchanted by the boy's keen intelligence, and perhaps also by the desire, by the hope, of being able to pass on the vast knowledge he was afraid would die with him.

Why had he left the prestigious university at Bologna? He was honest enough to admit that he had been motivated by foolish arrogance. The works of the great Greek, Jewish and Arab doctors of medicine had been translated in Salerno and Bologna. However, despite the wealth of knowledge generated by these previously unheard-of works, the West had persisted in using practices that owed more to superstition than to science. Joseph had gradually convinced himself that he would be the harbinger of this medical revolution. He was mistaken. He had settled in Paris in 1289 in the belief that his wish to propagate his art for the common good would protect him from the anti-Semitism that was rife in France. Again he was mistaken. A year later, the situation grew worse after the case of Jonathas the Jew,[52] who was accused of spitting on the Host, even though so-called witnesses were unable to describe the exact circumstances in which the supposed sacrilege had taken place. Jews were once again portrayed as enemies of the faith in the same way as the Cathars. Besides the everyday humiliations and official discriminatory measures, they lived in fear of being stoned by a hostile mob that would readily tear them apart with impunity. Abandoning his possessions, like so many others, he had chosen the route to exile. He considered going to Provence, which was known for its tolerance, and where many of his people already enjoyed a peace they mistakenly believed would be lasting. But Joseph's age had caught up with him and his journey had ended in Perche. He had set down his meagre baggage in a small town not far from Authon-du-Perche, and had tried to remain inconspicuous. He had occasionally treated people, though without employing his full knowledge for fear of arousing suspicion, and yet was so much more successful than the local apothecaries and doctors that news of his reputation soon reached the chateau. Artus had summoned him, and Joseph, not without trepidation, had obeyed.

The tall, withdrawn, broken man had stood before him and

studied him in silence for a few moments before declaring:

'My only son died a few months ago. I wish to know whether you could have saved him, esteemed doctor.'

'I cannot say, my lord. For, although I am aware of your terrible loss, I do not know the symptoms of his illness.' The tears had welled up in the old physician's eyes and he had shaken his head and murmured: 'Ah, the little children. It is not right when they die before us.'

'And yet, like his mother, he had a frail constitution and often became ill and feverish. His skin was deathly pale and he bled profusely even from the smallest scratch. He complained of tiredness, headaches and mysterious pains in his bones.'

'Did he feel the cold?'

'Yes. To such an extent that his room had to be heated in summer.'

Artus had paused before continuing:

'Why did you, a Jew, choose to practise in this part of the world?'

Joseph had simply shaken his head. Artus had gone on:

'To be a Jew at this time in the kingdom of France is a frightening thing.'

'It has long been the case and in many kingdoms,' the physician had corrected, smiling weakly.

'Together with the Arabs you are reputedly the best doctors in the world. Is such a reputation justified?'

'Our patients must be the judges of that.'

For the first time in many months, Artus, whose grief had been unrelenting since Gauzelin's death, allowed himself a witty rejoinder:

'If they are able to judge, it is because you have cured them, which is more than can be said for the majority of our physicians.'

He had taken a deep breath before asking in a faltering voice the question that had been plaguing him all along: 'He, my physician, was fond of bloodletting. It worried me and yet he swore by its effectiveness.'

'Oh, how fond they are of bloodletting! In your son's case it was pointless, I fear, though, judging from your description of his symptoms, the little boy would have died anyway.'

'What was he suffering from in your opinion?'

'A disease of the blood mostly found in very young children or those over sixty. It is quite possible that the same sickness in a less severe form also took your wife. The condition is incurable.'

Strangely, Joseph's diagnosis had eased the Comte's terrible suffering. Gauzelin's death had not been due to his physicians' – and consequently his own – shortcomings, but to a twist of fate that they had been powerless to prevent.

Joseph had subsequently found sanctuary at the chateau. The Comte granted him full use of the library and the freedom to come and go as he pleased and this, together with the Comte's influence, made him feel secure. Gratitude had gradually given way to respect, for Artus d'Authon was a man of his word and, one day, in the course of conversation he had said to Joseph:

'Should your people's plight worsen – as I fear it may – then I strongly advise you, for appearance's sake, to convert. My chaplain will attend to it. Should the idea prove abhorrent to you, Charles II d'Anjou, King Philip's* cousin, whilst complying in Anjou with the monarch's severe treatment of the Jews, is far more tolerant in his earldom of Provence and his kingdom of Naples. Charles is a cautious but shrewd man and the Jews bring him wealth. Naples seems far enough away to offer more safety. I would help you travel there.'

Joseph could tell by the solemn look in the eyes gazing intently at him that, come what may, he could trust this man's word.

The Comte enjoyed such robust health as to make him the despair of any doctor wishing to practise his art. And so Joseph treated the minor ailments of the Comte's household or the more serious illnesses afflicting the serfs, which were mostly caused by deprivation or lack of hygiene. The old physician had long given up trying to fathom the contradictions in man and had reached the conclusion that it was a futile search. His patients showed their gratitude by bringing him small gifts and bowing as they passed him on the street. They took him for an Italian scholar or powerful sage, called upon by their master to look after their health. Children would run along behind him, taking hold of his robe as though it were a lucky charm. Women would stop him, shyly informing him in hushed tones of a recovery or a pregnancy, and slip him a basket of eggs, a bottle of cider or a milk roll sweetened with honey. Men would bare an arm or a leg to show him that a skin ulcer he had treated had disappeared. Joseph chose not to scrutinise their smiles, their awkward speech, their faces, to avoid identifying those who would have denounced him to the secular authorities had they known he was a Jew.

He walked over to the large lectern where Clément, his mouth gaping in astonishment, was in the process of devouring a Latin translation.

'What is it you are reading that so surprises you?'

'The treatise on fraudulent pharmaceutical practices, master.'

'Oh yes, the one by Al-Chayzarî that dates back two centuries.'

'It says here that in order to increase their earnings pharmacists were in the habit of cutting Egyptian opium with *Chelidonium* or wild lettuce sap or even gum arabic to make it go further. The deception can be detected by mixing the powdered form with water. *Chelidonium* gives off a smell of saffron, lettuce a slightly sickly odour and gum arabic makes the liquid taste bitter.'

'Fraudulent practice has existed since time immemorial, and I suspect it always will – there is much money to be made from being dishonest. A good physician, or pharmacist, should know how to detect it in order to be sure of the effectiveness of the medicine he prescribes to his patients.'

Clément looked up and, unable to contain himself any longer, asked him the question he had been burning to put to him since their first meeting:

'Master … Your knowledge is so vast and so varied … Have you ever heard of a scholar by the name of Vallombroso?'

Joseph knitted his bushy grey eyebrows and replied:

'Vallombroso is not a man but a monastery in Italy. I am told they have carried out some astonishing mathematical and astronomical studies there, and that the friars are excellent at medicine.'

'Oh …'

Disappointment was written all over the child's face. Now he would never be able to understand the scribbled notes in the big red journal.

'Why do you ask?'

'I …' Clément stammered.

'Is it as bad as all that?' Joseph coaxed him gently.

'I read somewhere that … but please do not imagine for a moment that I give any credence to such nonsense, I read that Vallombroso was the name quoted in a theory according to which the Earth is not fixed in the heavens …'

The colour drained from the physician's face and he ordered sharply:

'Be quiet! No one must ever hear you speak of such things.'

Joseph glanced around nervously. The large, bright room, freezing cold in winter, which they were using as a study, was empty.

He moved closer to the child and bent down to whisper in his ear:

'The time is not yet ripe. Mankind is not ready to hear and accept the truth ... The Earth is not fixed. It spins on its own axis – thus explaining the existence of day and night – and moreover it rotates around the Sun, always following the same course, which is what produces the seasons.'

Clément was stunned by the perfect logic of it.

'Do you understand, Clément, that this is a secret? If anyone were to find out that we share this knowledge, it could cost us our lives.'

The child nodded his agreement then spoke in a hushed voice: 'But does this mean that the astrologers are all mistaken?'

'All of them are. What is more, it seems logical to assume that other planets exist which we do not yet know about. And this is why you should not put your faith in astrological medicine's current teachings.' Joseph paused briefly before continuing: 'It is now my turn to ask you to let me into a secret ... young woman.'

Clément's cry of astonishment rang out in the soundless room.

'For you are indeed a girl, are you not?' Joseph continued in a whisper.

Clément, still speechless, was only able to nod.

'And you will soon be eleven ... Has anybody ever explained to you the ... physiological peculiarity characterising the fair sex?'

'I don't know. I know I'll never grow a beard and that there exists a fundamental physical difference between boys and girls,' the child ventured.

'I thought as much. Well now, let us start with that – cosmogony can wait!'

Clément's shock quickly gave way to panic, and in an almost inaudible voice he tearfully implored:

'No one must know about it, master. No one.'

'I realise that. Do not fear. We are joined together by dangerous secrets now, as well as by our thirst for knowledge.'

They turned as one towards the door as it creaked open. Ronan ventured a few steps into the room before offering an apology:

'I trust I have not interrupted you in mid-experiment, revered doctor.'

'No, indeed. We had just finished a demonstration.'

'My Lord Artus has asked to see young Clément.'

'Well, run along, my boy. The Comte wishes to see you. You mustn't keep him waiting.'

'Thank you, master.'

'Come straight back whenever it pleases His Lordship. We have not finished for today.'

'Very good, master.'

The Comte was working in his beloved *rotunda*. When Clément came in, he looked up from his ledgers and nodded gratefully to Ronan.

'Zounds! What a thankless task is that of a paymaster. It puts me in a most foul mood,' he muttered. 'And yet I should be overjoyed and grateful that we have avoided disaster. The harvests were good and the calving season more encouraging than last year.'

As he finished writing a sentence, Clément could not help

noticing the elegance of his cursive script.[53] It was then that he recalled the bold handwriting in the notebook – the rotunda lettering reserved for scientific, legal or theological treatises; in brief, for scholarly works in Latin. If, as he had always suspected, it was the knight Rioux's script, could this mean he had been a theologian in the Hospitaller order? And if he had been, how would that knowledge further Clément in his investigation? He did not know, but he felt instinctively that it was important.

The Comte replaced his quill in the beautiful silver inkwell shaped like a ship's hull that was sitting in front of him. His face, already pensive, became tense, and the child was filled with apprehension. Why this hesitation? What news was he holding back? The Comte spoke in a faltering voice which he tried unsuccessfully to control:

'Madame de Souarcy has arrived at the Inquisition headquarters at Alençon where she is being held in *murus strictus.*'

Clément leaned against a bookshelf, trying to catch his breath. His whole body seemed to tremble. A firm hand grasped his tunic just as he felt his legs give way under him. The next thing he knew he was sitting in one of the small armchairs dotted around the circular room.

'Forgive me, my lord,' he stammered as he regained consciousness.

'No. It is I who should apologise. I fear that keeping the company of men and farmers has left me wanting in manners and consideration. Stay seated,' he insisted as Clément tried to stand up. 'You are still young, my boy … And yet you must be aware that some people are obliged to leave behind childish things sooner than others. I must ask you as a matter of urgency to search your memory. You told me how that rascal Eudes de Larnay and his loyal servant plotted to have Agnès arrested by the Inquisition. It would appear that she unwittingly gave refuge to a heretic, a certain ...'

'Sybille.'

'Yes.'

Clément bit his lip before blurting out:

'She was my mother.'

The Comte looked at him and murmured:

'Now I understand why Madame Agnès was so keen to send you away from her entourage.'

A curious tenderness welled up in Artus, who for days had been gripped by fear. He had known men, soldiers, who would willingly have denounced a child to the Inquisition in order to spare themselves the threat of a trial. And yet she, a helpless woman, or so she thought, had stood up to them. She must know of the conflict that raged in the minds of certain friars. Torn between their carnal desire and their vow of chastity, they feared or loathed women and their seductive powers, and absolved themselves of the temptation they felt in their presence by holding the devil responsible. However, having met Florin, Artus did not believe he was the sort to be troubled too much by self-denial. Yet, indeed, this loathing of women, this need to exercise a destructive power over them, was itself a form of carnal desire.

The Comte felt sickened and angry by turns. Ever since he had first seen Agnès dressed in peasant's breeches calming the bees as she harvested honey, he had dreamed in the early mornings of that long pale neck, of breathing its scent, of brushing its flesh with his still-slumbering lips. He dreamed of her long, fine hands holding the reins gently but firmly, like a true rider. He dreamed of them holding his belly and his loins. The image had become so vivid, so inappropriate, that he would banish it from his thoughts, knowing that it would creep back the moment he lowered his guard.

'In the letter you brought with you, Madame de Souarcy suggested a hidden influence far greater than that of her scheming half-brother.'

'Indeed, my lord. We came to that conclusion. Eudes de Larnay could pay the inquisitor but not guarantee him any influential backing. His power extends no further than his tiny estate and is far less than your own. It stands to reason that someone intervened to reinforce Florin's position.'

Artus walked over to one of the windows with their tiny asymmetrical leaded panes, unusual for the time. Hands clasped behind his back, he stood gazing out at the gardens ablaze with the russet browns and ochres of autumn. In the distance, a pair of swans floated on the pond, so perfectly elegant in their watery element and yet so ungainly on land. One day he would walk there with her, holding her arm. He would introduce her to the capricious swans, the proud peacocks and the albino deer who would peer at them shyly with their big brown eyes as they approached. One day he would recite to her: 'I love to walk among this fragrance and behold the marvel of these flowers,'[54] and she would reply, imbuing the words of Monsieur Chrétien de Troyes* with all the strength of her feeling: 'I was testing your love. Be sad no more, for I love you even more as I know you love me from the very depths of your heart.'[55] One day. Soon.

Defeat Florin. Kill him if necessary.

He found himself speaking to the child as though he were a man of his own age:

'And yet Florin must be aware of my childhood association and friendship with the King of France. His impudence, his ... immunity must come from Rome. Remember, though, that the

Pope is dead and we do not know who his successor will be. It comes as no surprise, then, that it is not a pontiff, but somebody who wields great influence in the Vatican. The late Benoît* was a merciful man, a reformer. He might have advocated compassion and clemency in our case. They gave him no time. His reign lasted but eight months … I am convinced that its brevity was intentional. And … I sense that his enemies are also ours.'

'But who?' Clément asked.

'We will find out, my boy, I promise you. Go now.'

Templar commandery at Arville was situated in the middle of what had once been the land of the Carnutes on the pilgrim's way to Santiago de Compostela, and was one of the first of its kind to be established, thanks to the generous donation of almost two and a half acres of woodland by Geoffroy III, a noble from Mondoubleau. A small band of knights, together with a few equerries and lay brethren[56] – mostly shepherds and herdsmen – had settled there from 1130 onwards.

The commandery served a triple purpose: as a farm estate that provided meat, grain, wood and horses for the crusaders in the Holy Land; as a recruitment centre and training camp for the Templars waiting to leave for the crusades; and finally it re-established the religious life that had vanished from the once-thriving Gallic community formed by the three towns of Arville, Saint-Agil and Oigny after it had been razed by the invading Romans.

Further donations by the Vicomtes de Châteaudun, the Comtes de Chartres, de Blois, and even the Comtes de Nevers, of woodland and arable land, as well as the right to harvest timber, bake their own bread and trade, had transformed the commandery into one of the richest in the kingdom of France. Notwithstanding past generosity, the lords of Mondoubleau – the Vicomtes de Châteaudun – had begun to resent the Templars' increasing wealth, and in 1205 their growing concern threatened to undermine the order's state of grace. The dispute worsened to the extent that in 1216 Pope Honorius III excommunicated Comte Geoffroy IV, who was intending to prohibit the Templars at Arville from driving their convoys outside the Mondoubleau estate, from owning a bread oven, from selling their merchandise at the marketplace and from harvesting bracken for animal fodder. Geoffroy IV had finally yielded to papal authority, but not before leading a small uprising.

The knights' activities had soon attracted an extended population as, in exchange for a nominal rent and a few services, they offered bread and dwellings with a smallholding.[57] In the year of 1304 seven hundred souls lived outside the commandery's stout ramparts.

The sun was high up in the sky when Francesco de Leone emerged from Mondoubleau Forest, which was adjacent to Montmirail Forest. The old mare he had hired at Ferté-Bernard moved along at a sluggish pace. The poor animal had already walked so far carrying his weight that he hadn't the heart to goad it on to arrive more quickly. His growing stomach pangs were a reminder that he hadn't eaten since the previous morning when he had finished the bag of provisions his aunt, Éleusie de Beaufort, had handed him just before he slipped away unseen from Clairets Abbey. Leone would never have allowed himself to describe what he felt as 'hunger', out of respect for the ravages of true hunger. He knew he would be offered food upon reaching his destination. This was the one Christian act no monk-soldier could disregard, despite the difficult, not to say hostile, relations between the Knights Hospitaller and Templar.*

Of course Leone could not ask the Templars to help him in the quest that had driven him for so long, a quest brought to him from the underground tunnels at Acre moments before the bloody defeat that heralded the end of Christendom in the Orient. Before joining the slaughter raging above their heads, a Knight Templar, sensing his imminent demise, had entrusted Leone's godfather, Eustache de Rioux, with a journal containing a lifetime of research, questions and unsolvable mysteries. He had spoken of a papyrus scroll written in Aramaic – one of the most sacred texts in all civilisation – and indicated that it was safely hidden at one of the Templar commanderies.

Under no circumstances must the commander at Arville suspect Leone's true motives. As for any hospitality he might receive, Leone was certain that it would be minimal and circumspect. Before his journey had even begun, Leone predicted that it would end in failure. Vain hope was not enough to explain his determination to carry on regardless. He wanted to breathe in the atmosphere of the place, and was convinced that once inside the church he would feel the presence of the secret, the key, that was hidden there – perhaps the papyrus.

He walked up the pebble path leading to the towering ramparts encircling the various buildings. The drawbridge was down over the surrounding moat, fed by the nearby river Coëtron. To the left stood the stables – reportedly large enough to house fifty or more horses, destined to be transported to the Holy Land on special vessels, which they would board via a drop-down door in the transom. Beyond the stables lay the kitchen and physic garden that supplied the Templar community with a few of its vegetables and most of its medicaments. To the right of the gateway, squeezed between the church and the utilitarian buildings, a smallish dwelling with tiny arrow-slit windows was most likely the preceptor's[58] abode. A little further on stood the church's circular watchtower, built of dark chalk-stone – a mixture of flint, quartz, clay and iron ore. This Temple of Our Lady, whose name invoked the Templars' cult of the Virgin, had been set apart from the ramparts, allowing the villagers to attend services without entering the commandery, thus respecting the Templar monks' cloister. In turn, another, smaller door permitted the monks to enter without ever leaving the enclosure. The two-tiered bell tower was supported by a pointed arch with its three rounded arches symbolising the Trinity. At the centre of the enclosure was the tithe barn, where a tenth of all the local harvests collected as taxes were stored. Behind the barn another stout watchtower stood guard over this amassed wealth. Close by, the bread oven – the focus of so much acrimony – defied the Vicomtes de Châteaudun with its presence.

Leone approached what he took to be the commander's dwelling.

His black surcoat with its eight-pronged white Maltese cross did not go unnoticed. A young equerry glanced up at him and the colour drained from his face. He looked around frantically as though searching for help from some quarter, and Leone half expected him to flee. He smiled sadly: how often they had fought side by side, come to one another's aid, laid down their lives for each other without a thought for which colour cross the other wore. Templars and Hospitallers had died together by the thousands, their mingled blood seeping into the soil of foreign lands. Why in times of peace did they forget their brotherhood during those bloody conflicts?

He called out to the young boy:

'Pray, take me to your commander, Archambaud d'Arville.'

'My lord ...?' the young man stammered.

Sensitive to the boy's discomfort, Leone added:

'Tell him that Francesco de Leone, Knight of Grace and Justice of the Order of Saint John of Jerusalem, is here. Hurry. My mount and I are both weary.'

The equerry ran off and Francesco dismounted. Nearly half an hour passed, during which time Leone began to doubt whether the preceptor would in fact receive him. Of course he must. To send him away would be a very unwise move on his part in view of the delicacy of the current political situation.

The man who walked through the gateway had an imposing physique, emphasised by a white mantle adorned with a red cross with four arms of equal length, and a long tunic reaching down to the floor. A sword hanging from a wide leather belt swung against his calf. It was difficult to guess the age of the furrowed face, framed by a thick mane of hair and a grizzled beard; forty, forty-five, older perhaps. The commander smiled politely and Leone thought he saw the man's eyes light up as he made his introductions. Indeed, he enquired:

'Are you the Francesco de Leone who was expected to become one of the pillars of the Italian-speaking world in your order?'

Leone was not overly surprised by a commander knowing of the Hospitallers' internal affairs; both military orders contrived as discreetly as possible to find out what they could about the other. But that he should acknowledge it so openly was perplexing.

'It was an honour and a responsibility of which I considered myself unworthy at the time, and which I consequently declined.'

'Proving that, in addition to your reputation for piety and bravery, you are a wise man. To what do we owe the pleasure of this visit, brother?'

Leone had decided to offer a simple excuse in order not to arouse any suspicion. Since he was unable to request a bed for the night at a Templar commandery he had no other choice but to content himself with a brief visit.

'To the need for prayer, a halt for my weary horse and a rumbling stomach, I confess. I am on my way to Céton and do not expect to be there before nightfall,' he lied.

Leone had no way of telling whether Archambaud d'Arville believed him. Nevertheless, he replied:

'You are a welcome guest. One of our people will attend to your mount. As for you and I, we shall begin by sharing a meal.'

'I must leave soon after none[+] if I am to find lodgings at Céton. I shall visit the abbey there tomorrow morning.'

'Your visit will be a brief one, then, I fear,' announced the other man in a voice that sounded too cheerful to be true. 'But please follow me – I am failing in all my duties.'

Leone walked with him towards the building to the right of the main gateway. So it was the preceptor's dwelling.

Two equerries were seated at the table in the main hall. They bent over their bowls of soup and busily finished the remainder of their meal, clearly keen to leave the room at the first opportunity.

The Templars' table, though far from lavish, was reputedly less frugal than that of the Hospitallers. For the Templars, unlike the Hospitallers, had always been a military order, and since soldiers must be well nourished if they are to fight like lions, the practice of fasting among its members had always been restricted.

A lay brother soon arrived and placed a goblet of hippocras in front of Leone and a thick slice of poor men's bread[59] made of wheat, rye and coarsely sifted barley in front of Archambaud d'Arville. After tracing a cross on the piece of brown bread with the tip of his knife, the commander sliced it in two and gave half to the Knight Hospitaller. They both thanked God for this blessing.

The lay brother then served a slice of spinach-and-bacon pie on each of these trenchers, followed by ox tongue roasted in verjuice.

The faint feeling of bewilderment the knight had been experiencing since he arrived was gradually turning into one of unease. There was something unnatural about the lack of interest Arville showed in his reasons for being there and in his journey in general. Under normal circumstances he would have attempted to glean as much information as possible, knowing that Leone was a prominent figure in the Hospitaller hierarchy.

Their meal took place in awkward silence, punctuated by an occasional comment on the dishes they were eating, or on that year's harvest or the unlikelihood of there being a new crusade.

Arville agreed with Leone's reservations regarding the matter, adding:

'We cannot feed more than fifty animals and are obliged to sell our horses at the market.'

Leone found this idle chitchat disturbing. Something else lurked behind the smug façade of civility. And yet it was unthinkable that the commander knew anything about the reason for his visit, still less about his quest. Had the other man sensed his unease? Whatever the case, his manner changed abruptly to one of forced joviality, adding to Leone's suspicions about his host of a few hours. Archambaud d'Arville began to describe in great detail his own calamitous arrival at Perche-Gouet four years before: his departure from Italy – a country dear to his heart – the neglectful state in which he had found the commandery when he arrived. Indeed, he had been obliged to mete out cautions and minor punishments, alternating bread-and-water penances with two-day fasts – the worst offenders being made to eat their meals on the floor. In this way, the commander explained, he managed to call to order certain monks guilty of committing venial but routine sins. He guffawed as he recalled one greedy Templar sergeant who would sneak out at night and raid the honey, plunging his hands into the barrels. They had discovered him asleep one morning after gorging himself, his body covered in ants. It had taken four days for the swellings from the bites to go down. Another, whose fondness was for the demon drink, would be so inebriated before the first service of the day he had to prop himself up against a pillar in the Temple of Our Lady, and hiccupped after each word as he intoned, '*Salve, Regina, Mater misericordiae; vita, dulcedo et spes nostra.*'[60] Then there were those who had a tendency to ignore their duties, preferring instead to play court tennis in the spacious loft above the stables that had been converted into an area devoted to leisure. Leone smiled politely as he tried to glimpse the reason behind the preceptor's garrulousness. Something was not right; despite the cool weather the other man was perspiring and had already poured himself a third cup of hippocras.

It was getting late. Leone stopped speculating and politely interrupted Archambaud d'Arville's futile but relentless anecdotes:

'Despite the pleasure it gives me to remain in your company, brother, I must soon take my leave. I have a long journey ahead of me and would like to pray before setting off again.'

'By all means, by all means ...'

And yet, Archambaud's displeasure was palpable. Was Leone nearing his goal or merely being misled by false impressions?

He thought he saw a sudden look of real grief darken the commander's forced cheer as he proposed:

'I cannot allow you to leave without tasting our cider. It is legendary throughout the region.'

Leone accepted with good grace.

Shortly afterwards, they left the tiny building for the temple. They entered through the pointed archway, reinforced by four salient buttresses. The church had been inspired by the austerity of Cistercian buildings and consisted of a nave made up of four spans, ending in a semicircular apse. Light flooded in through the high round-arched windows. There was only an altar, no benches even. And yet as Leone walked between its pillars he knew that he had arrived. He felt a strange and wonderful light-headedness, and let out a sigh of relief. The commander apparently misconstrued the gesture and held on to his arm to steady him.

'You are weak from exhaustion, brother.'

'Indeed,' he lied. 'Might your generosity extend to granting me one last favour? I would like to spend a few moments alone before thanking you one last time and continuing my journey.'

The Templar walked out into the afternoon sunlight shrugging his shoulders and said:

'I shall go and see to it that your mount is ready. Meet me in front of the stables.'

A sea. A warm, tranquil sea. A cradle of light, welcoming, calming. He had waited so long to run his hand over those vast black and brown stones that he was almost afraid to touch them now. He would not begin searching or lose himself in pointless speculation. Not today. The time had not yet arrived. He was tempted by a sudden feeling of sluggishness to lie down on the broad, dark flagstones and sleep. Today he would allow himself to be bathed, lulled. Today he would reflect upon how privileged he was to be there in the presence of the key. Like Eustache de Rioux before him, Leone was unsure of its exact nature. Could it, as he had sometimes imagined, be a doorway to a labyrinth traced in the stones, visible only from a precise angle? Or was it a manuscript pillaged from some library and brought there by a monk or soldier? Was it the papyrus in Aramaic purchased from a Bedouin in the souks of Jerusalem, as described by the Knight Templar in the tunnels below Acre? Was it a cross or a statue covered with secret symbols? Was it a simple object?

Not today. Archambaud d'Arville would come back to look for him if he tarried. And yet Leone had found what he had been searching for: the certainty that his quest would begin again in that place.

Tomorrow he would think of a way to return and remain there.

As he walked out to join the commander, the light from the sun made him wince. He had an unpleasant hollow feeling in his chest and imagined that the unbearable separation from his quest was once again weakening him.

Archambaud d'Arville was waiting for him in front of the stables. A young lay brother held his mare's reins. Leone sensed from the commander's sudden restlessness that the man was in a hurry to see him leave. He thanked him once again and climbed into the saddle.

Vicinity of the Templar commandery at Arville, Mondoubleau
Forest, October 1304

Francesco de Leone was not unduly disturbed by his encounter with the commander, the prospect of which he had found daunting from the outset. Admittedly, the man's strange behaviour had puzzled him, and he had not been taken in for a moment by his garrulous sociability. But then Leone had not expected any generous cooperation from the Templar order and, besides, Archambaud d'Arville could not possibly be aware of the presence of any key – under whatever guise – or he would never have allowed Leone to remain in the Temple of Our Lady alone.

Leone needed to think up a way of gaining free and unlimited access to the commandery in order to achieve his aim of unearthing the secret.

He patted the neck of the hired nag that was carrying him. The animal, unused to such gestures of affection, whinnied and jerked its head nervously.

'Steady, old girl. We are not in any hurry now.'

Could the pretence he'd been obliged to keep up have wearied him to such an extent? He was finding it increasingly difficult to remain upright in the saddle. The horse responded to the slight pressure of his leg and lengthened its stride.

Francesco de Leone was under the impression that he had only just left the commandery enclosure and yet the forest and the night were already beginning to close in on him. He was dripping with sweat and shivering. An unpleasant dryness made his tongue stick to the roof of his mouth and occasional giddy spells caused him to sway in his saddle. Above his head the sky and the treetops turned in circles. He tried to summon up his strength, clutching the reins, and as his body slipped from the saddle he realised that he had been drugged: the fraternal bowl of cider. He wondered whether the drug would kill him or merely render him unconscious and smiled at the thought before collapsing onto the blanket of dead leaves covering the forest floor.

A few dozen yards away, Archambaud d'Arville dismounted. He felt a mixture of disgust and terror. To kill a brother, a man of God who had willingly risked his life to defend their faith, seemed to him an unpardonable sin, and yet he had no choice. The future of the commandery, perhaps even the existence of their order in France, depended on this crime for which he would never be able to forgive himself. The ghoulish figure who had visited him two days before had been unequivocal: Leone must die and his death be made to look like the work of brigands. Arville was unaware of the reasons for this killing, but the missive containing the order to carry it out, which the apparition had handed to him, bore the seal of the halved bulla, which legitimised acts and letters in the interim preceding the election of a new pope. The Templar had already killed, but honourably, as a soldier face to face with his enemy, sometimes taking on five men single-handed. Even as his flesh had been torn and seared, his soul had remained unscathed. To have drugged this formidable swordsman in order to be sure of overpowering him was abhorrent to him, and for the first time in his life he despised himself. He had become a vile executioner, and the knowledge that he was acting on the orders of the papacy did nothing to diminish his guilt.

He drew his dagger and approached his brother's inert body. Horrifying memories of throngs of men, hideous images of battlegrounds transformed into mass graves came back to him.

He heard for the thousandth time the screams of the dying, the ferocious cries of the victors, intoxicated by the smell of blood, crazed by the kill. So many dead. So many dead in the name of eternal love. Would their souls be enriched as a result as they had been led to believe? Was there no other way than slaughter? And yet if he began to doubt now, hell would open at his feet.

The movement behind him was so swift and soundless that he did not notice it. An explosion of pain in his chest. He raised his hand and snagged it on the tip of a short sword. He could feel the metal sliding out of his flesh, only to be plunged in a second time.

He slumped to his knees, vomiting blood. A youthful voice clear as a mountain spring, the voice of a young girl, spoke to him, imploring:

'Forgive me, knight. Forgive me out of the goodness of your heart. It was my duty to save him. His life is so precious, so much more precious than yours or mine. I could not challenge you directly for I was unsure of being any match for you. But I promise you, knight, that I have saved your soul. Grant me forgiveness, I beg of you.'

Archambaud d'Arville had no doubt that the girl was speaking the truth, that she had saved him from the torment of eternal guilt. She had chosen in his place, freeing him from the need to disobey the apparition and the missive from Rome, freeing him from the need to obey.

'I ... pardon you ... sister ... Thank you.'

Esquive d'Estouville remained with the dying man until his last gasp, the tears from her amber eyes dropping onto his surcoat. She knelt down beside him in order to stretch out his body and place his hands upon his bloodstained chest, and gazed at the handsome supine figure. She did not know how long she prayed through her tears for the Templar's soul and for her own.

When she finally rose to her feet, the moon was full. She walked over to Leone's sleeping body and lay down beside him. She embraced him and kissed his brow. She drew her cape over him to protect him from the damp night chill, and spoke in a whisper:

'Sleep, my sweet archangel. Sleep for I am keeping watch. And then I shall vanish once more.'

Esquive d'Estouville closed her eyes, trembling with emotion as she lay next to the big slumbering body that was oblivious to her presence. Was she sinning? Undoubtedly, and yet her sin was a reward for the long years of waiting, for the unbidden, disturbing dreams that she no longer even tried to resist now that they had permeated her waking hours. Ever since she had appeared to him in Cyprus in the guise of a grubby beggar girl capable of deciphering the runic prophecy, her only thoughts were of him. She had devoted her body and soul to their quest but her heart belonged to this man who was near to being an angel. He was ignorant of her feelings, and it was better that way. The mere suggestion of any love that was not motherly, sisterly or born of friendship would have saddened him, for he did not want it and could not return it. But what did it matter? She loved him more than her own life, and this love that she had discovered thanks to him filled her with joy and strength.

Dawn was breaking when Leone came round. His head was gripped by a vicelike pain and his mouth filled with an acid saliva. He managed to sit up. He felt dizzy and tried to suppress a growing sense of panic as his mind drew a complete blank. Where was he? Why was he lying in the middle of the forest in the early morning? He struggled with his hazy recollection of the previous day, forcing himself to retrace his steps. Gradually, faces and words began to emerge from the fog of his thoughts. He had gone to the Templar commandery to meet Archambaud d'Arville, whose garrulousness and false bonhomie had made his head spin. And yet behind all that fraternal cheer Leone had momentarily sensed the man's anguish and despair. The commander had offered him a bowl of cider before he went on his way.

Upon entering the nave of the Temple of Our Lady, Leone had been seized by the wild hope that he would receive a sign proving that the secret he had been pursuing all these years lay within those walls, among those flagstones and pillars. Was the sudden giddiness and the incredible calm he had felt in the temple confirmation of such a sign or simply the first effects of the drug?

Where was his worn-out mare? He rose to his feet, staggering slightly, and looked around. The mare was staring at him a few yards away, tethered to the trunk of a silver birch, refreshed after her night's unencumbered rest. He had collapsed, fallen to the ground. But who had tethered the mare? It was then he noticed the brownish-red patch seeping from beneath a small pile of leaves. He drew his sword from its scabbard as he approached it. He flicked the leaves aside with the blade, already knowing what he would find there. He dropped his sword and fell to his knees beside Archambaud d'Arville's body, then swept away with his hands the flimsy remains of his leafy tomb. Leone was able to deduce what had happened from the two identical stab wounds in the commander's chest, the bloodstains on his white mantle and the compassion and respect with which the killer had treated the corpse. The Knight Templar had trailed him with the clear intention of killing him as soon as the drug had taken effect. But why? Somebody had been there and had shown no compunction in killing a Templar commander in order to defend Leone's life – a protector, then, rather than a rascal or evil brigand. But who and why? Had his champion then fled on the commander's mount? Leone had a vague recollection, but the image escaped him. He tried in vain to summon it back, slowly stroking his finger across his brow.

He was stirred by the thought of the torment this man of God, this warrior, must have endured: to poison a brother and then like an abject executioner to slay him. Who had the authority to compel a Templar commander to perpetrate such villainy?

Assuming Arville's orders had come from his Grand-Master or his chapter, they would still have required the Pope's approval. But the Pope was dead, and Benoît would never have endorsed such a dishonourable act: Leone had known, respected and loved him well enough to stake his life on it.

In the absence of a pope, who possessed sufficient authority to arrange the murder of a Knight Hospitaller? The answer was so glaringly obvious that it struck him with the full force of its monstrosity.

The King's counsellor and confidant Guillaume de Nogaret's*
initial surprise at Francesco Capella's absence had turned
to concern and then quickly to anger. What had become of this
young man in whom he had begun to place his trust? The day
after his new secretary's unexplained disappearance, Nogaret had
dispatched a messenger to his uncle, Giotto Capella, carrying a
missive whose unequivocal content bristled with threats. Had a
sudden illness confined Francesco to his bed? To Nogaret's mind
there could be no other acceptable explanation for his absence,
and he would hate to have to hold Giotto Capella responsible
for misleading him by extolling the virtues of a nephew whose
behaviour had turned out to be so rude and unreliable.

The letter had thrown Giotto Capella into a panic, and his first
impulse had been to leave France without further ado. Then he
had taken to his bed, curling up under a pile of counterpanes as he
envisaged his life hanging by a thread were the King's counsellor
ever to discover his role in this deception. He had spent hours
snivelling and trembling as he sweated under the heavy coverlets,
justifying his actions with any excuse he could find. What else
could he have done faced with Francesco de Leone's blackmail
threat? Leone and the other Knights Hospitaller knew that he
was responsible for the Mamelukes breaking through the last
defences of the Saint-Jean-d'Acre stronghold. What other choice
did he have but to obey Leone by passing him off as his nephew
and providing him with the false identity he needed in order for
Seigneur de Nogaret to engage him? Naturally, the moneylender
had suspected that the knight's intention was to spy on the

King's counsellor. But what good would it have done to admit it? None at all. At least not as far as he was concerned. Weary of his own despair, Capella had decided to crawl out of bed and compose a blustering reply. In it he related his nephew's sudden interest in a young lady and his equally unexpected departure from Paris in order to follow her to Italy. He portrayed himself as the despairing uncle, fearful of having offended Monsieur de Nogaret, and ended with a bitter diatribe against the recklessness of youth. Monsieur de Nogaret had been unconvinced, regarding his reply as no more than a feeble excuse.

The King's counsellor felt a cold rage welling up inside him as he put down the page of spidery scrawl. In fact, he could not forgive himself for having allowed a fellow feeling to develop between him and this Francesco Capella, for having deemed him intelligent and possibly divulged too many secrets. He had reflected long and hard on the information he had shared with him and felt reassured when he recalled nothing of any importance. Nevertheless, he would give that weasel Giotto cause to regret recommending his relative. Nogaret would see to it personally that the scoundrel never obtained the post of Captain General of the Lombards of France that he had so long coveted.

That morning Guillaume de Nogaret was still in a bad mood: he had lost a diligent secretary as well as an agreeable companion. He immersed himself in his accounts. His thin lips became twisted in a grimace of displeasure as he drew up the inventory of the King's brother's most recent expenditure of treasury money. How could he put a stop to Charles de Valois's* extravagance without angering the monarch? Valois dreamed of war, of reconquering lost territories; in brief, of raising and commanding armies. Francesco Capella was right to have expressed concern.

Just as he was recalling his vanished secretary, he heard a loud bark coming from the royal quarters. One of Philip's lurchers. Nogaret swung round to face the tapestry on the wall behind him and the red stitching of the dogs' mouths on the blue background. He rose to his feet and lifted the hanging. What if Francesco Capella had been sent to spy on him? But by whom? Certainly not by Giotto Capella. He examined the padlock on the safe built into the wall and could see nothing suspicious. Still, he was assailed by doubt. He seized the key hanging on the chain he kept around his neck at all times, and placed it in the small opening. The lock seemed stiff, though he could have been imagining it. He opened the safe and rifled through its contents. Nothing was missing. But why was the black calfskin notebook on top of the pile of letters? Surely he had written or received these since he had last consulted the notebook. Logically it should have been somewhere underneath or in the middle of the pile. Could he be sure of this? After all, the lock had not been forced. The habit of power had made him more mistrustful. Francesco's sudden departure and his uncle's clumsy explanation had heightened his suspicions. Since he could no longer question the nephew he would force the uncle to talk.

Nogaret walked over to the door of his office with the intention of calling an usher, but changed his mind as he clasped his fingers round the handle. Would it not be a mistake in these dark and troubled times to admit to a possible lapse in judgement, a mistake for which he might pay heavily? Enguerran de Marigny, who was already the King's chamberlain, was manoeuvring himself into the monarch's good graces with the help of the King's beloved wife, Queen Jeanne of Navarre, to whom he was both confidante and trusted ally. Nogaret, the fearful, timid worrier, envied his rival's self-assurance. Marigny possessed the ability to converse, argue and theorise with such poignancy or passion that his audience took his every word to be gospel. Guillaume de Nogaret knew he was incapable of matching the man's eloquence and manner. If he admitted to the King that he had been spied upon by a man whom he himself had engaged, Marigny would be sure to use this blunder to undermine his reputation. He might feel avenged by delivering Giotto Capella into the hands of the executioners, but it would only weaken his position at court.

After all, nothing in the safe had gone missing. No doubt he was scaring himself unnecessarily.

And yet how on earth did that notebook come to be on top of a bundle of confidential letters he had only recently placed in the safe?

Nogaret sat down at his desk again and studied the nib of his quill pen. No, the shadowy figure whose services he employed was not resourceful enough to be of any use to him in this matter. The King's counsellor detested that cowled sycophant who had admittedly served him well hitherto. And yet the henchman's palpable loathing, bitterness and thirst for revenge made his blood run cold. Hurting others appeared to relieve his tormented soul. Nogaret was no villain. If he were guilty of scheming or worse, his motivation, and perhaps his justification, was always to serve the greatness of the monarchy.

No. He could not use the cowled figure to dig out the truth about Francesco Capella. As for the usual spies, they were all in the employ of the King and most of them also reported to Marigny for a fee. Any inquiry undertaken by Nogaret was in danger of being brought to the attention of his main rival, who would not hesitate to use it against him at the first opportunity.

For the moment his best course of action was to pretend that nothing had happened.

Nogaret sighed with exasperation. He needed a spy, one not driven by envy or fanaticism, an intelligent spy. His isolation at the Louvre was weakening his position. He had gained the King's respect, possibly even his gratitude, but had failed to win his friendship. Nogaret, who found emotions deeply puzzling, had nonetheless learned something important from observing them: however foolish or misguided, emotions were what dictated people's actions. Intelligence only came into play after the fact, to justify or absolve. He need look no further than the King's own weakness on the subject of his warmongering brother, Monsieur de Valois.

A spy. He must find a clever spy who would answer only to him. How would he go about it, knowing that his enemies were watching his every move?

Clairets Abbey, Perche, October 1304

Éleusie de Beaufort, the Abbess of Clairets, shivered despite the heat given off by the fire in the hearth in her study. She had been chilled to the bone ever since first setting eyes on that inquisitor Nicolas Florin. The old nightmarish visions had found their way back into her waking thoughts, and assailed her to the point where she feared those moments of semi-consciousness that precede sleep.

If the Abbess had ever entertained any doubts as to the purity of the quest that bound her, her nephew Francesco and the late and good Benoît XI together, the arrival of that evil creature had silenced them for ever. But would the light they were striving to restore to the world be enough to defeat the Nicolas Florins who had darkened the centuries since the dawn of time? Francesco, whom she had brought up as her own son, was convinced that it would. And yet he had so little in common with other mortals; he was so much more like an angel who had come down from another world. And what did angels know of rage, terror and physical suffering?

Her eyes grew misty with tears.

Claire, my dear sister, your son is so like you. And yet he is so otherworldly. We are groping blindly through an endless labyrinth. We turn in circles, searching for the guiding thread. I am plagued by questions to which I can as yet find no answers. Why did you die at Saint-Jean-d'Acre? Why did you not foresee the massacre and flee? What did you know that I did not?

My nights have become a graveyard where I meet you all, my beloved ghosts: Henri, my sweet love, my husband; Philippine, whose precious blood runs through our veins; Benoît, my dear Benoît; Clémence, Claire, my sisters, my warriors.

And she who is one of us. What does she really know of her true destiny?

I am tormented by anguish, Claire, by the thought that we might be mistaken, that it is all an illusion. What if there is no key, no door?

We are like that game of tarot the Bohemians have recently brought back from Egypt, or China. We play our cards without knowing their real significance. For who can truly claim to know?

I am afraid, Claire, and yet I cannot name my fears. There is a danger emanating from these stout walls, these sombre archways where I believed I would find peace. I sense it in every passageway, on every stair. An evil beast inhabits these places now. No one can see or hear him and few of us are aware of his presence. It would take Clémence's courage or your foresight to defeat him. Or Philippine's triumphant resolve. I am merely a frightened old woman, who has convinced herself she is erudite and therefore knows all there is to know about the human soul. And look at me now, alone, my limbs crippled with pain, plagued by visions I am powerless to comprehend, terrified by the depth of the abyss into which I find myself staring. I shiver with an inner cold that tells me evil is among us. It escorted Florin through these doors. It crept into our midst and has been spying upon us ever since, infiltrating our conversations, even our prayers. It is biding its time. Why, I do not know.

Do you remember the small town in Tuscany our parents took us to when we were young? Do you remember the peasant children brandishing a devil made of brightly coloured cloth and how it petrified me? I screamed and sobbed and refused to move. You rushed over and snatched it from them, and they looked on in anger as you hurled it to the ground and trampled on it. Then you walked towards me smiling and said: you give him strength by believing in him. The devil is generous. He is the scapegoat for all our sins and accepts the blame at no great cost to us.

You were right, dear sister, and I would be excommunicated if anyone were ever to find out what I believe. That there is no devil. That the eternal battle between good and evil exists in man alone. I have met one of evil's willing adepts; I have touched him. He smiled at me and he was beautiful.

I am afraid, dear Claire.

Adélaïde Condeau, the sister in charge of the kitchens and meals at Clairets Abbey, scoured the contents of one of the cabinets in the herbarium, which was crammed with phials, sachets made of jute, earthenware flasks and a host of other receptacles. She almost felt guilty for being there without first asking permission from the Abbess or the apothecary nun, Annelette Beaupré, who treated the herbarium as if it belonged to her. She defended it jealously and at times with surprising vehemence. It was rumoured that Annelette, whose father and grandfather had both been physicians, had never accepted not being allowed in turn to practise their art and had joined the abbey because it was the only community that permitted her to do so. Adélaïde could not swear to the truth of these statements, though they might explain in part the apothecary nun's arrogance and bitterness. Whatever the case, Adélaïde was in need of some sage with which to season the magnificent hares sent by a haberdasher[61] from Nogent-le-Rotrou the previous day, and which she was planning to liven up with a purée made from plums picked after an early frost.

Sage was a common remedy used in the treatment of headaches, stomach pains, paralysis, epilepsy, jaundice, swellings, aching legs, fainting fits and a host of other ailments. The apothecary nun must have stocked up on it during the summer months, especially since this medicinal herb also made a delicious sauce when mixed with white wine, cloves, ginger and black pepper. Adélaïde searched in vain for a large bag embroidered with the words *Salvia officinalis*. She found *Pulicaria dysenterica*, *Salicaria*, *Iris foetida*, nettle, borage and betony, but no sage. Exasperated, she wondered whether the apothecary nun had placed the bag on one of the top shelves. After all, she was as tall and robustly built as any man. The young nun dragged over a stool and clambered onto it. She saw no sign of any sage. Groping with her fingers behind the first row of sachets and phials, she discovered a jute bag that had fallen down the back. She pulled it from its hiding place.

Adélaïde jumped off her perch and emptied the contents of the little bag onto the table used for weighing and making up preparations. The sour-smelling yellow-brown flour had to be rye, but what were those little black flecks? She leaned over to smell it and the pungent odour made her recoil.

'Sister Adélaïde!' a voice rang out behind her.

The young nun almost leapt into the air and clasped her hand to her chest. She turned to face the apothecary nun, whose vast medicinal knowledge was no excuse for her tetchiness, not in Adélaïde's eyes anyway.

'What are you doing here?' the other woman continued in an accusatory tone.

'I just ... I just.'

'You just what, pray?'

The young girl in charge of meals finally managed to stammer out an explanation as to what she was doing in Sister Annelette's jealously guarded sanctuary.

'In short, I was looking for some sage for my sauce.'

'You could have asked me.'

'I know, I know. Only I couldn't find you anywhere so I decided to look for it myself. I even stood on a stool and …'

'If you had a modicum of good sense, dear sister,' remarked the other woman disdainfully, 'you would know that I am hardly likely to keep a remedy I use so frequently in such an inaccessible place. Sage is …'

Annelette paused in mid-sentence. Her eye had alighted on the mound of flour on the table top. She walked over to it, frowning, and demanded:

'What is this?'

'Well, I confess I don't know,' said Adélaïde. 'I found that bag on the top shelf. It had fallen behind the others.'

Incensed, Annelette sharply corrected the girl:

'My bags and phials do not fall; they are arranged in perfect rows after being weighed and listed in my inventory. You must be aware that some of these preparations are highly toxic and I need to be able to identify their content and usage at a glance.'

It was the apothecary nun's turn now to lean over the small mound of powder. She pushed aside the blackish clusters with the tip of her forefinger. When she raised her head again, her face had turned deathly pale. Her voice betrayed none of its usual arrogance as she stammered:

'D-dear God!'

'What!'

'This is ergot.'

'Ergot?'

'Ergot is a fungus that grows on rye – small kernels form on the ears. Ancient texts claim that it causes gangrene, giving the limbs the blackened and withered aspect of charred skin. The corpses look as though they have been burnt. Some scholars attribute "St Anthony's fire"[62] to it – the violent delirium accompanied by hallucinations[63] we hear so much about, which some fools take to be visitations or possession. This powerful poison is probably responsible for wiping out entire villages.'[64]

'But what do you use it for?' asked the increasingly anxious Adélaïde.

'Have you taken leave of your senses, Sister Adélaïde! Do you really imagine that I would prepare such quantities of a harmful substance like this? Admittedly, I always keep a small sachet of it – for it possesses excellent properties. It relieves headaches,[65] incontinence and haemorrhages[66] in older women. But never as much as this.'

'How should I know … Please don't be angry with me,' spluttered the young girl, on the brink of tears.

'Oh, pull yourself together! Spare me your floods of tears. This is a serious matter and I'm in no mood to have to comfort you.'

At this, Adélaïde went running into the garden where she burst out crying.

Annelette's eyes were riveted on the contaminated rye so she scarcely heard the young nun's sobs. Who had prepared this flour and to what end? Who had hidden it in the herbarium and why? In order to incriminate her should it be discovered? More importantly, who but she was well versed enough in poisons to know about ergot's horrific properties?

Should she inform the Abbess? She was in no doubt. Éleusie de Beaufort was one of the few women at the abbey whom Annelette considered truly intelligent and for whom she consequently felt a combination of affection and respect. For this reason she was reluctant to upset her. The past few months had been a trying time for the Abbess, and the inquisitor's arrival appeared to have sapped her usual strength.

First of all she must think. What better place than a medicine cabinet to conceal poison. Moreover, it was conceivable that an intruder had managed to enter the abbey enclosure and slip into the herbarium. On the other hand, the idea of someone returning regularly to fetch the hidden substance was absurd. The poisoner must be attached to the abbey. The chaplain who took the services was an improbable candidate owing to his age, his near-blindness and his increasing tendency to fall asleep. This meant that the poisoner had to be a woman.

During the next half-hour, Annelette went through a mental list of all the sisters. She began by eliminating the lay servants who had been dedicated to God. Not one of them could read or would be capable of preparing a poison whose existence was known only to a handful of scientists. She forced herself to ignore personal likes and dislikes, limiting herself to complete impartiality and objectivity – no small achievement for someone who tended to judge her fellow human beings harshly.

Nonetheless, she immediately struck Éleusie de Beaufort off her mental list. Éleusie was a learned woman but her total lack of interest in the sciences made her a poor candidate. And Éleusie's faith was so exacting that it would not tolerate any imperfection. She ruled out Jeanne d'Amblin on the same grounds, despite the antipathy she felt towards the woman – an antipathy she was honest enough to admit sprang from her envy of the extern sister's freedom from the cloister. She doubted Jeanne even knew ergot existed. As for that sweet but silly girl Adélaïde, whom if anything she found exasperating, she was at a loss in any situation that did not involve plucking a bird, skinning a hare or scalding the bristles off a baby pig. And Blanche de Blinot, the senior member of the abbey who was Éleusie's second in command, as well as the prioress, was so ancient that she looked as though she might crumple up at any moment. Her deafness, a source of occasional mirth to the younger sisters, infuriated Annelette to the point where she avoided talking to her for fear of being obliged to repeat the same sentence five times over. In contrast, the cellarer nun, Berthe de Marchiennes, with her permanent expression of devoutness, was a more than likely suspect. She was educated, the youngest member of a large but impoverished family that had looked upon her – the eleventh child and a female into the bargain – as superfluous. Berthe was one of those women who grow more graceful with age but who when young are extremely plain. Lacking both a dowry and good looks, the monastic life had offered itself as a last resort. Annelette froze. Couldn't this be a description of her own life? The abbey had been the only place where she could exercise her talents. Another face replaced that of the perpetually pained cellarer nun: Yolande de Fleury – the sister in charge of the granary. Who was better placed than she, whose task it was to oversee the sowing of the crops, to have knowledge of crop disease and access to the contaminated rye? By the same token, Adèle de Vigneux, the granary keeper, must be considered a prime suspect. Likewise the treasurer nun, the infirmary nun and the sister in charge of the fishponds and henhouses, and so on … And yet, opportunity alone could not explain such a heinous crime as poisoning. The culprit needed a motive, but above all a killer's instinct. Despite the low esteem in which she held her fellow human beings, Annelette was forced to admit that the majority of the other sisters possessed no such instinct.

Night was falling when she left the herbarium, after removing the troublesome flour from the table top. She had whittled her list down to a few names, faces, possibilities. Still, Annelette Beaupré was clever enough to realise that she had very little evidence to back up her suspicions. She had simply used a process of elimination to exclude those she considered unlikely killers.

After she had recovered from her fright and stopped crying, Adélaïde Condeau made what she considered an important decision: she would do without the sage and therefore avoid any further confrontation with that shrew Annelette. How unpleasant she was when she set her mind to it, that overgrown creature! Adélaïde immediately reproached herself for having such uncharitable thoughts. She screwed up her face as she finished the cup of lavender and cinnamon tea sweetened with honey that Blanche de Blinot, the senior nun, had kindly brought her. She had put too much honey in and it tasted sickly, especially taken cold. Her face broke into a smile: Blanche was very old, and it was well known that old people developed a taste for the only sweetness they had left in life.

Rosemary was a perfect herb, and went well with game. Moreover, she had enough of it stored in the kitchens to make another visit to the herbarium unnecessary. Three novices had spent the morning gutting and quartering the hares that now lay in a macabre heap on one of the trestle tables. This was Adélaïde's favourite time of day; vespers[+] was about to begin and the novices, who, like her, were excused from attending the service in order to prepare supper, were busy laying the table in the great hall under the watchful eye of the refectory nun. A moment of calm descended upon the enormous vaulted kitchen, broken only by the roar of the fire in the great hearth, the occasional patter of a sister's feet hurrying to the scriptorium, the crackle of the stove or the gurgle of pipes.

Adélaïde had been daunted at first by her promotion to head of kitchens and meals; it seemed to be more about accounts and inventories than pots and pans. Sensing her hesitation, the Abbess and Berthe de Marchiennes – the cellarer nun to whom she reported directly – hastened to assure her that her primary duty would continue to be that of providing them with food. For Adélaïde loved to chop, mix, prepare, purée, simmer, braise, thicken and season. She loved preparing food for people, nourishing them. No earthly pleasure could compare in her eyes with trying to invent new recipes for soup or crystallised fruit, as she frequently did. Perhaps the root cause was her precarious start in life; she had been close to starvation when a cooper discovered her at the edge of Condeau Forest.

The long wooden spoon she was holding made a hollow sound as it slipped from her hand and bounced off the tiled floor. The bread. The rye bread she had secretly given the Pope's emissary to nourish him on his journey. She had not ordered any that week from Sylvine Taulier, the sister in charge of the bread oven. So where had the little loaf come from? A sudden giddy spell nearly caused her to lose her balance and she clutched the edge of the table just in time. What was happening to her? She felt as though thousands of pins and needles were pricking her hands and feet, jabbing at her face and mouth. She tried to make a fist with her hand, but her limbs felt numb. Her stomach was on fire and a cold sweat poured from her brow, drenching the collar of her robe. She was finding it difficult to breathe. Still holding on to the edge of the trestle table, she attempted to move towards the door, towards the others. She wanted to cry for help but no sound came out of her mouth.

She felt herself slump to the floor and she put her hand on her chest. She couldn't feel her heart. Was it even beating? She opened her mouth and tried to breathe, but the air refused to flow into her lungs.

Why had she been saved by that man, only to be poisoned a few years later? What sense was there in that?

A last prayer. May death take her quickly. Her prayer would not be granted.

For more than half an hour Adélaïde veered between pain and incomprehension. Fully conscious, the sweat running down her face, she could make out the other sisters flooding into the cavernous kitchen, frightened, shouting, weeping. She saw Hedwige du Thilay cross herself and close her eyes as she held her crucifix up to her lips. She recognised Jeanne d'Amblin's distraught face, and saw her press her hand to her mouth to stifle a cry. She saw Annelette leaning over her to sniff her mouth and smell her breath. She felt Éleusie's soft lips brushing her forehead and her tears dropping onto her hand. Annelette lifted a finger moist with saliva to her mouth and tasted it.

The tall woman rose to her feet, and for the first time the young girl in charge of the kitchens thought that underneath her sister's gruff exterior was an inner warmth. She heard her murmur:

'My poor child.'

The apothecary took the Abbess aside and Adélaïde could no longer hear what they were saying:

'Reverend Mother, our sister has been poisoned with aconite.

She is suffocating to death. Unfortunately, she will remain conscious throughout. There is nothing we can do except to gather round and pray for her.'

Adélaïde Condeau struggled in vain against the creeping paralysis that was slowly immobilising her whole body, up to her cheeks, trapping her voice in her throat. She tried with all her might to utter a single word: bread.

As the nuns knelt around her and she was given absolution, the single, precious syllable echoed in her head: bread.

When she could no longer draw breath, when she opened her mouth wide to suck in the air that was denied to her, she imagined that she had finally managed to utter the word.

Her head flopped to one side, cradled in Éleusie's arms.

Dressed in a sumptuous sapphire-blue robe adorned with a fur trim and embroidery as fine as that of any princess, Mathilde de Souarcy strutted up and down in front of the ladies and gentlemen of her imaginary court, alternately curtseying and putting on a coquettish air.

As she now considered herself a grown woman, she had instructed her servant to braid her hair into coils around her head.

She clucked with delight. How boring it had been stuck inside that bleak abbey where her mother had thought fit to send her after the Grand Inquisitor from Alençon had come to inform her that the time of grace had begun. How tedious to have to get up so early and go to church, and be forced to help make beds and fold linen for love of thy neighbour! And yet, there were plenty of lay servants to relieve well-born girls like her of those duties. During what she considered a scandalous imprisonment, which had lasted less than a week, Mathilde's biggest fear had been that she might end her days amid the dreary, bustling activity of Clairets. However, she had not counted on the devotion of her dashing uncle Eudes. God only knows how relieved she had felt when she learned of his arrival at the abbey. He had immediately demanded that the Abbess hand over his niece, and Éleusie de Beaufort had been unable to resist the order for very long. Eudes was Mathilde's uncle by blood and in the absence of her mother became her official guardian. Indeed, owing to her uncle's generosity she had lived like a princess for the past few weeks. The bed chamber he had provided for her had been that of the late Madame Apolline. It was spacious and well heated thanks to the large hearth, which was the height of modernity, possessing as it did two small shutters, one on either side, allowing the heat to circulate more efficiently. On the bare stone walls, brightly coloured hangings depicting ladies taking their bath kept out the damp. She slept every night in the vast bed, and felt a little uneasy when she tried to imagine the activity that must have taken place there – for she could only assume that it was here Madame Apolline had received her husband. What had gone on between those sheets? She had attempted to find out by occasionally probing Adeline or Mabile. The two fools had burst into fits of giggles and told her nothing. A mirror stood on a dainty jewellery dresser with sculpted legs. Her miserable rags had been stored in two large chests flanking the hearth until, one day, her uncle had angrily demanded that they be burnt and his niece dressed in keeping with someone of her status. True, some of the finery he had given her had belonged to her late aunt Apolline. But she did not resent her uncle for having the dresses altered to fit her. What a deplorable waste it would have been to throw them away, especially since poor Apolline, who was naturally ungainly, had done them little justice. Multiple pregnancies had only increased her agonising clumsiness. She had always given the impression of being trussed up in her robes and veils, and would stand like a peasant woman with her hands supporting her back, weakened by so many swollen bellies. In contrast, when worn by Mathilde, the linen and silk fabrics floated like delightful clouds.

An unpleasant thought blighted her good mood. Her mother was now in the hands of the Inquisition, and although Mathilde was unaware of the precise nature of the task of these friars, she knew them to be unforgiving and that anyone unfortunate enough to enter their headquarters was unlikely ever to emerge again. However, they were men of God and the Pope's emissaries.

If her mother had incurred their wrath, then it must be seen as punishment for a grave sin she had committed. Indeed, now she came to think of it, Mathilde was indulging her mother by not resenting her even more than she already did, for if Agnès de Souarcy was found guilty, the scandal threatened to taint her by association and thus jeopardise her future.

At least she was free of that good-for-nothing Clément. Mathilde had often felt sickened by her mother's weakness for that common farm hand, son of a lady's maid. How arrogant he had been towards her, though she was the sole heir to the family name! And he was mistaken if he thought she hadn't noticed the expression of pained sympathy on his face when she spoke to him sometimes. The fool! Now she was enjoying her sweet revenge! He had fled the manor like a thief, proving in Mathilde's view that his conscience was not clear. She had gleaned from Adeline that, besides the draught horse his mistress had supplied him with, he had taken only some food and a blanket. He must have left his crossbow, for serfs were not permitted to carry weapons. Yet another of her mother's stupid ideas! A gleeful thought crossed the young girl's mind. The forest was an unsafe place full of two-and four-legged predators. What if the ugly brat had been ripped to shreds?

This happy thought was interrupted by the cautious entrance of the servant Barbe, provided for her by her uncle.

'Well, what do you want?' Mathilde snapped.

'Seigneur Eudes requests the honour of being permitted to visit you in your chamber, Mademoiselle.'

Mathilde's face lit up at the mention of her beloved uncle.

'The honour is mine. Well, don't stand there – go and tell him!'

No sooner had the girl left the room than Mathilde rushed over to the mirror to check her hair and the fall of her dress.

Eudes chuckled as she lifted her arms and twirled around to let him see how his gift showed off her pretty figure to advantage.

'You are a vision of loveliness, dear niece, and your presence here brightens up my household,' he declared, forcing a note of concern into his voice.

The young girl was flattered by the compliment and fell straight into the crude trap he had laid for her.

'And yet you seem so serious, uncle.'

Eudes was delighted to have so easily got her right where he wanted her.

'It concerns your mother, my little princess, whom, as you know, I love as a sister. You see, her impending trial will have unfortunate repercussions for us all. If, as I fear, Madame Agnès is found guilty of heresy, it will bring shame upon us both. I know you are a clever child. You will therefore understand that a verdict such as this would not favour our dealings with the King of France – not to mention the disgrace that would tarnish the family name for ever. My life is done, but yours is only just beginning, and it would be a terrible injustice if …' He ended with a sigh of despair.

Mathilde lowered her head in dismay. So, her uncle was confirming her own fears of the past few weeks. On the verge of tears, she murmured:

'How unfair it would be indeed for us to be associated with my mother's sins. Is there nothing we can do, uncle …?'

'I have mulled over the alternatives during the last few nights when I was unable to sleep. It seems to me there is only one sure way … but it pains me to tell you what it is.'

'Pray do, dearest uncle, I entreat you. The situation is serious.'

'It is … Oh, the suffering I am about to cause you, you whose happiness is closest to my heart …'

Mathilde did not doubt his words. Far away from Manoir de Souarcy's cold, gloomy interior, she was at last living the life she had always longed for: fine clothes, a servant to do her hair each morning, twice-weekly baths in milk and water scented with rosemary and violets, greeted like a young lady wherever she went. No! She had been deprived of it for long enough by her mother's stubbornness and she refused to allow what was rightfully hers to be taken away from her! Moreover, she had an equal duty to protect her uncle, her benefactor.

'I implore you … Nothing could be more terrible in my eyes than to see you publicly disgraced as a result of my mother's mistakes – especially after you have been so good to her – too good.'

Magnificent! The pretty little fool had fallen straight into his lap!

'You are so good, my radiant princess. What a comfort you are to me in my hour of torment. This painful solution would seem, then, to be the only one left to us. An accusation.'

Mathilde showed no surprise, for she had already thought of it herself. Had not Pope Honorius III advised in one of his encyclicals: 'Let each draw his sword and spare neither his fellow man nor even his closest relative'? She saw nothing wrong in obeying the orders of God's representative on earth.

'As you know, niece, in the eyes of the Inquisition, failure to denounce a heretic is tantamount to complicity … It pains me to torment your sweet soul with such a decision.'

'No, uncle. If my mother had not foolishly given refuge to that … that traitor Sybille, who was pregnant to boot, then you and I would not be in this situation. And after all … perhaps that devilish fiend, that succubus, did sow the seeds of heresy in my mother's soul, condemning her to eternal damnation, which is far more terrible than any trial. I shudder at the thought.'

The first few days of the month had been warm and exceptionally wet. The slightest shower of rain would send evil-smelling torrents of mud hurtling through the streets, and yet Nicolas Florin did not yearn for Carcassonne's sunnier climes. He had, as he liked to think of it, 'sown the seeds' of some very lucrative affairs, whose crop he would harvest once Agnès de Souarcy's trial was over. Indeed, he was at any moment expecting a visit from one of his future guarantors of wealth.

Nicolas Florin had given instructions for Agnès de Souarcy to be left alone for a week in her cell in the dungeon underneath the Inquisition headquarters. She was not permitted to wash herself, and her chamber pot was to be cleaned out only every three days. Besides water, her diet would consist of three bowlfuls of milk soup made with root vegetables,[67] and a quarter portion of famine bread, which Agnan, his secretary, had ordered especially from the baker. The man, surprised by such an odd request in a year when harvests were good, had assumed it was part of a penance.

Florin had been a little disappointed for he was sure that she would refuse such lowly nourishment. And yet she had dutifully finished every last crumb. He knew why: Agnès de Souarcy was preparing to hold out for as long as she could. Good ... It would only make his game more enjoyable. A week. It was a long time to spend alone in the dank gloom with only one's own thoughts for company, thoughts that turn in circles and always end up imagining the worst. Nicolas's plan was a simple one, and had until then proved effective. Keep the accused in wretched isolation, terrify them for a few days, interrogate them and then allow a few visitors to bring them an agonising taste of what they were missing: freedom, their loved ones' faces, the realisation that life outside, however hard, was sweet by comparison. In fact, this strategy was aimed at breaking down the most stubborn resistance in order to obtain a confession and he did not expect a confession from the beautiful Agnès, who was guilty of nothing more than refusing to yield to her half-brother's lust. However, these bullying tactics would give the affair the appearance of an authentic trial, and he had spent hours relishing the thought of his victim's face already twisted with fear.

He gave a sigh of contentment as he cast his eye over the narrow room that served as his office. His small desk, made of a second-rate wood that had begun to split, was almost buried under a pile of casebooks. These were indispensable to the inquisitor, who was obliged to record in them every last action, meeting, witness accusation, punishment meted out or torture employed. The aim was not so much to ensure the thoroughness of the procedure as to make sure that no case would ever be lost. If the accused were eventually found innocent, who was to say that he might not be tried again for some other crime?

His secretary, Agnan, entered silently, his head bowed, and waited for Florin's permission to speak.

'Well, Agnan. What is it?'

'Seigneur Inquisitor, your visitor has arrived.'

'Bring her in.'

The other man slipped soundlessly out of the room.

Marguerite Galée belonged to a wealthy family of burghers from Nogent; shipbuilders who no doubt had taken their name from the vessels they constructed.[68] Nicolas had carefully researched the state of their finances.

The lady cut a fine figure in her fur-trimmed coat, too warm for the time of year. She could not have been more than twenty-two. Twenty-four at the most. The perfect oval of her face was framed by the sheerest of veils. A hint of vulgarity in her eyes belied the unassuming elegance of her posture, her upper body leaning backwards slightly so as to avoid stepping on the narrow train attached to the front of her dress, as worn by ladies of the nobility. The tiny silk slippers covered in mud that peeped out at every step were additional proof of her wealth, for by evening the sludge in the streets would have irrevocably ruined them.

Nicolas stood up to greet her and, holding out his hand, guided her to the chair on the other side of his desk. She sighed and gave a pretty shrug of her shoulders as she spoke hesitantly:

'A distant relative, Baron de Larnay, heartily recommended you to me, Seigneur Inquisitor. I find myself in a very delicate situation from which I know not how to extricate myself. I have come to you ... for advice, Seigneur Inquisitor. Your wisdom, which is equalled only by your indulgence, has been remarked upon among a ... discreet circle.'

How exhilarating life was becoming: this ravishing, exceedingly rich young woman lowering her gaze before him and addressing him by his title 'Seigneur Inquisitor' at the end of every sentence; and as for the Baron de Larnay, well, he was turning out to be more interesting than he had first thought.

'You flatter me, Madame.'

'No, Seigneur Inquisitor. On the contrary, I ... This is such a delicate matter ...'

He paused. Marguerite Galée had been testing the water ever

since she arrived and caution told him that he should continue feigning an inquisitor's disinterested observation. However, he was afraid the lady might take fright and renounce her plan, in which case he risked seeing the generous compensation he was hoping for go up in smoke. The predatory look in her eye when she first arrived encouraged him to throw caution to the wind:

'Madame, pray look upon this office as a confessional. I have listened to many stories in here, few of which have surprised me. It is not always easy to bring about justice. Is it not my role to remedy such matters ... and my reward to receive the gratitude of such pure souls as yours?'

She raised her head and a knowing smile played across her lips, as alluring as an exotic fruit.

'What a relief, Seigneur Inquisitor ... The first of my worries is that, unhappily, I have as yet been unable to conceive. The second is that my husband is very ill ... the doctors fear that the pain in his chest, which has left him breathless for weeks, will grow worse ...'

She paused and bit her lip. Florin encouraged her to go on with an affectionate gesture.

'Despite his advanced age, my husband's father enjoys such perfect health that I am beginning to find it suspicious.'

So, this was the reason for the lady's visit. Her father-in-law must be extremely wealthy. If her husband were to die before his own father without leaving an heir, this avaricious beauty wouldn't see a penny of the old man's money. Florin felt a nagging doubt. There were plenty of poisons available with which to rid oneself of an old man who clung stubbornly to life, which a woman such as she would have no difficulty in procuring. On the other hand, he had witnessed it many times: it was much easier to arrange for someone else to carry out a murder than to perpetrate it oneself. Even so, he was a little disappointed in her. Admittedly, though, an inquisitorial procedure was above suspicion, whereas a case of poisoning might incriminate the beneficiary.

'Suspicious, you say?'

'Indeed, as is my inexplicable sterility. You see, my father-in-law … Well, I would be putting it mildly if I said that he is not overly fond of me.'

'Do you suspect him of improper practices?'

'Most emphatically.'

'Of practising magic? I am referring to black magic, the use of incantations and the invocation of evil spirits. Is this what you mean?'

'Just so. I even suspect him of having a hand in my poor dear husband's illness.'

Whom you will dispatch the moment the old man has given up the ghost, thought Nicolas, affecting an air of deep disquiet.

'This is a most serious accusation, Madame. Indeed, a witch resembles a heretic in his worship of demonic idols. Have you any proof ?'

'Well, he …' She appeared to hesitate, but went on: 'He eats meat on fasting days …'

A sensible man, for fasting days are a most tiresome invention, Nicolas thought to himself. He was going to have to help the beautiful Marguerite, for she had clearly not thought out this stage of her offensive.

'A most valuable piece of evidence. There exist others even more damning. For example, do you suspect that your father-in-law undermined your husband's health and prevented you from conceiving with wax figurines?' he suggested.

She nodded.

'Good. In your opinion, does he summon demons in a cellar or a burnt-out chapel?'

'There is one not far from where he lives.'

'It is common in these places to find evidence of black masses, such as inverted crucifixes and candles blackened with soot. You will need to verify this in the presence of a notary. Do you suspect him of taking part in sexual acts of a depraved and unnatural nature?'

'I am convinced of it … with me he tried to …'

And a man of good taste into the bargain, Florin reflected approvingly, if indeed there was any truth in the accusation.

'Why, the scoundrel! However, I had more repulsive, bestial acts in mind.'

She raised her eyebrows questioningly.

'For example, involving animals such as goats …'

During the next half-hour, Nicolas Florin listed every piece of evidence Marguerite needed to plant so that the men-at-arms and the notary, whose testimony was crucial to the inquisitors, could find it without any difficulty.

She was beaming as she stood up to leave. She approached his desk, her hands outstretched in a gesture of gratitude. He grasped them, raised one to his lips and ran his tongue over her palm. She closed her eyes in ecstasy and murmured:

'This affair promises to be most intoxicating, Seigneur.'

'I am ready to intercede at a moment's notice, Madame.'

She threw him a beguiling look as she left the room, and he unfolded the note she had slipped into his hand. Printed on it was a sum: five hundred pounds. There was no need for any contract. Who would be foolish enough to default on a debt to an inquisitor – pecuniary or otherwise?

*

The would-be Marguerite Galée walked along sedately until she turned the corner of the Inquisition headquarters, when she felt her legs give way beneath her. She leaned against the enclosure wall for a moment and took a deep breath. She heard a low voice like an instantly soothing balm, a voice she associated with a past miracle.

'Come, there's a tavern nearby. You look pale. Come and rest awhile, my friend.'

The tall cowled figure put his arm around the waist of the false Marguerite Galée and helped her along the few remaining streets. The young woman could not stop shaking and was unable to speak until they had sat down at a corner table of the establishment, which was almost deserted at that time of day. She nearly spilled the wine she was sipping from a goblet down her beautiful hired coat. The alcohol helped rid her of her feeling of nausea. Francesco de Leone removed his heavy cloak and asked:

'How do you feel, Hermine?'

'I was so afraid.'

'You're a brave woman. Drink some more and catch your breath.'

Hermine obeyed. How strange that this magnificent man, the only man ever to have refused her when all she had to offer by way of gratitude was her body, could calm her with a look or one of his inscrutable smiles. How strange that he alone had helped her feel at peace with her own soul – and even with those of others.

She was able to summon up that afternoon of pure terror as vividly, painfully and perfectly as if it had taken place only yesterday.

He had not judged her, the beautiful archangel; he had barely spoken. He had stood between this woman whom he did not know and an angry volley of stones. The blood had trickled down his forehead and onto his cheek. He had not protested or backed away or drawn his sword from the scabbard swinging against his calf. He had simply looked at them, and his piercing blue gaze and the cross above his heart had made even the most vehement of her tormentors bow their heads.

Stoned. They wanted to stone her to death. Hermine had belonged to a Cypriot lord – bought and paid for like a bolt of silk, a pack of hunting dogs or a censer. When he died, his frantic widow claimed that Hermine had bewitched him, had stolen him from her bed and killed him with her caresses and love potions. The ludicrous nature of these accusations had deterred no one: they were reason enough for an execution. A horde of men, women and even a few children had chased her for hours along the cliffs, shouting and jeering merrily as they passed each other bottles of wine. Finally they had cornered her in a cove. Exhausted, Hermine had curled up like a terrified animal, shielding her head with her arms. She had recognised the excitement in their eyes. The thrill of sanctioned murder. A shower of stones rained down on her. Then all of a sudden he had appeared and thrust her behind his back and they had scuttled away like crabs, those evildoers turned executioners, intoxicated by a taste of power.

It was strange. She would have travelled to the ends of the earth for her knight and yet he had only wanted her to go to the end of the street, as far as the Inquisition headquarters.

Hermine held out her hand and Francesco clasped it between his. This simple contact made the young woman close her eyes. He released his grip, and she murmured:

'Forgive me.'

'It is I who must ask your forgiveness for placing you in a dangerous situation.'

'You warned me. Pleasing you is so sweet to me.' She smiled apologetically before continuing: 'I enjoy being eternally indebted to you. I owe you my life and you can never forget me – for the lives of those we save belong to us. We cannot change this however much we may wish to.'

It was his turn to smile now. Like Éleusie, and his mother and sister before her, Hermine unknowingly reawakened his compassion, allowed him to lower his guard, to fall asleep without clasping the hilt of his sword. Hermine and the other women who lived in his memory had the power to wash away for a moment the Giotto Capellas of this world and all the baseness he encountered.

'What is your opinion of him?'

'It is not a question of opinion, dear knight, but of fact. He is the worst kind of vermin. No. Vermin is not the right word. He is vile, corrupt, beyond redemption.'

'I understand. Things have been made even easier for the likes of him since the Pope granted inquisitors the right to absolve each other of any blunders or transgressions.[69] And this generosity has been extended to allow them to preside over torture sessions, which was previously forbidden. I'll wager Florin could not have wished for a more appetising gift.'

'They frighten me,' murmured Hermine.

'They frighten everybody and the fear they inspire is their main weapon. Tell me about the meeting.'

She recounted every detail of her encounter with Florin, including the moist caress he had left on the palm of her hand. He listened, nodding occasionally.

'There is something I don't quite understand, Francesco,' she continued. 'You must have already guessed all this from what your aunt told you about Florin's dealings with Larnay.'

'Of course, and …' He paused, then changed his mind: 'You see, my dear Hermine, a man is being condemned and I must know whether his cruelty is the result of a sickness of the soul or of the mind. Thanks to you, I am now certain that there is nothing wrong with his reason since he sells trials for personal gain. I shall make one more appeal to him … and if he fails to respond, his time of grace will be up.'

She paused before asking the dreadful question:

'Is he to die?'

'I do not know. I … do not plan an enemy's death. It either happens or it does not.' He grew silent for a moment before continuing: 'The landlord has agreed to let you change upstairs. My dear friend, it is time for you to return to Chartres. I have hired a horse-drawn carriage for you. I do not know how to thank you enough.'

'By not thanking me at all. As I have already said, we are responsible for our debts whether we are lenders or borrowers. You will never be rid of me or of the memory of me, my handsome knight.'

He studied her in silence for a moment and then closed his eyes and smiled:

'I have no wish to be, Hermine. Until we meet again, my fearless one.'

Her eyes brimming with tears, she tried to disguise her emotion, declaring in a sharp voice:

'Don't forget to return the fur-trim coat to the draper's and above all to get back the outrageously high deposit. These people would suck us dry if they could! On the other hand, the shoes are in a pitiful state and they are sure to demand compensation.'

'I knew Florin would notice them.'

The grime sticking to her hands and legs disgusted her. Her scalp itched and the stench of her dress, soiled with sweat and sour milk from the soup she ate each evening with a spoon she could not see, sickened her. She had removed her veil, dipped a corner of it in the ewer of water and tried to wash herself as best she could. How long had she been there? She had lost all sense of time. Three, five, eight, ten days? She had no idea and clung to the thought that sooner or later the inquisitor would have to interrogate her. And then ... No. She must avoid thinking about what would happen then. Florin was counting on using fear to break her and make his task easier. There is nothing more destructive than despair – except perhaps hope.

Had it been night or day when she slept? The nightmares had kept coming, but she had discovered a way of keeping her waking fears at bay by reliving the most precious moments in her life. They were few and far between and she was obliged to conjure up the same ones over and over again: gathering flowers, harvesting honey, the birth of a foal, Clément's knowing smile. She had spent hours reciting the ballads of Madame Marie de France,* starting again from the beginning when she forgot the words. She had recreated entire conversations of no import: stories Madame Clémence had told her, instructions she would give for a dinner, soothing words she used with Mathilde, a discussion on theology with the chaplain. Nothing of any import. Her life amounted to nothing of any import.

Agnès jumped. The sound of heavy footsteps on the stone stairs that she had descended she could not remember when, followed by Florin who was eager to show her her cell. She stiffened, listening hard, trying to interpret every sound. Was he coming to interrogate her?

The steps ended long before they reached her door. The sound of something sliding and the shuffle of feet. A heavy object being dragged. She rushed over and pressed her ear to the wooden panel and waited, straining to hear through the silence.

A shriek followed by a wail. Who was it? The man who had begged her to die quickly?

The shrieking began again and continued for what seemed to her like an eternity of pain.

The torture chamber was right next to the cells.

Her mind became awash with dark, screaming, bloody images. Agnès slumped to her knees in the mud and wept. She wept as though the world were about to end. She wept for that man, or another, for the weak and innocent – she wept because of the power of brutes.

She did not pray. She would have needed to invoke death for her prayer to have any meaning at all.

Was it morning when she awoke on her pallet with no memory of having dragged her body there? Had the endless torment just finished? Had she fainted? Had her mind mercifully allowed her a moment's oblivion?

So, the torture chamber was right next to the cells. In this way the torments of other prisoners fed the fear of those still waiting in the evil-smelling darkness of their cells.

She felt a slight sense of relief in that place that tolerated none. There would be the weeks of questioning first. The intrinsic obscenity of the thought shocked her: those others she had seen crouched on the floor were being tortured, not her, not yet.

The intention of Florin and the other inquisitors became clear. They wanted to break them, to reduce them to pitiful, terrified, tormented souls in order to convince them that salvation lay in siding with their executioners, in confessing to sins they had never committed, in denouncing others, in destroying their innocence.

Break. Break their limbs, their bones, their consciences, their souls.

Someone was approaching. Her heart missed a beat as the footsteps paused in front of her cell. A wave of nausea made her throat tighten as the bolt grated. She stood facing the door. Florin stooped to enter the tiny space, a sconce torch in his hand.

The inquisitor enquired directly in a soft voice:

'Have you made peace with your soul, Madame?'

The frightened words 'Indeed, my Lord Inquisitor' echoed in Agnès's head and yet she heard herself reply calmly and unfalteringly:

'My soul was never in turmoil, Monsieur.'

'It is my job to find that out. I consider the interrogation room more suitable for the initial cross-examination of a lady than this cell which' – he sniffed the lingering odour of excrement and stale food in the air and screwed up his face – 'which smells like a sewer.'

'I have become habituated to it, as you assured me I would when I arrived. However, the other room would allow you to sit down and me to stand up straight.'

'Do you give me your word, Madame, that you do not need shackles or a guard?'

'I doubt that it is possible to escape from the Inquisition headquarters. Besides, I am weak from these few days of semi-fasting.'

Florin nodded then turned to leave. Agnès followed him. A

fair-haired youth was waiting a few feet away, carefully holding an escritoire upon which stood an ink-horn and a small oil lamp. He was the scribe charged with recording her declarations.

As they passed the barred cells, Agnès searched in vain for the man who had grasped her ankle. Her eyes closed in a gesture of quiet relief as she realised that he must be dead. He was free of them.

The nearer they came to the low-ceilinged room, the more Agnès felt as if the air were coming alive. It felt lighter, more vibrant. They crossed the enormous room to the hallway. She felt curiously elated at the sight of a patch of sky heavy with rain clouds, seen through the tiny windows looking out onto the courtyard. They turned right and walked up another staircase made of dark wood. When they reached the landing, Florin turned to her. The effort of climbing fourteen steps had left Agnès breathless. Florin observed:

'Fasting allows the mind to soar free.'

'You are living proof of it.'

She bit her lip in fright. Had she taken leave of her senses? What did she think she was saying? Surely, if she angered him, he would wreak his revenge. He had all the means at his disposal.

Florin lost his composure for an instant. This was the other woman speaking, the one he had already glimpsed behind Agnès's pretty face. He could have sworn that she was completely oblivious to the transformation. He was mistaken. An inexorable calm washed over Agnès, flushing away the seeds of terror Florin was attempting to sow; the powerful shades whose presence she had felt during her first encounter with the inquisitor had returned.

They stopped before a high door, which the young scribe hurriedly opened. Agnès walked through, looking around her as though she were a curious visitor. For the past few moments, she had been overwhelmed by an odd sense of unreality, as though her mind were floating outside her body.

Agnès stood in the middle of the freezing, cavernous room, her mind a complete blank. Strangely, the exhaustion she had felt when she left her cell had given way to a pleasant languor.

Four men sat waiting impassively at a long table: a notary and his clerk, as required by the procedure, and two Dominicans, besides the inquisitor. The mendicant friars sat staring down at their clasped hands resting on the table, and Agnès thought to herself that despite the difference in age they could almost be twins. It was in Florin's power to call upon two 'lay persons of excellent repute', but such people were less well versed in theology and so less intimidating to the would-be heretic. Four austere-looking men dressed in black robes sitting together formed a threatening wall.

Monge de Brineux, Comte Artus d'Authon's bailiff, would not be present at the interrogation as Florin had neglected to invite him.

The inquisitor sat down in the imposing, ornately sculpted armchair at one end of the table, while the young scribe settled himself on the bench.

She listened through a fog to Florin's booming voice:

'State your Christian names, surname and status, Madame.'

'Agnès Philippine Claire de Larnay, Dame de Souarcy.'

At this point the notary rose to his feet and read out:

'In *nomine Domini, amen*. On this the fifth day of November in the year of Our Lord 1304, in the presence of the undersigned Gauthier Richer, notary at Alençon, and in the company of one of his clerks and two appointed witnesses, Brother Jean and Brother Anselme, both Dominicans of the diocese of Alençon, born respectively in Rioux and Hurepal, Agnès Philippine Claire de Larnay does appear before the venerable Brother Nicolas Florin, Dominican, Doctor in Theology and Grand Inquisitor appointed to the region of Alençon.'

The notary sat down again without glancing at Agnès. Florin continued:

'Madame, you are accused of having given refuge to a heretic by the name of Sybille Chalis, your lady's maid, of having helped her escape our justice and of having allowed yourself to be seduced by heretical ideas. Further accusations have been made against you which we consider it preferable not to discuss here today.'

The procedure allowed him to keep that trump card in case she managed miraculously to clear herself of the charge of heresy.

'Do you admit to these facts, Madame?'

'I admit to having employed in my service one Sybille Chalis, who died in childbirth during the winter of 1294. I swear on my soul that I never had the slightest suspicion of her heresy. As for the seductive power of such heretical abominations, I know nothing of it.'

'We will be the judge of that,' Florin retorted, suppressing a smile. 'Do you confess to having kept the son of this heretic, a certain Clément, who in turn entered your service?'

'As I have already stated, I did not suspect his mother's heresy, and saw in the gesture an act of Christian charity. The child has been brought up to love and respect the Church.'

'Indeed … and what of your own love of the Holy Church?'

'It is absolute.'

'Is it indeed?'

'It is.'

'In that case why not prove it here and now? Do you swear on your soul and on the death and resurrection of Christ to tell the whole truth? Do you swear that you will conceal nothing and omit nothing?'

'I swear.'

'Take heed, young woman. The seriousness of this oath far outweighs any you have sworn thus far.'

'I am aware of that.'

'Very well. Since it is my job to try by every means possible to clear you of the charges, I must ask you before we begin to tell me whether you know of any persons who might seek to harm you?'

She stared at him, feigning puzzlement through her exhaustion. Brother Anselme, the younger of the two Dominicans, believing the point needed explaining to her, cast a searching glance at the other friar before venturing:

'Sister, do you believe anyone capable of gravely perjuring themselves in order to harm you, out of hatred, envy or sheer wickedness?'

A second trap. Clément had warned her. It was better to supply a long list of potential informers than to absolve out of hand a close friend or relative who might turn out to be her fiercest accuser.

'I do. And for reasons so disgraceful that I am ashamed to mention them.'

'Pray give us their names, Madame,' the Dominican demanded.

'My half-brother, Baron Eudes de Larnay, who has hounded me with his incestuous desires since I was eight. His servant Mabile, whose surname I do not know and whom he introduced into my household in order to spy on me. Finding nothing to satisfy her master, she invented tales of heresy and shameful carnal relations in order to tarnish my name.'

Agnès went quiet as she tried to think who else might wish her harm. She hoped that her chaplain, Brother Bernard, had spared her, but after all she did not know him well. How could she be sure?

'Who else?' Brother Anselme insisted.

'My new chaplain, who does not know me well, might have misjudged me. Perhaps one of my serfs or peasants resents paying me tithes. My servant girl Adeline. I cannot imagine what possible grudge she could hold against me, but I have reached the point where I trust no one. Perhaps she took offence when I told her off one day.'

'Oh, we know that sort with their vipers' tongues. They turn up at every trial and their accusations are treated with caution. In contrast, a man of the cloth ... However, we shall see. Anybody else?'

'I am not guilty of any discrimination.'

'If this is the truth, then God's acknowledgement will enlighten us accordingly. Anybody else, Madame?' Brother Anselme insisted, glancing again at the other Dominican, who remained impassive.

Agnès thought quickly: Clément, Gilbert the simpleton, Artus d'Authon, Monge de Brineux, Éleusie de Beaufort, Jeanne d'Amblin and many others occurred to her, but no one who was capable of perjuring themselves out of sheer spite. Gilbert, perhaps. He was a gentle soul but weak and malleable enough for an inquisitor easily to put words in his mouth. She added regretfully:

'Gilbert, one of my farm hands. He is a simpleton and understands very little of anything. He lives in a world of his own.' Suddenly fearful of endangering him, she corrected herself: 'But his soul has always remained faithful to Our Lord, who loves the pure and innocent ...'

She weighed her words. She must avoid implying that Florin was assembling false accusations or biased testimonies. She was still unsure whether the two friars Anselme and Jean were Florin's henchmen, but she did not want to risk vexing them by incriminating a representative of their order, a doctor in theology moreover.

'... He is dull-witted and slow of speech and it would be easy to draw stories out of him that might appear strange or even suspicious.'

'Madame ...' the Dominican chided her softly in a sad voice.

'Do you truly believe that we would consider the accusations of a simpleton?'

She was sure they would not, but this way the notary was obliged to record that Gilbert was a simpleton. Any accusation forced out of him, then twisted to show his lady in a bad light, would be considered suspect.

'Is that all, Madame?' Anselme insisted again, turning quickly to look at Friar Jean. 'Think hard. It is not the aim of this court to entrap the accused by deceitful means.'

She bit her lip, narrowly avoiding blurting out the words that were on the tip of her tongue:

'God will recognise his true people, and you are not among them.'

Instead she affirmed:

'I can think of no other informant.'

Florin was ecstatic. Even before Agnès entered the interrogation chamber he knew it would never occur to her that her own daughter might be her most vehement accuser. The young girl, pampered by her uncle, had filled a page with well-turned phrases written in appallingly bad script containing enough poison to deal her mother a deathly blow. The girl's accusations – a mishmash of heresy, sorcery and immoral behaviour – smacked of Eudes de Larnay's scheming and Florin had not been taken in for a moment. On the contrary, he was certain of Agnès's innocence. It was a source of comfort to him that such a pretty exterior could conceal so much malice, resentment and jealousy, for the flawed natures of the majority of his fellow creatures guaranteed him a long and fruitful career. He was already savouring the thought of Agnès's devastation upon reading this ignoble calumny. Her own daughter, whom she had made every effort to protect, was prepared to send her to the stake without the slightest hesitation. What a delightfully amusing thought.

He approached Agnès and handed her the Gospels. She placed her hand on the enormous black book bound in leather.

'Madame, do you solemnly swear before God and upon your soul to tell the truth?'

'I do.' She recalled the words Clément had taught her, and added: 'May God come to my aid if I keep this vow and may He condemn me if I perjure myself.'

Florin gave a little nod to the notary, who rose to his feet and declared:

'Agnès, Dame de Souarcy and resident of Manoir de Souarcy, having been read the accusation and having placed her right hand upon the Gospels and sworn to tell the whole truth concerning herself and others, will now proceed to be cross-examined.'

Florin thanked the notary with a polite gesture and studied

Agnès at length, half closing his eyes, as though in prayer, before enquiring in a soft voice:

'Madame de Souarcy, dear child, dear sister … Do you believe that Christ was born of a virgin?'

The cross-examination had begun with all its ruses and pitfalls; if she replied 'I believe he was' it could be interpreted as a sign that she was unsure. Clément had read her a list of all the trick questions. She replied in a steady voice:

'I am certain that Christ was born of a virgin.'

A flicker of annoyance showed on Florin's face. He continued:

'Do you believe in the one Holy Catholic Church?'

Again, it was necessary to rephrase the sentence in order to prevent any unfavourable interpretation:

'There exists no other church than the Holy Catholic Church.'

'Do you believe that the Holy Ghost proceeds from the Father and the Son as we believe?'

She remembered Clément reading her the exact same sentence as though it were yesterday. Most of the accused responded in good faith, 'I do.' The Grand Inquisitor then pointed out that they were skilfully twisting the words in the manner of heretics and that by 'yes, I do' they really meant 'yes, I believe that you believe it' when in fact they believed the contrary.

'It is clear that the Holy Ghost proceeds from the Father and the Son.'

Florin continued in this vein for a few minutes before realising that he would not catch her out. He declared in a loud voice for all to hear:

'I see that Madame de Souarcy has learned her lesson well.'

Before he could interrupt her, she retorted:

'To what lesson are you referring, Seigneur Inquisitor? Are

you suggesting that faith in Jesus Christ is learned by rote like the alphabet? Surely we are born with it, of it. It is what we are. It illuminates and pervades us. Might you have learned it as another learns a meat recipe? I shudder to think.'

The colour drained from the inquisitor's face and he clenched his jaw. He stared at her darkly through his soft eyes. It flashed through her mind that he would have hit her if there had been no witnesses.

The Dominican friar who had questioned her cleared his throat awkwardly. She had scored a victory over Florin and he would be merciless. But she had also gained some time and, without knowing why, the need to hold out as long as she could seemed imperative.

Florin, struggling to regain his composure, ordered her to be taken back to her cell. As she descended into her daily hell, she kept repeating to herself:

'Knowledge is power. The most invincible weapon, dear sweet Clément.'

The moment the guard had pushed her into her cell and slammed the heavy door behind her, she fell to her knees, clasped her hands together and tried to comprehend where the strength to hold her head up high and stand firm had come from.

'Clémence … My sweet angel … Thank you.'

Back in the interrogation room, Florin was seething. He could not understand how the week of fasting and solitary confinement he had inflicted on his prey had not worn down her last resistance. This female had questioned him, ridiculed him in front of two of his brothers. He reviled her and – why not admit it? – he was beginning to fear her.

After she had gone he tried to manoeuvre himself back into a position of strength by declaring in a passionate voice filled with regret:

'Such a clever tongue is a sure sign of a perverse and devious mind, and points more clearly to heresy than any accusation. We have seen how these lost souls defend themselves thanks to the deviant teachings they receive, and how they try to confuse us with their antics. Women, who by their very nature are treacherous and scheming, are even more expert at it.'

Maître Gauthier Richer, the notary, gave a little nod of approval. In his view, the cunning, calculating nature of women made them prime recruits for the devil. However, Nicolas Florin sensed that his little speech had not entirely convinced the two Dominican friars who had been summoned as witnesses. In particular Brother Jean, who had not yet spoken and refused to catch the inquisitor's eye.

Brother Anselme spoke again in a soft voice:

'Let us reconsider, brother, my Lord Inquisitor, young Mathilde de Souarcy's damning testimony.'

'Damning indeed,' Florin repeated, pleased by the choice of adjective. 'In it Mademoiselle Mathilde ...'

'A direct reading of it might prove more enlightening, brother,' interrupted Jean de Rioux, speaking for the first time.

Florin searched for a hint of suspicion, hesitation or even complicity, in the man's voice, but found nothing to betray his witness's attitude. A fresh concern was added to the rage the inquisitor had felt during Agnès's declaration. The presence of religious witnesses belonging to the same order as the inquisitor made a mockery of justice. Indeed, Florin could not recall a single occasion during any trial where the former had contradicted the latter. This was the real reason why he had chosen not to summon lay witnesses. Even so, everything about Brother Jean de Rioux worried him: his thoughtful silence, his composure, his unwillingness to look Florin in the eye, even his hands, which were oddly robust for a man of letters approaching fifty. Moreover, Anselme de Hurepal appeared to seek his approval before each of his interventions. He chided himself: he was behaving like a frightened child again. It was only natural for these two fools to take their role seriously, but he would give them short shrift as he had the others.

He approached the table and plucked Mathilde de Souarcy's statement from under a small pile of papers. He began reading aloud:

'I, Mathilde Clémence Marie de Souarcy, only child of Madame Agnès de Souarcy …'

He did not see Jean glance at Anselme. The younger man interrupted on cue:

'Pray, Brother Inquisitor … We are able to read. I believe that it would be most helpful if we acquainted ourselves with Mademoiselle de Souarcy's words in quiet contemplation, the better to consider their significance.'

Florin almost uttered a curse. What! Did these two fools dare to cast doubt on his word? Brother Anselme insisted:

'Are we to understand that this young girl is not yet of age?'

'She will be soon – in a year's time. Besides, the accusations of children against their parents are not only admitted but strongly encouraged regardless of their age. Indeed, who is better placed to judge corruption than those who live with it, who put up with it day in, day out?'

'Indeed,' the Dominican conceded, stretching out his hand. Florin reluctantly passed him the statement. Brother Anselme read it first and then handed it over to Brother Jean. The Dominican's impassive expression and his slowness in reading exasperated Florin. Finally, Brother Jean looked up and remarked:

'These words are enough to condemn her without further ado.'

The inquisitor felt as though a weight had been lifted off his shoulders and said, smiling:

'Did I not tell you? She is guilty and although it pains me greatly to say it I hold out little hope of her salvation.'

His relief was short-lived.

'Even so … Is it not extraordinary that this young girl who barely knows how to hold a quill and whose script is so clumsily executed expresses herself with such consummate skill? Let us see … "My soul suffers at the thought of the constant abominations committed by Madame de Souarcy, my mother, and her persistent sinfulness and deviance make me fear for her soul" or "The young chaplain, so devout the day he arrived, oblivious to this shadow of evil hanging over us …" or "God granted me the strength to resist living with evil despite my mother's constant example …" Gracious me! What convincing rhetoric.'

Brother Jean raised his head and for the first time Florin's eyes met his. The man's gaze was infinite and he had the dizzying sensation of walking through a never-ending archway. Florin blinked involuntarily. Jean declared in a firm voice:

'May I share our concern with you, Brother Inquisitor? Although we are only present in an … advisory capacity, we would find it very distressing if your purity and ardent faith were manipulated by false witnesses. We therefore strongly recommend that Mademoiselle de Souarcy be brought here to the Inquisition headquarters to be questioned before this assembly without her uncle being present.'

Florin hesitated for a fraction of a second. It was in his power to refuse this precautionary measure, but such a refusal would come back to haunt him. An unpleasant thought occurred to him. What if these two monks had been secretly placed as witnesses by Camerlingo Benedetti, to whom he owed his departure from Carcassonne and his new post at Alençon? What if they were in fact papal inspectors, like the ones sent by the Holy See to settle internal disputes in the monasteries or to ensure the smooth running of trials? Nicolas's career was too promising for him to take any unnecessary risks. He was in no doubt that the wretched little Mathilde would stand by her testimony and that Eudes could be counted upon to help her. However, the Dominican's request would mean a delay in proceedings. Still, the cloaked figure who had insisted Agnès de Souarcy must die had not specified any precise date.

The most prudent course of action would be to comply.

'I am grateful to you, brother, for your concern. The knowledge that others are at hand to ensure the purity and integrity of the inquisitorial tribunal is invaluable to one such as I who presides in solitary judgement. Scribe ... record the summoning of the witness and send for Mademoiselle de Souarcy.'

Another thought cheered him.

Once Mathilde had arrived he could arrange a confrontation between mother and daughter. What a delightful spectacle that promised to be.

Éleusie de Beaufort closed her eyes. A warm tear trickled down her face into the corner of her mouth. Blanche de Blinot, the senior nun, clenched her fist spasmodically and repeated as though she were reciting a litany:

'What is happening, what is happening? She is dead, isn't she? … How could she be dead? She was still so young!'

Gentle Adélaïde's corpse lay in its coffin, which was resting on a pair of trestles in the middle of the registry, waiting to be taken to the abbey's Church of Notre-Dame. Annelette Beaupré had struggled with the dead girl's stubborn tongue, which protruded gruesomely, and had finally resorted to gagging the dead girl with a strip of linen in order to keep the thing inside her mouth. Consequently the dignity refused to her in death was restored.

They had all paid their respects, tearfully, silently or in prayer, to the young woman who had been in charge of the kitchens and their meals. Annelette had studied their different demeanours, the uneasy, distant or forlorn expressions on their faces, determined to discover the culprit among them, for she was convinced that her theory was correct and had shared her thoughts with the Abbess.

Éleusie had protested at first, but had soon yielded to the apothecary's implacable logic and accepted the unacceptable: they were rubbing shoulders every day with the goodly Adélaïde's killer. Her fear had given way to painful despair. Evil had slipped in with that creature of darkness Nicolas Florin. She had felt it.

The Abbess had remained at her desk for many hours, unable

to move, unsure of how to act, of where to start. She had learned that no amount of prayer or lighting of candles could drive out evil. Evil would only recoil in the face of pure unflinching souls who were prepared to fight to the death. The titanic battle had no end; it had existed since the beginning of time and would go on raging until the end. Unless …

The time for peace had not yet come. Éleusie was going to fight because Clémence, Philippine and Claire would have taken up arms without a second thought. Why was she still alive when the others would have been so much better equipped for battle?

Early that morning, Jeanne d'Amblin had left on her rounds to visit the abbey's regular benefactors and new alms givers.[70] The extern sister had been reluctant to leave the Mother Abbess alone to face whatever came next. Éleusie had used all her authority to persuade Jeanne to go. Now she regretted her decision. Jeanne's competence, her energy, her firm but gentle resolve were a comfort to her. She raised her eyes and glanced at Annelette, who was shaking her head.

She walked over to the apothecary, pulling Blanche behind her, and said in a hushed voice:

'I want everybody, without exception, in the scriptorium in half an hour.'

'That might prove dangerous,' replied the tall woman.

'Might we not do better to lead a more … discreet investigation?'

'There is no greater danger than refusing to see, daughter. I want everyone to be there except for the lay women. I will see them later.'

'The murderess might lash out if she feels cornered. If she fears discovery, she might attack another sister, perhaps even you.'

'That is precisely what I'm hoping, to make her panic.'

'It is too risky. Poisoning is such a subtle art that even I am powerless to prevent it. Could we not …'

'That is an order, Annelette.'

'I … Very well, Reverend Mother.'

A wall of still white robes ruffled only by a slight draught. Éleusie made out the tiny faces, brows, eyes and lips of the fifty-odd women, half of them novices, who were waiting, wondering why they had been summoned. And yet Éleusie was sure that no one but the murderess had suspected the true magnitude of the tidal wave that was about to engulf the scriptorium. Seated at one of the writing desks, Annelette lowered her head, fiddling absent-mindedly with a small knife used for sharpening quill pens. One question had been nagging at her since the evening before. Why would anyone find it necessary to kill poor Adélaïde? Had she uncovered the identity of the poisoner? Had she seen or heard something that implicated her killer? For the cup of herbal tea, which the apothecary had discovered, had been given to the sister in charge of meals at a time in the evening when she was alone in the kitchens. The murderess must have taken advantage of this fact to bring her the fatal beverage. In addition to these questions another worry was plaguing Annelette: what if the poisoner had taken the drug from her medicine cabinet in the herbarium? The apothecary nun was in the habit of treating pain, facial neuralgia and fever[71] with dilutions of aconite.

'Daughters … Sister Adélaïde is with Our Lord. Her soul, I know, rests in peace.' Éleusie de Beaufort breathed in sharply before continuing in a strident voice: 'However, the suffering endured by whoever has usurped the will of God will be eternal. Her punishment in this world will be terrible and the ensuing torment inflicted upon her by the Almighty unimaginable.'

Some of the sisters glanced at one another, unable to grasp the meaning of this judgement. Others stared at their Abbess with a mixture of amazement and alarm. The morbid silence that had descended was broken by a flurry of voices, feet scraping the floor and stifled exclamations.

'Silence!' thundered Éleusie. 'Silence, I have not finished yet.'

The astonished nervous whispers instantly came to a stop.

'Our sweet sister Adélaïde was poisoned with a cup of honey and lavender tea that contained aconite.'

Fifty gasps rose as one and reverberated against the ceiling of the enormous scriptorium. Éleusie took advantage of the ensuing hubbub to examine the faces, searching in vain for any sign that might reveal the culprit.

'Silence!' Éleusie exclaimed. 'Silence this instant! As you would expect, I do not intend to ask which of you brewed the tea as I doubt I would receive an answer.' She paused and looked again at the fifty faces staring back at her, her gaze lingering on Berthe de Marchiennes, Yolande de Fleury, Hedwige du Thilay, but most of all on Thibaude de Gartempe. 'However, you – and by you I mean the person responsible for this unforgivable crime – have underestimated me. I may not know your name yet, but I shall find it out before long.'

A tremulous voice broke the profound silence following this promise:

'I don't understand what's going on. Will somebody please tell me what our Reverend Mother is saying?'

Blanche de Blinot was fidgeting on her bench, turning first to one sister then another. A novice leaned over and explained to her in a whisper.

'But ... I took her the tea!' Thrown into a sudden panic, the old woman groaned: 'You say she died from a cup of poisoned honey and lavender tea? How could that be?'

Éleusie looked at her as though a chasm were opening at her feet.

'What are you saying, Blanche dear? That it was you who brewed the tea for Adélaïde?'

'Yes. Well ... No, it didn't happen quite like that. I found the cup on my desk when I was preparing to go to vespers. I sniffed it ... and well, I have never really cared much for lavender tea, it is too fragrant for me,' she said in a hushed voice, as though confessing to some terrible sin. 'Although I am partial to verbena, especially when it is flavoured with mint ...'

'Blanche ... The facts, please,' Éleusie interrupted.

'Forgive me, Reverend Mother ... I digress ... I am getting so old ... Well, I assumed Adélaïde had prepared it for me and so I took the cup back to the kitchen. She is ... was such a considerate girl. She said it was a shame to waste it and that she would drink it herself.'

Éleusie caught the astonished eye of the apothecary nun. Who else besides the two of them had understood the significance of this exchange? Certainly not Blanche, the intended victim, who was agonising over having handed the poisoned tea to her cherished sister. Somebody had wanted to get rid of Blanche. But why? Why kill a half-deaf old woman who spent most of her time snoozing? Éleusie could feel a pair of hate-filled eyes boring into her from she did not know where. She made a monumental effort to carry on:

'I am now in possession of the evidence I needed in order to follow up my suspicions. My theory of how to unmask the culprit is based upon the identity of the victim. Adélaïde's death, however terrible, was a mistake. It is all becoming clear. You may go now, daughters. I shall write directly to Monsieur Monge de Brineux, Seigneur d'Authon's chief bailiff, informing him of this murder and providing him with the names of two likely suspects. I shall demand that the culprit be given a public beating before being executed. May God's will be done.'

No sooner had she closed the door of her apartments than her show of authority, her bravado, crumbled. She sat on the edge of her bed, incapable of moving or even thinking. She waited, waited for the hand that would administer the poison, for the face filled with bottomless loathing or fear. She heard a sound in the adjoining study, the faint rustle of a robe. Death was approaching in a white robe, a wooden crucifix round its neck.

Annelette stood in the doorway to her bed chamber. Visibly upset, she stammered:

'You ...'

'I what?' murmured Éleusie, her weary voice barely audible.

Trembling with rage, the tall woman roared at her:

'Why did you make such a claim? You have no more idea who is responsible for this horrific act than I. Why make believe that you do? Have you taken leave of your senses? She will kill you now to avoid being unmasked. You have left her no other option.'

'That was my intention.'

'I am helpless to protect you. There exist so many poisons and so few antidotes.'

'Why did she try to poison Blanche de Blinot? The question haunts me, yet I can think up no answer. Do you think that Blanche ...'

'No. She still hasn't realised that she was the intended victim. She is too upset by Adélaïde's death. I have taken her back to her beloved steam room.'

'And what about the others?'

'The few who possess a modicum of intelligence suspect the truth.'

'Who would do this?'

'Don't you mean why?' corrected Annelette. 'We are all in danger until we unravel this deadly plot. We must stop looking at the problem from the wrong angle. I, too, confess to concentrating on scrutinising the other sisters, but it is not the right approach. If we discover the motive, we will have the culprit.'

'Do you think you will succeed?' asked Éleusie, feeling reassured for the first time by the imposing woman's forbidding presence.

'I shall do my utmost. Your meals will no longer be served separately. You will help yourself from the communal pot. You will neither eat nor drink anything that is brought or offered to you. What were you thinking! If the murderess gives any credence to your declarations and thinks she's been unmasked, she'll ...'

Éleusie's exhaustion gave way to a strange calm. She declared resolutely:

'I have cut off her retreat. Now she is forced to advance.'

'By killing you?'

'God is my judge. I am ready to meet Him and have no fear.'

'You seem to place very little importance on your own life,' said Annelette disdainfully. 'Death is a trifling matter, indeed ... It comes to us all and I wonder why we fear it so. Life is a far more uncertain and difficult undertaking. Have you decided to renounce it out of convenience or cowardice? I confess I am disappointed in you, Reverend Mother.'

'I will not permit you to ...'

Annelette interrupted her sharply:

411

'I don't give a fig for your permission! Have you forgotten that when you accepted your post you vowed to watch over your daughters? Now is not the time to go back on that vow. What were you expecting? That your time here at Clairets would pass by like a pleasant stroll in the country? It might have but it didn't. Until we discover the intentions of this monster we will all be in danger.'

'I thought death was a matter of indifference to you?'

'It is. However, I confess that I place great value on my life and I haven't the slightest intention of giving it away to the first killer who comes along.'

Éleusie was preparing a sharp rejoinder but was deterred by the sombre look in Annelette's usually clear eyes. Annelette continued in a low voice:

'You surprise me, Madame. Have you already forgotten all those who went before us? Have you forgotten that our quest outweighs any one of us and that our lives and deaths are no longer our own? Would you yield so easily when Claire chose to perish on the steps at Acre rather than surrender?'

'What are you talking about?' whispered Éleusie, taken aback by this unexpected declaration. 'Who are you?'

'I am Annelette Beaupré, your apothecary nun.'

'What do you know about the quest?'

'Like you, Madame, I am a link in the chain. But a link that will never yield.'

'What are you talking about? A link in what chain?'

'In a thousand-year-old chain that is timeless. Did you really believe that you, Francesco and Benoît were alone in your search?'

Éleusie was dumbfounded.

'I ...'

412

'I believe Benoît was aware of every link down to the last rivet.'

'Who are you?' the Abbess repeated.

'My mission is to watch over you. I do not know why and I do not ask. It is enough for me to know that my life will not have been in vain, that it will have been one of many fragments joining together to form the foundation of the purest and most noble sanctuary.'

A silence descended on the two women at the end of the confession. The Abbess's incredulity was swept away by the sudden revelation. So, others besides Francesco, Benoît and her were working in the shadows and fearful of being discovered. Annelette's chain conjured up a more far-reaching enterprise than Éleusie had ever imagined. How blind she had been never to have suspected. She wondered whether her nephew had been more perceptive. No. He would never have left his beloved aunt in the dark. This explained the frequent coincidences that had guided Éleusie's life all these years, as well as Francesco's sometimes inexplicable discoveries and Benoît's help, even her appointment at Clairets. Éleusie had never requested the post, and yet it was here that the secret library was located. And Manoir de Souarcy was a stone's throw from the abbey.

Agnès.

'Annelette ... Tell me more about this ... this chain.'

The large woman sighed before confessing:

'I have told you most of what I know, Reverend Mother. For a time, I believed that our dear departed Benoît was in charge of its organisation. I was mistaken. Indeed, I am not even sure how apt the idea of a chain is.'

'In that case who ordered you to watch over me?' Éleusie was growing exasperated.

'Benoît, of course.'

'Our Pope, Nicolas Boccasini?'

'Yes.'

'How could that be? Did you know him?'

'I belonged to his entourage when he was Bishop of Ostia.'

'But he knew nothing about me ... I was a mere intermediary.'

'Perhaps.'

Éleusie's annoyance was gradually giving way to alarm. She was beginning to feel that they were all unknowingly caught up in an enormous spider's web. She stammered:

'Are we not unwitting pawns on a chessboard we cannot even perceive?'

'What does it matter if the chessboard is glorious? That is not the question. I am convinced that the person bringing death to our abbey is also responsible for the demise of the papal emissary whose apparently charred corpse was found in the forest with no signs of any fire nearby ... Ergot of rye.' Annelette appeared to reflect for a moment before adding: 'Did you feed that messenger, the one who came here to see you?'

The Abbess understood instantly what the apothecary nun was driving at, and her heart sank at the thought that she might have unconsciously aided the poisoner. She exclaimed:

'Dear God ... you don't suppose the bread I gave him ... Could the oats, barley and spelt wheat used to make our daily bread have been contaminated?'

'Ergot can infect other plants, though it is rare. And the flour Adélaïde found in the herbarium was unquestionably rye. It remains to be seen who gave the man the poisoned bread.'

Éleusie chided herself for feeling selfishly relieved.

'It seems likely that the monster also killed the emissaries that were sent before and after the one you received here,' Annelette continued.

Éleusie stared at her in silence. It was clear to her, too, and she could have kicked herself for not seeing it sooner. Tears of deep despair welled up in her eyes. Clémence, Claire, Philippine … You who have carried me all these years would be so disappointed by my weakness now.

'Do you think there may also be a connection with Madame Agnès's arrest and the arrival of that inquisitor?' she heard herself ask in a muffled voice she barely recognised as her own.

'It would not surprise me at all, Reverend Mother. However, I must know more before I can decide. Who is Madame de Souarcy really? And why is she so important to you? The secrecy we swore for our own protection complicates matters. You know that my task is to protect you and yet I know nothing of yours. Now that Benoît is dead, I think we must change the rules of the game.'

Éleusie paused:

'What do you know about … What did Benoît tell you about …'

The apothecary smiled sadly and declared:

'It is a difficult subject to broach, is it not? You cannot be sure how much I know, and I have no notion of the extent of what has been revealed to you. We observe one another, both reluctant to break our vow of absolute silence. I, too, have been hesitating for a long moment, Madame. I veer between the certainty that in the face of this partially glimpsed danger we must inevitably confide in one another, and the fear of making a disastrous error of judgement by unreservedly giving you my trust.'

Annelette's words perfectly captured Éleusie de Beaufort's own thoughts.

'Then we must be brave, daughter, for it takes courage to trust others. What did Benoît tell you about the quest?'

The apothecary's gaze strayed towards the window:

'In truth, not a great deal. Benoît was afraid that too much knowledge might endanger the brothers and sisters who had joined his cause. No doubt he was right. His death is painful evidence of it. He revealed a few of the facts to me, but in such a disjointed way that I cannot be sure of having grasped everything. I can only relate them to you as they were related to me, over time. He spoke of a thousand-year-old struggle between two powers. Since the discovery of a birth chart, or rather two birth charts that are now in our possession, this secret but bloody war has been moving steadily towards its climax. One of the two planetary alignments concerns a woman whose whereabouts will become known during a lunar eclipse. Up until now the estimation of these two birth dates has been hindered by an erroneous astrological calculation. This woman must be protected, even at the cost of our lives. You play a key role in her protection, and I in turn am your guardian. That is all I know.'

Annelette turned her gaze from the gardens and studied Éleusie before concluding: 'Why did I not think of it before? The woman is Agnès de Souarcy, isn't she?'

'We think so ... but we are not entirely sure. All of Francesco's research and calculations point to it being her.'

'Why is her life so precious?'

'We still do not know despite our endless speculations. Madame de Souarcy has no link with the Holy Land ... Therefore she does not belong to the holy lineage as we had first supposed. Come and sit down here next to me, Annelette.'

The towering woman moved a few paces from the door with what seemed a heavier step than usual. Éleusie enquired:

'Are you afraid?'

'Of course I am, Reverend Mother. And yet doesn't human

greatness lie in the ability to conquer that inborn fear which makes us want to hide in a hole and never come out, and carry on fighting?'

Éleusie gave a wistful smile.

'You might be describing my life. I have always been afraid. I have tried hard to be brave and have failed more often than I have succeeded. I increasingly regret that death spared me and not one of my sisters. Any one of them would have been so much stronger and more resolute than I.'

Annelette sat down beside her on the edge of the bed and said softly:

'How can you be sure of that? Who knows where or to what end we are being moved on the chessboard of which you spoke?'

The apothecary nun let out a sigh. The two women sat in silence for a moment. Éleusie was the first to speak:

'I feel as if I am surrounded by an impenetrable fog. I have no idea what to do or which way to turn.'

Annelette sat up straight, declaring in her usual commanding tone:

'We are not alone now. There are two of us, and I have no intention of allowing that evil snake to strike again with impunity. No! She will have me to contend with, us, and we will show her no mercy!'

The Abbess felt some of the same self-assurance – the same anger even – that she detected in Annelette. She too sat up straight and asked:

'What can we do?'

'Firstly, we must increase our vigilance in order to guarantee our own safety. As I told you, Abbess, our lives are no longer ours to do with as we please, and certainly not to make a gift of to any murderess. Secondly, we shall conduct an investigation.

Benoît is dead. We are therefore on our own and can expect no more timely help from him. The criminal is cunning. I suspect that she pilfers my remedies from the cupboard in the herbarium, which proves that she is well versed in the art of poison. I plan to remove the contents of certain bags and phials. We will need to store them in a safe place …'

Éleusie immediately thought of the library. No, she would keep the knowledge of that secret place even from Annelette.

'Then I will lay a little trap of my own for that snake.'

'What trap is that?'

'I prefer it to remain a surprise, Reverend Mother.'

Annelette's caution reassured Éleusie: the apothecary nun would not be taken in by anybody. So she did not insist upon being told her plan and simply nodded.

'And now,' her daughter continued, 'we must turn our thoughts to Blanche de Blinot. Why would anyone want to murder a senile old woman who is going deaf and forgets everything she says or does from one moment to the next?'

The portrait was scarcely a charitable one, but Éleusie was beyond the customary petty reproofs it had been her task to mete out before.

'Blanche is our most senior nun,' the apothecary continued, 'and your second in command, as well as acting prioress during her moments of lucidity, which are becoming few and far between.'

Annelette jumped up. A sudden thought had occurred to her. She pointed an accusatory finger at the Abbess and all but shouted:

'And she is guardian of the seal!'

'My seal!' Éleusie cried out in horror, also jumping up. 'Do you think somebody might have taken it? A seal breaker![72] My seal can be used to send secret messages to Rome, to the King, to sign deeds, even death sentences … and any number of other things …'

'When Blanche is not using the seal to authenticate minor documents in your name in order to lighten your chores, where is it kept?'

'In my safe with my private papers.'

No sooner had she spoken than it dawned on her. Annelette appeared not to notice her unease for she insisted:

'And is it there now?'

'No … I mean, yes, I am certain it is,' confirmed the Abbess, touching her chest to make sure that the key she always wore on its heavy chain was still there.

The sudden change in her voice alerted Annelette, who studied her attentively and waited for her to continue.

'As an extra precaution, every abbey safe has three keys. The lock will not open without the combination of all three. It is the custom for the Abbess to have custody of one, the guardian of the seal another and the prioress the third.'

'Am I to understand that as guardian of the seal and prioress Blanche keeps two keys?'

'No. Our senior nun's waning faculties induced me to take one back and entrust it to the cellarer nun, who answers directly to me and whose position in the abbey hierarchy makes her the obvious next choice.'

'That spiteful creature Berthe de Marchiennes! I wouldn't trust her with my life.'

'You go too far, my child,' Éleusie chided half-heartedly.

'And what of it? Have we not gone beyond polite pleasantries? I don't trust the woman.'

'Nor do I,' the Abbess confessed, 'and she is not the only one.' Éleusie paused for a moment before recounting the curious scene she had stumbled upon some weeks before: the exchange between the schoolmistress, Emma de Pathus, and Nicolas Florin, whom she had been obliged to lodge at the abbey.

'Emma de Pathus actually spoke to the inquisitor whose presence we were forced to endure?' echoed Annelette Beaupré, stunned. 'The man is evil. He is one of our enemies. What could they have been talking about? Where might she know him from?'

'I have no idea.'

'We must keep a close watch on her, then. But firstly we must ensure that nobody has stolen the key from Blanche.'

'The safe cannot be opened without my key.'

She could read in her daughter's strained expression the thoughts that she was keeping to herself. Éleusie voiced them for her:

'Indeed ... If Berthe de Marchiennes ... I mean, if the murderess is already in possession of the other two keys, then I am the last remaining obstacle,' she concluded. 'Let us go and question Blanche ... Dear God, poor Blanche ... what easy prey.'

They found the old woman in the steam room as they had expected. Blanche de Blinot sought relief for her aching bones in the only room that was heated at that time of year. She had made a little niche for herself in the corner where, with the aid of a lectern, she was able to sit and read the Gospels instead of standing up on painful limbs. The senior nun looked up at them, her eyes red from crying, and stammered:

'I would never have believed that I might one day live through such a terrible thing, Reverend Mother. Poor little Adélaïde, a poisoner in our midst, and one of our own. Has the world come to an end?'

'No, dear Blanche,' Éleusie tried to comfort her.

'Everybody is convinced that I am gradually losing my faculties and no doubt they are right. But my mind hasn't stopped working entirely. That tea was meant for me, wasn't it?'

The Abbess paused for a moment before admitting:

'Yes, dear Blanche.'

'But why? What have I done to make anyone wish to kill me? I, who have never offended nor harmed even the smallest of creatures?'

'We know, sister. Annelette and I have considered this atrocity from every angle and have gradually come to the conclusion that it wasn't a personal attack on you. Do you still have the key I gave you? The key to the safe.'

'The key? So this is about the key?'

'We think it might be.'

Blanche sat up straight on her lectern, trying not to wince with pain.

'What do you take me for!' she exclaimed in a voice that brought back to Éleusie some of the woman's former determination. 'My mind might wander sometimes, but I am not senile yet, contrary to what some say.' She shot Annelette a withering glance. 'Of course I still have it. I can feel it all the time.'

She pulled a leg out from under the lectern and thrust an ungainly leather shoe at the apothecary nun.

'Come on. Since you're still young, take off my shoe for me and roll down my stocking.'

The other woman obeyed. She discovered the tiny key under the sole of Blanche's foot. The metal had left its indentation in the pale flesh.

'This can only add to your aches and pains,' Annelette remarked.

Intent upon scoring a victory, Blanche retorted:

'That may be so, but I can be sure I'll never mislay it. Do you really think you are the only one in this abbey with an ounce of common sense?'

The apothecary nun stifled a smile she deemed incongruous in these perilous circumstances, and confessed:

'If indeed I did entertain such thoughts, you have proved me wrong.'

Blanche acknowledged her sister's rejoinder with a nod of satisfaction and declared:

'Your honesty does you credit.' A sudden sadness extinguished the old woman's fleeting contentment. 'You are right about one thing, though. I am very old and prone to falling asleep. No. I do not resent any remarks you might have made about my enfeebled state.' Turning to the Abbess, she concluded: 'Reverend Mother, you are aware of the friendship, esteem and affection I feel for you. Pray relieve me of the burden of this key. If I found this painful hiding place, it was because there were times when during my too frequent naps I felt something brush against my neck or waist. Perhaps it was merely an impression, as in a dream. But I took it seriously enough to choose … my shoe.'

'And it was very wise of you, Blanche,' Éleusie praised her. 'Let us entrust the key to our apothecary. We will publicly announce that you have been disencumbered of it at your own request without revealing who its new keeper is and in this way …'

'No one will try to kill me in order to steal it,' the old woman finished the sentence for her.

'What a shrewd idea of yours, sister, to keep it in your shoe. I shall do the same,' Annelette lied.

She had already decided upon a hiding place. She regretted lying to poor Blanche but continued to believe that the old sister's advanced age had weakened her faculties and was concerned lest she give herself over to idle and dangerous chatter. Only she and the Abbess would know where she planned to keep the key.

They left Blanche de Blinot, safe in the knowledge that she would sleep more easily.

Back in her study, the Abbess said:

'Lend me your key for a few moments. I am going to ask the cellarer nun for hers, too. I want to make sure that my seal is safe. I shall see you afterwards, Annelette.'

The other woman understood that she was being dismissed and did not take offence. No doubt the safe contained private documents. Moreover, she had to prepare her little trap, as she had chosen to refer to it.

Éleusie de Beaufort found Berthe de Marchiennes, the cellarer nun, by the hay barn. She was overseeing the counting of the hay bales being stacked in a pile by four serfs. Éleusie was instantly puzzled by Berthe's expression. She could detect no hint of sorrow on her face, or indeed any emotion whatsoever. Éleusie stifled a growing feeling of hostility. Berthe had not been close to Adélaïde, nor was she to any of the sisters. The cellarer nun was muttering under her breath:

'For goodness' sake! What idlers! At this rate we'll still be here at nightfall.'

'The bales are heavy.'

'You are too charitable, Reverend Mother. The men are slothful, that's all. All they think of is eating their fill at our expense. My father was right to ...'

Berthe stopped in mid-sentence. Her father had beaten the living daylights out of his serfs, blaming them for all his own mistakes. He had starved them and left them to die like animals and the Abbess knew it. Just as she knew that the late Monsieur de Marchiennes had taken one look at his newborn baby girl before declaring her ugly as sin, without prospects, and never giving her another thought. Berthe clung to a dream she knew to be impossible. She still aspired to the life she felt she had been deprived of, a life in which she would have been beautiful, the life her name predisposed her to, had it not been for her father's indifference and stubborn foolhardiness, which had been the ruin of the family.

'My dear Berthe, would you please lend me the key to the safe which I put in your charge.'

Éleusie thought she saw a flicker of hesitation on the cellarer's face, and was surprised by the woman's sudden awkwardness as she stammered:

'Why, naturally … I … I always keep it with me. Why … Of course it is not for me to question your reasons for opening the safe, but …'

'Quite so,' interrupted Éleusie sharply. 'The key, if you please.' The Abbess was becoming uneasy, on edge. Was Berthe going to tell her she had lost it? Had her silent reservations about the cellarer nun been justified? She held out her hand.

The other woman's crumpled, embittered little face creased up even more. She unbuttoned her robe, pulled out a long leather thong and lifted it over her veil. On the end of it hung the key.

'Thank you, daughter. I shall return it to you the moment I have finished with it.'

*

A quarter of an hour later Éleusie was shaking so much as she jiggled the three keys into position in the lock that it took her two attempts. She scarcely glanced at the seal, but let out a loud sigh of relief as her hand alighted on the *pergamênê*[73] containing the plans of the abbey. It was the only record of the existence and location of the library, and the Abbess was no longer in any doubt that this was what the murderess was looking for.

Château de Larnay, Perche, November 1304

Eudes de Larnay reread for the fifth time the brief summons signed by the inquisitor, Nicolas Florin.

What was the meaning of this new development? When Florin had advised him to produce a written statement from Mathilde de Souarcy, he had understood that the young girl would not be required to appear before her mother's judges. It was not so much that the baron wished to protect his niece, but that he was afraid that the tissue of lies he had filled her with might begin to unravel during a cross-examination.

And what of it! Florin had enough evidence to keep Agnès rotting in prison for a few months and to dispossess her of her dower! Since he was now Mathilde's legal guardian, her inheritance belonged to him for the time being. Time enough for him to achieve his aim. That flighty little madam wouldn't have a penny left to her name once he had finished with it. And when her uncle had tired of her youthful charms, he would send her to a nunnery whether she liked it or not. After all, girls there were fed and clothed and at least no one could hear them lamenting their fate.

He felt that the inquisitor was treating him very lightly. He even appeared to make barely veiled threats. Eudes reread the note aloud:

'... You will bring your niece to the Inquisition headquarters at Alençon without further ado and leave her alone in our company so that we may determine the reliability of her suspicions and grievances regarding Madame her mother ...'

There was no entreaty, no polite phrasing.

Eudes was seething. It meant taking Mathilde all the way to Alençon. No doubt they would have to arrange a wagon since the foolish girl was terrified of horses and slumped over the neck of her mount like a straw doll hanging on to the reins. Agnès was like a centaur in comparison, undaunted even by the perilous ladies' side-saddles. The fastest, most spirited destriers responded to the pressure of her calf as though they had at last found their true master. It was Eudes, no one else, who had taught her to sit in a saddle from the age of five. She had shrieked with laughter, ducking to avoid low branches, fearlessly fording river beds, clearing hedges and was often the victor when they raced each other.

Suddenly, he felt aghast at the stupidity of his plan. What had he been thinking! Besides money and the power it brings, all that had ever mattered to him was Agnès. How had it come to this? What did he care for that foolish, heartless girl strutting about in cast-offs while her aunt, who had died giving birth, was barely cold in the ground? Agnès would rather have put on the clothes of a beggar than accept such unseemly gifts. She would have held her head up high, a queen among queens clothed in rags, and all would have bowed before her. She would have slept on bare boards like a dog rather than occupy the deserted conjugal bed. Dear God, how had it come to this?

Was it him or their blood ties that repulsed her so? It must be their blood ties. If he believed otherwise, it would drive him mad. Yet what did she really know of her true origins? Agnès's mother might have lied in order to force the late Baron Robert to recognise her child. In any case, his father Robert, his grandfather, and now Eudes himself, the last in the male line of the de Larnay family, had sired so many bastards that he sometimes wondered whether he might not be bedding his sisters, nieces, cousins, aunts, even his own daughters. And what of it? In the end were they not all descended from Adam and Eve? Had not Adam and Eve borne two sons, one of whom had killed the other? They all shared the same blood.

A thought was slowly forming through his rage and jealousy, through the pain of his unrequited love and frustrated desire. Until then he had believed he was the sole originator of his plan, but had he not in fact been manipulated? True, he had for years dreamed of wreaking his revenge on Agnès, of making her pay for her arranged marriage to Hugues de Souarcy by robbing her of her dower. But never of handing her over to the Inquisition. He trawled his memory.

Incapable of admitting that he was an animal driven by his passions and brutalised by his lack of intelligence, Eudes discovered the one person he could blame: Mabile.

He raced up to the servants' quarters, where his mistress and accomplice had been holding court since her return to the chateau. She had cleverly insinuated to the other servants that not only did she serve her master in his kitchen but also in his bed, thus making them respect her more, since none could be sure of the true extent of her influence.

Eudes found her sprawled on her bed, dipping her finger in a pot of honey and licking it. She greeted his arrival with a suggestive smile and opened her legs beneath her dress. Under other circumstances such an invitation would have produced an immediate effect. Not today. He seized the girl by the scruff of her neck and slapped her with such force that she moaned:

'What …?'

'You lied to me! You've been lying to me from the start,' he exploded.

Bewildered, Mabile snapped back:

'Well, that makes two of us.'

Another blow, this time from his fist, sent her hurtling to the floor.

The servant understood that her master's anger was real and that he was quite capable of giving her a thrashing. Dragging herself up onto all fours, she cried:

'My lord ... what is it?'

'The truth. I want the truth this instant. If you lie to me again, I'll kill you.'

The girl's fear gave way to rage. That loathsome Agnès. She should have known. She sat back, her legs folded under her, and hissed:

'Is my lord feeling pricked by remorse? Well, it's a little late for that.'

Eudes walked over to the crouching girl and kicked her in the chest, eliciting a cry of pain. She fell forward, and even as she gasped for breath her body shook with malicious glee as she spluttered:

'I'll wager the lovely Agnès isn't quite so full of herself these days. And, if you don't mind me saying so, I wouldn't bother trying to save her. The punishment reserved for perjurers is scarcely better. And the same goes for that haughty little madam you treat as though she were the lady of the house. It's too late, I tell you! That lynx Agnès de Souarcy is going to die and it serves her right.'

'Who told you that?'

'I found your mysterious visitor's suggestion most appealing, a real ghoul he was ... Though not unreasonable. He spoke of such punishments and abuse as I could never have dreamed of inflicting upon the lovely Agnès, and then gave me the name of the Grand Inquisitor you were to see.'

Eudes realised that Mabile's hatred would only end when her rival was dead. He understood that he had been used, that he had fallen headlong into a trap he had wrongly believed was of his own making.

'Why ... Why do you hate her so much?'

'Why?' she hissed venomously. 'Why? Because without even having to ask she received everything I begged to be given. Because she grudgingly deigned to accept what I wanted so desperately I was prepared to kill for it. Because when you bed me, you want me to be her. Need I go on?' She let out a spiteful laugh before concluding: 'I'm not without brains ... It was I who stole her pretty little handkerchief and planted it a few yards from where the bailiff's men found that corpse. The fools ... They didn't even realise that if they didn't find it the first time they looked, it was because somebody had hung it on a low branch after the murder. If the bastard manages to escape the clutches of the Inquisition, which I doubt, she will fall directly into the hands of secular judges.'

Eudes felt as though a huge abyss were opening up in front of him. He enquired in a trembling voice:

'She never really lay with her chaplain, did she?'

'What of it? Provided people believe she did, that's good enough for me. As for that pest Clément's mother being a heretic, it is more than likely, but I couldn't give a fig either.'

Eudes felt an icy chill descend on his thoughts and declared blankly:

'You have half an hour in which to leave the chateau. You will take with you only enough food for a day's consumption. You will be searched before you go. Should you dare to return here or communicate any of our shameful secrets, you will meet a slow and painful end.'

With these words he left the room. Mabile remained motionless for a few moments, unsure whether to cry tears of rage or sorrow. Rage prevailed for she had learned long ago that tears offered no protection.

She rose to her feet, vowing through clenched teeth:

'You'll pay for this a hundredfold, my master!'

Fortunately, the money she had been squirrelling away for years was hidden in a safe place at Clairets. Together with what she knew about Eudes, from whom she intended to exact a high price in exchange for her silence, it would enable her to start a new life elsewhere on a good footing. Pleased at her own foresight, she prepared to leave, putting on several layers of clothing.

'You'll pay for this, I swear upon my soul.'

Eudes lay slumped over the table in the main hall, his head resting in a red pool that was too watery to occasion any alarm on the part of Monsieur Manusser, Madame Apolline's former apothecary. Furthermore, the empty pitcher lying beside him suggested that his master's sleep was not due to tiredness. He tapped Eudes on the shoulder then quickly stepped back. Eudes groaned in his drunken stupor then sat up, his eyes half closed.

'What is it?' he roared.

'Mabile left an hour ago, my lord; she took the road north. You instructed me to inform you.'

'Is it dark yet?'

'Almost.'

'Was the hussy searched before she left?'

'Your orders were carried out to the letter. Barbe searched her thoroughly, including her private parts. Mabile could not have concealed anything of value or any document about her person. We provided her with an oil lamp, as you requested, and with enough food for a day.'

'Good. Is my horse saddled?'

'Just as you instructed, my lord.'

Eudes stood up, a little unsteady on his feet, and said:

'I need to clear my head. Have a bucket of cold water sent to me at once. I must … visit my mine.'

Sceptical but eager not to provoke his master's rage, the apothecary bowed and left.

Eudes's fist came crashing down on the table.

'Ugly whore! Your evil scheming is over! Prepare to commend your soul to God – if indeed he does not reject it in disgust, for it must be putrid.'

He had given her an hour's start to enable her to put a good distance between herself and Château de Larnay. The light from the oil lamp would help him find her.

Eudes rode through the forest. The sky was clear and the night air fresh and invigorating. A fine evening for an execution. Mabile had become too dangerous. Even so, he would follow her advice. It was impossible for him to retract his accusations, still less those he had put into his silly little niece's mouth. He soon spotted her. She was following the road, keeping close to the edge of the forest, ready to sneak into the undergrowth at the slightest sound. She swung round to face the thunder of hooves, and Eudes raised his arm to put her at ease. He slowed his mount, stopping a few paces from her.

'I let my temper get the better of me,' he conceded gruffly.

Mabile raised her lamp so that she could see her master's face. Reassured, she gave a grin of triumph.

'Let us return,' Eudes ordered.

He dismounted and walked towards her. She wriggled coquettishly and pressed her body up against his. Two hands gripped her throat. She gasped and tried to struggle, scratching at his eyes, her legs thrashing about helplessly. He pressed as hard as he could, grunting with the effort. He felt something give in the girl's throat. Mabile kicked one last time then went limp. He released his grip and her lifeless body slumped to his feet like a bundle of rags.

He dragged her into the bushes. Looking back one last time without a trace of sorrow or remorse on his face, he left her lying a few yards from the road with her skirts hitched up. If anybody found her before the animals got to her, they would conclude that she had been raped and left for dead by some vagabond. Her peasant's dress would rule out any thorough investigation.

Eudes felt relieved as he climbed back into his saddle. After all, she was just a servant, a strumpet who had turned out to be a little cleverer than the others. What's more, she had been presumptuous and, above all, foolish enough to have lied to him about the chaplain. He should have got rid of her sooner. He had been far too indulgent. They were all the same, these harlots. Give them an inch and they take a mile!

Night was falling. A sharp wind had risen and was rattling the wooden shutters on the herbarium door. A pensive Annelette examined the contents of her tall medicine cabinet. She enjoyed these peaceful moments of solitude, this feeling of using her intelligence to rule over a domain that might be limited to the stout walls of the tiny building, but was hers.

Her fear had abated, as had her concern for the Abbess's life. They had discussed the threat; now it was time to act. She was faced with a cunning enemy, clever as well as crafty – in short a worthy adversary. What had begun as a mission to protect the Abbess had turned into a personal challenge, a sort of wager with herself. Would she turn out to be the stronger, wilier opponent? Annelette's foe, unbeknownst to her, had provided her with the chance to prove her ability. Annelette had waited all these years for an occasion to test the extent of her superiority, but had lacked any objective yardstick. Deep down, she was convinced that she was confronted with a creature whose brain worked exactly like hers, with the enormous difference that her opponent had chosen to serve evil. The apothecary nun had submitted fairly easily to the monastic rules of this community of women whom she mostly despised – just as she would a community of men. For her it was the lesser of two evils. And yet the thought of doing battle with another mind thrilled her. She would leave the prayers and supplications to others and make use of the intelligence God had given her. This was the most glorious mark of appreciation, the most complete form of allegiance she could show Him.

Annelette let out a sigh of contentment: the battle was about to begin and she would show no mercy. She would bring to bear all her scientific knowledge, her intellect and her loathing of superstition in the bid to combat her enemy's cunning wickedness. She experienced a frisson of elation: when had she ever felt this free, this strong? Probably never.

She began by taking down all the bags of dried, powdered plants, the phials and jars containing the solutions, decoctions, spirits and extracts she had prepared during the spring and summer seasons. On the edge of the stone slab, she set aside for later use a small ampoule with a brown wax seal and then sorted the other remedies into two separate piles on the larger table. On the left, she placed those preparations which could not prove fatal in the tiny quantities a poisoner would use if adding them to food or drink: dried sage, thyme, rosemary, artichoke, mint, lemon balm and a host of others used to flavour food, as well as for treating minor ailments. On the right, she put the toxic substances that she would give to Éleusie to put in a safe place. Curiously, the phial of distilled Aconitum napellus root, which she used to treat congestive inflammations, general aches and pains and gout, did not appear to have been tampered with. Where, then, had the murderess procured the aconite that had killed poor Adélaïde? Unless she had been planning this for some time and had stolen the liquor the year before. Annelette then carefully examined the embroidered red lettering on the bags whose contents were toxic, and wondered which of them she might have chosen had she harboured evil intentions. Her gaze lingered on the crushed *Digitalis purpurea*[74] leaves she used for treating dropsy and heart murmurs, the *Conium maculatum*[75] she prescribed for neuralgia and painful menses, and the powdered *Taxus baccata*[76] she mixed with handfuls of wheat in order to exterminate the field mice that attacked their granary. She was startled by how light the last bag felt. She hurried to the lectern where she kept her bulky register. In it she recorded the details of every prescription and what each bag weighed at the end of the week. She should have ten ounces[+] of *Taxus baccata*. She rushed over to the scales. The bag weighed just over nine ounces. Nearly an ounce of yew was missing – enough to kill a horse, and therefore a man or a nun. Who would be the next victim? She scolded herself. She was looking at the problem from the wrong angle again. There were two possibilities. One was that their enemy was allied to the forces of darkness struggling to put an end to their quest. If this were the case, the poisoner would run into two obstacles in the form of her and Éleusie de Beaufort. The other possibility was more mundane but no less lethal. The poisoner was motivated by hatred or jealousy, in which case the next victim's identity would be far more difficult to predict. Another thought occurred to her and she checked her register again for the date when she had last weighed the bag. She could now completely rule out one of her least likely suspects: Jeanne d'Amblin. The powdered yew could only have been stolen during the two days preceding Adélaïde's murder – that is to say during one of the extern sister's rounds. In any event it was a clever choice for there was no antidote. The symptoms of yew poisoning were nausea and vomiting followed by shaking and dizziness. The victim would quickly plunge into a coma before dying. The discovery confirmed Annelette's suspicions: the murderess was knowledgeable about poisons … Or else she had been advised by someone who was, but who?

She must reflect, find a method of counter-attack. The bitter taste of yew could only be disguised in something very sweet and heavily spiced. In a cake. Or – and this would be the height of criminal ingenuity – in another bitter-tasting medicinal potion.

Thus whoever drank the nasty-tasting brew would not suspect that it contained poison.

It took Annelette a good hour to finish stacking the lethal substances in a big basket and replacing their phials and bags with harmless ones. She swapped aconite for sage, digitalis for milk thistle and filled with verbena the bag marked *Daphne mezereum*,[77] that beautiful red-flowering plant, three berries of which were enough to kill a wild boar. The murderess could pride herself on having alleviated her next victim's cough, colic or cramp if she decided to use it.

A smile spread across Annelette's lips. She had come to the final stage of her plan. She removed the piece of cloth covering the crate of eggs she had filched from under the nose of the sister in charge of the fishponds and the henhouses. Poor Geneviève Fournier would probably have a fit when she discovered that fifteen of her beloved hens had not laid. She saw in the number of eggs she collected each morning proof of her good ministering to her birds and of the Lord's munificence in her regard. The more eggs they laid, the more puffed up with pride she became, until she took on the appearance of a plump, contented mother hen. Annelette frowned at herself for thinking such uncharitable thoughts. Geneviève Fournier was a charming sister, but her harping upon the necessity of singing canticles to her hens, geese and turkeys in order to fatten them up for eating bored the apothecary sister as rigid as the necks of the ducks Geneviève crammed with grain.

She looked up as she heard a muffled sound coming from outside. It was well after compline.[+] Who was up at this time of night? She lowered the covers of the two lighted sconce torches and walked towards the herbarium door. The sound started

437

up again: cautious footsteps on the pebble paths that formed a cross separating the herb beds. She pulled open the shutter and found herself face to face with Yolande de Fleury, the sister in charge of the granary and one of her prime suspects, for who could obtain contaminated rye more easily than she? The plump woman turned white with fright and clasped her hand to her chest. Annelette demanded in an intimidating voice:

'What are you doing here at this time of night, sister, when all the others are in bed?'

'I ...' the other woman stammered, her cheeks turning red.

'You what?'

Yolande de Fleury gulped and seemed to spend a long time searching for an explanation as to why she was there:

'I ... I felt an attack of acid stomach coming on just after supper ... and I ...'

'And you thought you might find the right remedy yourself.'

'Blackthorn usually ...'

'Blackthorn can be used for a range of ailments. It possesses diuretic, laxative and depurative qualities, as well as being very good for curing boils. You aren't suffering from boils or acne by any chance, are you, sister? As for acid stomach ... Milk thistle, centaury and wormwood are preferable. In short, any number of medicinal herbs other than blackthorn. I will therefore ask you again: what are you doing here?'

'I confess that my excuse was a clumsy one. The truth is that I am upset about what has been happening, about poor Adélaïde's terrible death, and I needed to take the air, to think ...'

'I see. And despite the hundreds of acres of land around our abbey you felt it necessary to "take the air" outside the herbarium?'

The other woman appeared even more distraught, and

Annelette thought she might burst into tears. And yet something in her manner, although secretive, convinced Annelette that Yolande de Fleury was not prowling around in the hope of stealing poison from her medicine cabinet. Moreover, the murderess must already be in possession of the powdered yew.

'That's enough, sister! Go back to your dormitory this instant.' Yolande then astonished the apothecary by clutching the sleeve of her robe and whispering nervously:

'Will you report my presence here to the Abbess?'

Annelette pulled her arm free and, stepping back, retorted:

'Naturally.' She felt suddenly angry and scolded the other woman sharply: 'Have you forgotten, sister, that there's a monster in our midst? Don't you realise that the murderess may have procured the poison from my cabinet, the poison that caused the horrific death of the sister in charge of the kitchens and meals? Or are you simply hare-brained?'

'But ...'

'No buts, sister. Go back to the dormitory straight away. The Abbess will be duly informed.'

Annelette watched the young woman's hunched, weeping figure vanish into the darkness. What had the foolish woman really been doing there? Her inept excuses had made Annelette frankly doubt that she could be the poisoner. And yet ... What if her clumsiness were a clever façade?

She went back into the herbarium to finish preparing her masterstroke. She replaced the bags containing the switched contents in the cabinet, and pulled a face as she picked up the tiny ampoule with the wax seal that she had set aside earlier. Cracking the eggs one by one, she separated the slippery whites into an earthenware bowl before adding a few drops of the almond oil which she had had sent from Ostia and used for treating chilblains and cold sores. She stirred the mixture vigorously then sighed as she held her breath and opened the phial. The foul stench of rotten teeth or stagnant marshes filled her nostrils instantly. The substance was essence of *Ruta graveolens* – commonly known as fetid rue or herb of grace. Annelette suspected that the plant's alleged effectiveness as an antidote to bites from poisonous snakes or rabid dogs[78] did not explain the appellation herb of grace, choosing to give credence to a more mundane explanation: despite the Church's condemnation, humble folk for whom another mouth to feed would spell disaster used fetid rue as an abortifacient. In a more concentrated or wrongly administered dose it could prove fatal. She quickly emptied the contents into the foamy egg whites and stirred the mixture vigorously again with her spatula, trying hard not to retch. Finally, when she was satisfied, she spread a layer of the mixture on the floor directly in front of her medicine cabinet. The oil would prevent it from drying too quickly and make it stick better to leather or wooden soles. She then heaved the big basketful of lethal substances onto her hip and left without locking the door behind her.

The Abbess was expecting her. Annelette Beaupré listened attentively as she walked through the darkness, guided only by the feeble light of a sconce torch. In fact, she did not really feel afraid. The murderess was almost certainly not endowed with the kind of physical strength that would enable her to carry out a direct attack, certainly not on somebody her size.

Mathilde de Souarcy had arrived an hour earlier escorted by Baron de Larnay, who Nicolas Florin thought was in a lamentable state. His purple-streaked face suggested he had been drinking. The inquisitor was delighted. The signs of human weakness always put him in a good mood. The young girl's sumptuous fur-lined coat, more suitable for a married woman, was evidence that her uncle treated her like an elegant kept woman. Agnan had left them waiting in a tiny, freezing-cold room.

Eudes de Larnay was growing increasingly uneasy, despite the outward display of calm he had affected in order not to scare his niece. He had gone out of his way to be charming to her during the long journey to Alençon, complimenting her on her figure, her appearance, her melodious voice. He had gone through her accusation with her and done his best to point out any possible pitfalls it contained. Finally, he had reminded her that at the slightest sign of any retraction the inquisitorial tribunal had the power to declare her a false witness, which would have dire consequences for them both.

The repulsively hideous young clerk who had shown them into the room reappeared. Eudes stood up as though to accompany his niece, knowing full well that she had been summoned alone. Agnan blushed and stammered:

'Pray remain seated, my lord. Mademoiselle de Souarcy has been requested to appear alone before the tribunal.'

Eudes slumped back in his chair and cursed under his breath. The anxiety he had managed to suppress throughout the voyage was beginning to gain the upper hand. What if Mathilde let herself be intimidated by this Grand Inquisitor? What if he caught her out with clever arguments, on the finer points of doctrine? No. Florin would receive a generous payment once Agnès had been found guilty. The young girl's claims were a godsend and it was not in his interests to cast doubt upon them. But who were these other judges? Had Nicolas Florin guaranteed their complicity out of his own pocket? After all, Mathilde might be desirable but she was a halfwit.

He had no reason to be alarmed. Mathilde was determined not to do anything that might send her back to that pigsty, Souarcy.

How appealing indeed was the pretty young damsel who was feigning coyness for their benefit; quite the little lady in her sumptuous dress of purple silk, set off by a diaphanous veil of shimmering azure. She stood with her head slightly bowed and her graceful hands clasped over her belly in an admirable show of false modesty. Florin silently approved Eudes de Larnay's taste and wondered whether he had bedded her yet.

He walked over to the young girl and declared in a mellifluous voice:

'Mademoiselle ... Allow me firstly to praise your courage and unwavering faith. We are all able to imagine just how agonising this must be for you. Accusing a mother is a most painful thing, is it not?'

'Less painful than witnessing her transgressions, it must be said.'

'Quite so,' said Florin ruefully. 'I must now ask you to state your Christian name, surname, status and domicile.'

'Mathilde Clémence Marie de Souarcy, daughter of the late Hugues de Souarcy and of Agnès Philippine Claire de Larnay,

442

Dame de Souarcy. My uncle and guardian, Baron Eudes de Larnay, kindly took me in after my mother's arrest.'

At this point the notary stood up to give his little recital:

'In nomine Domini, amen. On this the eleventh day of November in the year of Our Lord 1304, in the presence of the undersigned Gauthier Richer, notary at Alençon, and in the company of one of his clerks and two appointed witnesses, Brother Jean and Brother Anselme, both Dominicans of the diocese of Alençon, born respectively in Rioux and Hurepal, Mathilde Clémence Marie de Souarcy does appear before the venerable Brother Nicolas Florin, Dominican, Doctor in Theology and Grand Inquisitor appointed to the region of Alençon.'

The aforementioned inquisitor thanked him with a perfunctory smile and waited for him to sit down again on the bench. He glanced at the two Dominicans. Brother Anselme was staring at the young girl. As for Brother Jean, whose hands rested on the table before him, he appeared lost in the contemplation of his fingernails. Nicolas stifled his amusement: none of them had the slightest idea of the little tragedy he had arranged, which was about to be played out before them.

Nicolas Florin picked up the big black book that lay on the table and walked up to Mathilde until he was almost touching her:

'Do you swear upon the Gospels to tell the whole truth, to conceal nothing from this tribunal and that your testimony is given freely without hatred or hope of recompense? Take heed, young lady, for by swearing this oath you commit your soul for eternity.'

'I swear.'

'Mademoiselle de Souarcy, you declared in a letter written by your own hand and dated the twenty-fifth of October, I quote:

"My soul suffers at the thought of the constant abominations committed by Madame de Souarcy, my mother, and her persistent sinfulness and deviance make me fear for her soul," and then, "The young chaplain, so devout the day he arrived, oblivious to this shadow of evil hanging over us, has much changed under her influence." While reassured in your regard, our concern for your mother grows when we read your words: "God granted me the strength to resist living with evil despite my mother's constant example, but my heart bleeds and is in pain." Are these your exact, unaltered words?'

'Indeed, my Lord Inquisitor,' Mathilde acknowledged in an infantile voice.

'Do you wish to retract, tone down or in any other way modify your accusation?'

'It is an exact reflection of the truth. Any change would be mistaken and a terrible sin.'

'Very good. Scribe, have you recorded the witness's consistency?'

The young man nodded timidly.

'You are still so young, but I implore you to try your best to help us by remembering. When did you first notice that Madame de Souarcy's soul was being contaminated by evil, and what were the signs?'

'I cannot give a precise date … I must have been six, possibly seven. I …' Mathilde lowered her voice to a whisper as though the enormity of the words she was about to pronounce made her breathless: 'On several occasions I saw her spit the host into her handkerchief during Mass.'

A horrified murmur rose from the men seated around the table. Florin secretly praised Eudes de Larnay. He could hardly have thought up a better idea himself.

'Are you certain your eyes were not playing tricks on you? It is so … monstrous.'

'I am certain.'

The grate of a bolt, less rasping than usual. Agnès, exhausted and trembling from lack of food, mustered all her strength and stood up. The slightest effort left her breathless. She had spent the past few nights in a fever and the rancid smell of sweat, mixed with the stench of excrement from the latrine, made her feel sick. Fits of coughing had left her throat raw and she shivered uncontrollably. Her scalp itched so much that she could no longer tell whether it was simple dirt or if her head was crawling with lice. Her dress hung loosely from her body and, despite the coat Florin had given her in a show of kindness, the icy cold pierced her to the bone.

She immediately recognised the gaunt, unsightly face of Florin's clerk, but could not recall the name Florin had used to address him on the evening they had arrived at the Inquisition headquarters – an eternity ago.

'What …'

Her teeth were chattering feverishly and she was unable to end her sentence. The words seemed to elude her, like faint sparks flickering in her mind.

'Hush, Madame. I am not supposed to be here. If he ever found out … I have been going over the evidence for your trial … It is a stain on our Holy Church, Madame, a parody, worse still, a wicked deception; every witness statement in your favour, including that of the Abbess of Clairets, my lord the Comte d'Authon, your chaplain Brother Bernard and many more, has gone missing. To begin with I thought they must have been mislaid, and I duly informed the Grand Inquisitor, only to be rewarded with his anger and contempt. He insisted that he had no recollection of them and made it clear that, if any evidence had gone missing, I was to blame …'

A remote feeling of relief. Agnès swayed; her head was spinning. It took all her strength of mind to comprehend what the young man with the weaselly face was telling her. And yet she had not forgotten the flicker of compassion that had rendered him almost beautiful.

'He cleverly insinuated that, if I mentioned this loss to anyone, I would be held accountable and punished for my incompetence, adding that out of his compassion and affection for me he would say nothing. I do not fear punishment. My soul is free from sin. Do you know that I was afraid when this beautiful man chose me to be his clerk? I believed … I believed him to be an angel come down to earth. I believed that behind the repulsive façade others see he had sensed my purity and devotion. I believed that he had seen my soul as only angels can. Poor fool that I was. He delights in my ugliness for it makes him appear even more beautiful. He has a wicked soul, Madame. He threw out the testimony in your favour. Your trial is a tragic farce.'

'I don't … What is your name?' she asked in a dry, hoarse voice.

'Agnan, Madame.'

She cleared her throat:

'Agnan. I am so weak that I can barely stand. He is … He is more than just a wicked soul. He is an incarnation of evil. He has no soul.'

She felt herself topple forward and just managed to steady herself by holding onto one of the wall rings used to chain the prisoners' arms above their heads.

Agnan retrieved a lump of bacon and two eggs from his sleeveless cassock and handed them to her.

'Eat these, Madame, I implore you. Gather your strength … And clean your face. What you are about to endure is … villainous.'

'What …'

'I can tell you no more. Farewell, Madame. My thoughts are with you.'

All of a sudden he had gone and the door was bolted so quickly after him that Agnès was unsure of having even seen him leave the cell. She stood trembling, clutching the precious bacon and eggs to her chest, unable to make any sense of his parting advice. Why should she wash her face? What did it matter if she appeared dirty and stinking before her judges, before Florin's paid puppets?

The cross-examination had been going on for over an hour. Florin and Brother Anselme had alternated points of doctrine with questions of a more personal nature in an improvised duet.

'And so,' Florin insisted, 'Madame de Souarcy your mother considered that Noah's inebriation after the flood was sinful, even though he was pardoned for not having known of the effects of wine upon the mind, having never tasted it before?'

'My mother thought him guilty anyway and managed to convince Brother Bernard.'

'Did Madame de Souarcy believe the wisdom of her judgement to be above that of God? That constitutes blasphemy,' the inquisitor concluded.

'Yes,' Mathilde acknowledged, adding ruefully, 'but there is so much more, my Lord Inquisitor.'

Brother Anselme glanced at his fellow Dominican, who had raised his head for the first time since the beginning of the cross-examination and now prompted Anselme to speak with a blink of his eyes:

'Mademoiselle de Souarcy, you write, and I quote: "The young chaplain, so devout the day he arrived, oblivious to this shadow of evil hanging over us, has much changed under her influence. During Mass he utters strange words in a language I cannot understand but which I know is not Latin." Do you recognise these words as your own?'

'I do. They are an exact description of the truth.'

'You are aware that those who have turned from God and gone the way of the devil are sometimes rewarded with the power to speak in strange tongues in order to assist them in their dealings with the devil,' Florin emphasised.

'I did not know,' Mathilde lied convincingly, her uncle having already stressed its importance.

'It is a significant point, which may result in the arrest of Brother Bernard. In your opinion did the two accomplices engage in sinful invocations?' the inquisitor insisted.

Mathilde pretended to hesitate before confessing in a tremulous voice:

'I fear they did.'

'Pray, be more precise, Mademoiselle. Your testimony must help us to shed light upon the true extent of their corruption. We will then be in a position to determine whether your mother is guilty of latria[79] or of dulia,[80] for we do not consider these two heresies in the same light, a further example of our extreme tolerance.'

Mathilde stifled a sigh of relief; two days ago she had no idea what these terms meant and would have been at a loss for words. Her uncle, fearing she might be questioned on this point, had explained them to her, emphasising the extreme seriousness of the crime of latria and insisting that her mother must be accused of it along with the other charges laid against her.

'It pains me greatly to have to tell you. They invoked devils during Mass and recited loathsome prayers in a sinful language, as I wrote in my accusation, then they knelt and sang their praises.'

'In front of you?'

The young girl trembled, seemingly on the brink of tears, as she stammered:

'I believe my mother wished to lead me down the path to hell.'

More shocked gasps rose from the men seated on the bench.

Mathilde heaved a sorrowful sigh before adding:

'One day ... the servant whom my uncle had been kind enough to give us came to find me. She was so upset she could barely speak. I followed her to the little sacristy in the chapel. A pile of chickens lay there with their throats cut.'

'So, they offered sacrificed animals!' exclaimed Florin, who had been enjoying himself immensely since the cross-examination had begun.

This young girl was a sensation. Her uncle could turn her into a sideshow.

Mathilde nodded and continued:

'In that case they are guilty of latria and this is no doubt the most painful confession I shall ever make.'

Brother Anselme studied her for a few moments before asking:

'Do you believe that Sybille Chalis is to blame for Madame de Souarcy's crimes against the faith?'

'My mother repeatedly told me of her attachment to the girl and of the sorrow she had suffered at her death. Indeed, she always showed an exaggerated fondness for Sybille's posthumous son, Clément.'

Florin chimed in:

'The boy fled even before Madame de Souarcy's time of grace was up, a clear sign of his overwhelming guilt. Pray continue, Mademoiselle.'

'It is my belief that Sybille sowed the seeds of heresy in my mother, for which she will be damned, and that her son continued her work using all his guile.'

Just then, the door to the vast room opened and Agnan slipped in, hugging the walls until he reached the Grand Inquisitor's armchair. He leaned over and whispered to him that Madame de Souarcy was on her way up the stairs to the interrogation room. Nicolas nodded and rose to his feet:

'Mademoiselle, your bravery is equalled only by your purity. For this reason I do not hesitate to put you face to face with the enemy of your soul. I feel certain that the ensuing exchange will greatly enlighten the noble members of this tribunal, if indeed there is still any need.'

Mathilde stared at him, trying to grasp the meaning of what he had just said. Her puzzlement was fleeting. Her mother walked slowly into the room. No one else present noticed the deep sorrow in the looks exchanged by Brother Anselme and Brother Jean.

Agnès had heeded Agnan's baffling advice after gobbling up the only proper food she had received since her imprisonment.

The bacon and eggs had given her a feeling of inner warmth she had not had for days, and her shivering had subsided. She had then managed to give her face a cursory wash and to braid her tangled hair, sticky with grime.

When she saw Mathilde, her pale face brightened and she smiled for the first time since her arrival. She rushed towards her daughter, arms outstretched. The young girl recoiled and turned away. Confused, Agnès came to a halt. She felt a shudder of panic. Had they arrested her daughter, too? Had Eudes perpetrated a second and no less heinous crime? She would kill him, even if it meant eternal damnation.

Suddenly she became aware of a pair of eyes boring into her, and she turned to face them. Brother Jean, the one she had never heard speak, was staring at her. It puzzled her when he shook his head slightly, but she would soon understand.

Florin walked towards her nimbly and gracefully, as though he were gliding over the flagstones.

'Madame de Souarcy. Your dishonesty and the cunning eloquence you have displayed here will be of no use to you now. An angel has guided us to this pure young girl,' he concluded, gesturing towards Mathilde.

Agnès looked at the inquisitor and then at her daughter. What was he saying? She would hold the girl in her arms. Everything would be all right then, she was sure. Life would return to normal then. She would protect her, she would do battle with them all, and the young girl would emerge triumphant. Agnès would not tolerate her being imprisoned, forced to endure the same suffering as her mother. It was only then that she noticed Mathilde's clothes: the sumptuous dress of heavy silk, the veil so sheer she could not recall having seen one finer, her fingers laden with rings. Madame Apolline's magnificent square turquoise, the Bohemian garnets she had worn on her index finger, her thumb ring studded with grey pearls.

She did her best to ignore the voices clamouring inside her head and the truth they were trying to foist upon her. One voice broke through her stubborn refusal to hear – that of Clémence – and said in a whisper: 'Do you see the magnificent amethyst crucifix draped around her neck, my dear? It was left to Madame Apolline by her mother. She wanted to be buried with it. Why do you think Eudes has given it to your daughter? Those pretty wine-coloured beads bought her betrayal.'

The crucifix. Poor sweet Apolline. She would often kiss it while she prayed, as though somehow it restored some of the love of her mother, snatched from life so young.

A sigh in her head. Not hers. The voice's.

Her own sigh rising up her throat. Agnès felt the floor give way beneath her feet. A cold, dark shadow descended over her thoughts. A stony silence filled her head. She collapsed. During the infinite moment when she saw the flagstones flying towards her, during the infinite moment it took for her to hit the ground, she repeated to herself: what have they done to you, my child? Damned. They are damned and will pay a hundredfold for what they have turned you into.

When she came to, she was in a tiny room heated by an ember pot. Agnan handed her an earthenware bowl whose contents she swallowed without saying a word. The fiery alcohol made her cough and suffused her chilled body with warmth.

'The cider is strong but you will find it invigorating.'

'How long ...'

'Nearly half an hour. You are not with child, are you, Madame?'

Agnès shook her head and murmured:

'You offend me, Monsieur, I am a widow.'

'Upon my soul, I beg your pardon. Madame ...Mademoiselle your daughter has gone to take lunch with Baron de Larnay. The hearing will resume upon their return.'

She said in a voice she scarcely recognised, a calm, strangely resolute voice:

'So, she was not arrested.'

'No indeed, dear lady, she is your most fearsome accuser … I read her letter to Florin. It is pure poison, so sulphurous that it burns the eyes and fingers. I could not …'

'I understand,' she interrupted, 'and I am grateful to you for your brave and daring attempt to warn me.'

She reached out and touched his hand. The young man blushed and grasped her fingers which he held to his lips. Choked with tears, he stammered:

'I thank you, Madame, from the depths of my soul.'

'But … it is I who am indebted to you. Why do you …'

'No. You are living proof that my life has not been in vain, and for this I can never thank you enough. As God's weak creature, I will have found greatness if my miserable efforts help to save innocent souls such as yours, for you are innocent, of that there is no doubt. One as ugly as I could hope for nothing more.'

Suddenly his expression changed. The emotion that had made his voice catch gave way to an unbending resolve:

'Mademoiselle de Souarcy has learned her lesson well, but she is as foolish as she is wicked. This is your only weapon against her.'

'I …' Agnès tried to reply but Agnan cut her short:

'There is no time, Madame. They will be sending for you shortly.'

He related her daughter's damning testimony. She was choked with sobs at first. Then she tried to think who could have so thoroughly corrupted her daughter, and felt overcome by a murderous desire to kill the demon, to cleave his heart in two with her short sword, a gift from Clémence that had remained sheathed since her marriage. She envisaged him falling at her feet, a pool of blood spreading underneath him. That demon Eudes. That demon Florin. And then the truth she had been trying to avoid from the moment she first saw Mathilde in the interrogation room thrust itself upon her. Mathilde had joined the forces of evil, bartering her soul for a few colourful trinkets. As her mother she was at least partially to blame. Undoubtedly she had not prepared her daughter well enough, had not provided her with the means to resist the frivolous yet powerful allure of such trivial things. Perhaps she had lavished too much care and attention on Clément's education.

I love you so dearly, Clément. Live, Clément. Live for me.

We are so alike, Clément. Why are you the only light that enters my cell, the one I cling to in order to stay sane? Live, I beg you. Live for my life's sake.

'It appals me to be the bearer of this cruel blow, Madame,' Agnan apologised.

'No, Monsieur. On the contrary, you have made me feel that I am not alone in this hateful place, and whatever becomes of me I cannot thank you enough for that. You have helped me prepare for an event I would never have dared envisage. Thank you, Agnan.'

He lowered his eyes, profoundly grateful that such a beautiful lady would call him by his Christian name.

When Agnès came face to face with Mathilde, she was immediately struck by the change in her. Where was the little girl she had brought into the world, had brought up – admittedly fickle and given to tantrums and yet so gay? Before her stood a little woman – a little woman who was no longer her daughter, who was intent upon sending her to the stake. The hatred and resentment she felt for her mother boiled down to a few bits of finery, a few glistening trinkets on her fingers. Agnès had hoped the young girl might try to avoid her gaze. She would have seen in it evidence of some lingering affection or regret, perhaps. Instead Mathilde stared brazenly at her mother with her light-brown eyes, raised her head and pursed her lips.

What followed had been a nightmare skilfully staged by Florin. The horrors, the absurdities Mathilde had uttered in order to seal her mother's fate had left Agnès speechless, unable to respond. Thus, if the flesh of her flesh were to be believed, in addition to heresy she was guilty of sorcery and lechery. A strange torpor had overtaken Agnès. She had refused to fight back or even to defend herself. When, after each new lethal outburst from her daughter, Florin had asked her triumphantly: 'What have you to say to that, Madame?' she had limited herself to replying repetitively: 'Nothing.'

What did the euphoria she sensed in Nicolas Florin matter? Or the brief smiles of encouragement he gave to Mathilde? Nothing. Nothing now.

'If we have understood correctly, you claim that Brother Bernard sprinkled his prayers and sermons with words from a strange, demonic tongue?' the Grand Inquisitor insisted.

'Yes. It certainly wasn't Latin, still less French.'

'Did your mother also speak in this evil tongue?'

'I heard her use it, though not as often as the chaplain.'

'It is common knowledge that women have less of an aptitude for languages than men.'

Maître Richer nodded as he did whenever Florin made a spiteful remark about the fair sex. His ill-tempered little face contorted with petty satisfaction.

'Mademoiselle de Souarcy, I should like to refer back to

Clément, who has so … opportunely disappeared,' the Grand Inquisitor continued. 'Do you think that he too was seduced by evil?'

Mathilde, weary after two hours of cross-examination, felt a renewed vitality. She made a supreme effort to hide the instinctive hatred she felt for that loathsome wart of a boy. In a voice filled with sorrow, she declared:

'I am sure of it. After all, he could have been contaminated in his mother's womb.'

Why hadn't her uncle Eudes anticipated her being questioned about that vile brat? She paused for a moment before elaborating:

'He, too, spoke in that sacrilegious tongue, and with consummate ease. Indeed, now I come to think of it I am convinced he was the sly but determined architect of my mother's downfall.'

Agnès felt a pain, like a knife striking her chest. She began to stir as though from a long sleep. Clément. Mathilde was attacking Clément. A sudden rush of energy caused the Dame de Souarcy to stand bolt upright. Never!

'Ah! The undeniable proof !' Florin boomed. 'A trio of devil worshippers. I thank eternal Providence for having allowed us to discover them before they were able to poison innocent souls. The boy must be found, arrested and brought before us.'

All of a sudden, the vicelike grip that had been choking Agnès dissolved. Her body forgot the weeks of imprisonment and starvation, the feverish nights. Mathilde, her daughter, her own flesh and blood, not content to manoeuvre her into the merciless clutches of the Inquisition, was throwing Clément into the jaws of those ruthless beasts. Never!

She raised her head and stared coldly at her daughter. Pronouncing each syllable crisply, she retorted:

'My daughter scarcely knows how to spell in French. She has such difficulty reading her prayers that I have been forced to make her learn them by heart. As for the letter she supposedly wrote, there is no doubt in my mind that it was dictated to her or that she copied it out. Since she does not understand a word of Latin, not even dog Latin, how could she be fit to judge the strangeness of any language, whether profane or sacred?'

Florin tried desperately to counter-attack, but could only hiss:

'A feeble defence, Madame!'

'It's a foul lie!' Mathilde screeched.

A slow, deep voice boomed through the room. The others all turned to face Brother Jean, who had risen to his feet and was speaking for the second time during the hearing:

'*Te deprecamur supplices nostris ut addas sensibus nescire prorsus omnia corruptionis vulnenera.* How would you render this, Mademoiselle?'

Mathilde decided that this was the moment to burst into tears. She stammered:

'I am … exhausted. I can't go on …'

'What has become of your recently renewed vigour? How would you render this very simple phrase, Mademoiselle? Did you at least recognise it as Latin and not a profane language?'

A silence descended. Florin searched desperately for an argument, cursing himself for getting carried away by his predilection for games. Incapable of remaining annoyed with himself for very long, he quickly turned his rage on Mathilde. What a fool, what an idiot to have mentioned Latin when she couldn't understand a word of it!

'Madame,' said Brother Jean, turning to Agnès, 'how would you render this sentence?'

'We beg of You humbly to endow us with the unwavering

ability to shun all that might corrupt the holy purity.'

'Notary, in accordance with the precautions laid down by the inquisitorial procedure, which state that if any part of an accusation is shown to be false the entire accusation must be called into question, I challenge that of Mademoiselle Mathilde Clémence Marie de Souarcy. I have no doubt that our judicious Grand Inquisitor will endorse this precaution.'

Brother Jean waited. Florin clenched his jaw in anger. Finally he spoke:

'Indeed. The accusation of this young woman is called into question.' He struggled with the urge to hurl himself at Mathilde and beat her, adding: 'Scribe, make a record of the fact that this tribunal has expressed grave doubts regarding Mademoiselle de Souarcy's sincerity and is concerned that she may have already perjured herself. Write down also that the same tribunal reserves the right to bring charges against her at a later date.'

Mathilde cried out:

'No …!'

She took a few paces towards the inquisitor, her hands outstretched, and stumbled. Agnan rushed to grab her and led her outside to where Eudes was, rashly, savouring his imminent victory.

Brother Jean tried to catch Agnès's eye, but she was far away. She had plunged into a world of unimaginable pain. She had lost Mathilde and doubted she would ever find her again.

She clung to her last source of hope, of strength: Clément was out of harm's way, for now.

'The fool!' Eudes bawled. 'The unbelievable fool! Why didn't he warn me that he intended to put you face to face with Agnès? I would have dissuaded him … You are no match for her.'

Jostled by the movement of the wagon rolling down the road alongside Perseigne Forest, which led to the eponymous abbey, Mathilde had not stopped crying and snuffling into her deceased aunt's lace handkerchief, embroidered with the letter A in pretty sea-green thread. Her uncle's last remark cut her to the quick and she stared up at him, her face puffy from weeping. How pink and unsightly she looked, he thought, just like a piglet – a shapely piglet, perhaps, but a piglet all the same.

'What was that you said, Uncle? Am I no match for my mother?'

This was not the moment to upset the little woman. After all, until Agnès had been found guilty he remained her provisional guardian.

'What I mean, my dear girl,' he corrected himself, patting her hand, 'is that you are still young and relatively ignorant of the shrewd tactics used by certain people. It is a great credit to you that you still have scruples.'

'How true, Uncle,' agreed Mathilde obsequiously.

'Your mother … well, we both know her well … She is cunning and manipulative … In short, I admire you for having stood up to her. What an ordeal it must have been for a young girl such as you.'

Mathilde was slowly beginning to feel better. Once again she was cast as her mother's victim – a role she liked so much that she believed in it more and more.

'Yes. But …'

'I could have shown that clown of an inquisitor which questions would be favourable to us! But no, the fool was intent on playing his own little game,' interrupted Eudes, still annoyed.

'Something the inquisitor said worried me, Uncle. He threatened to charge me with perjury.'

Had it not been for that depleted mine of his, which was ruining his financial as well as his political prospects, he would have happily left her to her fate.

'What of it? Another two hundred pounds will see to it. Anything to please you, dear niece.'

'Another?'

Eudes attempted to extricate himself:

'Yes. Two hundred pounds here, another two hundred pounds there, a hundred more for the abbey, and so on …'

Mathilde realised in a flash that her mother's trial had been arranged from the beginning, paid for by her uncle. The knowledge comforted her, made her feel secure. The power of money was so tremendous that she determined never to be without it again, at whatever cost.

Yolande de Fleury, the sister in charge of the granary, stood, pale-faced, holding her tiny frame as upright as possible, before the Abbess's desk. Éleusie de Beaufort turned towards the windows. The fine layer of early-morning frost that covered the gardens had not yet melted. A mysterious silence appeared to have enveloped the abbey. The Abbess strained her ears: no laughter rang out behind the heavy door to her apartments, breaking off as an admonishing finger was raised to a pair of lips. Sweet Adélaïde had taken with her into her icy tomb the gaiety which these austere, unyielding walls had never managed to stifle. Éleusie had not seen fit to do so either, contrary to the recommendation of Berthe de Marchiennes, the cellarer nun, who would no doubt have preferred everybody to wear her own perennially miserable expression. Claire and Philippine had always been so cheerful, Clémence, too – at least before she married that wretched oaf, Robert de Larnay. Each stifled giggle or suppressed smile from her nuns reminded Éleusie of her sisters and their carefree childhood. It was without doubt Adélaïde's cheerfulness, her daily wonderment, her ceaseless chatter even, that had made her one of Éleusie's favourite daughters.

The insistent gaze of the sister in charge of the granary brought her back to her study, back to the present.

'I shall repeat the question, dear Yolande. What were you doing wandering around outside the herbarium at night?'

'What a nasty tell tale,' murmured the sister, her little round chin quivering.

'Our apothecary was only doing her duty. It was imperative

that I be informed of your nocturnal foray, which is all the more worrying in the light of … the present circumstances.'

'Reverend Mother, you don't imagine that I went there with the intention of stealing poison!'

'I didn't imagine that a poisoner would rob us of our dear Adélaïde either,' the Abbess retorted sharply. 'Answer me.'

'I felt dizzy … and terribly restless … I needed to take the night air.'

Éleusie heaved a deep sigh:

'So you insist upon sticking to that unlikely tale. You are not making it any easier for me, Yolande, but worse still you are making it more difficult for yourself. You may go now, daughter. Return to your barns, but do not imagine that I've finished with you yet.'

Yolande de Fleury left without further ado. A few moments later Annelette Beaupré walked into her study, accompanied by Jeanne d'Amblin. Despite Blanche de Blinot's role as second in command at the abbey, Éleusie had not invited her to this meeting. Poor Blanche had scarcely uttered a word since discovering that someone had tried to poison her.

Éleusie gave them a summary of the short, unsuccessful conversation she had just had with the sister in charge of the granary.

Annelette said sharply:

'Why does she insist upon behaving in a way that can only make us suspicious?'

'I do not believe for a moment that she could be this … this monster,' declared Jeanne, shaking her head.

Annelette retorted instantaneously:

'In that case, what was she doing at night outside the herbarium?'

'I don't know ... Perhaps she really did need some fresh air. It is possible. What do you think, Reverend Mother?' the extern sister asked, turning to Éleusie.

'What should I think ...? Naturally I do not see Yolande de Fleury as a *toxicatore*.[81] But then I do not see any of my daughters in such a wicked role. As for Yolande, I am beginning to wonder whether her stubbornness might not conceal ... a ... how should I say ... Goodness, how embarrassing ...'

'Pray explain to us, Reverend Mother,' said Jeanne d'Amblin, trying to make her feel less awkward.

'Well, as we all know in every cloistered community where celibacy is the rule ... and this applies no less to our brother monks ... I mean ...' She adopted a more matter-of-fact tone.

'Rome is aware that in some monasteries, a lack of emotion and physical contact can lead some of us to engage in relationships with ... a fellow nun or monk of the same sex.'

Jeanne d'Amblin stared at the hem of her dress and Annelette declared:

'Are you suggesting that Yolande might be carrying on an ... improper relationship in a place of prayer and meditation?'

'I have no idea, daughter. It is simply a thought that occurred to me, if only because I far prefer it to the idea of Yolande as a poisoner. One is a minor misdemeanour we can only hope is passing, the other a vile murder requiring flagellation and death.'

A brief silence descended. Annelette Beaupré knew all about such practices. A blind eye was turned to them in the hope that they would remain hidden, above all from the outside world. She herself had been the object of furtive glances and smiles that were more than expressions of sisterly warmth. Such infatuations of the heart and the senses baffled her, and reinforced her general lack of respect for her fellow human beings. Why this need for fleshly contact and kisses when there were so many marvels waiting to be studied and understood? If she had managed to avoid being bedded by a man, it was certainly not so as to be bedded by a woman. Jeanne d'Amblin broke the uneasy silence:

'I can make no sense of this dreadful business! Why would anyone want to poison Adélaïde and why try to kill Blanche, if she really was the intended victim? Unless ... unless this is a case of insanity or' – she paused to cross herself before finishing her sentence – 'demonic possession ...?'

The apothecary glanced at Éleusie, seeking her consent, which Éleusie gave with a nod. Annelette explained:

'Assuming that madness does not lie at the root of this murderous act, the only motive we can think of, and which bears some weight ... are the keys to the safe containing our Reverend Mother's seal. It is customary for the guardian of the seal, our senior nun, to be entrusted with one of these keys. A second is kept by Berthe de Marchiennes, and the third, naturally, is in the hands of our Reverend Mother.'

Jeanne d'Amblin's eyes opened wide with astonishment, and she murmured:

'Falsified documents? But that's terrible ... That seal can send innocent people to the gallows! And ... And a lot more besides ...'

'Undeniably,' Éleusie interrupted. 'But rest assured, Jeanne, the seal is safe; it has not been moved.'

'Oh, thank God ...' she whispered.

Éleusie could not tell whether the momentary relief this piece of news brought her outweighed their common concern.

Annelette intervened impatiently:

'Yes! If indeed we have discovered the murderess's true motive, we are confronted with a difficult choice. If the seal is what she wants, she will try again. As we plan to announce later, I am now in possession of our senior sister's key. Our Reverend Mother will hold on to hers and the third will remain in the keeping of Berthe de Marchiennes.'

A sudden flash of comprehension registered on Jeanne d'Amblin's face and she all but cried out:

'But that means ... that means ... she will try to kill all three of you? Oh no ... oh no, I couldn't bear it!'

'Do you have a better idea?' asked Annelette, who was becoming irritated.

'Well ... Well, I don't know ... I'll think of something, be patient! You say that she tried to poison Blanche in order to take her key. I've got it. Why not hide them somewhere instead of keeping them under our robes or around our necks? Let's hide them in a secret place that only one of us will know about, our Reverend Mother, for example. That way we will trounce the monster at her own game. Poisoning our Abbess won't help her discover the hiding place.'

The logic of the idea should have convinced Annelette, and she was surprised when it didn't. Even so she was honest enough to wonder, fleetingly, whether this was not because she resented Jeanne for thinking of it first.

'Your idea is a good one,' she conceded. 'Let us think about it. Before we do, there is another rather more urgent matter that requires our attention.'

Éleusie cast a bemused glance at her apothecary daughter, who continued:

'First of all, Jeanne, I should inform you that almost an ounce of yew powder has gone missing, the powder I use for killing the rats and field mice that attack our granary.'

'Why was I not told about this earlier?'

'It was stolen during your rounds.'

'Sweet Jesus,' murmured Jeanne d'Amblin. 'She could ...'

'Yes, she could easily kill one of us with it ... Which makes me think that another murder is imminent.'

'"Urgent" is certainly the right word!' the extern sister remarked.

'Jeanne, there is a favour I should like to ask of you.'

The sudden hesitancy in the apothecary nun's usually forthright voice alerted the other two women. Having not been consulted beforehand about the appropriateness of any request, Éleusie wondered what she could be about to say.

'I trust that our Reverend Mother will not be offended by my asking you this without giving her prior warning. I ... Let us just say that I have formed my own suspicions regarding some of the other nuns – suspicions which I am aware may be wholly unfounded ...'

Such circuitous, cautious speech coming from Annelette, who was normally so blunt, made the other two women uneasy.

'... Our Reverend Mother has not influenced my suspicions in any way. To cut a long story short,' she continued more boldly, 'I have very little trust in Berthe de Marchiennes.'

'You go too far,' murmured Éleusie, incredulous.

'Well, that is how I see it,' Annelette retorted, not without a hint of resentment. 'In any event I would like you to keep her key, Jeanne.'

The extern sister looked at her as if she had gone raving mad before exploding:

'Have you taken leave of your senses? Absolutely not! And become the murderer's target in Berthe's place? I refuse! If you were to ask me to guard our Reverend Mother's key in order to protect her life, I would accept. Not without trepidation, I confess, but I would accept. But do not imagine for a second that I would do the same for Berthe … Never!'

Despite the gravity of the circumstances, Éleusie found herself stifling a smile. This was the first time she had ever seen Jeanne lose her calm. She said reassuringly:

'My dear Jeanne, I am grateful to you for wanting to protect me. I am grateful to you both. It has taken these terrible events to show me who my true friends are. As for my key … I will keep it. Nobody else should bear the burden of responsibility I took on when I joined Clairets.'

Jeanne lowered her eyes to hide her sorrow. Éleusie tried to put her mind at rest:

'My dear Jeanne, this is not my funeral oration. I have no intention of being poisoned before this evil has been eradicated.'

A few moments later when they took leave of one another, Éleusie conveyed to the apothecary with a meaningful look that she wished to speak to her alone. Annelette accompanied Jeanne d'Amblin along the corridor leading to the scriptorium then took leave of her on the pretext of wanting to verify something, and returned via the gardens.

Éleusie de Beaufort was still standing behind her heavy oak table, apparently not having moved.

'And this little trap you are setting, daughter, when will you give me the results? Time is running out. I can sense the beast is about to strike again.'

'Soon … I am waiting, watching and waiting.'

Nicolas Florin studied the Comte Artus d'Authon, seated on the other side of his tiny desk, with an air of bored politeness.

'I regret, Seigneur, that since you are not a direct relative of Madame de Souarcy I cannot allow you to visit her. I assure you that it pains me not to be able to indulge you in this matter, but I am obliged to follow strict rules.'

Florin waited to see the effect of this barely concealed snub. Artus remained calm, contriving not to betray his simmering rage to the inquisitor. The evil rat was revelling in his power.

'I understand that Madame de Souarcy's cross-examination has already begun.'

'Yes.'

'Do you suppose the trial will go on for long?'

'I fear it will, Seigneur Comte. But do not ask me any further details. The inquisitorial procedure, as you know, is shrouded in the utmost secrecy. We are most keen to preserve the honour and dignity of those brought before us until formal proof of their guilt has been established.'

'Oh, I do not doubt for an instant that Madame de Souarcy's honour and dignity are of the utmost concern to you,' retorted Artus d'Authon.

Florin clasped his hands on his black robe and waited to see what the powerful lord would do next. Would he attempt to bribe him as he had during their first meeting? Would he threaten him or beg him? And he, Florin, which would he prefer? A combination of all three, of course.

But instead of this, Artus's fleshy lips parted in a strange smile, a smile that bared his teeth. Suddenly he stood up, much to the surprise of Florin, who automatically followed suit.

'Since, as I anticipated, my request has been in vain, I would not want to waste any more of your time. I therefore bid you goodbye.'

After the Comte had left, Florin sat brooding. What had in fact occurred? Why had the arrogant fool not begged him? Had he not received a stinging insult? He certainly felt the blood rush to his cheeks as if he had just been slapped. Who did that Comte think he was! So, he wanted to see his female, did he? Well, he should come back in a few days' time. Since she had failed to confess under cross-examination her torture would begin the very next day.

Seized by a murderous rage, he sent his desk flying. Stacks of files and notes lay scattered about the office. He shrieked:

'Agnan, come here this instant!'

The young clerk rushed in and gazed incredulously at the disarray. Florin growled ominously:

'Don't just stand there, you fool, pick it up!'

It was almost none when Francesco de Leone, who was standing in a porch, saw Nicolas Florin leave the Inquisition headquarters. The Dominican responded to the polite greetings of a few passers-by with an unassuming smile then turned into Rue de l'Arche. Leone pulled his cowl over his face and straightened the short, waisted peasant's tunic he was wearing underneath the thick leather apron of a smith. He fell in behind the inquisitor, maintaining a few yards' distance between them. A grubby-looking boy passed him by, then slowed down all of a sudden and sauntered along with his arms behind his back, gazing up at the surrounding buildings. Leone wondered for a moment whether he wasn't up to some mischief.

The knight had no real plan – as he had assured Hermine after her performance as the wealthy Marguerite Galée, eager to send her father-in-law to a better world. He was not sure whether he was hoping to discover compromising evidence that would force Florin to back down or waiting for a situation to arise that would require killing him. Leone was aware that he was allowing himself to be guided by the other man's actions, which might or might not lead to his death. This was not a hypocritical attempt to evade responsibility. Leone had been responsible for many deaths, but had never chosen his victims. Florin, however undeserving, would enjoy what he had been unable to offer the others: a private judgement of God. If he were not meant to die, he would be spared. This was what the Hospitaller sincerely believed.

The inquisitor lengthened his stride, as though he were in a hurry to get somewhere. Perhaps, also, now that they were further away from the Inquisition headquarters he was no longer worried lest somebody question his haste. Curiously enough, the little beggar boy had also quickened his pace and was keeping the same distance between himself and Florin. Leone's soldierly instinct alerted him.

Florin turned right and walked up towards Rue des Petites-Poteries. All of a sudden, he slipped into Rue du Croc. Leone hurried after him but by the time he reached the cobbler's shop on the corner, Florin had vanished and he found himself face to face with the little rascal who was looking equally bemused. Just as the boy was about to run off, Leone leapt forward and grabbed him by the tunic.

'Who are you following?'

'Who, me? Nobody, I swear!'

The knight took hold of the boy's ear and, leaning over, whispered:

'You were following the Dominican, weren't you? I'm a man of little patience so don't lie to me. Who sent you?'

The boy panicked. He certainly didn't look very friendly, this smith. He tried unsuccessfully to wriggle free from his grasp.

'Let go of me!' the boy protested, trembling with fear.

Putting on a threatening voice, Leone said:

'If you tell me the truth, I'll give you three silver coins and let you go. However, if you continue lying to me, I'll give you a good thrashing and throw you in the River Sarthe.'

The little urchin's eyes filled with tears at the thought, but he replied astutely:

'And why should I believe a smith when he says he has three silver coins? I've already got one from my client and he promised me another when I tell him what he wants to know, but he looks like a real lord.'

Without letting go of the boy's ear, Leone reached into his purse with his other hand and took out three coins.

'All right,' the child muttered. 'But let go of my ear. You're hurting me, you brute.'

'If you attempt to run off ...'

The child interrupted him, shrugging his shoulders:

'Why would I choose a dip in the Sarthe when I can earn proper money?'

Leone stifled a grin and released his ear, but remained ready to pounce at the boy's slightest movement.

'Who paid you to spy?' Leone asked him again.

'He offered me two silver coins to follow the Dominican.'

'Do you know his name?'

'No.'

'What did he look like?'

'Very tall. A big man, bigger than you. And dark, with dark eyes, too. He wears his hair shoulder-length and dresses in fine clothes and carries a sword. A powerful man by the looks of him. I'd say he's a baron, possibly even a count.'

'What age?'

'A lot older than you.'

'What exactly did he ask you to do?'

'To follow the inquisitor without being seen and find out where he lives.'

What was Artus d'Authon doing mixed up in this affair, for Leone was almost certain it was he? His aunt Éleusie de Beaufort had alluded briefly to Agnès de Souarcy's meeting with her overlord just before the young woman's arrest.

'Where are you supposed to meet him?'

'At a tavern called La Jument-Rouge, it's …'

'I know where it is.'

Leone handed the boy the coins, which quickly disappeared under his tunic.

'I advise you not to go back and warn your client in order to try to get the other silver coin or I'll …'

'I know … you'll throw me in the Sarthe!'

The boy turned on his heel and vanished before Leone had decided what to do next.

Was Artus d'Authon a friend or foe? Now was not the time to worry about that.

Which of the buildings had Nicolas Florin slipped into? Leone did not believe that he had discovered he was being followed. He could do nothing but wait, crouched in the shadow of a nearby wall. Sooner or later the man would have to come out again.

A good half-hour went by, during which the knight managed to empty his mind of the endless calculations, theories, questions. Not thinking is a strenuous and exhausting exercise for a man of thought. Accepting nothingness, inviting it, becoming the void, is to allow oneself to experience infinity. Time then passes in a random way. The little barefoot girl who lifts her thick cotton dress, tied with a piece of string at the waist, and squats in the gutter to empty her bladder as she stares at you fills the whole universe. How much time passed before she stood up and ran off ? A little ball of hemp blown across the cobblestones comes to a stop then rolls on for a few feet[+] before stopping again then rolling again, until it reaches a wall where somebody's foot treads on it and carries it who knows where; for a few split seconds that ball becomes the most important thing in the world.

Francesco de Leone almost didn't recognise the beautiful Nicolas. He cut a dashing figure. He was without question one of the finest-looking creatures Leone had ever seen. His willowy body was perfectly suited to lay clothes. Indeed, it appeared Florin was well acquainted with the latest town fashions. He had swapped the black habit and long white cape of the Dominicans for a silk shirt, on top of which he wore a short tunic that set off his dark-purple leggings and breeches. Elegant Parisians referred to these as *hauts-de-chausses* and *bas-de-chausses*. Over his tunic he wore a bodice lavishly embroidered with gold thread, and a jacket of fine dark-green wool gathered at the waist by a belt covered in gold work and with slits in the sleeves to allow a glimpse of the bodice. The whole was topped off by a greatcoat, open at the front and sides, that would have been the envy of the finest lords, and a hood of a softer green than the jacket, which concealed his tonsure, and whose pointed end he wore hanging down in the style of the young dandies at court.

Francesco de Leone recalled the clothes they were given when they joined the Hospitaller order. Besides bed and table linen they received two shirts, two pairs of leggings, two pairs of breeches, a bodice, a fur-trimmed jacket and two coats, one with a fur lining for winter, as well as a cape and a belted tunic coat. Only when the clothes or linen became threadbare did they take them to the administrator, who would duly replace them. In exchange they handed over their fortune to the order, and in Francesco's case this had been a substantial one inherited from his mother. And yet he had no doubt that the bequest would have pleased the remarkable woman who had given birth to him. As for him, leaving behind his worldly goods had been such an immense relief that he had spent the whole night following this final rite of passage wide awake and in a state of bliss. Clearly the inquisitor did not share his fondness for self-denial.

Claire. As he grew older so the memory of his mother seemed to grow clearer. Her elder sister, Éleusie de Beaufort, resembled her, though she was less pretty, less vivacious. Small things – a made-up poem, a beautiful flower, a child's words, the unusual colour of a ribbon – would elicit his mother's ready laugh. And yet that pale and lofty brow concealed such intelligence and wisdom, some of which Leone liked to believe he had inherited. Added to this was her intuition, which Leone had not been endowed with. He saw in this the price he had to pay for his physical strength and masculinity. She had 'sensed' the twisting currents sweeping along all their lives long before they became apparent. As a small boy Leone had been convinced that this mysterious gift came from the angels. Had she also sensed her own slaughter and that of her daughter at Saint-Jean-d'Acre? No. It was unthinkable, for if she had had such a premonition, she would have escaped in time with her child.

There was so much he did not know about that beautiful, noble woman who had held him in her arms and called him 'her brave knight of the white cross' when he was only five or six years old. Had she already known that he would one day join the Hospitaller order? How was that possible? Had they not simply been loving words from a mother to her son?

Lost in such sweet, painful memories, Leone realised just in time that he was stalking his prey too closely, and running the risk of the other man turning round and seeing him. Florin must not be able to recognise him later on. He slowed his pace.

Did the inquisitor rent a bachelor's apartment in this well-to-do, discreet part of town where he could transform himself at his leisure and perhaps even keep the company of ladies?

He had lined his purse well with the blood of others.

Nicolas Florin was hurrying now. He entered one of the neighbourhoods where the passers-by leave as dusk sets in and the peaceable atmosphere dissolves as another type of creature comes to life. The modest corbelled dwellings appeared in places to form arches above the alleyways. The front of each building was occupied by stalls or workshops. Leone began to notice women whose appearance betrayed their calling*, as required by the Church and civic authorities. Their gaudy, low-cut dresses and the absence of the type of jewellery and belts worn by burghers' wives or noblewomen, which they were prohibited from wearing, marked them out as purveyors of the flesh. Leone deduced that there was a bordel nearby, as in the big cities.[82] A strumpet, scarcely older than fourteen, approached Florin. He sized her up from head to toe as he would a horse. The knight flattened himself in a doorway and observed the transaction taking place a few yards away, hardly daring to imagine what the poor girl would be put through in exchange for a few paltry coins, for he was certain that Florin's sexual preferences would also entail violence and torture. They finally moved away, disappearing into a hemp-and-linen draper's stall that must have fronted a house of ill repute.

A good half-hour passed before the inquisitor re-emerged alone, wearing a look of sly satisfaction, and Leone wondered whether the poor girl was still able to stand. The pimps who supplied the wine and candles never interfered with their customers' antics, however abusive, so long as they got their money.

Florin walked back the same way he had come, Leone following behind, only instead of turning into Rue des Petites-Poteries he went straight on until he reached Rue de l'Ange where he slipped through the doorway of a well-to-do town house. Leone waited a few moments before approaching. The ground and first floors were made of stone with a half-timbered second floor above. The newly tiled roof had no doubt replaced the original thatched one, suggesting that the owner was extremely wealthy. The little dormer windows were wooden and protected by oilcloth, and all the interior shutters were closed, apart from those on the first floor. The pipes draining dirty water from the kitchen onto the street were dried up, as were those funnelling human waste into sewers or pits. The handsome-looking dwelling seemed to have been recently abandoned.

Florin must have rented a tiny room in Rue du Croc where he could transform himself into a rich burgher and then come to this smart house. But who did it belong to and why did nobody appear to be living there?

It took Leone one hour and much lying to find out the answers to these questions from the various shop owners on Rue des Petites-Poteries and Rue de l'Ange. Monsieur Pierre Tubeuf, a rich draper, having been very opportunely found guilty of heresy and dealings with the devil, had had his property confiscated by the Inquisition. Terrified that any objection on their part might prompt the inquisitor to charge them with the same crimes, his wife and two children had fled the town. Leone had no doubt that this was what would have happened. Florin had awarded himself a magnificent house at the cheapest price.

The knight left the neighbourhood. Now he knew where Agnès's torturer lived.

Artus d'Authon waited, the barely touched cup of buttered ale in front of him. What was the child doing? He should have reported back long ago. The Comte made a supreme effort to suppress his anger and above all his despair. Had the little beggar boy tricked him? And yet the prospect of another silver coin should have been incentive enough. Perhaps Florin had suspected that he was being trailed and the boy had given up. He felt a flicker of fear for the boy's safety, but reassured himself. Those young street urchins were quick on their feet and catching one would be no easy task. He raged against himself. What could he do now? Florin would recognise him instantly if he took it into his head to follow him. He cursed his ineptitude as a man of honour. He was capable of provoking a duel, fighting and winning, yet scheming and subterfuge were foreign to him, and he felt powerless against a sly snake such as the inquisitor. His chief bailiff, Monge de Brineux, was too much like him to be of any use. The solution came to him in a flash. Clément! Florin had never seen the boy and Clément had already shown that he possessed both courage and intelligence. Moreover, he would do anything to save his beloved mistress. Artus felt a great sense of relief and celebrated by swigging back his beer. He would return to Alençon with

Clément the day after tomorrow. Come evening, Florin would be back where he belonged – in hell. The Comte would invoke the judgement of God, and Agnès would be freed, her accuser having been struck down by the hand of God. He leapt up, almost overturning the table, and rushed out to the astonishment of the other customers.

The knight Leone found Rue des Carreaux, which led to his meeting place at the Bobinoir[83] Tavern, Rue de l'Étoupée. He was guided there by the crier[84] whose job it was to announce the price of wine served at the tavern.

Landlords were commonly named after their establishments and Monsieur Bobinoir, who was no exception, looked up as the knight walked in and wondered what a smith was doing coming into his tavern, which was a meeting place for haberdashers, a guild that was growing in wealth and status and whose members were now considered to be on a par socially with the burghers. Maître Bobinoir paused. His regular customers did not care to rub shoulders with a member of the lowly professions. Then again, as long as the man was not a tanner whose clothes were impregnated with the stench of rotting flesh, or even a common dyer, he did not feel obliged simply to ask him to leave. Besides, something about the man's appearance intrigued Monsieur Bobinoir – a sort of effortlessness, an ease devoid of arrogance. No doubt the other customers sitting at the tables that day felt it too, for after giving him a second glance they quickly returned to their conversations. The smith looked around the room for a place to sit then turned silently to the landlord, who motioned with his chin towards an isolated table.

When Monsieur Bobinoir went over to take his order, he made

a point of speaking in a loud voice so as to reassure his regular customers:

'We keep good company here, smith, and Bobinoir is pleased to welcome you today. If tomorrow you still have a thirst, be a good fellow and slake it in the tavern serving people in your own trade.'

The smith's deep-blue eyes gazed up at him and Maître Bobinoir, gripped by a sudden anxiety, had to resist the urge to draw back in order to avoid being humiliated in front of his customers. And yet slowly the man's face creased into a smile:

'You are too kind, Monsieur Bobinoir, and I thank you. I accept your hospitality and will remember that it is an exception.'

'There's a good chap,' the landlord boomed, pleased at having more or less stood his ground. 'Will you take some wine?'

'Yes, bring your finest. I am waiting for a friend … a Dominican friar. Like me he is not a haberdasher, but …'

'A friar!' interrupted Maître Bobinoir, then pronounced solemnly, 'I am honoured to receive him in my establishment.'

A few moments later, Jean de Rioux, the younger brother of Eustache de Rioux, who had been Leone's godfather in the Hospitallers, walked into the tavern. Monsieur Bobinoir now began to fuss over the Dominican, whose arrival he saw as open confirmation that his establishment attracted the salt of the earth and was far from being a den of iniquity.

As his old friend approached the table, the knight stood up to embrace this courageous, honourable soul who had not hesitated to lower himself to spying if it meant remaining true to his faith and that of his departed brother.

'I am angry at fate, Jean, for my pleasure at seeing you after all these years is spoiled by the circumstances that drove me to request your help. But, most of all, I am eternally grateful to you for not hesitating to offer it, despite your duty of obedience to your order.'

'Francesco, Francesco ... What a joy to behold you, too! As for my help, it is only a mark of the friendship and respect I have always felt for you. Eustache thought of you as a son, and you are like a younger brother to me. No request of yours could be anything but pure, which is why upon receiving your brief missive I did not hesitate for a second to offer you my help, likewise Brother Anselme.'

Jean fell silent as Maître Bobinoir approached and set down a cup of frothy beer in front of him. He nodded politely to the man and waited for him to leave before continuing in a hushed voice:

'As for my duty of obedience to my order, it can never outweigh that which I owe to God. Do not think, dear Francesco, that just because we willingly submit to the rule we become sheep. Do not think that we cease to have minds of our own. Many of us, Dominicans and Franciscans alike, question the bloody path that the Inquisition has taken. What was once firm conviction has turned into ferocious zeal. Defending the faith is one thing, coercive violence another, and it makes a mockery of the Gospels.'

'It was Benoît XI's intention to rein in the Inquisition.'

Jean de Rioux looked at him, incredulous. 'And revoke Innocent IV's papal bull *Ad extirpanda*?'

'Precisely.'

'But the political risk would have been enormous.'

'Benoît was aware of that.'

'A rumour is spreading that he died a natural death from internal bleeding,' Jean de Rioux added.

'It was to be expected ... And yet he was murdered, he died

from eating poisoned figs,' corrected the knight. 'The defenders of the imperial Church are rid of an embarrassing reformer and Christianity is deprived of one of its purest souls.'

They sipped their drinks in silence, then the Dominican spoke again in an almost inaudible voice:

'What you tell me, brother, increases the unease I feel and yet am unable to define. Something is being prepared, something whose true nature is still unclear but which goes far beyond fraudulent trials in exchange for money. Florin feels invulnerable, and that cannot be explained merely by the fee he will receive from that oafish baron.'

'You and I have reached the same conclusion. Only I believe I am able to put a name and a face to this menacing shadow.'

'Who?'

'The camerlingo Honorius Benedetti.'

'Surely you are not suggesting that he is behind the sudden death of our beloved late lamented Benoît XI?'

'I am almost sure of it, although I have no way of proving it and doubtless never will.'

They parted company an hour later at the top of the tavern steps. Jean had told Leone in detail about the cross-examination of Agnès de Souarcy that he had attended. He was in no doubt as to the trumped-up nature of the absurd charges and of the trial itself. Jean had made special mention of the shameful role played by Agnès's daughter.

They had to act quickly. The preliminary questioning would not go on for much longer, especially now that Florin's key witness, the malicious but foolish Mathilde de Souarcy, had made such a bad impression upon the judges.

They shook hands upon parting and Jean held on to Leone's. The knight hesitated for a second before asking:

'Jean, my friend, do you believe as Eustache did, and as I do now, that no act in defence of the Light can be considered profane?'

'It is my firm conviction, and it would hurt me if you were to doubt it,' the Dominican murmured solemnly.

Leone handed him a small package wrapped in a piece of cloth, and advised:

'Do not open it here, brother. It contains your preferential treatment and no doubt Agnès de Souarcy's salvation. There is a note with it. If you feel that … Well, the content of the note may endanger your life and I would never forgive myself if …'

A faint smile lit up the furrowed face that reminded Leone of his Hospitaller godfather.

'You know as well as I do, Francesco, that danger is a fickle mistress. She rarely appears where we think she will – hence her allure. Give me the package.'

Vatican Palace, Rome, November 1304

It was strange … He who suffered so much from the heat had begun to feel chilled to the bone after Benoît's death.

It was as though the sweet reminiscences that had up until then moved and comforted Honorius Benedetti, the deceased Benoît XI's camerlingo, during his darkest hours had been sucked into a bottomless pit. Where was the memory of the exquisite lady's fan he had put away in a drawer, and the swim in the icy river from which he and his brother had emerged pink with cold and delight, only to discover that their feet were bleeding? Honorius, who had been five at the time, had screamed out that they were going to die. Bernardo had quickly rallied, taking his younger brother in his arms and explaining that the crayfish had cut them, but that they would get their own back by having them for lunch. They had gorged themselves on the grilled creatures before falling asleep. Their mother … The intoxicating smell of her hair rinsed in honey and lavender water, which made them want to breathe it in, put it in their mouths and swallow it. What had become of these comforting memories?

Exaudi, Deus, orationem meam cum deprecor, a timore inimici eripe animam meam.[85]

It was Benoît. Benoît had taken them with him when he died. If only Honorius could resent him for it then his beautiful memories would come flooding back. But he could not. Benoît and his angelic obstinacy. Benoît and his gentle determination.

A wave of sadness filled his eyes with tears. Sweet Benoît.

I loved you dearly, brother. The eight months I spent in your company were my only solace in this palace full of loathsome, sickening fools. Why did you force me to kill such purity, Benoît? I didn't care about the others, mere insects borne by the wind. When I held you in my arms, when you spewed your blood, I knew that this cold would haunt me for ever.

Benoît, did you not see that I was right, that I was fighting for us both? Why should we welcome revolution, we who cherish continuity? Why should we give up everything in the name of a supposed truth, a truth so vague that it can only seduce madmen? I defend the established order, without which men would once more be plunged into the chaos we have saved them from. Surely you did not believe that they loved Truth? That they prayed for Justice? They are weak, dangerous fools.

Oh, Benoît … Why did you have to resist me, to oppose me unwittingly. If only we had seen eye to eye, I would have laboured tirelessly to seat you on the throne of God, as I did Boniface* – whom I did not even like. I would have been the indefatigable means for you to reign over our world. God illuminated you with His smile, but He gave me the strength to continue fighting. Why did you have to persist in your dream?

I cried for nights on end before giving him the order to slay you. I prayed for nights on end. I prayed that the scales would finally fall from your eyes. But you were blinded by the light. Your death throes were the longest hours of my life. Your suffering wounded me so deeply that I vow to obliterate from my vocabulary for ever the words 'torment, affliction, ordeal'.

Without you, Benoît, my world is empty. You were the only one who might have been a kindred spirit, but your love for Him separated us. And yet I, too, love Him more than my life, more than my salvation.

I drugged myself so that my vile executioner might enter the secret corridor leading from my office to your chamber. Even as I drank the bitter potion I prayed it would kill me. But death turned its back on me. They blamed my faltering speech on the opium when I was choking with grief.

Remember how I watched you eat those figs one by one. You beamed at me like a child as you recalled the sweet days spent at Ostia. With each shred of purple skin that you spat out into your hand another drop of life drained from you. I counted the number of breaths you had left, and as the poison spread into your veins so my soul drained from my body.

I have no place in my heart for regret, Benoît. Still worse, I have no regrets because I could never have allowed you to strip away our majesty, our supremacy, in the name of some splendid Utopia. Still worse, because since your death I no longer live, I toil. That is all I have left, together with this terrible emptiness.

If in His eyes and yours I acted wrongly, in the eyes of mankind I did what was right. I will accept my punishment. It can be no worse than my present suffering.

Beloved Benoît, may your sweet soul rest in peace. I implore you even as each fibre of my being cries out for an end to this most fervent of its desires.

Honorius Benedetti stood up and dried his face, which was moist with tears. The room was spinning, and he leaned against his enormous work table to steady himself. Finally the dizziness went away. He paused to catch his breath then pulled the braided rope behind the tapestries that brightened up his study. An usher appeared out of nowhere.

'Show him in.'

'Very good, Your Eminence.'

The cowled figure stepped into the room.

'Well?'

'Archambaud d'Arville is dead, run through with a sword. Leone has slipped through our fingers.'

The camerlingo closed his eyes in a gesture of despair.

'How could that be? Did you warn Arville to be on his guard? Leone is a soldier – one of the finest in his order.'

'He was supposed to drug him in order to render him weak.'

Benedetti grunted and asked:

'Do you think this is another intervention by one of theirs?'

'The idea had crossed my mind.'

'Why have none of my spies succeeded in flushing them out? I might be forgiven for thinking that they enjoy divine protection!'

'No, Your Eminence. God is on our side. Even so, our enemies are accustomed to secret warfare. We forced them back into their caves, crevices and catacombs. They turned this defeat to their advantage. They have become an army of shadows whose strength we cannot gauge.'

'In your opinion, does Leone know that his secret quest was in fact instigated by others?'

'It would surprise me.'

The prelate's irritation got the better of him and he demanded sharply:

'All the evidence suggests that that scoundrel Humeau sold the manuscripts he stole from the papal library to Francesco de Leone. Have you found them?'

'Not yet. But I am searching tirelessly.'

'Indeed! I would prefer it if you searched successfully.'

'Everything points towards Clairets Abbey.'

'What is Leone's connection to the place?' asked the camerlingo.

'The Abbess, Éleusie de Beaufort. Benoît XI appointed her

and I am beginning to wonder whether there might not be some other connection between her and the knight which we don't know about.'

'Make it your business to recover the Vallombroso treatise urgently. Without it we are incapable of calculating the dates of birth. And the work on necromancy, too … At this stage any help, however subversive, is welcome.'

'You don't intend to … I mean, you are not going to use that monstrosity?'

'You speak of monstrosities? And what do you suppose you are guilty of since you began working for me?'

The figure remained silent.

'And what of the woman?' the camerlingo continued.

The figure drew back his cowl. His face broke into a smile.

'At this moment in time, Your Eminence, there can't be much left of her and I wouldn't want to be in the place of what little there is.'

'Her suffering brings me no enjoyment. Suffering is far too precious a sacrifice to be wasted in vain demonstrations. I know one thing,' the prelate murmured, before continuing in a firmer voice: 'Agnès de Souarcy must die, and quickly, but her execution must be made to look like a just one. I have no need for a martyr on my hands.'

'I'll inform her torturer at once. He will be disappointed. He gets drunk on suffering like others do on mulled wine.'

'He has received handsome enough recompense for his obedience,' Benedetti pointed out sharply. 'I detest the enjoyment of torturers. Once his work is done I want him killed. We have no more need of him. His repulsive existence is a stain on my soul.'

'Your wish is my command, Your Eminence.'

Honorius was exasperated and said through gritted teeth: 'You are aware of my wishes, now carry them out – I pay you enough! I would hate to lose patience with you. Now go.'

The threat was plain enough and the figure pulled down his cowl and left.

The camerlingo waited a moment before angrily summoning the usher with an angry tug on the bell rope.

'Has she arrived?'

'Not yet, Your Eminence.'

Disappointment was written all over Benedetti's face and he muttered under his breath:

'Why is she so late? Let me know as soon as she arrives.'

'Very good, Your Eminence.'

One of Philip the Fair's huge lurchers was gazing at him balefully. Guillaume de Nogaret sat waiting in the King's study chambers, trying his best not to move for fear that the bitch with a white coat and brindled markings on her head might interpret his slightest gesture as a threat. These animals allegedly killed their prey with a single bite. He understood the need for them, though not what induced the ladies to keep the more decorative of these four-legged creature as pets, even going so far as to dress them in embroidered coats to keep them warm in winter.[86] It was true that to Monsieur de Nogaret's mind God's only true creature was man, and to a lesser extent woman, and the Almighty had put all other species on earth for him to use without ill-treating or doing violence to them.

The counsellor saw Philip the Fair's tall, emaciated figure appear at the far end of the gloomy corridor he had been staring down. He stood up to the immediate accompaniment of unfriendly growls from the bitch, which moved forward, sniffing vigorously at the hem of his coat.

'Down,' he ordered in a hushed tone.

This had the effect of making the dog growl even more loudly. As soon as her master entered the room, she bounded over to him and placed herself between him and this man whose smell she did not care for.

'There's a good girl, Delmée,' Philip said reassuringly, bending down to pat her. 'Go and lie down, my beauty. Did you know, my dear Nogaret, that she is the fastest of all my hunting dogs, and that she can snap a hare's spine with one bite?'

'A truly fine animal,' the counsellor conceded with such a lack of conviction that it brought a smile to Philip's lips.

'I sometimes wonder what other interests or amusements you have besides the affairs of state and the law.'

'None, Sire, which do not relate to your affairs.'

'Well, how do things stand regarding my pope? Benoît XI, or rather his sudden demise, has left me in an invidious position.'

Nogaret was in no way offended by this remark. And yet, if the Pope's unexpected passing had left anybody in a delicate situation, it was he. His plan to provide Philip the Fair with a Holy Father who was more concerned with spiritual matters than France's affairs of state was still not ready. Guillaume de Nogaret detested acting hastily, but the forthcoming election gave him no choice. He explained:

'On my behalf Guillaume de Plaisians has approached Renaud de Cherlieu, Cardinal of Troyes, and Bertrand de Got,* Archbishop of Bordeaux. These are our two most promising candidates.'

'And?'

'It will doubtless come as no surprise to you, Sire, to learn that they are both, and I quote, "extremely interested in serving our Holy Mother Church".'

'Indeed, it comes as no surprise, Nogaret. The papal crown confers countless benefits, including, I suppose, money. What do they demand for deigning to rule over Christendom?'

'They are both equally greedy ... Privileges, titles for family members, various gifts and certain assurances from you.'

'What assurances?'

'That their authority in spiritual matters should remain established and that you should no longer interest yourself in the administration of the French Church.'

'The French Church is in France and I am the ruler of France. The landed wealth of the French Church is so vast that it would make even my richest lords green with envy. Why should it enjoy even greater privilege?'

Nogaret equivocated:

'Indeed, Sire ... But we need a pope who will be well disposed towards you. Let us offer these assurances ... Do you really think that the successful candidate will come complaining and risk the negotiations that led to his election being revealed?'

Philip the Fair's pursed lips betrayed his ill humour.

'Which one do we favour?'

'If we have considered them both, it is because their willingness to serve us is unquestionable. Monseigneur de Got is certainly the shrewder of the two, though like Cherlieu a mild-mannered man, a trait, if I may say so, which influenced our choice.'

'Indeed, we do not want a strong personality. And what do they intend to do about that scourge, Boniface VIII? You are aware, Nogaret, of how keen I am for him to be deposed, albeit posthumously, in revenge for poisoning my existence. He systematically opposed my every order, and I am convinced he even went so far as to instigate the rebellion in the Languedoc by backing that troublemaker Bernard Délicieux.* Boniface ...' the King said with contempt. 'An arrogant blunder whose memory is a stain on Christianity!'

Their mutual loathing for Benoît XI's predecessor created a further bond between the two men.

'Plaisians has naturally broached the matter with tact and diplomacy. They both appeared to listen carefully to him, and in any event showed no hostility.'

'How will we choose between the two, for we are unable to move two pawns at the same time?'

'I would give my backing to the Archbishop of Bordeaux, Monseigneur de Got.'

'And your reasons?'

'You are better acquainted than I with his skill as a diplomat. Furthermore, the Gascons like him, which will earn us additional votes at no cost and with no need for open intervention. Finally and most importantly, Monseigneur de Got has come out in favour of reuniting all the military orders under one flag, and thus of ending the Templars' autonomy. Our motives may differ, but we seek the same end.'

'Let it be Monsieur de Got, then. We shall back him resolutely and discreetly, and make sure he shows his gratitude.'

Crouched in the corner of a tiny room, dark and dank, stinking of excreta and sour milk. Crouched on the muddy floor that has coated her skimpy dress, her calves and thighs with a foul greenish film. Crouching, straining in the darkness, trying to make sense of the sounds she heard. There had been a voice barking out orders, obscene laughter and cries followed by screams of pain. Then a terrified silence. Crouching, trying hard to merge into the stone walls, hoping to dissolve there, to vanish for ever. Steps coming to a halt outside the solid-looking low door. A voice declaring:

'At least they say this female's pleasing and comely!'

'She used to be. She looked more like a beggar when I brought her back down from the interrogation room.'

A loud rapping on the door. Why did they keep on when all they needed to do was pull the bolt across? The rapping grew louder and louder. Stop, I say, stop …

Éleusie de Beaufort managed to wrench herself free from the nightmare that had ensnared her. Drenched in sweat, she sat up in bed. Agnès. The torture. The torture was about to begin. What was Francesco doing?

Somebody was moving outside the door to her chambers. A voice cried out. It was Annelette:

'Reverend Mother, I beg you, wake up … Jeanne … Hedwige …'

She leapt out of bed and ran to open the door.

Thibaude de Gartempe, the guest mistress, was clinging to Annelette Beaupré's arm. Behind the two women stood Emma de Pathus and Blanche de Blinot, both deathly pale.

'What is it?' asked Éleusie, alarmed, as she straightened her veil.

Thibaude shouted in a rasping voice:

'They're going to die, they're going to die … Oh dear Lord … I won't stay in this godforsaken place a moment longer … I want to leave, now …'

The guest mistress, her eyes flashing and in the grip of hysteria, looked ready to hurl herself at the Abbess. Annelette tried to pacify her and snapped:

'That's enough! Let go of me! You're digging your nails into my arm. Let go, I say …'

The other woman cried out: 'I want to leave … Let me leave. If you …'

A stinging slap jerked the woman's head to one side. Annelette was preparing to raise her hand again when Éleusie intervened:

'Will somebody tell me what is going on!'

'It is Jeanne d'Amblin and Hedwige du Thilay. They are terribly ill. The vomiting began just after bedtime.'

The Abbess felt the blood drain from her face. She began shaking and in a barely audible voice asked:

'Yew poisoning?'

'It could be. I'm still not sure, although the symptoms appear to be consistent.'

Without a word Éleusie leapt out into the corridor and ran to the dormitories, followed by the four women.

Jeanne d'Amblin lay between sheets soaked in bloody vomit, her eyes closed, her chest barely lifting as she breathed, her face twisted into a grimace of excruciating pain. Éleusie placed a hand on the woman's icy brow then stood up straight, trying her best to stifle the sobs that were choking her.

Annelette roared:

'Where is the water I ordered?'

A petrified novice handed her a jug, spilling a quarter of the contents on the floor.

A cry rang out from the other end of the dormitory:

'She's leaving us … No, it's not possible … Somebody, do something …'

Éleusie rushed over. Hedwige du Thilay's head had just flopped onto the shoulder of the sister in charge of the fishponds and henhouses, Geneviève Fournier. Beside herself, powerless to accept the truth, she was shaking the treasurer nun's frail little body in an effort to revive her and whispering:

'Please, Hedwige dear, please wake up … Come along, Hedwige, come along now … Can't you hear me? It's me, Geneviève, remember, with my turkeys, my eggs, my carp and crayfish. Please try, I beg you. You must breathe, Hedwige dear. Look, I'll help you. I'll loosen your nightshirt and you'll feel more comfortable.'

With surprising gentleness, Annelette attempted to free the poor woman's skinny corpse, but Geneviève refused to let go. Annelette sniffed the bluish lips and stuck her finger in Hedwige's mouth in order to smell her saliva. Then she kissed Geneviève's brow, which was slick with sweat, and murmured:

'She's dead. Let go of her, please.'

'No. No!' shrieked the sister in charge of the fishponds. 'It's not possible!'

She clung on to her sister, almost lying on top of her lifeless body and buried her face in the woman's neck, repeating in a frantic voice:

'No, it's not possible. The Lord wouldn't allow it. He wouldn't allow one of his sweetest angels to be taken like that. I know he wouldn't! No, dear Annelette, you're mistaken – she isn't dead at all. She's fainted, that's all. It's just a nasty turn. You know what a frail constitution she has. Dead! … What nonsense!'

Éleusie was about to intervene, but Annelette discouraged her with a shake of her head and instructed:

'We must see to Jeanne now that I think I know which poison we are dealing with.' She added in a whisper so that Geneviève Fournier would not hear: 'Not a word to Jeanne about Hedwige's death. You know how close they were. Our extern sister's life is hanging by a thread and there is no point in weakening her chances by dealing her a terrible blow.'

They turned away for a time from the woman who refused despair, knowing that the respite would be short-lived and that the gentle Geneviève's grief would soon hit her with all the force of an implacable truth.

Jeanne was suffocating. Waves of nausea filled her mouth with bloody saliva that oozed down her chin. She let out a cry:

'Dear God, the pain … My stomach is bursting. Bless me, Reverend Mother, for I have sinned … I beg you, bless me before … it's too late … Water … I'm so thirsty … Bless me …'

Éleusie made the sign of the cross on her brow and murmured:

'I bless you, my daughter, my friend, and hereby absolve you of your sins.'

A faint relief slackened the grimace of pain etched on Jeanne's face. The dying woman managed to whisper:

'Is Hedwige any better?'

'Yes, Jeanne, we hope that she may live,' Éleusie lied.

'We … we were poisoned at the same time.'

'I know … Rest, preserve your strength, daughter.'

Jeanne closed her eyes and spluttered:

'Damn her …'

'She is damned, now try to be quiet.'

Annelette picked up the ewer of water and ordered Jeanne to be held down and her mouth forced open.

The dying woman tried feebly to resist, and groaned:

'Let me die in peace. I am at peace.'

For the next quarter of an hour, the apothecary nun forced her to drink, ignoring her pathetic protestations and the gagging that made her cough and spit. Two novices took turns to fetch water from the kitchens. After Jeanne, whose strength was waning fast, had swallowed several pints of fluid, the apothecary nun stood up straight, the front of her robe soaked in water and bloody vomit. Pointing a threatening finger at Emma de Pathus and Yolande de Fleury, who had been standing silently, transfixed, beside the bed since the nightmarish scene began, she ordered:

'Sit her up and keep her upright.'

The two nuns pulled Jeanne's inert body into a sitting position.

'You two,' she commanded, turning towards the quaking novices, 'open her mouth and keep it open until she starts vomiting.'

They all obeyed, incapable of uttering a word.

Annelette thrust her fingers down Jeanne's throat, faintly disgusted by the fetid yet sweet smell of her breath, and fingered her uvula until the poisoned woman's diaphragm began to contract. She waited until her hand was bathed in a flood of warm liquid from the intestines before releasing her sister, who was gradually regurgitating the contents of her stomach.

Half an hour later when they lay Jeanne back comfortably, her heartbeat was still irregular and her limbs were shaking, but she was having less difficulty breathing.

Éleusie followed Annelette down the corridor. Blanche de Blinot was leaning up against one of the pillars and weeping into her hands. She raised her head when she heard them coming and wailed:

'I'm a coward. A cowardly old woman. I am so afraid of death. I feel ashamed.'

'Blanche, do not be so hard on yourself,' Éleusie sighed. 'Death is a worry to us all, even though we know that a wondrous place awaits us beside Our Lord.'

Turning towards Annelette Beaupré, the old woman asked:

'Will Jeanne die too?'

'I don't know. Hedwige was frailer and older than Jeanne. And she may have swallowed more of the poison. We won't know until we have found out how they ingested it.'

'But why?' whispered the senior nun, sniffling.

'We do not know that either, dear Blanche. And if I had formed a theory, it now needs reappraising in light of the two new victims' identities,' the Abbess suggested, thinking of the plans of the abbey locked in the safe.

For if the murderess's aim was to steal them, then why poison Hedwige and Jeanne who did not have the keys? She did her best to comfort Blanche, adding:

'Go and rest for a while. The novices are watching over Jeanne. They will inform us of any change in her condition.'

Huddled up beside the great hearth, the only source of heat in the immense study chamber, Joseph de Bologne and Clément were performing an exercise in smelling. The old physician had pushed a beaker containing a foul reddish-yellow liquid under his apprentice's nose. He said impatiently:

'Come on, be more precise. What does it smell like?'

Stifling a desire to retch, Clément replied:

'Oh … I think I'm going to be sick …'

'Scientists aren't sick, they consider, they use their noses. More importantly, they remember what they smell,' Joseph interrupted him. 'Use your nose, Clément. It is the doctor's best tool! Come on, what is it?'

'Rotten egg, very rotten egg.'

'And where do we find this unpleasant odour? For let us not exaggerate – there exist far more evil-smelling ones.'

'In the faeces of patients suffering from digestive haemorrhage.'

'Good. Let's try another more difficult one.'

'Master …' interrupted Clément, whom these experiments were powerless to distract from his one obsession, which he thought about day and night, sobbing in his bed when he knew he was alone: 'Master …'

'You're thinking about your lady, aren't you?' said Joseph, who had consciously increased the number of experiments and lessons in the hope of offering his brilliant student some reprieve from his torment.

'She scarcely leaves my thoughts. Do you think … that I shall ever see her again?'

'I would like to believe that innocence always triumphs over adversity.'

'Do you really believe that?'

Joseph de Bologne studied the boy, and was overwhelmed by an infinite sadness. Had he ever witnessed the triumph of innocence? Probably not, and yet he was ready to lie for the sake of this young girl disguised as a boy whom he had come to love as his only spiritual son:

'Sometimes … Though generally when it is helped along. Come, my boy, let us continue,' he said, striving to give his voice a ring of authority.

He crossed to the other side of the vast room and poured some amber liquid into another beaker before submitting it to Clément's olfactory expertise:

'What do we smell? What does that pleasant odour tickling the nostrils suggest?'

'Apple juice. *Pestis!* [87] The smell on plague victims' breath. Well, the majority, others smell of freshly plucked feathers.'

'Try your best to remember both smells. I am telling you, that dread disease has not finished with us yet. And what must you do?'

'If a bubo forms, I must cauterise it with a red-hot knife, taking care to wear gloves, which I must incinerate, and to scrub my hands and forearms vigorously with soap. If the plague has infected the lungs, then there is nothing I can do except to avoid going within two yards of the victim. In effect, the plague victim's saliva forms tiny bubbles, which are expelled into the air and breathed in by the person to whom the sufferer is speaking.'

The old physician's wrinkled face beamed and he nodded. A good master doth a good pupil make.

Suddenly they both jumped. It felt as if a whole army had just invaded the room. Artus called over:

'May I draw near without fear of contracting some deadly disease? What is that evil smell?'

'Rotten egg, my lord.'

'You scientists certainly do engage in some extraordinary activities. Esteemed doctor, I wish to speak to your assistant urgently.'

'Should I leave the room, my lord?'

'On the contrary, I will leave you to your evil smells and take him to my chambers, which are protected from such noxious vapours.'

Once they were inside the little rotunda, Artus went straight to the point:

'I need your help, my boy.'

Clément could tell by the Comte's solemn expression that this related to Agnès. For a split second he froze with fear. No. No. She couldn't possibly be dead. In that case he would be dead, too, for his life depended so much on that of his lady.

'I-is it very bad news?' he stammered, doing his best to stifle the sobs that were rising in his throat.

'It is not good, but no worse than yesterday or the day before, so do not begin to despair yet. Madame de Souarcy is still alive … But the torture will begin shortly.'

Artus looked murderously around the room, searching for something he could break, something he could smash to pieces in an attempt to calm his fury. He brought his fist down on the table, upsetting the inkpot in the shape of a ship's hull. Clément stood still, watching the ink run slowly along the grain of the wood and drip on to the floor. Artus stood next to him and they both looked on in awe as the tiny dark stain spread ominously across the floorboards. Black ink, not red, Clément kept saying to himself. Ink, not blood, just ink. Even so, he pulled from his belt the piece of coarse cloth he used as a handkerchief, and rushed over to soak up the inky pool.

Artus raised his eyes, as though Clément's simple gesture had broken the evil spell riveting their gaze to the floor. He continued where he had left off:

'Florin must die, Clément. There is no other solution. He must die, and soon.'

'Give the order to saddle me a horse, my lord, and I'll leave at once. I'll kill him.'

The child's blue-green eyes staring at him conveyed his fierce determination. And, strangely, Artus knew that he was capable of doing it, even if it meant being killed himself.

'I will be the one to wield the sword, my boy. It is an old friend that has never failed me. What I need is someone to trail Florin, for he knows me. I thought I had found a little helper, but he vanished into thin air.'

Clément grew excited:

'I can replace him. Just give the order, my lord!'

'We leave for Alençon at dawn tomorrow.'

'But it is more than twenty leagues+ from here … Will we arrive in … time?'

Clément stumbled over the last word, which sounded like a death sentence.

'Twenty-three to be exact, and I'll be damned if we don't arrive in time! If we ride our horses hard, we'll arrive the day after tomorrow at dusk.'

Vatican Palace, Rome, November 1304

The feeling of agonising numbness that scarcely left Camerlingo Benedetti was cut short by the arrival of an usher:

'Your visitor is here, Your Eminence.'

A sigh of relief stirred Honorius. He felt as though this blessed announcement had finally allowed him to reach dry land, to leave behind the turbulent seas that had been buffeting him for the past few days and nights.

'Give me a moment to say a short prayer and then show her in.'

The other man bowed and left.

And yet, the camerlingo had no intention of spending the time in quiet contemplation. He wanted to savour it, be aware of its every nuance.

Aude, the magnificent Aude. Aude de Neyrat. The mere sound of her name worked on him like a magic charm. The tightness that had gripped the prelate's throat for months abated. He could breathe the almost cool air again, exhilarated. The insistent throbbing pain in his chest vanished, and for the first time in what seemed an age he dared to stand up and stretch without being afraid he might shatter.

To behold Aude, to smile at her. Unable to contain himself any longer, he rushed over to the tall double doors of his office and flung them open, to the astonishment of the usher, who was waiting outside with Madame de Neyrat.

'Come in, my dear, good friend.'

The woman stood up with an exquisitely graceful movement.

Honorius thought to himself that she was even more stunningly beautiful than he had recalled. She was quite simply miraculous. One of those miracles that occur once in a lifetime, and whose perfection leaves the onlooker humbled. A mass of blonde locks framed a tiny, angelic, perfectly oval-shaped face. Two almond eyes like emerald-green pools stared at him joyfully, and a pair of heart-shaped lips broke into a charming smile. Honorius closed his eyes in a gesture of contentment. That graceful figure, that domed forehead concealed one of the most powerful, most sophisticated minds he had ever encountered.

She walked towards him, her feet barely touching the ground, it seemed to him. Honorius closed the doors behind them.

Aude de Neyrat took a seat and smiled, tilting her ravishing head to one side:

'It has been such a long time, Your Eminence.'

'Please, Aude, let us pretend that time, which has scarcely left its mark on you while turning me into an old man, never really passed.'

She consented with an exquisite gesture of her pretty hand, and corrected herself:

'Gladly … It has been no time at all, then, dear Honorius.' Pursing her full lips, she declared in a more solemn voice:

'Your letter delighted me at first and then, I confess, I found it troubling.'

'Forgive me, I beg you. But I am plagued by worries, and no doubt it showed through in my words …'

The camerlingo paused and looked at her. Aude de Neyrat had led a turbulent life. Only a miracle could explain how she bore no signs of it. Orphaned at an early age, she had been placed under the tutelage of an elderly uncle who had quickly confused family charity and incest. The scoundrel had not enjoyed his niece's charms for long, and had died a slow and painful death while his protégée stood over him devotedly. At the tender age of twelve Aude discovered she had a flair for poison, murder and deception, equalled only by her beauty and brains. An aunt, two cousins who stood to inherit, and an elderly husband had shared the same fate as the hateful uncle, until one day the chief bailiff of Auxerre's men had become suspicious of the series of misfortunes befalling her relatives. Honorius Benedetti, a simple bishop at the time, happened to be in the town during her trial. Madame de Neyrat's striking beauty had made him recall the follies of his youth, during which he would leave one lady's bed, only to fall into the bed of another. He had insisted on questioning her, arguing that his robe would encourage a confession. She had confessed to nothing but had spun a web of lies which, as a connoisseur, had impressed him. In his view such cunning, such astuteness, such talent should not end up with a rope round its neck, still less burnt like a witch at the stake. He had moved heaven and earth, using money, threats and persuasion. Aude had been released from custody and cleared of all suspicion. She had been the prelate's only carnal transgression since his renouncement of the world. He had joined her a week later in the town house she had inherited from the husband she had sent to an allegedly better world. For a moment, Honorius had been afraid that she would not willingly take part in his violation of the rule. He had been mistaken. And, as he had secretly hoped, she did not feel indebted or under any obligation to spend those few hours with him naked and sweating between the sheets. She had done him the honour of offering herself to him because he was a man, not her creditor. During these hours of perfect folly, they had discovered one another, sized one another up like two wild beasts of equal stature. They had made love as one makes a pact.

Typically, Aude had considered that the ends justified the means. Had she not confided during the early hours:

'What else was I to do, dear man? Life is too short to allow it to be ruined by spoilsports. If only people were more sensible, there would be no need for me to poison them. I am a woman of my word and a woman of honour – admittedly in my own peculiar way. Consequently, my uncle, who believed he had the right to take away my innocence and my virginity, paid with his life. I had no say in the deal he struck over my young body and therefore I saw no need to ask his opinion regarding his death. Promise me that you are a sensible man, Honorius. I would hate it if you disappeared … You are far too special and precious not to be part of my life.'

He had roared with laughter at the charming threat. He had not had many reasons to laugh since; his life had veered out of control and become bleak and joyless. In the end, Aude's cheerful vivacity revived the only memory that allowed him to breathe freely.

'What I am about to tell you, my radiant Aude …' he began before she interrupted him with a look of glee:

'Must never leave this room? Surely you know me better than that, my dear man.'

He exhaled slowly. Could he have dreamed of a more perfect confessor than Aude? The one person he could trust. He closed his eyes and continued with difficulty:

'Aude, my wonderful Aude … If only you knew … Benoît is dead and I am responsible. His death wounds me, gnaws relentlessly at my insides, and yet it had to be done.'

'Why?' she asked, apparently untroubled by his admission.

'Because Benoît was a purist, whose obstinacy threatened to undermine the foundations of our Church. He had a dangerous dream and clung to his idea of evangelical purity at a time when we are threatened from all sides, at a time when, on the contrary, we need to strengthen the authority of the Church in the West. Dialogue, exchange and openness are no longer appropriate ... Indeed, I ask myself whether they ever have been. A reform of the Church, a display of *mea culpa* would be fatal to us, I am convinced of it. Aude, we are the guarantors of an order and a stability without which mankind cannot survive. We are confronted by forces which I consider to be evil, and which are attempting to undermine our power. A number of European monarchs, including Philip the Fair, are intent upon weakening our authority, my dear. However, they are not my main concern. We will succeed in forcing them back. It is the others, I confess, who make me afraid.'

'The others? What others?' enquired the splendid young woman.

'If I knew who they were, my worries would be over. I can feel them closing in on all sides. I see evidence of them in the proliferation of heresies, in the zealous austerity of some of the mendicant friars, in the benevolent attitudes towards their ideas on the part of nobles and burghers. I seek them out tirelessly ... Already the hopes of the wealthy and erudite minorities rest with these reformers. The others, the poor, will soon follow suit, seduced by their grotesque theories of equality. We fend off and will continue to fend off heretical movements, but they are merely the outer expression of a deeper hatred of us and of what we stand for.'

'And yet, the Inquisition has never seemed so active,' his guest pointed out.

'The Inquisition is a jack-in-the-box used to scare people. There have been past uprisings against it, proving that the people will react if they find a ... leader.' Honorius paused before continuing: 'A leader or a miracle. Just imagine, my friend ... Just imagine ...'

'What is it you are not telling me? I sense your fear and it alarms me.'

The young woman's perceptiveness convinced him to tell her everything:

'I am involved in a struggle which at times I fear will be in vain. I fear imminent failure. It would only take a miracle – a convincing miracle – to tip the scales.'

'What kind of miracle?'

'I don't know. I doubt whether even Benoît understood the true nature of it, and yet he was ready to protect it with his life, as is one of his key combatants, the Knight Hospitaller Francesco de Leone.'

He looked at her intently for a moment before continuing:

'If my explanations seem vague and uncertain, it is because for years I have been searching blindly. A text, a sacred prophecy fell into our hands and was spirited away. It contained two birth charts. After long years of futile searching and disappointment, Boniface became aware of the existence of an astronomical treatise written by a monk at the Vallombroso Monastery. The revolution contained within its pages could under no circumstances be propagated. The work was locked away in our private library. We were making headway in our calculations, which would have allowed us to decipher both charts, when the treatise was stolen by a chamberlain and sold to the highest bidder ... Leone. The fact remains that we were able to interpret the first chart and, thanks to an eclipse of the moon, to find the person it referred to: Agnès de Souarcy.'

'Who is she?'

'The illegitimate recognised child of a lowly baron, Robert de Larnay.'

A disbelieving frown creased Madame de Neyrat's pretty brow.

'What an absurd story. What possible part could a minor French noble play in a clash between the forces of conservatism and reform within the Church?'

'An admirable summary of the chaos into which I have been plunged for years.'

'Moreover, a woman. What are women in the eyes of a prelate? Saints, nuns or mothers on the one hand, and whores, delinquents and temptresses on the other. What possible importance could a woman have?'

Honorius said nothing as she reeled off her list. He was clever enough to know that she was right. Be that as it may, what other role could a woman play? Was not she, Aude, the charming murderess, living proof of this?

'I am hopelessly in the dark, my dear. All I know about the woman is that she represents a terrible threat, the exact nature of which escapes me. She must die, and quickly.'

'And you want me to carry out her execution?' Madame de Neyrat enquired with a smile.

'No. I took care of that long before I called upon you.'

'What is it you want from me, then, dear Honorius?'

'I need that Vallombroso treatise. I need it urgently so as to be able to calculate the second birth chart and pre-empt my enemies. I engaged the services of a henchman whose incompetence worries me and is beginning to exasperate me. I counted upon his anger, his bitterness, his need to exact revenge on life for the injustice of which he believes he is a victim.'

A brief silence followed this admission. Aude de Neyrat responded thoughtfully:

'Honorius, Honorius, it is wrong to place your trust in fear and envy. They are the attributes of a coward, and cowards are the worst traitors.'

'I did not have much choice, my lovely woman. Will you help me?'

'I told you once that I am a woman of my word and a woman of honour. I always repay my debts, Monsieur,' she replied unsmilingly for the first time. 'Moreover, very few of those I have incurred I hold dear. I will help you ...' and then, aware that the tone of her conversation had become rather serious, she added light-heartedly: 'And, who knows, I might even be doing our future pope a service.'

He shook his head before replying:

'I prefer to remain in the shadows, my dear. I am waiting anxiously behind the scenes for a man whom I can serve better than I serve myself. Benoît ... Benoît, though I loved him dearly, was not this man.'

'And what shall I do with your spy?'

'Eliminate him if the need arises; he has given me proof enough of his ineptitude.'

'I find the idea quite appealing, Honorius.'

Aude stood up, and the camerlingo followed suit, clasping her hands before raising them to his lips. She murmured:

'I will remain in Rome for two days in order to rest. Do not hesitate to pay me a discreet visit if you so wish.'

'I think not, my dear. We know each other too well, but above all we like each other too much.'

She closed her eyes and, flashing one of her most dazzling smiles at him, whispered:

'Why would I have given you the same reply had you been the one to make such a brazen proposition?'

'Precisely because we know each other too well and like each other too much.'

Hunched behind his wooden work table in the entrance to Nicolas Florin's office, Agnan knew the moment he looked up and saw him. The image of a noble sword flashed through the young clerk's mind. For days he had been praying for a miracle, an unlikely miracle, and now his prayer had been answered in the form of this man staring down at him with his dark-blue eyes, eyes that changed from deep sea blue to sapphire according to the light. Eyes which Agnan knew contained secrets, terrible but noble secrets of which he had no knowledge, but which stirred him to the depths as he sat behind his little table.

'Would you be so kind as to announce Francesco de Leone, Knight of Justice and Grace of the Order of Hospitallers of Saint John of Jerusalem? I have come to ask after Madame de Souarcy.'

Without thinking or really knowing what drove him to act so rashly, Agnan heard himself say:

'Save her, I beg you.'

The other man studied him for a moment then frowned. 'Is it so easy to read my thoughts? You worry me.'

'You are a great comfort to me, knight.'

The young clerk disappeared then reappeared in a flash. He moved closer to Leone and murmured:

'He is more corrupt and dangerous than any incubus.'

'Do you really think so?' replied Leone with a smile. 'The advantage is that this one is mortal.'

Since his clerk had announced the man's arrival, Florin had been wondering what a Knight Hospitaller could possibly be doing at the headquarters of the Inquisition. That Agnès de Souarcy woman had caused him nothing but trouble. Her torture would begin presently and end too soon for his taste in the eternal rest of the accused. Death. A few hours of inflicted pain, of screams, would bring him some compensation at least. He could have strangled her in her cell, of course, and pretended that she had hanged herself in order to avoid being tortured – this was not an uncommon occurrence. No. She had upset and annoyed him enough. Hers would not be an easy death.

Leone followed Agnan into the inquisitor's tiny office. The young clerk immediately left the two men. Contrary to what he had decided, Florin felt compelled to stand up when the knight entered. The man's striking beauty and palpable strength left Florin speechless. The absurd but irresistible idea occurred to him that he would love to seduce this man in order to destroy him. And why not? Of course he preferred to bed young girls, but what a remarkable demonstration of his power if he managed to lead the handsome Knight Hospitaller astray. After all, for him sex was merely a way of confirming his dominance.

'Knight, I am greatly honoured.'

'The honour is mine, Lord Inquisitor.'

Leone was filled with a sense of excitement, which made him feel ashamed. The excitement that precedes the most gruelling battles. Giotto Capella had been a weak adversary. In comparison the man standing before him was one of the most dangerous, most unpredictable he had ever encountered. Giotto Capella was a broken man, Florin a poisonous snake. He frowned at his sudden perverse desire to defeat the lethal creature by using his own weapons.

'Pray be seated, knight. My clerk informs me that you are

concerned about the fate of Madame de Souarcy.'

'Not about her fate, Monsieur, for I am sure it rests in the most capable of hands.'

Florin was flattered by the compliment and bowed his head graciously.

'Nonetheless, Madame de Souarcy's mother was a great friend of my aunt's, and since I was passing through your beautiful province on my way to Paris on Hospitallers' business, I thought I might comfort her with a prayer.'

'Hm…'

Florin was no longer listening. He was busy trying to think of the best way to seduce this beautiful man opposite him.

'Would you do me the favour, brother, of allowing me to see Madame de Souarcy?' Leone asked in a soft, cajoling voice.

Suddenly sobered by the request, Florin forced a smile:

'Certainly, knight, I feel powerless to refuse you such a simple favour. I greatly appreciate the generosity of some of the representatives of your order.'

Nicolas Florin was seething. Why was this knight meddling in his trial? He had no authority. He was furious at being forced to yield. However, since it was impossible to know whether a Knight Hospitaller travelling alone, especially a Knight of Justice and Grace, held the rank of commander or was a mere soldier, he had best tread carefully. Florin had reached a crucial stage on his ascent up the ladder to power but he knew that he had many more rungs to climb. Only then would he be above everything, above other men and the law. It would be better if he handled this stranger with care and made a show of welcoming his judgement with disinterest and gentle humility. He continued:

'You understand that since you are not a direct relative of the accused this constitutes a breach of procedure. I would therefore request that your visit be brief. Madame de Souarcy's trial is still in progress.'

Leone stood up and thanked him, gazing into the inquisitor's soft brown eyes. Florin asked:

'Will you come and take your leave of me, knight?'

'Naturally, Monsieur ... I am surprised you even ask,' Leone replied in a hushed tone.

Agnan hurried ahead of him, mumbling unintelligible words of gratitude as he stumbled down the stairs leading to the cells. The young clerk's fingers were trembling so much that Leone was obliged to draw back the bolt for him.

'Go now and be blessed,' the knight thanked him. 'I can find my own way back. I have so little time, but it will suffice ... for now.'

'I prayed so hard that you would come, Monsieur,' the other man stammered. 'I ...'

'Go, I tell you. Hurry back so as not to arouse his suspicions.'

Agnan vanished behind a pillar like some benevolent shade.

Leone did not notice the stench that pervaded the jail. Nor did he see the dirt, the deathly pallor, the dark shadows under the eyes of the woman who stood with great difficulty before him. She embodied the strength, the infinite resilience of womankind. Those blue-grey eyes studying him were recompense enough for all his pain and toil. It occurred to him that she was the light, and that he had waited all his life to see her. He fell to his knees in the filthy sludge, gasping for breath, overwhelmed by the emotion raging inside him, and murmured:

'At last ... You, Madame.'

'Monsieur?'

Her exhaustion had left her too weak to respond. She tried

desperately to find some explanation for this extraordinary show of reverence, for this man's presence in her cell. Nothing made sense any longer.

'Francesco de Leone, Knight of Justice and Grace of the Hospitaller Order of Saint John of Jerusalem.'

She stared at him quizzically.

'I have come a long way in order to save you, Madame.'

She tried to moisten her cracked lips and cleared her throat before speaking:

'Pray rise, Monsieur. I don't understand … Who are you? … Did the Comte d'Authon …'

So, Artus d'Authon was one of her friends. The thought comforted Leone.

'No, Madame. I know the Comte only by name and by his fine reputation.'

'They occasionally send clever spies to extort confessions,' she whispered softly, leaving Leone in no doubt as to her own astuteness.

'The Abbess of Clairets, Éleusie de Beaufort, is my aunt or should I say my second mother, since it was she who brought me up after my own mother, Claire, died at Saint-Jean-d'Acre.'

Despite her extreme fatigue, Agnès had a vague recollection of Jeanne d'Amblin mentioning that the Abbess had taken in a nephew after the bloody defeat that heralded the end of Christendom in the Orient. Finally feeling she could relax, she leaned against the wooden partition. He added:

'We have so little time, Madame.'

'How did you manage to persuade that wicked creature to allow you to see me?'

'By playing him at his own game. There are few possibilities open to us, Madame. One is the right of appeal …'

She cut across him:

'Come, Monsieur, you know as well as I do that it would be futile. Inquisitors antedate their records to ensure that no appeal ever reaches the bishop in time. And even if it bore fruit, which I doubt, I will be dead before they assign another inquisitor to my case. In addition to which, the man would bear me a grudge for having challenged one of his colleagues.'

Leone held the same opinion. He had only alluded to this legal tactic in order that she accept more readily what was to follow. He looked at her again through the gloom, moved by what he saw, by what she was unaware of in herself. He thanked God for being the one whose life would be sacrificed in order to save this woman, this woman who had no notion of her extraordinary importance.

'The torture will begin presently, Madame.'

'I know. Should I confess my terror? I endured their screams for days on end. That man … He must be dead. I despise my cowardice. I fear I will behave ignobly, that I will be reduced to a screaming wreck, ready to confess to the worst sins in order to stop the pain …'

'I am sure of my courage, and yet I, too, would feel afraid. However, we may both misjudge ourselves … I adhere to the principle of leaving nothing to chance where man is concerned … It generally brings disappointment.'

She tried to interrupt, to beg him to explain, to clarify his last remarks, but he stopped her with a gesture of his hand.

'Madame … you must endure the pain. You must hold out until tomorrow, for the love of God.'

'Tomorrow? Why tomorrow and not today?'

More than anything she regretted her words, which were born of her anticipation of the suffering to come. But after all she was only flesh and blood.

'Because tomorrow His judgement will be done.'

She did not even attempt to grasp the meaning of the knight's words. She was beginning to feel so strange, so unreal. He continued:

'The judgement of God can be invoked, Madame.'

'Do you still give it credence?'

'Naturally, since I am His instrument. If Florin were to disappear before your torment began, he would quickly be replaced and the trial would continue and might even be extended to include those closest to you who have supported you …'

Agnès understood the allusion to Clément and did not even feel surprised that this strange knight should know of the child's existence. She shook her head.

'… However, if God smites him down in retribution for your unjust suffering, no one – not even Rome – will want to continue with the accusation …'

'Rome?'

'Time is running out.'

He took from his surcoat a tiny ochre cloth bag and emptied its contents into his hand. He held out a greenish-brown ball the size of a large marble.

'Chew this before the torture begins. Chew it, I beg you. You will barely feel the sting of the lash. This substance found its way to me from China after many misadventures. The resin tastes bitter, but it works like a charm if used properly.'

'Who are you really? Why are you risking your life to help me?'

'It is too soon to speak of that …'

He added to her confusion by declaring:

'… Purity cannot exist without inflexibility, otherwise it leads to sacrifice, and it is too soon for that. You must live. It is my honour, my faith and my choice to protect you until my last dying breath.'

There was a knock at the ominous door. They could hear Agnan's muffled voice behind the thick panelling:

'Hurry, please! He is beginning to get restless and will come down soon.'

'Live, Madame. Oh dear God! Live, I implore you!'

Agnès slipped the little brown ball of paste between her breasts. After the door had closed behind him, she wondered whether she had been hallucinating. She felt for the ball under her dress in order to convince herself that the meeting had been real.

She lay down and closed her eyes, refusing even to try to comprehend the meaning of their exchange. She was only made of flesh and blood, and the obscure interlacing patterns she was beginning to sense above her made her mind reel.

A clear voice like a waterfall echoed in her head. Clémence. Clémence de Larnay.

Live, my precious. The hideous beast's end is nigh. Live for us, live for your two Clémences.

I will live, my sweet angel, Agnès murmured as she began to fall asleep.

A shadow slipped through the darkness of the vast dormitory, hesitating, listening for the sounds of deep breathing and snoring. It glanced at the three rows of cubicles separated by curtains that offered the sisters a little privacy in which to undress. At the centre of each cubicle stood a bed.

Bees. A hive of bees busy doing what? A swarm of insects whose individual existences had no meaning. An unchanging world of rituals, routines and orders. The shadow felt overwhelmed by anger and resentment. How it loathed them all. To leave that place, to flee the mediocre monotony of a life that was no life at all. To live at long last.

The shadow moved forward a few paces. Its bare feet made no sound on the icy floor.

It paused, listening intently, then drew back the curtains to one of the cells.

Prime[+] had just ended. Annelette leaned over Jeanne d'Amblin's shrunken frame and listened to her still-faint breathing. The extern sister's exhaustion following her fight against the poison had kept her bedridden. And yet, thanks to the care lavished on her by the apothecary, and all the sisters' prayers, Jeanne had managed the evening before to swallow a little chicken broth without instantly bringing it up. Annelette checked her pulse, which seemed more regular.

'Jeanne, dear Jeanne, can you hear me?'

An almost inaudible voice replied:

'Yes … I feel better. Thank you, my dear, thank you for all your care. Thank you all, my sisters.'

'Is your stomach still hurting?'

'Not as much.'

A sigh. Jeanne had fallen asleep again and the apothecary thought that it was for the best. As soon as she had regained some of her strength, she would be told the dreadful news of Hedwige's death. Éleusie had instructed them all to keep quiet about it because of the long friendship between the two women.

The tall, sullen woman was overcome by a deep sense of sorrow. Adélaïde Condeau was dead and so was Hedwige du Thilay. Jeanne had narrowly escaped following them to the grave, and as for Blanche de Blinot, she owed her life to her dislike of lavender tea. The poor old woman was gradually losing her wits and had been plunged into a kind of retrospective terror. The constant expression of fear she wore gave her face the appearance of a death mask. As for Geneviève Fournier, she had become a shadow of her former self after witnessing the shocking death of Hedwige, to whom it appeared she had been a great deal closer than Annelette had previously thought. Indeed, it was as though all the vitality had been drained out of the amiable sister in charge of the fishponds and henhouses. Geneviève wandered through the passageways like a tortured little ghost, scarcely noticing the other sisters as they tried to smile to her.

In contrast, the treasurer nun's gruesome death appeared to have restored the Abbess's determination, which had waned since the arrival of the inquisitor. Annelette felt a nagging concern: what if Éleusie de Beaufort had made up her mind to fight to the death? What if she had foolishly decided to sacrifice herself in order to eradicate the evil beast that was attacking them from within? She could not allow it. The Abbess must not die, and Annelette would do everything in her power to ensure that she did not.

Annelette Beaupré entered the herbarium to make the first of her two daily inspections. The bell for terce[+] had just rung and she had been excused from attending the service.

She paused in front of the medicine cabinet. A sudden excitement made her almost cry out with joy. She had been right! The mixture of egg white and almond oil she had been preparing each night had worked its magic. A sudden sadness dampened Annelette's enthusiasm. Geneviève Fournier had stopped scolding her hens. Their unreliability and the dwindling number of eggs she found each morning in the nests left her indifferent.

Pull yourself together, woman! Save your tears for when you've trapped this vermin.

Two black footprints were encrusted in the sticky substance. So, somebody had entered the herbarium sometime between compline the previous evening and that morning. Somebody who had no business being there and therefore could only have been up to no good.

The apothecary rushed outside and headed straight for the Abbess's chambers.

Éleusie listened, open-mouthed, hanging on her every word. After Annelette had finished telling her about her trap and what she had discovered, the Abbess said:

'Egg white, I see ... And what now?'

'Give the order for everybody to assemble in the scriptorium and take off their shoes without mixing them up, and have a novice bring in two warming pans full of hot embers.'

'Warming pans? Do you mean the ones we put in our beds to dry out the damp sheets?'

'The very same. And I want them red hot. It will be quicker than taking everything into the kitchen and unmasking the culprit there.'

A tentative row of white robes waited. The sisters stood in their stockinged feet, their shoes lined up in front of them. Loud whispers had broken out when the unexpected order had been given:

'Take our shoes off? Am I hearing things?'

'What's going on?'

'The floor's freezing …'

'I'm sure Annelette is behind this madness.'

'Whatever could they want with our shoes …?'

'My stockings are filthy. We don't change them until the end of the week …'

'I doubt this is a hygiene inspection.'

'There's a hole in one of mine and my toe's sticking out. I haven't had time to darn it. How embarrassing …'

Éleusie had ordered them to be quiet and waited while a bemused-looking novice went to fetch the warming pans she had requested. Finally they arrived from the kitchens, smoking from the embers inside.

Annelette, accompanied by the Abbess, approached the left-hand side of the row of bemused or irritated women. She picked up the first pair of shoes and rubbed them over the lid of the piping-hot pan. She repeated the same procedure with each of the sisters' shoes in turn, ignoring their murmured questions and astonished faces. Suddenly, there was a sound of sizzling, and a horrible stench like rotten teeth or stagnant marshes issued from one of Yolande de Fleury's shoes. Annelette continued brushing it over the pan until a flaky white coating formed on the wooden sole. She felt her face stiffen with rage, but forced herself to continue the experiment until she reached the end of the row of white robes. No other shoe reacted to the heat of the embers. She charged over to Yolande, who was as white as a sheet, and boomed so loudly that some of the sisters jumped:

'What were you doing in the herbarium?'

'But ... I wasn't ...'

'Will you stop!' the apothecary fumed.

Éleusie, fearing a fit of violence on the part of the big woman, intervened in a faltering voice:

'Yolande, come with us to my study. You others, go about your tasks.'

They had to drag the reluctant Yolande, who tried to defend herself, insisting that she had not set foot in the herbarium.

Annelette pushed the young woman into the Abbess's study and slammed the door behind them. She leaned up against the door panel as though afraid Yolande might try to escape.

Éleusie walked behind her desk and stood with her hands laid flat on the heavy slab of dark oak. Annelette barely recognised her voice as she exploded:

'Yolande, I am at the end of my tether. Two of my girls are dead and two more have escaped the same fate by a hair's breadth, and all this within a matter of days. The time for procrastination and pleasantries is over. Any other attitude would be recklessness on my part. I demand the truth, and I want it now! If you insist on prevaricating, I shall have no other choice but to turn you over to the secular authority of the chief bailiff, Monge de Brineux, since I refuse to pass judgement on one of my own daughters. I have requested the death penalty for the culprit. I have asked for her to be stripped to the waist and given a public beating.'

Despite the apparent harshness of the punishment, it was in fact relatively lenient for a crime of poisoning; execution was usually preceded by torture.

Yolande stared at her with tired eyes, incapable of uttering a word. Éleusie almost screamed at her:

'I am waiting for the truth! The whole truth! I command you to answer me this instant!'

Yolande stood motionless, her face had drained of colour and was turning deathly pale. She lowered her head and spoke:

'I did not set foot in the herbarium. The last time I went anywhere near the building, Annelette surprised me and reported my nocturnal outing to you. I've not been there since.'

'You're lying,' said Annelette. 'What do you think those white flakes on the soles of your shoes were? The cooked egg whites, which I spread on the floor in front of the cabinet containing the poisons. What do you think that evil smell was? It was the fetid rue I mixed into the preparation. I found the shoe prints in the mixture this morning – your shoe prints.'

Yolande only shook her head. Éleusie came out from behind her desk and walked right up to her. She spoke in a stern voice:

'Time is running short, Yolande. You are doing yourself no favours. I will tell you the two suspicions I have formed about you. Either you are the murderess, in which case my wrath will follow you to the grave and you will never find peace, or … you have developed an excessive attachment to one of your fellow nuns, an attachment that drives you to seek privacy outside the dormitory walls. Such an attachment would result in the two of you being separated, but that is all. I am waiting. You may yet be saved if you confess your sins. Seize this opportunity, daughter.

Hell is more terrible than your worst imaginings. Quickly, I am waiting.'

Yolande, her eyes brimming with tears, looked up at this woman she had once so admired and who terrified her now. She closed her eyes and let out a deep sigh.

'My son ...'

'What?'

'Somebody occasionally brings me news of my son.' A smile lit up the pretty, round face, ravaged with sorrow. She continued:

'He is well. He is ten now. My father brought him up. He passed him off as one of his bastards so that he wouldn't be stripped of the family name. My sacrifice saved him. I thank God for it every day in each of my prayers.'

The other two women received this unexpected confession in stunned silence. The bewildered Éleusie murmured:

'But ...'

'You wanted the whole truth, Reverend Mother, but some truths are better left unsaid. But now I've started I'll go on. I was fifteen when I fell passionately in love with a handsome steward. The inevitable happened. I fell pregnant by a peasant, outside the sacraments of marriage. The man I was supposed to marry spurned the dishonoured girl I had become. There was no excuse for me, it is true, as I had given myself with complete abandon. My beloved was beaten and driven away. Had he remained he would have been castrated and wrongly branded a rapist. He was so caring, so passionately loving. My father shut me away for the last five months of my pregnancy. Nobody was supposed to know. My son was taken from me immediately after he was born and entrusted to a wet nurse. After that I lived in the servants' quarters, on the pretext that I was no better than a beggar and deserved to be treated like one. And then my little Thibaut, whom I would occasionally glimpse at the end of a corridor, was struck down, and I saw in his illness a sign of God's wrath. I resolved to do penance for the rest of my days to atone for my sins.' She seemed not to notice the tears rolling down her cheeks. She clasped her hands with joy and continued: 'My sacrifice did not go unheeded, for which I am eternally grateful. My little boy is glowing with health. He can ride a horse now, just like a young man, and my father loves him like a son. I pray for him, too. He was so hard and unforgiving. Perhaps the love in his heart has been reawakened thanks to my child.' She straightened up and concluded: 'That is the whole truth, Reverend Mother. You, too, have known sensual joy, the love of a husband. I realise that in the eyes of mankind I was unwed, but I swear to you that when my beloved bedded me for the first time I was convinced that God was witnessing our nuptials. I was wrong.'

The revelation had shocked Éleusie de Beaufort. She felt hurt that Yolande had not confided in her. She attempted to comfort her, aware that it was futile.

'Dear Yolande … The Church accepts that its sons and daughters have known physical attraction and the pleasures of the flesh within and even outside wedlock in some cases. It is enough that we vow to banish it from our thoughts for ever when we take the cloth. As our holy Saint Augustine …'

'You don't understand!' Yolande cried out, suddenly becoming agitated. 'I would never, do you hear, never have sought the deceptive calm of your nunneries, never have yielded to your stupid rules and regulations if I had not feared for my son's life, if I had married my beloved. Never!'

She flew into a hysterical rage, hurling herself at the desk and sweeping up the papers with both hands, crumpling them, tearing them to shreds, banging her fists down on the oak table and wailing:

'Never, never … I hate you! Only the memory of Thibaut and my beloved keeps me alive in this place.'

She turned on the Abbess, her face twisted with rage. She raised her hands to claw the woman she had so respected during the long years spent in the nunnery, the long years of what in her eyes had been a less terrible form of imprisonment than any other simply because Thibaut had survived thanks to her atonement.

Annelette leapt in front of Yolande and slapped her twice hard on the face. The apothecary's deep, gruff voice rang out:

'Control yourself! This instant!'

Yolande stared at her with crazed eyes, ready to pounce. Annelette shook her and growled:

'You little fool. Do you imagine that piety is what brought me here? No, I came here because it was the only place where I could practise my art. Do you think Berthe de Marchiennes took her vows because she longed for a life of contemplation? No. Her family didn't need another daughter. Do you think Éleusie de Beaufort would have agreed to lead our congregation if she had not been widowed? And do you truly believe that Adélaïde Condeau would have chosen the monastic life if she had been well born instead of abandoned in a forest? And the others? You little fool! Most of us come here in order to avoid a life on the streets! At least we are close to God and lucky enough not to be hired out by the hour in some brothel in a town, ending our days riddled with disease and left to die in the gutter.'

The brutal truth of Annelette's tirade brought Yolande suddenly to her senses. She whispered:

'Forgive me. I humbly beg your forgiveness.'

'Who brings you news of your son?'

Yolande pursed her lips and declared categorically:

'I'm not telling you. You can threaten your worst but my lips are sealed. I've made enough mistakes already. I refuse to hurt someone who has shown only kindness by bringing me such solace.'

Annelette could tell from her tone of voice that it was pointless to insist. She wanted, however, to confirm the truth of what she had already deduced:

'And do these secret exchanges take place at night in front of the herbarium, which cannot be seen from our Reverend Mother's chambers or from the dormitory?'

'Yes. That's all I'm going to tell you.'

Éleusie felt appalled by the violence of the scene, but even more so by the discovery of yet another life destroyed. In a voice weak with exhaustion, she ordered:

'That will be all, daughter. Leave us.'

'Will your punishment …'

'Who am I to turn my back on you when He opened his arms to Mary Magdalene? Go in peace, Yolande. My only reproach is that it took you so long to tell us the truth.'

Suddenly anxious, Yolande stammered:

'Do you think that … if I had confessed sooner, Hedwige might have been …'

Annelette answered for the Abbess:

'Saved? I doubt it. There's no need for you to carry the burden of her death on your conscience. I suspect that she and Jeanne were a threat to the murderess and she decided to kill them. If we find out exactly why, we will discover who the poisoner is … or at least I hope so.'

After Yolande de Fleury had left, the two women stood facing one another for a moment. Éleusie de Beaufort was the first to break the silence:

'I am … Is it true?'

'Is what true?'

'That you would never have taken holy orders if you had been able to practise as a physician or apothecary in the world?'

Annelette suppressed a sad smile before confessing:

'Yes, it is. And if your dear husband had not passed away, would you be here among us?'

'No. But I have never regretted my choice.'

'Neither have I. Still, it was a second choice.'

'You see, Annelette, despite the climate of resentment towards the Church, these nunneries where we are allowed to live in peace, to work, to act, to make decisions are a blessing to women.'

Annelette shook her head.

'Behind this blessing lies a harsh reality: we women enjoy almost no rights in the world. Those who, like yourself, are better off might be fortunate enough to marry a man of honour, respect and love, but what about the others? What choice do they have? Freedom, it is true, can be bought like everything else. I was prepared to pay a high price for mine, but nobody was interested in my opinion, certainly not my father, who never even asked for it. As an unattractive spinster with no inheritance I could either look after my brother's children – my brother who was a mediocre doctor but a man – or join a nunnery. I chose the least demeaning of the two alternatives.'

'I'm afraid I must agree with Annelette,' a high-pitched voice rang out behind them.

They turned as one. Berthe de Marchiennes was standing

uneasily before them. She seemed to have lost her usual air of superiority.

'Berthe …'

'I knocked several times but no one answered so I came in. I only overheard the end of your conversation,' she added quickly.

She clasped her hands together, and it occurred to Annelette that this was the first time she had ever seen her stripped of her pious arrogance.

'What is happening, Reverend Mother? It feels as though the world is collapsing all around us … I do not know what to think.'

'We are as bewildered as you, daughter,' the Abbess replied, a little too sharply.

The cellarer opened her mouth, seemingly lost for words:

'I know that you don't like me very much, Reverend Mother, nor you, Annelette, nor the others. It pains me even though I know I only have myself to blame. I've … It's such a terrible thing to admit that you've never been wanted, loved. Even now at my age I don't know which is harder: to admit it to the rest of the world or to myself. God has been my constant solace. He welcomed me into his arms. Clairets has been my only home, my haven. I confess … I was jealous and resented your appointment, Reverend Mother. I assumed that my seniority and the faultless service I had rendered guaranteed my position as abbess – more than that, I felt it was my due. During these past few days I have begun to realise how much I overestimated my abilities. I feel so powerless, so pathetically feeble in the face of these lethal blows raining down upon us, and I am infinitely grateful to you, Madame, for being our abbess.'

This astonishing display of humility must have been difficult for Berthe de Marchiennes, and Éleusie reached out her hand, but the other woman shook her head. She moistened her lips with her tongue before continuing:

'I want to help you … I must. I know you don't trust me. I can feel it and I don't blame you; I deserve it.'

'Berthe, I …'

'Don't, Reverend Mother, let me finish. I deserve it because I am guilty of telling a cowardly lie in order not to … lose face. I cannot even give the excuse that I was afraid of upsetting you. No. My only motive was pride.'

Annelette refrained from intervening, having understood that this confession was not addressed to her. The cellarer took a deep breath before continuing:

'I … for a few days I mislaid the key to your safe that was in my charge. Or at least I thought so at the time. I was terrified that you might ask me for it in order to validate some deed. I searched high and low. I couldn't understand for the life of me how I had managed to lose that long leather thong I wore tied round my neck. I found it four days later at the bottom of a little mending basket I keep under my bed …'

The two other women stared at her in astonishment.

'I was so relieved that I did not stop to think how strange it was that I should find it there.'

'What do you mean?' Éleusie asked, fearing she knew the answer already.

'I had already twice emptied the contents of the basket onto my bed, thinking that if the thong had come untied, the key might have dropped down. The knot on the thong was intact. I am now certain that someone took it while I was asleep and then stuck it in the first hiding place they could find.'

'Not a very good hiding place since you had already looked there,' remarked Annelette.

'On the contrary, sister, a perfect hiding place, and one that shows the thief's contempt for me. She must have known that I had turned my bed, my mending basket, my whole cell upside down and she was counting on my pride, on my relief at having found the key without needing to admit my incompetence. I am therefore guilty of the sin of pride ... But if that monster thinks I'm a coward, she's very much mistaken.'

Agnès had been overcome with drowsiness soon after diligently chewing the bitter ball and forcing herself to swallow the mouthfuls of unpleasant saliva it produced. The nightmare she no longer wished to fight against had gradually given way to a sort of waking dream. She had let her body slide down the wall, slowing its descent with her hands.

Crouched in the corner of a tiny room, dark and dank and stinking. Crouched on the muddy floor that has coated her skimpy dress, her calves and thighs with a foul greenish film. Crouching, straining in the darkness, trying to make sense of the sounds she heard. There had been a voice barking out orders, obscene laughter, and cries followed by screams of pain. Then a terrified silence. And yet Agnès felt outside it all. She felt as though she were slowly sinking back into the wall. Crouching, trying hard to merge into the stone walls, hoping to dissolve there, to vanish for ever. Steps came to a halt outside the solid-looking, low door. A voice declared:

'At least they say this female's pleasing and comely!'

'She used to be. She looked more like a beggar when I brought her back down from the interrogation room.'

'Come on, let's take her. At least the women aren't as heavy to carry back as the men after they've fainted.'

The familiar sound of the bolt being drawn back. And yet she did not stir. She felt as though she were drifting, suspended in a foglike stupor.

'On your feet, Madame de Souarcy!' bellowed one of the men who had just walked into her cell. 'On your feet, do you hear?'

She would have preferred to remain like that, sitting in the stinking mud. But she knew instinctively that she must hide the nature of her apathy. Florin must not sense that she felt as if she were floating outside her body since she had swallowed the brownish ball. She managed to raise herself on all fours then rise to her feet. She was swaying like a drunkard. One of the men remarked sarcastically:

'You need less than my goodly wife to reach seventh heaven.'

The other man let out a coarse laugh of approval that Agnès did not understand. What in heaven's name were they talking about?

Her body was weighed down by a pleasant languor and they had to drag her along the corridor.

The other guard, the one who had laughed, declared:

'They shouldn't starve them like that ... then we wouldn't have to carry them. Look at her, she can barely put one foot in front of the other. I tell you she won't last out the first half-hour,' he predicted, referring to the timing of the torture sessions.

The procedural rules stipulated that there should be no more than half an hour of torture per question. It was an extra-ordinarily meticulous quantification of pain and one many inquisitors did not respect. They only needed to confess and be pardoned by one of their colleagues since each had the power to absolve the others.

They propped her up, holding her under the arms, while one of them opened the door to the torture chamber. What she saw inside made her blood run cold.

A long table, long enough for a human body to lie stretched out on. A long table glistening dark red. Beneath it a trough filled with a curious viscous substance. Blood. Blood everywhere.

Blood on Florin's face, blood on his forearms up to his rolled-up sleeves. Blood on the leather apron of the executioner, who was standing in a corner, arms crossed. Blood on the walls, blood on the straps hanging from the table. A sea of human blood.

Nicolas Florin glided towards her. His face was bathed in sweat and his eyes shone gleefully. Suddenly, Agnès understood the nature of his ecstasy: the blood, the screams, the endless torment, the ripped flesh, death.

She stared at him and declared calmly:

'You are damned, beyond atonement.'

He leaned forward and smiled, brushing her lips with his.

'Do you really think so?' he whispered into her mouth.

He turned round, walked gracefully over to the executioner and barked:

'That's enough chatter. There's work to be done and I have a burning desire to begin. What a fitting expression!'

A rough hand tore away the top half of her dress and pushed her towards the table. Another hand shoved her hard in the back and she lurched forward. The congealed blood on the wooden table touching her stomach plunged her into a bottomless pit of despair. She was bathing in the blood of another, in the martyrdom of another who had entered this hell before her. She barely felt the straps tighten across her back.

Florin twisted the mass of auburn locks that had lost their shine and tossed them to one side with regret. He misconstrued the cause of his victim's distress and in a purring voice declared:

'Come, come … We haven't started yet. A little nudity is surely nothing in comparison with the rest. You will soon see for yourself. Agnès Philippine Claire de Souarcy, née Larnay, you have been summoned here today before your judges to answer to the charges of complicity in heresy; individual heresy aggravated by latria; the seduction of a man of God, for which you are to be tried at a later date; sorcery and the invocation of demons. I ask you one last time, do you confess?'

The blood smelled of iron. Can a man be identified by the smell of his blood? Can one pray for him with one's mouth pressed into the pool of red liquid that was once his life?

'You do not confess your guilt?' Florin concluded hastily, for the contrary would have driven him to despair.

He felt a warm sensation spread across his belly and a rush of blood to his groin. He had waited so long for this moment. He struggled to hold back his mounting pleasure, to keep his eyelids from closing. He struggled not to hurl himself onto her back and bite into her, ripping at the beautiful pale flesh of his magnificent prey with his teeth until her blood ran down his throat.

'Clerk!' Florin shouted in the direction of an oil lamp that appeared to be floating a few inches above the floor. 'Note down that Madame de Souarcy refuses to confess and chooses to remain silent, a sure sign of her guilt.'

The young man sitting cross-legged on the floor nodded and recorded the refusal.

'Executioner, the lashes, quickly!' Florin snarled, thrusting his hand out towards the tall man in the leather apron. 'Clerk, note down that we are respecting proper procedure by first inflicting upon the accused the punishment reserved for women. If our generosity is not rewarded with a confession, we shall consider alternative methods of persuasion.'

Florin turned towards the open fire where some thin-bladed knives were being heated above the flames until they were red-hot.

Her body tensed when she heard the swish of the whip being

raised. She cried out as it struck her back with full force. And yet the sting of the thick leather thongs felt bearable. The blows rained down on her for what seemed like an eternity. Her body jolted with each punishing new wave. She could feel her skin splitting, but it seemed relatively painless. Something smooth and warm ran down her sides and dropped onto the table. Her flesh was smarting and yet it almost wasn't hers. A thought flashed through her mind, a soothing thought: her blood was mixing with the blood of the poor soul who had lain on that same table before her. She felt her torturer's hands kneading her raw flesh. She felt the powder being sprinkled onto her wounds. A crippling pain made her cry out despite the little brown ball. Salt. The wicked man was rubbing salt into her wounds.

She felt herself drifting into oblivion and willed it with all her might. Florin's hysterical screams came to her as if in a nightmare. He was gasping with pleasure, crowing as he ordered her to confess her sins. He cried out in a voice quivering with excitement:

'Executioner, this witch refuses God ... The irons ... The irons and let them be white-hot ...'

There was a loud knock at the door. Agnès let out a sob before plunging into merciful unconsciousness.

Jean de Rioux stood before the inquisitor. He avoided looking at the tortured woman, feigning disinterest.

Florin was panting, hunched over, his face covered in sweat, his eyes glazed over. The Dominican felt his gorge rise and struggled with an overwhelming urge to kill the man right there in that cellar that he had transformed into an unspeakable playroom for his own enjoyment. But Leone's instructions had been categorical: the judgement of God. He silently handed the missive to the torturer.

As soon as the inquisitor saw the seal, the glazed look in his eyes disappeared. Incredulous and excited, he murmured:

'The halved bulla?'

This message could only have come from one of the two camerlingos, and had almost certainly been sent by Honorius Benedetti himself. He trembled as he broke the seal. How extraordinary. Such was his power that the camerlingo now addressed letters to him in person.

He read and reread the contents, written in Latin:

'It is essential that the correct procedure be applied to Madame de Souarcy so that her trial cannot be judged null and void. We now share the same enemies and this links us definitively. My messenger will recover this missive. H.B.'

A sober Florin gazed up at the tall, grave-faced man. So, he was the camerlingo's secret emissary. This explained his objection to Mathilde de Souarcy's evidence. His mission was to ensure that Madame de Souarcy could not be saved due to some procedural error. Why had he not spoken up? If only Florin had known, he would not have wished him dead for demanding that the foolish young woman's accusation be thrown out. But Jean de Rioux was no doubt sworn to the utmost secrecy.

'We now share the same enemies and this links us definitively.' What a magnificent prospect ... Rome, greatness would soon be his!

Jean de Rioux's voice almost made him jump.

'Guards ... Take Madame de Souarcy back to her cell. Have her wounds cleaned and bandaged.'

The astonished guards looked questioningly at Florin, who chivvied them:

'Go on ... Do as you're told! The half-hour is up. The torture will resume tomorrow.' Then, turning to the Dominican, he added in a hushed voice: 'I shall walk back with you, my brother in Christ.'

A woman lay face down on the rack, the blood from the gashes on her back oozing to the floor. The woman was moaning. Her long fair hair was sticky with sweat and blood. A hand brushed against her martyred flesh, pouring a grey powder onto her wounds. The woman arched her back and went limp, fainting.

Éleusie de Beaufort clasped her hands to her mouth to stifle her growing impulse to scream. She fell forward onto her desk in a faint.

The same vision had come back to haunt her. She had mistakenly believed that she was the suffering woman. It was Agnès they were torturing at that precise moment.

She fell to her knees and prayed:

'Dear God ... dear God ... Dear, sweet Francesco ...'

A sudden wave of nausea made her stretch out on the broad dark flagstones where, unable to calm down, she repeated: 'The beast must die, Francesco, he must die! The beast must die, he must die!'

Annelette Beaupré sat on her stool in the herbarium, leaning against the cold stone wall with her arms crossed, pondering. Berthe de Marchiennes's confession that morning had baffled her. After the cellarer's departure, she and Éleusie de Beaufort had exchanged glances, unable to make head or tail of her story. The Abbess was adamant: her key had never left her person and she was too light a sleeper for anyone to be able to take it and return it while she was resting. And why replace Berthe's key when all three were necessary in order to open the safe where the seal was kept? Was Berthe lying to cover herself? Curiously, Annelette did not give that theory much credence, despite her dislike of the cellarer nun.

The answer came to her in a flash. Copies! Four days was plenty of time for a good smith to produce one. She suddenly had a worrying thought: what if Blanche de Blinot had also mislaid her key temporarily and said nothing? What if – given her mental deterioration – she had not even noticed its disappearance? What if a second copy had been made of the key for which Annelette had publicly accepted resonsibility? Her hand automatically reached up to touch the top of her robe. The small lump she felt there did not set her mind at ease.

The third and last key was hanging round Éleusie's neck. Assuming the theory of the copies was correct, it placed Éleusie de Beaufort above suspicion since she was free at any time to open the safe and retrieve her private seal. However, since her key was the only one of its kind she would be the next victim.

Something was not right. Some crucial element was missing. Why would the murderess insist on trying to take the seal when so many of them now thought this was her intention? Every deed, every letter would be scrupulously checked and rechecked by the Abbess. Moreover, if the poisoner killed her, her seal would automatically be invalidated.

There were so many loose ends and no clear way of tying them together. The whole affair seemed illogical. Annelette was unable to arrive at the truth. The murderess was both intelligent and extremely cunning. She had discovered the other sisters' weaknesses and strengths, their petty secrets and vanities, their deep resentments and turned them to her advantage. Yolande's Thibaut, Berthe's pride, Blanche's senility ... But why poison

Hedwige du Thilay and Jeanne d'Amblin? What part did these two friends play in these murderous equations? Two friends … What if only one had been targeted and their innocent habit of sitting together at mealtimes or taking tea together had sent the other to her grave? Which of the two had been meant to die, then, Hedwige or Jeanne? Hedwige du Thilay? Was her position as treasurer in some way connected? The paymistress managed the abbey's revenue, oversaw and paid the farrier, the singers and the veterinary doctor … In short, she was in charge of a good deal of money. It had not been unheard of in the past for monks to make veritable fortunes by falsifying deeds with stolen seals. No, she felt she was losing her way. Enrichment was not the murderess's motive, Annelette would have staked her life on it. And what of Jeanne d'Amblin, whose strong constitution alone had saved her from the poison? Jeanne had permission to leave the abbey in order to make her rounds. She met many of their donors, conversed with them and even became their confidante. Had she seen or heard something that had worried the poisoner? Something whose importance the extern sister had not realised at the time? Think … the answer was easily within her grasp.

Thibaut!

Thibaut, the beloved son for whom Yolande had been prepared to lie. Annelette must learn more about him and ask for the Abbess's help in order to do so.

Annelette had suddenly made great headway towards a solution. The poisoner must have discovered that the sister in charge of the granary slipped out at night to meet her informant near the herbarium. She had borrowed her shoes in order to point the finger at Yolande de Fleury. Annelette cursed for the first time in her life, stamping her foot petulantly:

'Zounds!'

Her theory didn't hold water, for it assumed the culprit knew that a trap had been laid for her, and yet Annelette had told no one of her plan, not even the Abbess.

Thibaut, Thibaut ... The answer, she was certain, lay in the pretty name of that illegitimate little boy.

An insistent ringing sound gradually brought her out of her thoughts: the sisters were being called for vespers.

She left the herbarium, more determined than ever to ingest nothing that she had not prepared herself in the kitchens. For, if her enemy were as clever as she gave her credit for, she would soon realise that Annelette was her most formidable enemy and would not hesitate to crush her.

A figure was crouching behind the hedging laid with chestnut branches that protected the medicinal herb garden from the wind.

Annelette, Annelette, thought the figure, how tiresomely tenacious you are. How it bores me. How would you like to die, dear apothecary? Just to please me, go on. Die!

Éleusie de Beaufort studied her apothecary daughter in silence.

'What you are asking me to do is so strange, Annelette ... Do you really think that this little boy can help our investigation?'

'I am convinced of it. We only need to send one of our lay servants. You mentioned that Yolande de Fleury's father lives on his estate in the vicinity of Malassis. It is not so very far from here. A good day's ride there and back.'

'And what is his mission?'

The tall woman sighed. She had no idea. And yet she instinctively persisted.

'I confess that I am not quite sure.'

'Annelette, I cannot send one of our servants out without telling him what I want him to do.'

'I am aware of that, Reverend Mother ... I want news of littleThibaut.'

'News. Is that all?'

'That is all. I am going back to the dormitory.'

Éleusie de Beaufort had become prey to a strange obsession. Whereas once she had avoided entering the perilous library, now she felt the need to check and recheck its contents several times a day. She was driven by an impulse she was powerless to resist. The abbey plans were locked in the safe, and, unless she was fiendishly clever, the murderess could not possibly know of their existence. Even so, the Abbess always ended up lifting the wall hanging and opening the door leading to the place which at once fascinated and terrified her.

She gazed at the oil lamp sitting on her desk. The feeble light it gave off was not enough to drive out the lingering shadows that seemed to cling to the shelves of books full of revelations. She rushed into the corridor and seized one of the resin candles. She needed a bright light if she was going to check the titles of all those books brimming with terrible truths.

Éleusie sighed wearily. She must remain steadfast. Only when she had finished would she allow herself a few hours' well-earned rest.

She took her time inspecting the books shelf by shelf, raising her candle aloft for fear of setting alight these precious but terrifying works.

The crouching figure's eyes were trained on the high horizontal arrow-slit windows, which for the last few minutes had been visible owing to a flickering light marking them out from the rest of the wall. A triumphant smile lit up the figure's face in the chilly gloom of the garden. The figure had been right and all this surveillance had finally paid off. The camerlingo would be pleased and, the figure hoped, would prove even more generous. The secret library was right next to the Abbess's chambers. The figure would soon be in possession of the manuscripts so coveted by Honorius Benedetti. There was no longer any reason to kill Éleusie de Beaufort in order to appropriate the third and last key. The figure was quite happy to grant the Abbess this pardon. Not because her brutal murder would have saddened the figure, but because Éleusie was a stubborn link in the chain. She formed part of the shadowy spider's web they were at pains to make out. The Reverend Mother might provide valuable information. That is, if she could be persuaded to reveal what she knew. Then again, they had every means of persuasion at their disposal!

N ight was slowly falling over Rue de l'Ange. Should he see in this street name a sign or simply another quirk of fate?

Francesco de Leone concealed himself in the porch of the handsome town house belonging to the late Pierre Tubeuf, the draper who had had the misfortune of crossing Florin's path. He waited for a moment then walked across the quadrangular courtyard towards the imposing building. The occasional flickering light of a candle passing behind the drawn curtains of the first-floor windows showed that the beautiful Nicolas was somewhere inside the house he had requisitioned for his own use.

The knight had not allowed himself to follow any plan, any strategy. His actions were guided by a sort of superstitious belief. It seemed essential to him that Florin should be the architect of his own doom, although he did not know where this conviction came from. It was not because he feared feeling any remorse, still less compassion. No. It was more like a vague intuition that nothing relating to or affecting Madame de Souarcy should be tainted or soiled, not even the death of her torturer.

Leone's eyes had filled with tears when Jean de Rioux had described to him the cellar, the outstretched body, the pale lacerated back, the blood dripping from her wounds. It had taken a moment for him to realise that he was crying. A miracle. This woman had already produced a miracle in him. How long had it been since he had felt that overpowering sorrow that was a sign of his humanity, proof that his soul had remained intact despite his being habituated to horror? He had witnessed so much death and suffering, had wallowed in it until it became invisible. Agnès's torment had shocked him into remembering the twisted, burnt bodies, the gaping mouths, the chests pierced by arrows, the amputated limbs, the gouged-out eyes. He was infinitely grateful for these memories which, before he met her, had been packed down so tightly they had become an indistinguishable mass. He no longer wanted to forget; he refused to take the easy escape and become inured to horror.

He walked towards the broad, gently rising steps leading up to the double doors of the hall and rapped with the heel of his hand.

He waited, his mind clear.

A crack appeared in the door before it swung wide open. Florin had changed into a sumptuous silk dressing gown embroidered with gold brocade which Leone was sure had once kept Monsieur Tubeuf warm on chilly evenings.

'Knight?' he asked in a deep voice.

'I shall be leaving Alençon shortly, and … the thought of not saying farewell … saddened me.'

'I would have been equally … sad had you left without saying farewell. Pray come in. Would you care for some wine? The … My cellar is well stocked.'

'A glass of wine, then.'

'This hallway is icy. Let me take you upstairs, knight. My principal rooms are on the first floor. I will join you directly.'

The vast reception room with its roaring fire was magnificent. An abundance of candelabra cast a harmonious, almost natural light. The exquisitely carved chests, the elegant pedestal tables imported from Italy, the tall bevelled mirrors and the lush tapestries hanging on the walls were evidence of the former owners' wealth. Leone sat in one of the two armchairs drawn up in front of the stone hearth. Florin returned carrying two Venetian glasses – a rare and splendid luxury seen only at the tables of the most powerful princes.

He pulled the other chair up to face his guest and sat down, brushing his knees against those of Leone, who did not recoil. The inquisitor was filled with a new kind of excitement. He had hooked his fish, and what a fine catch he was. If he managed to seduce this man, who could possibly resist him? The complexity of this game, the subtlety it required, intoxicated him more assuredly than any alcohol. He murmured in a deep, soft, seductive voice:

'I am … I was going to say honoured but suddenly the word displeases me.'

'Moved?' suggested Leone, leaning imperceptibly towards him.

'Yes. Moved.'

'As for me, I am stirred to the depths,' Leone confessed, and the sincerity Florin perceived in the knight's voice thrilled him since he misunderstood the reason for it.

'Stirred to the depths?' the inquisitor repeated, rolling the words greedily on his tongue. 'Is it not remarkable that our paths should have crossed like this?'

'Not really,' Leone corrected, narrowing his bright-blue eyes.

'Do you believe in fate?'

'I believe in desire and in satisfying desire.'

The long, slender hand, responsible for such torment, moved towards the knight's face. He watched it caress the air, the flesh transparent and orange against the firelight. Leone closed his eyes for a moment and a smile spread across his face. He took hold of Florin's wrist and stood up. The inquisitor followed suit and took a step forward so that his body was almost touching the Hospitaller's.

A sigh.

Florin's eyes, as deep as pools, widened and his mouth fell open without emitting any sound. He staggered backwards, staring down at the hilt of the dagger protruding from his belly, and gasped:

'But why ...'

Leone did not take his eyes off him. The other man pulled out the lethal blade and a flow of blood soaked the front of his fine dressing gown, making the gold brocade glisten.

'You should be asking who, not why. For the sake of the rose. So that the rose may live.'

'I don't ... You said ... Stirred ...'

'I am stirred to the depths of my soul. She has stirred me for eternity. I was not mistaken.'

Florin grasped the back of his chair with both hands to stop himself from falling. His thoughts were racing but he could make no sense of them.

'Agnès?'

'Who else? Do not even attempt to understand for it is beyond you.'

'The camerlin—'

'That evil pig, that vile executioner. There was no letter from the camerlingo. Jean de Rioux wrote the orders you received and the seal was taken from an ancient document in the library of a nearby abbey.'

A crimson bubble burst at the corner of the inquisitor's mouth, then another, followed by a string of ephemeral bright-red pearls. He coughed and a trickle of blood appeared and dangled from his chin. His features were twisted as the pain searing his insides exploded with renewed vigour. He groaned, stumbling over his words:

'It hurts ... It hurts so much.'

'All those tortured ghosts will finally be at peace, Florin. Your victims.'

'I ... I beg you ... I'm bleeding to death.'

'What? Should I put you out of your misery? What compassion have you ever shown that you should merit mine? Give me a single example. I ask no more in order to spare you the agony of a slow death.'

The blood was draining from the face that had once been so seductive. Leone wondered how many women, and men, had succumbed to the perfect mirage, only to discover the nightmare concealed within. How many had perished after an eternity of pain suffered at those long, slender hands? An infant's cries brought him back to the man now lying crumpled up before the hearth.

'It hurts ... It hurts so terribly ... I'm going to die, I'm so afraid ... For pity's sake, knight.'

The image of those blue-grey eyes encircled by sickly shadows flashed through his mind. For her sake, for the sake of the incomparable rose whose petals he had once sketched in a big notebook, Leone picked up the bloodstained dagger. He leaned over the dying man, loosened the neck of his gown and with a single movement slashed his pale throat.

A rattle, a sigh. Florin's body shook violently then went limp. Francesco de Leone paused to consider the torturer's corpse, searching deep inside himself to see whether this execution had given him any pleasure. None. Only a fleeting sense of relief. One beast was dead, but others would replace him, of this he was certain.

He picked up his glass from one of the little Italian pedestal tables and placed it carefully on the mantelpiece. Florin had fallen on top of the other and the purplish wine had mingled with the red of his blood. He stooped to pull off the luxurious rings that adorned the dead inquisitor's fingers. He kicked over one of the chairs, which fell on its side. He opened the blood-soaked dressing gown, baring the slender chest. This would give the appearance of a lovers' tryst that had gone wrong or a bloody burglary. Leone considered the scene he had staged, then removed his soiled surcoat and threw it on the fire before walking out into the night.

God would judge.

As for his fellow men, the knight was counting on their tongues loosening now that they no longer needed to fear the inquisitor, and on their thirst for revenge.

God would judge.

From the table perched on a dais that allowed a good view over the refectory, Éleusie's gaze swept over the sisters, who were seated at two long planks of wood resting on trestles, their faces lit up by the flickering flames of the resin candles.

The vast room would normally have been alive with the sound of whispering, inappropriate since meals were supposed to take place in silence. The odd misplaced giggle would normally have rung out, occasioning a call to order from the Abbess. The senior, cellarer and treasurer nuns would normally have shared the Abbess's table, but Blanche de Blinot rarely left her steam room now and Hedwige du Thilay was dead. The only one left was Berthe de Marchiennes, who, divested of her habitual air of superiority, resembled the ageing, pathetic woman she really was.

Éleusie de Beaufort had suggested to Annelette Beaupré that she occupy Hedwige's empty seat so as to spare her daughters a further painful reminder, but the apothecary nun had declined her offer. It was easier for her to survey the others, to observe their reactions from her end of one of the trestle tables, and she was sure that the murderess would be more cautious of the hierarchy sitting up on their dais.

Annelette Beaupré was keeping a close watch on Geneviève Fournier. The sister in charge of the fishponds and the henhouses was deathly pale, and the almost blackish-purple shadows under her big brown eyes betrayed the fact that she was not sleeping and not eating either, as she had swallowed next to nothing since Hedwige du Thilay's horrific death. This stubborn refusal to eat, which many attributed to the close friendship the two women had enjoyed, troubled the apothecary nun. Undeniably they had been close, as were many of the other sisters, but surely not to the point of starving herself to death. Annelette glanced along the table and felt a pang of grief when her eye alighted on the sprigs of autumn flowers marking Adélaïde Condeau's empty place, and that of Jeanne d'Amblin, who was recovering but still too weak to leave her bed.

Annelette watched Geneviève lift her bowl of turnip, broad bean and bacon soup to her lips, only to set it down abruptly on the table, her hands trembling. She looked around fearfully before lowering her head and pressing the crumbs of black bread between her fingers. The apothecary nun had seen enough; Geneviève was starving herself to death because, despite all the precautions they had taken, she was terrified. Two novices were posted as lookouts at the entrance to the kitchens while the new sister in charge of meals, Elisaba Ferron, prepared the food. Elisaba had just completed her noviciate and taken her final vows. The middle-aged woman, the widow of a rich merchant from Nogent-le-Rotrou, had received Annelette's backing for this post. She was burly enough to knock out anyone attempting to meddle with her pots. As for her stentorian voice, it struck fear into the hearts of more than a few when she placed her hands on her generous hips and boomed: 'My name is appropriate. It means joy in the house of God the Father. Don't forget it, God is joy!' Nobody in their right mind would contradict Elisaba for, despite her loud generosity, she was made of stern stuff, having spent her married life shaking up lazy clerks and putting impudent customers in their place.

Annelette perceived the worried, suspicious glances. They were all surreptitiously sizing one another up in an attempt to discover which familiar friendly face concealed the wicked beast.

She watched the furtive glances flying around the room, pausing occasionally and silently wondering. Would their hitherto peaceable, relatively harmonious congregation survive the insidious sickness of suspicion? Annelette was unsure. Indeed, if she were honest, she would have to admit that what kept them together was, above all, the shared conviction that this enclosure protected them from the outside world. But death had climbed in among them by stealth, shattering the stout ramparts and their belief that the world's madness could never enter there. In reality, though, what were the majority of the sisters most afraid of ? Being poisoned or finding themselves alone and destitute on the outside with no household willing to take them into service? Faith had unquestionably guided the majority in their choice. And yet, even they must have realised by now that the abbey had been their only refuge. And what would she, proud Annelette, do? She preferred not to think about it. Nobody was waiting for her on the outside. Nobody cared what became of her. Her sole existence, her sole importance was concentrated within these walls. This diverse congregation of women, whose members infuriated, amused and only occasionally interested her, had become her family. She had no other now.

The meal ended in an uneasy calm. Only the sound of the benches scraping against the floor broke the oppressive silence. Annelette was the last to leave the table and she followed Geneviève Fournier. Once outside the refectory the sister in charge of the fishponds turned left, cutting through the guest house and across the gardens to go and check her fish and poultry once more before going to bed. She walked slowly, stooped forward with her head down, oblivious to her surroundings. It was dark, and Annelette followed at a few yards' distance, taking care not to give her presence away. Geneviève crossed the cloisters and went past the relics' room. She walked alongside the stables until she reached the henhouses, which were near the entrance to the orchards. She stopped in front of the makeshift wooden fence and stood watching her beloved hens. Annelette, who had also come to a halt, was filled with a strange tenderness. What was her sister thinking about as she stood in the dark, chill night? About Hedwige? About death? Finally Annelette took the plunge. She strode over to Geneviève, and placed her hand on the woman's shoulder. The sister in charge of the fishponds and the henhouses jumped and stifled a cry. Annelette could see a look of terror in her eyes. Geneviève quickly regained her composure and let out a feeble laugh:

'How fearful I must seem. You gave me such a start ... Are you taking the air, dear Annelette?'

The other woman studied her in silence for a moment before declaring:

'Don't you think the time has come?'

'Pardon?'

'Why are you so afraid of being the next victim that you are starving yourself ?'

'I don't know what you're talking about,' the younger woman snapped.

'You know, or think you know, the cause of Hedwige's murder and Jeanne's near-fatal poisoning and that is why you fear for your life.'

'I don't ...'

'Be quiet! Can't you see that as long as you say nothing the murderess will want to eliminate you? But the more of us you let into your secret the less reason she will have to silence you.'

A huge tear rolled down the face of the sister in charge of the fishponds and henhouses, and she stammered:

'I can't go on …'

'Then tell me your secret. It is your only protection.'

Geneviève studied her. She so longed to believe her but was still so afraid.

'I … I saw you take my eggs, a large amount of them. At first, I was so upset that I even considered telling our Reverend Mother. But I waited. I asked Hedwige's opinion. It was only later, during the incident in the scriptorium when I saw you rubbing the soles of our shoes on the heating pans, that I understood the necessary part my eggs had played in the trap you had laid.'

'I see. Hedwige knew about my … borrowing from your hens, and as she was good friends with Jeanne she almost certainly mentioned it to her.'

Geneviève nodded nervously and murmured in a faltering voice:

'I am to blame … It's my fault they were poisoned.'

'No. Get that silly idea out of your head. Go back now, Geneviève. Go back and eat something. I will inform our Reverend Mother of this conversation. I advise you … I advise you to confide in some of the sisters about what has been worrying you.'

'But the poisoner … I might tell her.'

'That's precisely what I'm hoping. If she planned to get rid of you in order to stop you from talking, she'll realise it's too late and give up.'

A look of relief appeared on the diminutive sister's face and she flung her arms around Annelette who, embarrassed by this effusiveness, carefully extricated herself, smiling apologetically:

'I am not accustomed to such displays of affection.'

Geneviève nodded and confessed:

'Dear Annelette. I think that many of us have misjudged you. You seem so severe …' she added with a sigh. 'And yet you are without doubt the bravest, most intelligent woman I have ever known. I wanted to tell you that.'

With this she left, heading towards the gloomy buildings silhouetted against the moonlit sky.

Annelette stayed behind, watching the hunched figures of the hens asleep in their shelter. She did not doubt for a second the veracity of Geneviève's story. And yet she felt convinced that it didn't stand up either. Assuming Hedwige had mentioned Geneviève's concerns about her eggs to Jeanne, it followed that Jeanne must then have told somebody else in order to explain why both women had been targeted by the poisoner. Unless the two had shared food or drink that was only meant for Hedwige. The apothecary decided to put her mind at rest before going to bed. She went up to the dormitory, still deserted before compline, and entered Jeanne's tiny curtained cell. The extern sister was dozing. Annelette's foot knocked against something that made a hollow sound. She looked down and saw an empty soup bowl. Good. Jeanne was eating again and would soon recover her strength. She picked it up and went over to the sleeping woman's bedside. Something cracked under the thick leather sole of her shoe, and she was concerned lest the sharp noise rouse her sister. The hubbub of the other sisters returning to their cells after compline was sure to wake her and she would come back to talk to her then.

She left quietly, pulled the drapes closed behind her and went to the kitchen to return the soup bowl. It was then that she became aware of something squeaking as she walked. She looked under her shoe, assuming she must have picked up a pebble from the garden.

A tiny object glistened in the darkness. She tried to dislodge it and cried out in pain. At first she saw nothing. It was only when she went and stood under one of the lights in the kitchen that she noticed that her finger was bleeding. Upon closer inspection of her shoe she realised that the pebble was in fact a thick shard of glass. How had it got there? There was very little glass in the abbey. Only the scriptorium windows were glazed, and as far as she knew none of them was broken. Holding her finger above the sink, she doused it with water from a ewer, then bathed it with liquor made of thyme, rosemary, birch and sage,[88] a phial of which she carried in her belt at all times. A discreet cough made her swing round. A shy novice leaned forward and murmured:

'Our Reverend Mother wishes to see you. She is waiting in her study.'

The young woman disappeared immediately and Annelette spent a few moments dressing the tiny wound with a strip of linen before joining the Abbess in her study.

When she walked in, Éleusie rose to her feet, an inscrutable look on her face. Annelette raised her eyebrows quizzically.

'I have just received a most astonishing piece of news. I still do not know what to make of it. It feels as though the more we progress, the less I understand.'

Annelette waited. Something in the Abbess's manner intrigued her, alarmed her even. Éleusie raised her impossibly dainty hand to her brow and sighed:

'The child … little Thibaut de Fleury … He died nearly two years ago, a few months after his grandfather.'

Annelette felt her knees go weak. She slumped down onto the chair opposite the desk and breathed:

'Oh dear … But …'

'That was my first reaction, too, daughter. We have come up against a series of impossibilities. Why bring tales of a thriving happy childhood to his mother in that case? Who would be capable of such a monstrous act? And why did nobody notify her of her father's and then her son's deaths?'

'I am at a loss,' Annelette confessed. 'Above all, I don't know what to do. Should we inform Yolande that she is the victim of a grotesque farce?'

'And risk it killing her?'

'And risk it killing her … but also perhaps forcing her to give us her informant's name,' corrected the apothecary.

'Do you think that this informant is acting out of spite or is she simply passing on to Yolande information communicated to her by a third person?'

'I have no idea, and the only way of finding out is to discover her identity.'

Another silence descended. Annelette tried to bring order to the chaos of her thoughts, to find a link between the disparate, seemingly nonsensical elements. Éleusie de Beaufort was overwhelmed by an intense fatigue. She felt herself withdraw. Her world was gradually being reduced to ashes and she could only contemplate the wreckage. By dint of a supreme effort of will, she ordered:

'Go and fetch Yolande.'

Annelette found the sister in charge of the granary in the steam room folding bed linen with the guest mistress, Thibaude de Gartempe. Yolande stared at her coldly when she passed on the Abbess's request. The little woman, who had always been so cheerful, had not forgiven the apothecary nun for her suspicions. She followed her in silence and, much to Annelette's relief, did not even ask the reason for the interview.

Éleusie was standing, leaning back against her desk as though steeling herself for an attack. Yolande could tell from the concern on her face that something terrible had happened.

'Reverend Mother?'

'Yolande … my dear child … Your … Your father died nearly two years ago.'

Yolande lowered her eyes and murmured:

'Dear God … May his soul rest in peace. I hope he found it in his heart to forgive me …' Suddenly she asked: 'But … What about my son? What about Thibaut? Who looks after him now? I was my father's only child.'

'Your informant did not tell you, then?' the apothecary nun cut in.

Yolande turned towards her, a hard, inscrutable expression on her face, before saying through gritted teeth:

'I would prefer not to have to talk to you. I've never liked you, although I never expected to have any reason to distrust you.' She turned back to the Abbess, her voice softening again:

'Reverend Mother, pray tell me, who is looking after Thibaut?'

It was Éleusie's turn now to lower her gaze. Annelette barely recognised her voice as she uttered the terrible words:

'He joined your father shortly afterwards.'

Yolande did not understand what her Reverend Mother had just said to her. She insisted, puzzled:

'He joined him … how? Where? I …'

'He is dead, my dear child.'

An eerie smile appeared on the lips of the sister in charge of the granary as she leaned towards the distressed woman and asked:

'I don't … What are you saying?'

Éleusie felt a wrenching pain in her chest and she repeated in an almost aggressive tone:

'Thibaut is dead, Yolande. Your son died nearly two years ago, a few months after his grandfather.'

Annelette had the impression that Yolande's life was draining out of her as she watched the woman crumple. A strange sound like wheezing bellows filled the room, followed by a moan that gradually grew louder and louder until it exploded into a scream. Yolande whirled round in ever-faster circles, clawing at her face, unable to stop the piercing scream rising from her throat and pervading the room seemingly without her needing to take a breath. She slumped to her knees, panting uncontrollably as though she were choking to death. Annelette and Éleusie stood motionless, staring at her dumbstruck. How many minutes passed, filled only by the frenzied sobs of a grieving mother, the groans of a dying animal?

Suddenly the groaning stopped. Yolande looked up at them with crazed eyes, her face twisted with rage. She got to her feet using both hands. Éleusie rushed over to assist her, to embrace her, but Yolande leapt backwards, pointing her finger at her and snarling:

'How could you …? Cruel traitress, you're no better than your henchwoman, the apothecary. A couple of nasty, evil madwomen.'

Éleusie, incredulous, stepped back from her daughter. Yolande continued raging at her, and Annelette, afraid she might attack the Abbess, prepared to intervene.

'How dare you invent such a despicable lie? Did you have to sink to such depths? Do you think I am a fool? You made up this monstrous story in the hope that I would give you the name of the kind friend who brings me news. Never! I can see through your wicked ploy. And do you know how? Because my little boy is with me every second of the day. Because if he had died, I would have died instantly in order to be with him. Wicked monsters! You will be cursed for this!' She interrupted herself, clasping her hand to her mouth to stifle a hysterical laugh. 'I demand, Reverend Mother, that you request my immediate transfer to another of our order's abbeys. I wish to flee as soon as possible the stinking pit you and your disciples have dug in this place. I am sure I will not be the only one to demand a transfer. Others have seen through your despicable scheming.'

Annelette thought that Yolande had finally tipped over into madness. She interceded to try to calm her:

'Yolande, you are mistaken. We ...'

'Shut up, you demented poisoner! Do you suppose I don't know that you are the culprit? Oh, you are very clever and cunning, but you can't fool me.'

This accusation so took the apothecary nun by surprise that she was incapable of reacting. She tried, however, to reason with her sister:

'You don't understand ... If I am right, your informant ... well, it wouldn't surprise me if she was the poisoner we are tracking down. If so, then your life is in danger.'

The other woman hissed:

'A clever try, to be sure, but you'll have to do better than that to convince me. Murderess!'

Yolande flew out of the Abbess's study as if the devil were on her tail.

Annelette turned to Éleusie and murmured:

'I think she has lost her mind.'

The Abbess let out a sob and groaned:

'Dear God, what have we done?'

Annelette grappled with her own panic. For the first time in her life the tall imperious woman doubted herself. The accusations hurled at her by the sister in charge of the granary – during an unconvincing fit of grief – were unimportant. What was important was the crippling pain she and the Abbess had inflicted upon her. What mattered was the plan Annelette had thought up in order to force her to confess the name of her informant. She was filled with an excruciating sense of shame and heard herself say, almost imploringly:

'Reverend Mother, may I as an exception sleep in your chambers? I will make a bed on the carpet in your study. I realise that ...'

Her apothecary daughter's eyes, brimming with tears, her trembling lip and quivering chin spoke louder to Éleusie than any words. She agreed in a faltering voice:

'I dared not propose it myself. We are so alone tonight. And yet, Annelette, there is a battle raging outside, a merciless battle. I bitterly regret the pain we have caused Yolande, but she had to face the terrible truth, no matter what. Thibaut is dead and her informant has been lying to her for two years for reasons that are still unclear to me. In addition ... And may God forgive me for what is not heartlessness on my part, for I assure you that my heart bleeds for that poor grieving mother ... May God forgive me, but we are all in peril and Yolande's loss changes nothing. That poor little boy joined his Creator two years ago ... Our lives are in danger today or perhaps tomorrow. We will mourn our dead later. The beast must be killed first, and quickly.'

Annelette sighed and walked over to her Mother Superior, hands outstretched, and whispered:

'Thank you for voicing what I no longer dared to think.'

Adèle de Vigneux, the granary keeper, woke up shivering. The thin coverlet had slipped off her bed. She felt for it in the gloom, stifled a yawn and blinked, groggy from sleep. The dormitory was quiet except for the sound of breathing echoing from one end of the huge, icy room to the other. Occasionally somebody moving or coughing broke the monotonous rhythm. A loud snoring rose above the other sounds. It was Blanche de Blinot. Adèle de Vigneux smiled. Age seemed to protect Blanche from troubled dreams.

The young granary keeper pulled the coverlet over her and curled up snugly. Just as she drifted back into oblivion, a silhouette appeared behind the curtains around her cell.

Night was still keeping dawn at bay when they awoke to prepare for lauds.[+] Adèle pulled on her robe and adjusted her veil, her eyelids heavy with sleep. She drew back the curtain round her tiny cell and was surprised by the silence that prevailed in the neighbouring cell. Yolande de Fleury was still asleep. She had seemed so agitated the night before that Adèle had enquired after her wellbeing, only to be sharply rebuked. The other woman was so overwrought that the younger woman had not insisted. Yolande had said:

'Those two madwomen think I'm a fool but they'll soon discover how wrong they are. I would have felt it, you see. Those are things that a … I mean they are in the blood. Good night, Adèle. Please don't ask me to explain. I am in a foul mood and would hate to lose my temper with you, who have done nothing.'

Adèle paused. Perhaps a good sleep had helped her sister regain her composure. She pulled aside the drape and whispered:

'Yolande dear, Yolande … It's time to get up.'

There was no reply. She took a step forward. Something about the position of the sleeping woman alarmed her. She touched the hand lying on top of the coverlet.

A scream rang out through the dormitory. The nuns all stopped what they were doing and looked at one another. Berthe de Marchiennes was the first to emerge from this dreamlike trance. She rushed over to Adèle's cell. The young woman was repeating the same words, like a litany:

'Her hand is ice-cold … Her hand is ice-cold, it isn't normal, she's ice-cold, I tell you …'

Berthe drew back the cover sharply. Yolande de Fleury was lying with her mouth wide open. Purple-red scratch marks disfigured the pale skin on her neck. One of her legs was dangling over the side of the bed.

The cellarer nun closed the dead woman's eyes, turned to Adèle de Vigneux and said in a soft voice:

'She is dead. Please be so good as to fetch our Reverend Mother and Annelette Beaupré.'

Adèle stood rooted to the spot, her eyes moving between Berthe and the ice-cold corpse.

'That's an order, Adèle. Go and inform our Reverend Mother immediately.'

The young woman suddenly seemed to emerge from her stupor, and disappeared. Berthe sat down on the edge of Yolande's bed. She clasped her hands together in prayer:

'We are your humble devoted servants. Do not forsake us.'

The horses were exhausted and their riders scarcely any fresher by the time they reached the town of Alençon at dusk. The destrier, Ogier, was tossing his head and snorting; a cloud of vapour surrounded the stallion's flared nostrils and his chest heaved with the effort of breathing. Clément's mare, Sylvestre, quivered with tiredness, almost prancing as she walked, as though she were nervous of stumbling. Artus patted the neck of his magnificent mount and murmured:

'Steady! Steady! My brave steed. Our journey is done and I have found fine lodgings for you. My heartfelt thanks, Ogier. You are an even hardier beast than when I broke you in.'

The horse raised his head, shaking his pitch-black mane and flattening his ears in exhaustion.

Clément jumped down from his mare and stroked her muzzle – he was no less grateful to her for this punishing race against time, which was running short.

The ostler arrived to take the exhausted animals to be groomed. He tugged roughly on Ogier's bit and the horse threatened to rear up.

'Whoa, you oaf ! Nobody manhandles my faithful steed's mouth like that!' Artus shouted. 'Show him a little respect or he'll buck you at the first opportunity, and quite rightly. The same goes for the mare. Be careful. You can't ask an animal to give its all and then treat it like a beast of burden. These creatures have nearly killed themselves to get us here at breakneck speed. Treat them in the manner they deserve – and for which I am paying you handsomely – or you'll have me to answer to.'

The ostler did not need telling twice and gently cajoled the two mounts until they consented to walk on.

Clément followed Artus d'Authon through the streets of Alençon. How tall he was and what big steps he took, the child thought, as he did his best to keep up. All of a sudden Artus stopped, almost causing Clément to slam into his back.

'He should come out soon. I'll point him out to you. Follow him, and when you've discovered where he lodges make your way directly to La Jument-Rouge,' he said, gesturing towards a nearby tavern, 'and don't try anything, do you hear?'

'Yes, my lord.'

'... I'm warning you not to disobey me and try anything foolish, Clément. You may be brave, but you're not big or strong enough to take him on. I am. You will greatly harm your lady if you do not follow my instructions. Do you understand that if he slips through our fingers tonight, tomorrow Madame Agnès will die a thousand deaths?'

'I know, my lord. And then will you kill him?'

'I will. He has left me no other choice. It is a small matter in the end and I probably should have done it sooner. I could kick myself for hoping I could convince him.'

The Inquisition headquarters were strangely abuzz with activity when they arrived. Clerks were darting in and out of the place and men-at-arms with sullen faces rushed about for no apparent reason. Amid the general mayhem, the Comte d'Authon, flanked by Clément, walked towards the main entrance and went in. A skinny young friar, whom Artus did not recognise, came running up to them.

'M-my lord, my lord,' he stammered, giving a quick bow. 'He is dead. God be praised for doing justice. The wicked beast is dead.'

Sensing the Comte's bewilderment, he added:

'Agnan, my name is Agnan. I was chief clerk to that evil inquisitor. I was there when you came and tried to reason with him. I knew it was a waste of precious time. But it doesn't matter any more. He died as he lived, like a wicked sinner.' Agnan almost shrieked: 'God has passed judgement! His ineffable verdict has come down to earth like a revelation. The innocent dove, Madame de Souarcy, is free. Nicolas Florin's other victims, too. The judgement of God requires all his cases to be closed, permanently.'

'How did he die? When?'

'Last night. At the hands of a passing drunkard. It seems he invited the man into his house, the house he extorted from some poor soul whom he tortured to death. There was a struggle, ending in that devil's murder. Monsieur … We have witnessed a miracle … God intervened to save Madame de Souarcy, and … but it comes as no surprise to me. I looked into that woman's eyes, she reached out and touched me with her hand and I understood …'

'What did you understand?' Artus asked calmly, for the young man's exalted speech troubled him.

'I understood that she was … different. I understood that this woman was … unique. I am unable to describe it in words, my lord, and you must think me out of my mind. But I know. I know that I have been touched by perfection and that I will never be the same again. He also knew. He emerged from her cell stirred to the depths, his eyes shining with the indescribable light.'

'Who?' insisted Artus, sure that the young man had not lost

his mind, that his garbled speech concealed a profound truth.

'Why, the knight of course … The Knight Hospitaller.'

'Who?' the Comte d'Authon almost cried out.

'I assumed that you knew one another … I can tell you nothing more, Monsieur. With all due respect, please do not ask. No man has the right or the power to question a miracle. Madame de Souarcy is waiting for you in our infirmary. She has been through a terrible ordeal, but her courage is matched only by her purity. What joy you will feel in her presence! What joy … What joy I felt. Just imagine … She touched me, she looked straight into my eyes.'

Agnan wriggled free from Artus's restraining hand and ran off, leaving Artus and Clément speechless.

Agnès was raving, although the friar who was looking after her reassured them as to her physical health. Lash wounds were quick to heal. On the other hand, Madame de Souarcy was suffering from a fever that required her to spend a few days in bed, where she would receive the best care. Clément and Artus sat at her bedside. Occasionally, she would murmur a few incomprehensible words before sinking back into semi-consciousness. Suddenly, she opened her eyes, sat up straight and cried out:

'Clément … No, never!'

'I am right beside you, Madame. Oh, Madame, I beg you, please get better,' sobbed the child, his head in his hands.

Artus's heart was in his throat and his soul in torment; he was overjoyed that an alleged drunkard, whom he was certain was the Knight Hospitaller, had slain Florin, and at the same time devastated that the knight had got there before him. What a fool! He had tried to negotiate, to buy the man, when he should have stopped wasting time and unsheathed his sword. He had not saved Agnès, he had not earned her gratitude, and he would never forgive himself for it. He would have given his life for her, without hesitation. He was angry at the knight even as he felt grateful to him. Her other saviour had preceded him by a few hours, that was all, a few hours that had made all the difference. And that young friar Agnan, whose words Artus had not understood. Agnan, whose life had been illuminated because Agnès's hand had brushed against his hand or cheek. And suddenly Artus understood. He understood that this extraordinary woman who had stolen his heart and soul was unique, just as the young clerk had said. He understood that her attraction went deeper than her outward intelligence, courage, charm and beauty. And yet even as he held her slender hand between his, he could not help but ask who this woman really was. Everyone who knew her had been transformed in a way that could not be explained by love: Agnan, Clément, the knight, he himself … to name only those he knew. Who was she really?

In the days that followed tongues began to wag. Artus and Clément had found satisfactory lodgings at La Jument-Rouge. Everyone was talking, gossiping and conjecturing. The streets were alive with rumour and speculation. Even the local stoker and potter had revelations to make, tales to tell containing a mixture of truth and hyperbole. Nicolas Florin's brutality, his cruelty, his corruption, his taste for riches became common knowledge. He was even accused of sorcery, of having sold his soul in exchange for power, and it was rumoured that he had held frequent black masses. The humble folk unleashed themselves upon this man whom they had at first adored, then feared and finally come to hate. The episcopate, which had hitherto turned a blind eye, finally intervened, decreeing that the Grand Inquisitor's remains would not be buried in consecrated ground. This declaration reassured the masses, who, up until the day before, had bowed to Florin, also turning a blind eye to his notorious dealings, but now, no longer fearing reprisals, they turned against him as one.

Agnès's scars soon healed thanks to the constant attention of those around her. A few days after the death of her would-be executioner, she got out of bed and walked a few paces. Clément scolded her for rushing matters and Artus implored her not to overexert herself.

'Come now, dear gentlemen, I'm not as fragile as you think. It would take a lot more than this to finish off a woman like me. Any doubts I might have had about that have been dispelled.'

Despite the supplications of Artus, who longed for her to accept his hospitality, she decided to return directly to her manor in order to reassure her people and attend to the affairs she had been obliged to neglect.

The girl shied away in terror. Her cheek was stinging and Eudes's anger made her fear for her safety. A second blow sent her crashing into the door frame and she felt the blood streaming from her nose. She implored:

'Master ... I've done nothing wrong ... kind master.'

'Out of my sight, you whore! Vile whores, all of you!' shrieked Eudes, screwing up the letter the servant had just brought.

The young girl fled as fast as she could to get away from the madman's fists.

Eudes de Larnay was trembling with rage and regretted dismissing the servant girl. Beating her more would have brought him some relief.

The fools! The unutterable fools!

That wretch Florin had been handed this trial on a plate and had not managed to bring it to a successful conclusion. The fool had got himself stabbed by some brute – some drinking or orgy companion he had pulled from the gutter or from a cheap tavern. As for his gormless niece, who had nothing better to do than flutter her eyelids and prance about in her finery, she was too inept and stupid to have been seen fit to repeat what he had taken such pains to din into her. And as for that strumpet Mabile, who had led him on, made a fool of him, extorting his money with her lies. His entire household was useless, cowardly and stupid!

A sudden wrenching pain dispelled his anger.

Agnès ... my magnificent warrior. Why must you detest me so? I hate you, Agnès, for you are always in my thoughts. You haunt me. You dog my days and my nights with your presence.

I wanted you dead, yet what is there left for me if you die? He stifled the sob that threatened to choke him and closed his eyes. I love you, Agnès. Agnès. You are my festering wound and my only remedy. I hate you, I truly hate you.

He snatched up the pitcher from the table and drank without filling his goblet. The wine trickled down his striped silk doublet. The alcohol stung his insides, reminding him that he had not eaten since the day before. But the effect of the liquor soon sated him.

I have not finished with you yet, my beloved.

He would think up some other ruse. Quite apart from his resentment and his insatiable lust, he had no choice. He had no choice. His own survival depended on it.

Yolande de Fleury was resting in the ground. Every day Éleusie went to her grave to pay homage to her memory. Her grief was eased slightly by the thought that after a few moments of terrifying despair, the sweet Yolande had realised that her little Thibaut could not be dead. At least this is what the Abbess hoped Yolande had continued to believe until the very end.

Éleusie de Beaufort felt sure that Annelette was right. The sister in charge of the granary must have told her informant about the terrible scene that had taken place in the Abbess's study. She must have assured her that she had not revealed her name to them. It had never occurred to her that the kindly bringer of good news was none other than the murderess. Yolande had not suspected for a moment that by relating these events she was signing her own death warrant, for the informant could not risk being denounced.

The poor little angel had joined her son, and the day Yolande's coffin had been scattered with earth Éleusie had made a promise to herself. She would find out who had lied to Yolande and why. She felt that her daughter would not find peace otherwise. She felt that little Thibaut, whom she had never met, was pleading with her to do it for his mother's sake and his own. Suddenly, doing God's work in however small a measure and standing firm against the tides of evil seemed more important to her than anything else. Yolande de Fleury's informant was none other than the murderer of Adélaïde, Hedwige, Yolande herself, and of the Pope's emissaries. And yet, curiously, it was the lies the accursed woman had told in order to lull Yolande into a false sense of security that had come, in Éleusie's eyes, to represent an unforgivable sin. The Abbess had first wanted to eliminate any danger, to drive it outside the abbey's walls, and then, if she could, to see that justice was done. Now, she demanded atonement for these sins. Nothing less than execution.

The early-morning frost crunched beneath her feet as she walked back towards the main buildings. Before, an eternity ago, she had loved the peaceful indifference of winter. She would smile at the stillness of the snow that appeared to muffle every sound. The cold had not seemed to her unrelenting as it could be warded off by sitting beside a hearth or swallowing a bowlful of hot soup. That morning, she felt the deadly chill pierce her to the bone. She thought of all the deaths, all the creatures in the nearby forests that would perish before the advent of better weather. Death. Death was sliding, creeping, slipping all around. Her existence had become a graveyard and no amount of life would ever change that. She was the sole survivor in the mortuary that had implanted itself in her mind.

A few snowflakes pricked the skin on her hands before melting. She paused. Should she go to the herbarium to see Annelette? No, she hadn't the energy. Her study, however unwelcoming it might feel since the dreadful scene with Yolande, was still the only place where she could reflect.

The bells of Notre-Dame Church were pealing out. Sudden cries and an acrid smell made her turn her head in the direction of the guest house. She ran towards the building. Flames were rising out of the arrow-slit windows and she could hear the blaze roaring inside. Fire. A bevy of nuns was following Annelette's instructions and racing to fetch heavy pails of water. A human chain quickly formed. Pails, pans, every sort of receptacle passed from one pair of hands to the next. Annelette finally saw the Abbess and ran over to her, crying out:

'It's a diversion, I am sure. She is trying to divert our attention, but to what evil end I do not know.'

It came to Éleusie in a flash: the secret library. She ran in the opposite direction as fast as her legs would carry her.

The moment she opened the door and stepped into the cold room she sensed something was wrong. Her gaze fell upon the thick tapestry obscuring the tiny passageway and the door leading into the secret place. It seemed to be moving as though the biblical scene had come alive.

Who? Who had discovered her secret? Who had entered there? Dear God, the forbidden works, the notebook belonging to Eustache de Rioux and Francesco! It must under no circumstances fall into enemy hands. So, she had been right all along. The sole intention of the poisoner was to lay her hands on these works.

She searched frantically for any object she could use as a weapon. Her eye fell upon the stiletto knife she used to cut paper. She seized it and ran towards the hidden opening. A figure dressed in a heavy monk's habit, a cowl drawn over its face to avoid recognition, turned towards the Abbess, then made a dash for the door leading into the main corridor. Éleusie gave chase, still brandishing the knife, but the figure aimed a blow at her throat that left her fighting for breath. The Abbess struggled to seize the volumes wedged under the figure's arm, but to no avail. Bent double and gasping, Éleusie watched as the shadowy figure vanished at the end of the corridor. A sudden rush of energy she no longer thought herself capable of roused her, and she hurtled outside as though her life depended on it. She shouted at all the sisters she encountered who were on their way to help fight the fire:

'Go and instruct the porteress nuns[89] not to allow anybody out of the abbey under any circumstances. Failure to obey will be severely punished. This instant! Nobody must leave the abbey. That's an order!'

She herself raced to the main door and stirred the porteress, demanding that she bolt the heavy doors at once. The panic-stricken woman obeyed.

Éleusie sighed and dug her fingers into the painful stitch in her side to try to ease it. She bent double in a fit of nervous laughter and gasped:

'You'll not escape, you wretch! You thought you had got the better of us, didn't you, you vulture? I've got you now. I'll crush you like the vermin you are!' She turned towards the ashen-faced porteress and commanded: 'I am reinstating the strict cloister without exception. Nobody is to leave here without an order signed by me and only me. Every, and I repeat every, sister whom I authorise to leave must have her body as well as her bundles and cart thoroughly searched. Without exception.'

Éleusie suddenly turned on her heel and ran towards her daughters who were busy fighting the fire, snarling to herself:

'The manuscripts will stay in the abbey. Hide them … hide them as best you can, I will find them! You'll take them over my dead body.'

Agnès, who was still pallid and frail, looked at Clément and asked:

'What are you saying?'

'That we need to pay a visit to La Haute-Gravière, your health permitting.'

'I shall decide whether my health permits. Stop fussing over me like a mother hen.'

A joyous smile flashed across the child's face:

'So, Madame, you are my baby chicken now.'

Agnès laughed and ruffled his hair. She loved him so much. Had he not constantly been in her thoughts she would never have survived her imprisonment at Alençon.

'A big fat baby chicken, indeed!' She grew serious again, continuing: 'But we know nothing about the place, dear Clément.'

'Indeed we do, Madame. I learned from my remarkable teacher, the physician Joseph de Bologne.'

'Joseph again,' Agnès joked. 'Do you know, I think I am going to end up being jealous of that man?'

'Oh, Madame, if only you knew him ... You would immediately fall under his spell. He knows everything about everything.'

'Gracious me! What a flattering description. You miss him, don't you?'

Clément blushed and confessed:

'Never when I am with you, for that is where I always wish to be.' She could see him fighting back the tears. 'I was so afraid, Madame, so terribly afraid that I would lose you and never find you again. I thought I would die of sorrow a thousand times. And so, if I must choose, I prefer to stay here with you.' He paused before adding: 'Even so, Monsieur Joseph's teaching is without parallel. The man has studied the world with his mind, Madame. He has so much knowledge of science. Is it not wonderful and incredible that he should consider me worthy of receiving it and be willing to answer so many of my questions? Moreover ... he knows.'

'What does he know?' demanded Agnès, alerted by Clément's sudden seriousness.

'That I am not ... I mean that I am a girl.'

'Did you tell him?'

'Of course not. He found it out. He claims you can already see a woman's eyes in those of a child and that only a fool would confuse them with a man's eyes.'

Agnès grew anxious.

'Do you think he will tell the Comte?'

'No. He holds his lord in high esteem, but he gave me his word that he would say nothing And you see, Madame, you and he are the only two people whose word I completely trust.'

Agnès felt relieved and quipped:

'Don't say it too loud. You'll upset a lot of people.'

'Why should I care if I make you happy? Getting back to the subject of La Haute-Gravière, which is part of your dower, plenty of nettles grow there.'

'And little else,' the lady agreed with a sigh. 'Even the oxen won't graze there. I was thinking of buying some goats at the next livestock fair. At least we could make cheese from their milk.'

'Nettles thrive in ferrous soil.'

Agnès understood immediately what the child was implying.

'Really? Is Maître Joseph sure of this?'

'Yes. According to him, an abundance of nettles means the soil is rich in iron ore. We must find out, Madame. Is it the soil's composition or do the plants point to a deposit?'

'What must we do? How does one go about finding an iron-ore deposit?'

Clément pulled out of his thick winter tunic what looked like a dark-grey sharpening stone, and declared:

'By means of this wonderful, inestimably rare object Joseph lent me in order to help you.'

'Is it a piece of carved rock?'

'It is magnetite, Madame.'

'Magnetite?'

'A very useful stone that comes from a region of Asia Minor known as Magnesia.'[90]

'How can it help us, my dear Clément?'

'This little piece of stone you see here has the power to attract iron, or soil containing iron. It sticks to it. We don't know why.'

Rising from her bench, Agnès commanded:

'Saddle a horse! You will sit behind me on a pillion. You are right, we must find out immediately.'

Clément left at once. A smile spread across Agnès's lips, and she muttered to herself:

'I have you, Eudes. If, God willing, this is an iron mine, you will soon pay for the suffering you caused me.'

She drove out the images flooding into her mind, of Mathilde; her tiny nails when she closed her baby fist round her mother's finger; charging through the corridors at Souarcy, shrieking whenever a goose came up to her flapping its wings.

She must banish from her thoughts these happy memories that wounded her like a knife.

*

Where had the strange, beautiful man disappeared to, the Knight Hospitaller who had saved her, for she suspected that Florin's death had been more than fortuitous. If the story of the ill-fated encounter with a drinking or orgy companion had convinced those who wanted to destroy the inquisitor's already monstrous reputation, it had left Agnès sceptical. She had pondered for hours their brief exchange, attempting to reconstruct every detail, every word spoken. She had the bewildering certainty of having come close to a mystery that had then rapidly eluded her. Francesco de Leone was Éleusie de Beaufort's nephew, or rather her adoptive son. Would the Abbess agree to tell her more, to enlighten her about him?

Had Mathilde remained at Clairets, would her uncle have been able to corrupt her like that? Had she, whose only thought had been to protect her daughter, been at fault?

Stop!

Mathilde. Her cold eyes, her pretty fingers adorned with Madame Apolline's rings. Her lies aimed at sending her mother to the stake and Clément to the torture chamber.

No. She would cry no more. She was beyond tears.

APPENDIX I: HISTORICAL REFERENCES

Abu-Bakr-Mohammed-ibn-Zakariya al-Razi, 865–932, known as
Rhazes. Philosopher, alchemist, mathematician and prodigious
Persian physician to whom we owe, among other things, the
discovery and the first description of allergy-based asthma and hay
fever. He demonstrated the connection of the latter with certain
flowers. He is considered to be the forefather of experimental
medicine and successfully performed cataract operations.

Anagni, the Outrage at, September 1303. Pope Boniface VIII, who
challenged the authority of Philip IV (the Fair), was 'detained' in
Anagni. Guillaume de Nogaret happened to be in Anagni; he had
come to ask the Pope to convoke a general council in Lyon. The
origin of the conflict between Pope and King was the tithe that Philip
was trying to impose on the French clergy to support his war effort
against the English. (Some historians think, on the other hand, that
Guillaume de Nogaret orchestrated the sequestration of Boniface on
the orders of Philip the Fair, with the aid of the Colonna brothers,
who entertained a personal hatred for the sovereign pontiff.)

Archimedes, 287–212 BC. Greek mathematical genius and inventor
to whom we owe very many mathematical advances, including the
famous hydrostatic principle, which is named after him. He also gave
the first precise definition of the number pi, and set himself up to be
the advocate of experimentation and demonstration. Archimedes is
credited with being the author of several inventions, including the
catapult, the Archimedes screw, the pulley and the cog.

A palimpsest was recently auctioned at Christie's for US$2
million. It recounted the progress made by Archimedes in getting
to grips with infinity. The document, which had been overwritten

with the copy of a religious text, also contained the first crucial steps towards differential calculus, a branch of mathematics that had to be re-invented after the Renaissance. It is rumoured that Bill Gates was the successful bidder for the document, which has been donated to the Walters Art Museum in Baltimore, where it has been subjected to sophisticated analysis.

Ballads of Marie de France. Twelve ballads popularly attributed to a certain Marie, originally from France but living at the English court. Some historians believe she was a daughter of Louis VII or the Comte de Meulan. The ballads were written before 1167 and Marie's fables around 1180. Marie de France was also the author of a novel *Le Purgatoire de Saint-Patrice.*

Benoît (Benedict) XI, Pope, Nicolas Boccasini, 1240–1304. Relatively little is known about him. Coming from a very poor background, Boccasini, a Dominican, remained humble throughout his life. One of the few anecdotes about him demonstrates this: when his mother paid him a visit after his election, she made herself look pretty for her son. He gently explained that her outfit was too ostentatious and that he preferred women to be simply dressed. Known for his conciliatory temperament, Boccasini, who had been Bishop of Ostia, tried to mediate in the disagreements between the Church and Philip the Fair, but he showed his disapproval of Guillaume de Nogaret and the Colonna brothers. He died after eight months of the pontificate, on 7 July 1304, poisoned by figs or dates.

Boniface VIII, Pope, Benedetto Caetani, c.1235–1303. Cardinal and legate in France, then pope. He was a passionate defender of pontifical theocracy, which was opposed to the new authority of the State. He was openly hostile to Philip the Fair from 1296 onwards and the affair continued even after his death – France attempted to try him posthumously.

Calling. See Prostitution.

Carcassonne. In August 1303, when Philip the Fair paid a visit to the town, its population rebelled against the Inquisition, encouraged by the campaign of Bernard Délicieux, a Franciscan who was passionately opposed to the Dominicans and their Inquisition. He even took part in a plot to stir up the Languedoc against Philip. He was arrested several times and ended his days in prison in 1320.

Catharism. From *katharoi*, meaning 'the pure ones' in Greek. The Cathar movement originated in Bulgaria towards the end of the tenth century and spread as a result of the preachings of a priest named Bogomile. Viewed as heretics, the Cathars were pursued by the Inquisition. Very broadly Catharism was a form of Dualism. It contrasted irreversible Evil (matter, the world) with God and Goodness (perfection). Catharism condemned society, the family, the clergy, but also the Eucharist and the communion of saints. Although not definitive on the point, the first Cathars denied that Christ was human, seeing him as an angel sent to earth. Catharism was defined by an extreme purity, which encompassed, along with sexual abstinence, a ban on meat-eating, and was particularly appealing to the well-off and the cultivated who were suffering from spiritual malaise. From 1200 onwards the Catholic Church struggled to suppress the Cathars, after having condemned them in 1119 in Toulouse. The 'crusades' against the Albigensians followed. Simon de Montfort led the 'crusaders' from 1209 to 1215. This bloody war, taken up by the Inquisition, did not end until the surrender of the last strongholds of the Cathars, notably Montségur in 1244. The Cathar Church was never to recover from that, despite the attraction its ideal of purity exercised on the mendicant orders. Catharism died out around 1270.

Chrétien de Troyes, c.1140–c.1190. Poet from Champagne, sometimes described as the creator of the modern novel. He travelled widely and possibly visited England. He was closely associated with Countess Marie, daughter of Eleanor of Aquitaine who became Queen of England. Devoted to Ovid, he translated his *Art of Love* and reinvented narrative romance, injecting an element of psychological insight. He played with symbolism and crafted subtle plots, and in Cligès introduced elements of mythology. His best-known poem is probably *Perceval* or *The Story of the Grail*, but he also wrote *Lancelot, the Knight of the Cart*; Yvain, the Knight of the Lion and *Eric and Enid*.

Clairets Abbey, Orne. Situated on the edge of Clairets Forest, in the parish of Masle, the abbey was built by a charter issued in July 1204 by Geoffroy III, Comte du Perche, and his wife Mathilde of Brunswick, sister of Emperor Otto IV. The abbey's construction took seven years and finished in 1212. Its consecration was co-signed by the commander of the Knights Templar, Guillaume d'Arville, about whom little is known. The abbey is only open to Bernardine nuns of the Cistercian order, who have the right to all forms of seigneurial justice.

Délicieux, Bernard. Franciscan monk who fiercely opposed the Dominicans and their Inquisition. He was a good public speaker and his independence of spirit drew enormous crowds. He organised a demonstration against Philip the Fair when the King visited Carcassonne in August 1303. He went as far as to participate in a plot to enflame Languedoc against the King. He was arrested several times and ended his days in prison in 1320.

Galen, Claudius, 131–210, a Greek born in Asia Minor, was one of the greatest scientists of antiquity. He became chief physician to the gladiator school in Pergamum, and allegedly made use of 'volunteers' to perfect his knowledge of surgery. He served as physician to Marcus

Aurelius and treated the Emperor's two sons, Commodus and Sextus. Among other discoveries, Galen described how the nervous system works and its role in muscular activity, and the circulation of blood through veins and arteries. His most important discovery was that arteries carry blood and not air, as had previously been believed. He also demonstrated that it is the brain that controls the voice.

Got, Bertrand de, c.1270–1314. He is best known as a canon and counsellor to the King of England. He was, however, a skilled diplomat, which enabled him to maintain cordial relations with Philip the Fair even though England was at war with France. He became Archbishop of Bordeaux in 1299 then succeeded Benoît XI as pope in 1305, taking the name Clément V. He chose to install himself in Avignon, because he was wary of the politics of Rome, which he knew little about. He was good at handling Philip the Fair in their two major differences of opinion: the posthumous trial of Boniface VIII and the suppression of the Knights Templar. He managed to rein in the spite of the sovereign in the first case, and to contain it in the second case.

The Hospitallers of Saint John of Jerusalem were recognised by Pope Paschal III in 1113. Unlike the other soldier orders, the original function of the Hospitallers was charitable. It was only later that they assumed a military function. After the Siege of Acre in 1291, the Hospitallers withdrew to Cyprus then Rhodes, and finally Malta. The order was governed by a Grand-Master, elected by the general chapter made up of dignitaries. The chapter was subdivided into provinces, governed in their turn by priors. Unlike the Templars and in spite of their great wealth, the Hospitallers always enjoyed a very favourable reputation, no doubt because of their charitable works, which they never abandoned, and because of the humility of their members.

Inquisitorial procedure. The conduct of the trial and the questions of doctrine put to the accused are adapted from the work of Nicholas Eymerich (1320–1399) and Francisco Peña (1540–1612) – *The Inquisitor's Manual*.

The Knights Templar. The order was created in 1118 in Jerusalem by the knight Hugues de Payens and other knights from Champagne and Burgundy. It was officially endorsed by the Church at the Council of Troyes in 1128, having been championed by Bernard of Clairvaux. The order was led by a Grand-Master, whose authority was backed up by dignitaries. The order owned considerable assets (3,450 chateaux, fortresses and houses in 1257). With its system of transferring money to the Holy Land, the order acted in the thirteenth century as one of Christianity's principal bankers. After the Siege of Acre in 1291 – which was in the end fatal to the order – the Templars almost all withdrew to the West. Public opinion turned against them and they were regarded as indolent profiteers. Various expressions of the period bear witness to this. For example, 'Going to the Temple' was a euphemism for going to a brothel. When the Grand-Master Jacques de Molay refused to merge the Templars with the Hospitallers, the Templars were arrested on 13 October 1307. An investigation followed, confessions were obtained (in the case of Jacques de Molay, some historians believe, with the use of torture), followed by retractions. Clément V, who feared Philip the Fair for various unrelated reasons, passed a decree suppressing the order on 22 March 1312. Jacques de Molay again stood by the retraction of his confession and on 18 March 1314 was burnt at the stake along with other Templars. It is generally agreed that the seizure of the Templars' assets and their redistribution to the Hospitallers cost Philip the Fair more money than it gained him.

Medieval Inquisition. It is important to distinguish the Medieval Inquisition from the Spanish Inquisition. The repression and intolerance of the latter were incomparably more violent than anything known in France. Under the leadership of Tomas de Torquemada alone, there were more than two thousand deaths recorded in Spain.

The Medieval Inquisition was at first enforced by the bishops. Pope Innocent III (1160–1216) set out the regulations for the inquisitorial procedure in the papal bull *Vergentis in senium* of 1199. The aim was not to eliminate individuals – as was proved by the Fourth Council of the Lateran, called by Innocent III a year before his death, which emphasised that it was forbidden to inflict the Ordeal on dissidents. (The Ordeal or 'judgement of God' was a trial by fire, water or the sword to test whether an accused person was a heretic or not.) What the Pope was aiming for was the eradication of heresies that threatened the foundation of the Church by promoting, amongst other things, the poverty of Christ as a model way to live – a model that was obviously rarely followed if the vast wealth earned by most of the monasteries from land tax is anything to go by. Later the Inquisition was enforced by the Pope, starting with Gregory IX, who conferred inquisitorial powers on the Dominicans in 1232 and, in a lesser way, on the Franciscans. Gregory's motives in reinforcing the powers of the Inquisition and placing them under his sole control were entirely political. He was ensuring that on no account would Emperor Frederick II be able to control the Inquisition for reasons that had nothing to do with spirituality. It was Innocent IV who took the ultimate step in authorising recourse to torture in his papal bull *Ad extirpanda* of 15 May 1252. Witches as well as heretics were then hunted down by the Inquisition.

The real impact of the Inquisition has been exaggerated. There were relatively few inquisitors to cover the whole territory of the kingdom of France and they would have had little effect had they not received the help of powerful lay people and benefited from numerous denunciations. But, thanks to their ability to excuse each other for their faults, certain inquisitors were guilty of terrifying atrocities that sometimes provoked riots and scandalised many prelates.

In March 2000, roughly eight centuries after the beginnings of the Inquisition, Pope John Paul II asked God's pardon for the crimes and horrors committed in its name.

Mendicant convents. They were founded sometime between the twelfth and thirteenth centuries and were distinguished by their refusal to own land in common, promoting the return to evangelical poverty. They very quickly attracted a significant level of patronage, which led to a rivalry with the secular clergy, who considered that they had lost several of their regular donors to the mendicant orders. This conflict led to the suppression of many of the mendicant orders in 1274 (by the Second Council of Lyon); only the Carmelites, the Hermits of Saint Augustine, the Dominicans and the Franciscans were officially recognised by the Council. The Celestines joined the mendicant orders in 1294.

Nogaret, Guillaume de, c.1270–1313. Nogaret was a professor of civil law and taught at Montpellier before joining Philip the Fair's Council in 1295. His responsibilities grew rapidly more widespread. He involved himself, at first more or less clandestinely, in the great religious debates that were shaking France, for example the trial of Bernard Saisset. Nogaret progressively emerged from the shadows and played a pivotal role in the campaign against the Knights Templar and the King's struggle with Pope Boniface VIII. Nogaret was of unshakeable faith and great intelligence. He would go on to become the King's chancellor and, although he was displaced for a while by Enguerran de Marigny, he took up the seal again in 1311.

Peña, Francisco, 1540–1612. In citing this name, the author has knowingly committed an anachronism. Francisco Peña is the specialist in canonical law whom the Holy See charged, in the sixteenth century, with producing the new edition of The Inquisitor's Manual by Nicholas Eymerich.

Philip the Fair, 1268–1314. The son of Philip III (known as Philip the Bold) and Isabelle of Aragon. With his consort Joan of Navarre, he had three sons who would all become kings of France – Louis X (Louis the Stubborn), Philip V (Philip the Tall) and Charles IV (Charles the Fair). He also had a daughter, Isabelle, whom he married to Edward II of England. Philip was brave and an excellent war leader, but he also had a reputation for being inflexible and harsh. It is now generally agreed, however, that perhaps that reputation has been overstated, since contemporary accounts relate that Philip the Fair was manipulated by his advisers, who flattered him while mocking him behind his back.

Philip the Fair is best known for the major role he played in the suppression of the Knights Templar, but he was above all a reforming king whose objective was to free the politics of the French kingdom from papal interference.

Prostitution was reasonably well tolerated as long as it stayed within the limits imposed by the powers that be and religion. The canonical lawyers of the thirteenth century conceded that it was not immoral in certain circumstances, as long as the woman 'engaged in it only out of necessity, and did not derive any enjoyment from it'. In towns 'pleasure girls' had to live in particular districts and wear certain identifiable clothes. These attitudes to prostitution might seem contradictory. But when the mentality of the day is considered, they do make sense. For in those days men had many more options than women, and it was recognised, although not necessarily publicly, that women only fell into prostitution because they had no choice. So although the Church regarded prostitutes as sinners, it also considered men who married them to be doing a good deed. Prostitutes could be 'washed' of their old lives if they married or joined a convent. The rape of a prostitute was considered a crime and punished as such.

Robert le Bougre, also known as Robert the Small, was possibly Bulgarian in origin. He originally embraced Catharism and acceded to the highest rank and became an expert in that faith. But he later converted to Catholicism and became a Dominican monk. Gregory IX (1227–1241) valued him for his extraordinary ability to expose heretics. He seemed capable of trapping even the most skilled at concealment. In 1235 he was appointed Inquisitor General of Charité-sur-Loire, after his predecessor Conrad de Marbourg was assassinated, and was then responsible for cruel mistreatment and horrifying torture. The Archbishops of Sens and Rheims, among others, scandalized by the accounts that were reaching their ears, protested against Robert's behaviour. After the first written report on the methods used by Robert, he was stripped of his powers in 1234. Yet he returned to favour in August of the following year, and immediately took up his 'amusements' again. It was not until 1241 that he was definitively removed from power and imprisoned for life.

Roman de la Rose. A long allegorical poem written by two authors in two stages. Guillaume de Lorris started writing the love song of a courtier in around 1230. However, the part written by Jean de Meung between 1270 and 1280 is much more ironic, not to say cynical and misogynistic, with some barely disguised licentiousness. Jean de Meung did not hold back from attacking the mendicant orders by creating the character of a monk, named 'The Pretender'.

Saisset, Bernard, ?–1311. The first Bishop of Pamiers. Very unwisely, he tried to challenge the legitimacy of Philip the Fair's claim to the French throne, going as far as to hatch a plot to install the Comte de Foix as sovereign in Languedoc. Saisset refused to appear at his trial before the King, preferring to rely on the support of Boniface VIII to save him. In the end Philip the Fair exiled Saisset, who died in Rome.

Valois, Charles de, 1270–1325. Philip the Fair's only full brother.

The King showed Charles a somewhat blind affection all his life and conferred on him missions that were probably beyond his capabilities. Charles de Valois, who was father, son, brother, brother-in-law, uncle and son-in-law to kings and queens, dreamed all his life of his own crown, which he never obtained.

Villeneuve, Arnaud de, or Arnoldus de Villanova, c.1230–1311, born in Montpellier. Probably one of the most prestigious scientists of the thirteenth and fourteenth centuries. Raised in Spain by Dominican monks, he became a doctor, astrologer, alchemist and lawyer of very determined character who sparked controversy and did not hesitate to launch attacks on the mendicant orders. He only escaped the clutches of the Inquisition because he cured Boniface VIII, who pardoned him for his 'errors'. He remained the Pope's doctor until his death, then became doctor to Benoît XI, and then Clément V, all the while working on secret missions for the King of Aragon.

APPENDIX II: GLOSSARY

Liturgical Hours

Aside from Mass – which was not strictly part of them – ritualised prayers, as set out in the sixth century by the Regulation of Saint Benoît, were to be said several times a day. They regulated the rhythm of the day. Monks and nuns were not permitted to dine before nightfall, that is until after vespers. This strict routine of prayers was largely adhered to until the eleventh century, when it was reduced to enable monks and nuns to devote more time to reading and manual labour.

Matins: at 2.30 a.m. or 3 a.m.

Lauds: just before dawn, between 5 a.m. and 6 a.m.

Prime: around 7.30 a.m., the first prayers of the day, as soon as possible after sunrise and just before Mass.

Terce: around 9 a.m.

Sext: around midday.

None: between 2 p.m. and 3 p.m. in the afternoon.

Vespers: at the end of the afternoon, at roughly 4.30 p.m. or 5 p.m., at sunset.

Compline: after vespers, the last prayers of the day, sometime between 6 p.m. and 8 p.m.

Measurements

It is quite difficult to translate some measurements to their modern-day equivalents, as the definitions varied from region to region.

League: about 2 ½ miles (4 kilometres).

Ell: about 45 inches (114 centimetres) in Paris, 37 inches (94 centimetres) in Arras.

Foot: as today, 12 inches (30 centimetres).

Ounce: as today, about 28 grams.

APPENDIX III: NOTES

1. Jesus, we adore you.
2. The age of consent was thirteen for girls and fourteen for boys.
3. The customary usufruct of the deceased husband's properties awarded to widows. In the Paris region this was half of the husband's properties and in Normandy a third.
4. Meat was not eaten on Wednesdays, Fridays, Saturdays, feast days, or during Lent.
5. The dynastic name of Plantagenet was a nickname given to one of Edward's ancestors, Geoffroy, Comte d'Anjou, who transformed his lands into moors, planting, among other things, broom (Fr. genêts) in order to be able to hunt.
6. Water closet.
7. Practice of offering female children to convents.
8. The origin of the words 'saccharose' (the chemical name for sugar) and 'saccharine'.
9. Traditional word denoting beehives.
10. It was believed up until the end of the seventeenth century that the swarms surrounded a king and not a queen bee.
11. The Knights of Justice and Grace belonged to the Order of the Hospitallers of Saint John of Jerusalem.* A Knight of Justice must boast at least eight quarters of nobility in France and Italy and sixteen in Germany. The title Knight of Grace was bestowed on merit alone.
12. Friars were obliged to carry this when they travelled. Any friar unable to provide this pass when asked for it by a commander was summarily arrested and judged by the order.
13. Whosoever washes himself in the divine blood purifies his sins and acquires a beauty resembling that of the angels.
14. Unlike physics, surgeons, who were most often barbers, were looked down upon.

15. 12 June 1218.

16. The production of paper made of flax or hemp, although an invention of the Chinese, remained in the hands of the Muslims. In that capacity Christendom rejected it until the Italians invented a new method of fabrication towards the middle of the thirteenth century.

17. A non-cloistered nun responsible for the abbey's relations with the outside world.

18. A nun who answered directly to the Abbess and the prioress. Her function was to take care of the abbey's provisions and food stocks. She was authorised to buy and sell land and she collected tolls. She also took care of the barns, the mills, the breweries, the fish ponds and so on.

19. Place where visitors were received.

20. So be it. Have pity on us. Dreaded day when the universe will be reduced to ashes.

21. 'But immediately after the tribulation of those days the sun shall be darkened, and the moon shall not give her light, and the stars shall fall from heaven, and the powers of the heavens shall be shaken' (Matthew 24:29).

22. The nun responsible for educating children and novices was the only one authorised to raise a hand to them or mete out punishment.

23. A sort of short, sleeveless jacket with a buttoned neck, often richly ornamented, which men of stature wore over their short tunics.

24. And thus appeared the sign of the Son of Man.

25. Metal refiners whose job it was to beat bars into sheets before selling them on to manufacturers.

26. Grey-squirrel fur was prized at the time. Two thousand of the small rodents were needed to line one man's coat.

27. The sexual taboo between blood relations extended even to godparents.

28. Fine woollen or linen-and-wool garment worn over the chemise.

29. Probably a forerunner of the hurdy-gurdy.

30. Wind instrument akin to bagpipes.

31. Mellow-sounding string instrument.

32. Uranus, Neptune and Pluto were discovered later.

33. An apparatus for determining the positions of the planets in the system described by the Greek astronomer Ptolemy (second century BC). This fixed system, which was completely erroneous, was favoured by the Church and as such would remain in force during seventeen centuries.

34. Guy Faucoi 'le Gros' (in English 'Guy Foulques the Fat'), Pope Clément IV (late twelfth century–1268). A former soldier and jurist.

35. Inserts depicting a scene often in bold colours.

36. Large initial letters at the beginning of each chapter or paragraph usually decorated with interlacing.

37. Stylised decorative ornaments of intertwined leaves and vegetation.

38. Pigments and binding agents used in the making of inks.

39. Men were subjected above all to the strappado (which consisted in causing the condemned man on the end of a rope to fall repeatedly with all his weight), water and fire; women were generally whipped.

40. Neither autopsy nor dissection was practised, for religious reasons. Medicine was therefore based on the works of Hippocrates and Galen, professor of anatomy, and to a lesser extent those of Avicenna. Dissections began to be practised at the University of Montpellier in 1340.

41. Nun charged with keeping the accounts of the abbey's revenues, with overseeing and paying the farrier, entertainers and vets.

42. Divine Justice. Ordeals of fire and water or verbal duels before a court (the latter unrelated to duels of honour that became widespread during the eleventh century) intended to prove innocence or guilt. Fell largely into disuse by the fifteenth century.

43. The universe of angels contained three hierarchies.

44. Built on top of a sixth-century baptistery, Saint-Germain-l'Auxerrois dates back to the twelfth and thirteenth centuries. Of modest size during that era, it would later be enlarged.

45. Monastery where Galileo studied before going to Pisa to take up medicine.46. Uranus and Neptune.

47. Pluto.

48. 25 December was originally a feast day of pagans and saturnal plurimillenarians who celebrated the winter solstice. The Church decided around AD 336 to celebrate it as Christ's birthday.

49. Francisco Peña.*

50. Treatise for the Use of Inquisitors.

51. Francisco Peña.

52. Paris, 1290.

53. Otherwise known as 'bastard hand', it was used in the writing of deeds, letters, ledgers and any manuscript written in the vernacular.

54. Ballad by Marie de France.*

55. Chrétien de Troyes.*

56. Although these men did not take vows of poverty, chastity or obedience they enjoyed the privileges of the order in exchange for working on the land as craftsmen or servants at the commandery.

57. A piece of land given to a tenant farmer by a lord in exchange for rent and/or labour.

58. Preceptor was the name given in Latin texts for the commander.

59. Bread was an indication of social status. As such, a distinction was made between rich men's bread, knights' bread, equerries' bread, menservants' bread ... poor men's bread and famine bread.

60. Greetings O Queen, Mother of mercy; our life, our love and our hope.

61. A guild of wealthy merchants who sold fabric, clothing, *objets* and even gold work to the wealthy classes. They also dyed precious fabrics, like silk, which ordinary dyers did not deal in. Haberdasher became one of the most respected professions in the society of the time.

62. In 994, Raoul le Glabre described it as 'an illness which attacks a limb and consumes it before separating it from the body'.

63. Due to lysergic acid diethylamide, or LSD.

64. This direct link was not generally acknowledged until the seventeenth century.

65. Ergotamine is still used to treat migraine and headaches related to vasomotor function.

66. Haemorrhages due to fibroids.

67. Root vegetables (carrots, turnips, celeriac, etc.) were the food of peasants; the nobility ate only leaf vegetables.

68. A galliass or galleass was a heavy low-built vessel with sails and oars, larger than a galley, from where the word originates.

69. Granted in 1256 by Alexander IV and confirmed by Urban IV in 1264.

70. Those sentenced by a tribunal to pay money which was then distributed among the poor.

71. Aconite is no longer used to treat these symptoms, except in homoeopathy, owing to its extreme toxicity.

72. Malefactor who broke seals in order to change the wording on deeds.

73. Parchment. Hide prepared in Pergame. It remained in use after paper became more widespread and was used by the nobility for title deeds and official deeds until the sixteenth century.

74. Foxglove.

75. Hemlock, used for thousands of years to treat neuralgia.

76. Yew. Extremely toxic and used from ancient times onwards to coat arrow heads.

77. Species of flowering plant of the family Thymelaeaceae, once used as a purgative but which fell into disuse due to its toxicity.

78. It was equally used as an antiseptic and to bring on periods.

79. Latria: the worship given to God alone. Here it refers to the worship of the devil as though he were God.

80. Dulia: inferior type of veneration paid to saints. Here it refers to the act of praying to demons to intercede with the devil.

81. Poisoner.

82. Paris boasted approximately fifteen such establishments.

83. Winding frame.

84. Landlords employed criers to announce the price of the wine and sometimes the food they served in exchange for the right to drink there.

85. Listen to my prayer, O Lord, deliver my soul from fear of mine enemy.

86. The custom of ladies dressing their pet dogs to protect them from the cold began in the fourteenth century.

87. Plague. It is thought to have been rife, particularly in China, for three thousand years. In any case, the first known pandemic occurred in AD 540 on the shores of the Mediterranean where it also affected Gaul. The second pandemic, known as the black plague, lasted from 1346 to 1353. It started in India and killed 25 million people in Europe and probably as many in Asia.

88. Plants with antiseptic qualities that were used in the old days as well as lily, climbing ivy, bilberry and arnica.

89. Nuns or lay people in charge of opening and closing the doors to the enclosure or the buildings within the enclosure.

90. Wherein the word magnetism. The Greeks were familiar with magnets, which did not reach Europe until the twelfth and thirteenth centuries.